DANGEROUS GAMBLES

DANGEROUS GAMBLES

J. H. Sanderson

To Tony, the Best Big Brother anyone could ask for!

Acknowledgements

I would like to take this opportunity to thank my "Big Brother," Tony Heyes, for helping me work out the ideas that I had for this book. Sharing many road stories—and bottles of Jose Cuervo—helped to give the Roadhouse Sons their many adventures—both mentioned and alluded to—in this book. I should add the disclaimers that yes indeed, the names were changed to protect the ones that should have known better. In all seriousness, however, aside from the ones that I have specifically mentioned, all other characters and events in this book are entirely fictional and any resemblance to any person, living or dead, is purely coincidental.

Therefore, since I have thanked Tony, it is appropriate that I also thank his bands, *Section 8* and *Studebaker Hawk*—specifically, Dave Costa, Phil Hoefs and Stevie Smith, who provided the inspirations for some of the characters. The privilege of working with them was also a wonderful opportunity to gain an insight, however slight, into the world of the bands.

Another person that needs to be thanked is Mia Moravis (a/k/a "Cynthmia"), whose forensic science knowledge was invaluable to me, not to mention her extreme patience while editing and reviewing this manuscript. As she liked to put it, I was the one who built the house, she merely decorated it. Well, in that case, let me assure you, Mia, that you have excellent taste! She was also the main cheerleader who kept me focused and motivated when I was in danger of being overwhelmed and distracted by other things, and for that, as well, I am extremely grateful.

Music Foreword by Gardner Berry

In the mid '50s, Desi Arnaz produced a wildly successful and long-running TV series about his life as a New York City bandleader with a stunning and wacky wife. He was often portrayed as a buffoon.

In the early '60s, Richard Meltzer was kicked out of Yale for his wild pranks and for writing papers with rock music themes for his Philosophy class.

In the mid '60s, *The Monkees* became manufactured pop idols, and had televised fictional adventures for all of us to revel in. Happily, vernacular such as "ROTFL" was decades away.

In the early '70s, Bernard Slade brought *The Partridge Family* into our living rooms and, subsequently, brought Susan "Laurie" Dey into my dreams, but that's a story for another time. Also in our midst now are *Josie and The Pussycats*, *The Banana Splits*, and *Gorillaz*. The list goes on, but, quite frankly, I'm too old to watch cartoons anymore (I guess that's not specifically true, but the only cartoon I watch regularly is *The Family Guy*, which is light years away from the kiddie fare I grew up with).

A number of early TV sitcoms produced some relatively decent rock musicians. Most memorable were Ricky Nelson, Shelley Fabares, Paul Petersen, and *Happy Days'* Potsie and the gang at Arnold's drive-in. Okay, so some of it fell a bit short of decent, but my point is that rock musicians have rarely, if ever, been taken seriously as fictional heroes. And why is this? I have no rational answer. I suspect it's because non-musicians, or Muggles, as my band refers to them, have no idea what we're really like. They know our onstage persona (if we're lucky enough to have one), but what we do for the other 21 hours of the day is a mystery. I've been a working musician for 47 years, and I believe myself to be damned interesting. I have an enjoyable personal life and, by God, I'm capable of having adventures.

I find myself to be a bit of a snob when it comes to hanging out with non-musicians. I don't care about their kids, their jobs, their

401Ks, their boats, or their summer houses on the lake. I like to talk to musicians about their gear, their music and their experiences—good or bad—at shithole bars and in after-hours trysts that nobody in the "real" world knows about, or would believe, if they did.

I love my life. I look forward to going to work every day, or night, as the case may be. How many people can say that? So I was delighted to have an old friend send a manuscript to me which portrayed working musicians as the protagonists—not successful, spoiled, rich, millionaire rock stars; just regular struggling cover musicians eking out a living in bars, driving all night through sometimes miserable weather, and praying that the next gig doesn't get canceled.

We're real living, breathing people who, you might be surprised to know, are profoundly adept at solving problems and getting things up and running, sometimes against overwhelming odds.

We're musicians. We'll get it done. Actors can be Presidents, pro wrestlers can be governors, and stand-up comics can be Senators, so why not make musicians fictional heroes?

Why not indeed? You're cordially invited to read on…

Gardner Berry, New Hampshire
www.mamakicks.com

Law Enforcement Foreword by Peter Heed

The dirty little truth is that innocent clients are rare. This is one of the facts they do not focus on in law school. I know. After over 35 years as a criminal trial lawyer, both as a defense attorney and prosecutor, I can still count my truly innocent clients on the fingers of both hands. Perhaps I have just been unlucky, or perhaps my client selection has been incredibly bad. What is more likely true (that word again!) is that it simply goes with the territory.

The rare innocent client sticks out in your mind, stays with you. It changes things; raises the stakes; puts the pressure on. Simply doing the best you can with the evidence that exists (the customary standard) is not good enough. Now you MUST win. No excuses. No second-guessing. The consequences for the innocent client are too horrible to contemplate - and those consequences start right at the arrest.

Although, many years ago, I still remember my first innocent client and the stark look of trauma in his eyes from the arrest. He was sitting in a small dark holding cell at a local PD, shortly after being charged (falsely, it turned out) with bank robbery. He was shaking and obviously frightened. "I didn't do it," he said as soon as I sat down. "Sure," I replied. Even as a young attorney, I knew enough not to believe him. "It's got to be a fucking mistake!" "Right," I said, without any conviction. "Look, I'm your attorney, and I won't be able to help you, unless you cut the bullshit and level with me." He kept insisting. I started believing him. He appeared so genuinely frightened, so vulnerable, particularly when he explained how he was arrested. We've all been there. A police cruiser with flashing blue lights is coming up fast in the rear-view mirror. We pull over, hoping the cops are after someone else. Exactly what my client did. But then there were more cruisers and, with squealing tires, they pulled in front of and behind his car. Within seconds, he found himself looking down the business end of a Remington 12 gauge pump. It went downhill from there.

When things go wrong in the criminal justice system, it often turns out to be a problem with eyewitness identification. And so it was in this case. The good news is that I was quickly able to demonstrate this fact to the police and prosecutors, and the charges were dropped. The bad news is that, for my client, the trauma and damage would be long lasting. Yet it was the terror in my client's eyes, and his vulnerability right after the arrest, that struck me the most.

This is a vulnerability that J. H. Sanderson understands so well. Even rock 'n' roll musicians can be terrorized and frightened by the heavy hand of the criminal justice system. In *Dangerous Gambles*, Sanderson manages to skillfully blend the disparate worlds of law, espionage, and rock 'n' roll. The band members taste the dark side, and their vulnerability is the key that unlocks this door. Meticulous in detail and with authentic New England texture, Sanderson gets it right. He knows how to tell a story and drive it forward with characters that ring true. Innocence is not only rare, but can be irrelevant. Life is complicated, even for musicians. When the chips go down, who can you really trust?

Closely connected to my life in the courtroom has been my love of acting in local theater productions, for "telling a story" in an entertaining manner is one element in convincing the audience - the jury - that the story is worthy of belief. Sanderson also has an obvious grasp of this connection, for *Dangerous Gambles* is consistently entertaining. He would make a good lawyer; he crafts a compelling tale. I would be happy to serve on his jury.

Peter Heed
Westmoreland, New Hampshire

Table of Contents

CHAPTER ONE
"Busted"

On a sunny summer day in 1978, the whole world went to Hell. There was no preparation, there were no indications, and there were no warning signs. The effect was one of listening to an aria where the diva suddenly burped. No one knew exactly how it happened, and historians would debate for years what exactly triggered it. Nuclear tests by Russia in June were followed by protests in the West. Nuclear tests by America in July were followed by protests in the East, which were marked by reports of an "incident" in Eastern Europe, and ultimately Walter Cronkite's fatherly voice, announcing the Soviet Union's declaration of war.

In the immediate aftermath, there was panic. Everyone looked to the skies for the expected nuclear missiles, but none came, nor did any come the next day or the day after that. Since one side would not take the fatal step, the other decided not to, as well. The Third World War was turning out to be as conventional as the first two had been. This was especially so in its impact on the people. Faced with the need to supply fuel to its armed forces and in the grips of an oil shortage, coupled with the imminent threat to the Alaskan oil fields caused by a surprise Soviet invasion of the Aleutians islands and the Alaskan mainland, the United States implemented gas rationing almost as soon as war was declared, a decision that was soon followed by the rationing of rubber, sugar, coffee, and finally, meat and poultry. Americans felt the price of war immediately. More and more the American people sought distraction from their problems, and from movie theaters to dance halls, people turned out. However, due to wage and price freezes, the larger theaters and clubs went into decline, and things moved to smaller and smaller venues.

Such was the atmosphere in which the Roadhouse Sons performed. A few years prior to this, they had been opening for big name bands up and down the Eastern Seaboard, playing in front of thousands. Now in September, a mere few months later, they were playing to smaller clubs closer to home. With price freezes and shortages making concerts for the larger bands unaffordable for most Americans, cover bands like the Roadhouse Sons became quite popular on the club circuit. Working as a cover band for the larger, and now more expensive, big name bands, the Roadhouse Sons had quickly adapted to conditions and learned how to negotiate gas rationing and bartering into their contracts. They reduced their crew and equipment accordingly, yet still managed to put on the best performance that they could, or as their fans described it, 'rock out' almost every night. Not all bands had been able to adapt as they had, and a once crowded field became more open. However, these days, every joy came with a price, and the increased demand for travel strained their resources to the limit.

Despite this, if there was one thing that Cameron Walsh knew, besides music, it was how to make things work. As front man and lead guitarist, it often fell to him to make the tough choices for the band. When they realized they would have to reduce their road crew, he developed a test. Gathering the three roadies, he informed them that they received a call for a big show in Burlington, Vermont, but there was not enough gas to get them there from this gig in Queeche. If they made it, there would be a huge bonus; if they didn't make it, they'd be out of a job. They needed to figure out how to get the band to Burlington and do it by one o'clock that afternoon. Then he returned to his hotel room and curled up with a book. At twelve thirty there was a knock on his door and there stood Doug Courtland, his favorite roadie, bag in hand. Doug was the youngest roadie, at the ripe old age of 22, but his circumspection and ability to remain cool under pressure added years to his demeanor.

"We're ready," Doug said. "The truck is gassed, and since the oil was low, I put in a quart."

"Not so fast," Cameron said. "The other guys don't have gas for their car. We need two vehicles."

Without saying a word, Doug held up three gas coupons. Cameron didn't recognize the serial numbers on them and knew it was better not to ask to whom they belonged. His roadie had a knack for knowing how to find the things they needed—sometimes legal, sometimes not, and sometimes in between. Cameron had learned long ago that it was not a good idea to pry into it too much. As long as no one came knocking on his door, he, like many others, ignored it.

"Where are the other guys?"

Doug nodded his head toward the room where the roadies stayed.

"They haven't moved from there since you spoke to us," he said. From where they stood, Cameron could hear the loud, drunken voices of the other two, bitterly complaining about the injustices of life and how they had to "do everything."

"Wait for me in the truck," he told the roadie. Doug left without saying anything, but they were both well aware that the other guys were going to get the axe, and they had it coming. In bad times, if you want to keep your job, you don't have to be indispensable, just useful. They weren't.

Twenty minutes later, Doug noticed Cameron emerge from the hotel with his suitcase, followed by two other band members, Clyde Poulin, the rhythm guitar player (and keyboard player, when necessary), and Rich Webster, the bass guitarist. The drummer, Evan Dixon, was waiting in the other car. Of the other two roadies, there was no sign. Upon request, as he handed out the gas coupons, Doug told the others the gas stations at which to use the coupons. Cameron climbed into the cab with the roadie.

"They've got stuff to take care of," he explained. "We're going on ahead toward Rutland."

"I thought we had a show in Burlington?"

"Would you have gone to all that trouble to go to Rutland?"

Burlington, Vermont was a growing center for the music scene. Larger-than-average clubs were still in operation. The fact that it was not only a college town, but also accessible to Plattsburg Air Force Base, travelers to and from Montreal and the international airport, meant that there was more likelihood the band would be paid in cash and not "in kind." Rutland, on the other hand, was still home to smaller venues and did not offer as much opportunity.

"No, I guess not."

"I didn't think so," Cameron said, handing him the directions. "Let's go."

They drove on in silence for a while. At last, Doug spoke up.

"So, what exactly is this bonus you mentioned?"

"You keep your fucking job," Cameron yawned. Drawing his coat tighter, he leaned back in the seat to try and get some extra sleep.

He nodded off and slept fitfully, finally awaking when Doug pulled into the parking lot of the Batten Kill Roadhouse, a shop-worn building that had once been a dance hall, but now boasted a less refined clientele. Arriving a little after four thirty, Doug began unloading the back.

"Sorry to put all this on you," Cameron said. "We're going to have to make some adjustments, obviously. We'll help you as much as we can, but you're still going to have to do the work of the other guys."

"Do I get their pay, too?"

"Don't push your luck."

Doug shrugged. He didn't mind the loading and unloading part of his job; however, the setting up of the electronics did get him flustered. Fortunately, Cameron and the others had often insisted on doing that part themselves anyhow, so he didn't worry too much about it, and went about unloading the equipment and setting it up as near as he could guess to where they were supposed to play. The set-up was always basically the same; the lights and PA came out first, because they were positioned toward the back of the stage. The band always insisted on their own set-up, because even in the best of times, the quality of a venue's house system was often in question, and wartime was hardly the best of times. Some of the speakers were monstrous, but with the help of the dollies that they had, he figured it could be bearable.

After the lights and PA came the drum set, then the keyboard, then the amps, and lastly, the electronics cases and mics. Cameron had left his guitars in the truck the night before, so Doug set them aside and unlatched the cases, resting the lids on the latches so they were opened slightly to bring them gradually up to room temperature. Exposing a guitar to extreme temperatures causes warping, and while it hadn't been cold enough to freeze, he thought it best not to take chances.

Cameron carefully removed the lids to the PA and checked the settings. He was usually the one to oversee the loading and unloading of that equipment; the slightest disruption to the settings would have him spending valuable time readjusting and perfecting everything all over again. Rodger, the venue tech, still remembered the bawling out he had gotten the first time he worked for the band, and he didn't wish to repeat it. He had just finished unloading the truck when the other band members arrived.

As usual, the band came in the front door. They liked getting a good perspective on the room as well as the crowd so that they could make any special adjustments to their set list. A livelier club crowd would want simple down-and-dirty rock music, whereas some club denizens liked more blues, and still others appreciated a good mix. Tonight, as they suspected, it would be pure rock.

Not long after the war began, the Soviets launched an invasion of Alaska. From their air bases near the Bering Strait, MIG fighters attacked US Air Force bases in Alaska, as well as many of the ports. Cargo planes carried Soviet paratroopers, depositing them behind the lines, and enabling them to make tremendous gains, not only into the Alaskan coast, but also into the Alaskan wilderness and the Canadian northwest. Reports that filtered out showed that the Alaskan Resistance was making the Soviets pay dearly for every square inch of territory taken. A joint American-Canadian effort to push back the front had just opened up, and the public was in a fighting mood. Tonight's crowd would not be any exception.

With practiced nonchalance, the other three men began their usual pre-show routines. After greeting the crew that had already arrived, Evan, 27 years old and the more conservative of the group, would go to meet the owner. Based on his appearance, he was the logical choice. While his hair was shorter than the rest of the band, its tight curls still gave him a modern appearance that didn't seem out of place, even though he was clean-shaven. In addition, his clothes were usually less relaxed, preferring newer jeans and collared shirts. Being the only member of the band that was married, he tried to keep his options open in case the band should ever decide to break up and he was required to search for a more conventional means of employment, which, with the hard economic times, was an ever-present concern. In addition to being the drummer, he was the also the band's manager and handled the business aspect of things. Previously, they had employed an outside business manager, but after a while discovered that he had been negotiating his own deals, separate from what he had been telling them. Now, the Roadhouse Sons did everything in-house. Being a bit more conservative in appearance than the others, as well as having a background helping in his family's business, Evan had been the logical choice for the job.

Clyde would order a drink from the bar and make conversation with the bartenders, displaying an aptness for almost any subject of their focus. This, combined with his long blonde hair and dimpled smile that shone through his perpetual five o'clock shadow, and faux silver and turquoise bracelets that caused more than one woman to mention his resemblance to Robert Plant, helped him in his efforts to leave the masses with a favorable impression of him. All of it belied his young age of 24 years, and he had learned how to capitalize on that alluring success by making certain that both his jeans and shirts were as tight as he could manage to squeeze on. The skin-tight jeans, selectively and suggestively torn, assisted in provided some carefully orchestrated gyrations as the waitresses made their way past the stage. On more than one occasion, Clyde's attire had ensured that the band received the better brands of booze, as opposed to various homebrew varieties of the kind that bars were now trying to pass off as "top shelf."

Rich was the dark horse of the lot, in more ways than one. His skin and complexion were more on the swarthy side, whereas the others were more blonde and tanned. He, too, possessed a slender build on his 5' 11' frame. His dark features suggested a possible Native American heritage, and his dark hair, feathered back from his face, along with what some called a Fu Manchu mustache, sealed the assessment. His penchant for darker clothes and leather boots gave him an exotic appearance that many female patrons found exciting, and no one ever believed that he was only 25 years old. Never one to shy away from an audience, he would chat up the waitresses and find out their names before placing a drink order with them. He almost never approached the bar directly, but would make certain to deal directly with the servers throughout the show. Since these personnel were usually women, this helped generate a sense of competition with the female members of the audience, prompting them to get up and dance in hopes of attracting Rich's attention. To those that did not know him, Rich's reserved comportment made him seem indifferent to the attention that the audience tried to show him, yet another factor that made the ladies try even harder.

After they had done their preliminaries, the other three began to attend to their instruments, overseeing Doug's efforts and directing him to make whatever changes were needed. While this was unfolding, Cameron would begin his routine. Like Rich, Cameron had dark hair and dark eyes. However, unlike Rich, Cameron's skin was fair. Rich was the taller of the two, and Cameron, like Rich, sported a mustache, albeit a fuller model. Like most of the others, Cameron liked worn and tattered jeans and shirts, though he preferred his to be tattered from natural wear and tear. He favored motorcycle boots over the usual sneakers, and liked wearing woven bracelets. This feature, coupled with his shirts, bedecked with pop images or slogans, gave the impression of a more laid back, laconic individual, which was as far from the truth as it could be. He, 26 years old, was the second oldest to Evan, and they shared a quietly intense camaraderie and sentiment about all things Roadhouse Sons.

Even though Cameron would order a drink as soon as he arrived at the venue and addressed immediate concerns, he would always return to the bar to take a brief break. While there, he would make the acquaintance of the other patrons and spend time getting to know the bartender, finding out about them and buying the occasional round. This fostered an easy connection with the audience before the show even began, and provided the dual benefit of not only warming up the crowd, but generating and perpetuating a following that likely guaranteed the band return engagements with happy club owners. Once in a while, other band members would grumble that Cameron might pay too much time on his break, but he insisted that this was actually the most economical form of advertising. After all, you don't really have to pay for word of mouth.

When Rich began to tune his guitar, Cameron would return to the stage as well and begin his sound check. To the untrained eye, there was no cohesion to what was going on. The uncoordinated sounds, the individual movements of the band members, the stop-and-go efforts of the lights and the keyboard, and adjustments to one instrument after another, gave the impression that no one knew exactly what they were doing. Then, gradually, it came together. Doug would take his place at a table by the front of the stage, where he could have an unobstructed view. This was to ensure that he would know if he were needed onstage, either to deal with equipment or to deal with trouble. Individual notes were replaced with the opening chords of songs and the lights would begin to display a rhythm to their flashing. Before anyone realized the show was beginning, the stage lights would flash and a blast of sound would signal the opening song. As the shock wore off, the audience would respond with loud applause, as if to assure the band that they really had been paying attention all along. With a sly smile, Cameron would acknowledge their efforts and, almost as a reward, begin the show. The Roadhouse Sons were in the house!

The crowd was lively that night. As expected, they wanted to be worked up, and in recognition of it, the sets would go a little longer, and the sounds a little louder. The ladies danced and the men cheered. There were many new faces, but they also noticed some familiar ones. Despite the rationing and the war effort, or maybe because of it, there were those devoted fans who traveled to many, if not all, of the Roadhouse Sons' shows. There were the usual groupies that followed the band, but there were also some couples that also liked to keep up. Cameron noticed one such couple sitting in the corner and gave them a smile and wave. He often wished that he could catch them long enough to make their acquaintance, but they always seemed to leave before the show was over. It was a comfort to see familiar faces in troubled times, and the band made an effort to acknowledge each of them personally, if only with a "Hello" during the breaks.

In reality, the band played harder that night then they had in a while. The news on the war effort was a mixed bag; there was a push on the Alaskan Front, but Warsaw Pact forces had invaded neutral Austria. NATO forces were reinforcing Norway and Finland, and West Berlin had fallen after being under siege for the second time in thirty years. Presiding over all of this was the continued threat of nuclear attack. The people needed to be distracted, and the Roadhouse Sons would prove, once again, to be up to the challenge. Their voices were becoming hoarse and, despite having played for several days straight, Cameron's fingertips were almost raw, and he was at the point of exhaustion.

Once the set was over, Cameron made his way to the bar and ordered a drink. As expected, his favorite tequila was unavailable. Instead, he was offered one that the bartender said they had just gotten in the door that day. Cameron accepted it with a smile, but knew, even before he tasted it, that it would be horrible. The bitter, biting acid taste proved him correct, and he tried not to make a face as he sipped it. In the scramble to adjust to the war, one of the first things to come to the forefront, masquerading as "patriotic enthusiasm," were the black market dealers and racketeers, who offered "economic alternatives" to the more rare and expensive imported brands. "Protection booze" was flooding the market faster than bootlegged booze. In order to stay in business, bars usually had to buy liquor that was approved by the liquor agents. More often then not, the liquor was inferior alcohol either purchased cheap, or made and bottled in makeshift home distilleries It was purportedly against the law to make it that way, but with everything else going on, no one was going to spend much time worrying about bootleg alcohol, especially when its existence paid revenue to the states and municipalities that licensed it. So, like everyone else, Cameron had to settle for being screwed, while everyone concentrated on the big picture, which was just another way of saying, "If it doesn't affect me, I don't give a shit." That reality was as hard to accept as the horrid tequila was to drink. So when Evan approached Cameron just before the last set, Cameron was in no mood for bad news, and told Evan so.

"Well, you're going to get it anyway."

"If I am, there better be a fucking reason for it!" Despite the volume of the canned music that filled in for the band during their breaks, Cameron's voice was loud enough to attract some attention.

"Frank hasn't got the cash for us," Evan explained, his voice lowered. "The trucker strike has all but stopped his liquor shipments and he had to go with a wildcat outfit to stay open. He said they added a surcharge on top of the regular costs."

"Surcharge my ass," Cameron snarled "Bribe, say bribe damn it He's screwing us so he can pay his fucking bribe!"

"Keep your voice down!" Evan hissed. The "additional cost" of doing business these days was the elephant in the room. Everyone knew it was there, but no one wanted to talk about it in polite conversation. Some of the people standing nearby moved a few steps away, pretending not to hear.

"So, we're not getting paid? Is that what you're trying to tell me?"

"No," Evan assured him. "We're getting paid, just not all of it in cash."

"Oh, great, then. We're getting paid in what, may I ask? Chickens?"

"Will you please try to be reasonable?"

"Don't tell me to try and be reasonable!" Cameron demanded. "Are you going to have this same conversation with the others when you break the news to them, or am I going to be on my own?"

Evan took a deep breath, but said nothing.

"That's what I figured," Cameron said. "Do you mind telling me exactly what our reward for this last minute gig is? At least do me the courtesy of giving me a chance to think of how I'm going to explain it to everyone else."

"Well, he's wiping out our tabs, for one thing."

"Perfect," Cameron muttered, banging his glass on the bar to attract the bartender's attention. "Allie, bring me another and make it a double. Put it on my tab!"

"We're also getting some of their rations."

"I knew it! Chickens!"

"No. Regular commodities."

"This is a bar. What regular commodities could they have? Has the government started issuing peanuts now? Actually, since Carter's a fucking peanut farmer, I wouldn't put it past him to try and subsidize that. However, I'm still not interested!"

"Frank's the government distributer in town, and he can give us some of those things."

"We're back to the chickens, aren't we? Explain to me again why we picked you as our business manager?"

"Don't be difficult," Evan grumbled. "I'm talking about regular commodities that they give to everyone."

"Surplus peanut butter, surplus cheese and surplus powdered eggs," Cameron sneered, drinking deeply from the fresh glass placed in front of him. "I'd rather have the chickens. At least then I'd have fresh eggs!"

"We're also getting Government Issue gas coupons, and he's reopening the band house so we have a place to stay until the next show."

"Free gas, fleas and no charge for low grade booze; all this in exchange for cold, hard cash. A hard negotiator like you should consider working for the Teamsters; they haven't had anyone like you since Hoffa took off."

"Look, we're getting more than half of it in cash at least. That's better than nothing, right?"

"Are you content sending at least more than half of your pay back home?"

The color drained from Evan's face and his eyes went hard. He tried to keep his family life separate from the band. He often didn't engage in the wilder after-parties, and didn't associate with the groupies. Being on the road, and away from his wife and newborn daughter was painful for him. As a rule, the guys never pressured him to join them, nor did they interfere when he tried to get some time off to go home. Cameron knew that by making that remark, he had just crossed a terrible line.

"That was a cheap shot," Evan said. Torn between the high cost of childcare and the economic downturn, employment for Evan's wife was part-time, at best. Despite living with his mother, things were still difficult for them. The only steady income was what Evan sent home every week.

"No," Cameron said, looking him in the eye. "The Russian's attack on Anchorage was a cheap shot. This was a missile right in Red Square! You could have remembered that when they were giving you the sob story."

"Don't ever assume that I ever forget." Evan's voice was slow and even, and he returned Cameron's gaze. "I did the best that I could. If the money isn't there, it isn't there."

"Then what have we settled for?"

"Two hundred cash, one hundred in gas rations, another hundred in food."

"Four hundred total for a eight hundred dollar gig?! Brilliant."

"There's a war on, Cameron."

"No shit, really?"

"Don't be sarcastic!"

"Why the hell shouldn't I be?" Cameron demanded. "Why does everyone think we're the bottom of the totem pole? Why shouldn't I expect us to get paid what we've earned? Was I the only one that heard us kick ass tonight? Was I the only one who never saw that dance floor empty? Why the hell shouldn't I be royally pissed right now?"

"You should," Evan said, staring into his drink. "We all should. None of us should have to deal with this shit. In a perfect world, we wouldn't. But this isn't a perfect world, and it isn't a perfect situation, and I didn't get a more perfect deal and if you think you could have, then you are welcome to try."

Cameron studied him carefully. He knew Evan had tried to make a bad situation bearable.

"No," he said at last. "I think you did your best. Considering what you had to work with."

"What's that supposed to mean?"

"You'll see," said Cameron, setting down his drink. He headed around the bar to a door against the far wall, which opened onto Frank Boucher's makeshift office. There he found the supposedly beleaguered club owner counting out a large pile of money.

"I guess the strike is over?" Cameron snapped.

"What the hell do you think you're doing in here?" demanded Frank, tossing a towel over his desk.

"I'm here to get what I'm owed, and don't try any of your bullshit excuses with me!"

"I think you better get out of here. Right now, son, before you get yourself hurt."

"Are you threatening me, asshole?" Cameron challenged, taking a step toward him. "That would be a big mistake."

Frank regarded Cameron carefully, sizing him up, yet amused by Cameron's young and wiry frame.

The club owner was much older and more heavyset, with large arms and large hands. At first glance, one would have thought he was a former Marine or sailor. They both knew that he was a man who could take care of himself if trouble arose. Still, there is a certain sense of abandon that comes with youth, and there was no telling what risk the angry musician might take. Wisely, Frank wasn't about to display any weakness, or take any chances.

"I'm just going to say this one more time, son. Get out of here now."

Cameron didn't move, looking the club owner straight in the eye. He noticed Frank look quickly past him and knew that someone had stepped into the doorway. Cameron instantly regretted leaving his back to the door, and silently calculated how far he could jump to sidestep the expected attack. Then he heard a familiar deep voice.

"Everything all right?" asked Doug. Though immensely relieved, Cameron suppressed a smile at how the roadie tried to make his voice sound more menacing. For people that didn't know Doug, it was quite effective; for people that did know him, it was quite amusing. Cameron was glad that Frank didn't know Doug that well.

"Bringing reinforcements in won't help you any," warned Frank. "It will only make things worse."

"He's a roadie, not the Marines, you dumb fuck," Cameron sneered. Even as he did so, he caught the same menacing tone in his own voice. Unfortunately, he didn't know if it was affectation in his case, or real. No good would come from escalating the situation.

"I've got it under control, Doug," Cameron warned. "Wait outside, but don't let anyone else in here."

The two adversaries stared at each other, continuing to size each other up. Together, they created the familiar and age-old tableau of the younger generation struggling against the older one.

"If you negotiate a deal with me, old man, I would advise you not to try and renegotiate it later. You owe me money, and you're going to pay."

"I told your manager…"

"Save it, Frank!" Cameron snapped. "He didn't believe your bullshit and I don't either! If you were so strapped for cash, then what is that pile on your desk? You mind answering me that?"

"I don't have to explain anything to you," Frank answered. His voice was a low and glowering growl, and, for a moment, Cameron's mind flashed back to an old dog a neighbor had. He would give that same growl, just before he lunged at you. "Get out of my office or I'll call the cops."

"Go ahead. I'm sure they'd be quite interested in how you barter off government property to pay your bills."

"You can't prove that."

"State of Vermont says that a contract made in the presence of two witnesses is legally binding. You offered to pay us in government commodities in lieu of cash."

"Says who?"

"Our manager, our bass player, and me. I can add in the other guitar player and the roadie if you want. Hell, there are a half a dozen groupies that would swear to it, too, if they thought it would get them laid."

"If you want to play hardball, I would advise you to consider very carefully what you're doing. You might not get the chance to regret it."

The voice was the same low growl, but Cameron caught an additional edge to it, something more sinister than before.

Oh well… No fucking going back now.

"I'll worry about me. You worry about making certain I get what's coming to me."

Frank didn't say anything, nor did he move. Cameron also stayed where he was. The tension mounted, and they both knew that someone would have to do something to break it. Cameron felt the strain of the moment so clearly he was about to scream. Finally, the old man smiled.

"You're right," he conceded. "I'll see you get what you've got coming."

Turning back to his desk, the club owner rummaged around for an envelope and carefully counted out a small stack of hundred dollar bills. Tucking the flap inside, he handed it to Cameron.

"There's what you were owed, plus a little extra."

Cameron took the envelope and stuffed it into the back pocket of his jeans.

"Aren't you going to count it?"

"No."

"You trust me?"

"No. I'm just not going to count it right now. Plenty of time to do it later. Besides, I want to make sure I don't take my eyes off of you."

Frank's face registered the insult. His eyes darkened as he was about to respond. Then, at the last minute and as if thinking better of it, his face broke into a slight smile and he shook his head.

"Do you still want the rest of what I negotiated with your man?" Frank asked, trying to sound congenial.

"I don't need surplus peanut butter or toilet paper, buddy. Keep that shit. We'll be on our way just as soon as we tear down."

"But you've got three more days to play!" The shock in Frank's voice was genuine, and Cameron felt a surge of victory as he realized he had hit Frank where it hurt. Frank could not expect to draw people into his dive of a club if he didn't have something to offer, and the Roadhouse Sons were it. Judging by the fact that they had been asked to do this gig at the last minute, they might be the only hope Frank had.

"Scheduling conflict. Can't be helped," Cameron sneered.

Might as well press the assault.

"But we had an agreement!" Frank's voice was almost a screech now, and it was all Cameron could do not to smile.

Who's got who by the balls now, asshole?

"Don't try hiding behind a contract you just tried to wipe my ass with, old man. You might not like the atmosphere. Like I said, we'll be out of here as soon as we tear down."

Frank simply stood there watching Cameron, his mouth moving but no sound coming out. At last, he smiled again and held up his hands in a gesture of acceptance.

"It's late," the old man said calmly. "Hard to find a hotel this time of night. Might as well stay in the band house, at least 'til morning."

"I'll think about it."

"Look, son, no hard feelings, OK?" Frank said, holding his arms out. "Times are tough. We're all trying to make it. I tried something and it didn't work. No harm done, right?"

Frank's voice was much calmer now, more reasonable.

Almost sincere...

But Cameron didn't fall for it. Experience had taught him to be wary of sincere people.

"Whatever you say, Frank. I don't give a shit. I got my money and that is what I came in here for." But he still didn't make any moves toward the door. He decided to hold out and see where Frank would take it next.

"Tell you what. I'll still wipe your tabs. All your drinks are on the house, eh?"

"That's up to you. I could give a shit. They cost you an eighth of what you charged. You can afford to be generous."

Frank didn't register any response to that. Cameron knew then that he had been right about the protection booze. A strong man like Frank was not about to acknowledge anything that had him under its thumb. Or maybe it was his thumb in the first place.

"Then the drinks are on me, son. Deal?"

He held out his hand to the singer, who just shook his head.

"You're a piece of work Frank, you really are," Cameron sneered, realizing that Frank was unable to offer anything else. Frank was, therefore, probably unable to do anything to Cameron, officially at least. "Can't even remember you made both of those offers already. You still think you can screw me and make me thank you. Fuck off."

Stepping back into the hall, Cameron came face to face with the other members of the band as well as Frank's son, whom he noticed was sequestered away by Doug from the rest of them. The young man was trying to get around the roadie, who had a firm hand resting on the center of his chest. Doug could keep Frank's son at arm's length if the young man behaved, or he could drive his knuckles up into his windpipe if the youngster tried anything.

"No last set. Start tearing it down, guys" Cameron snapped. "We're out of here."

No one said anything as they struck the instruments and equipment. Except for what they needed to say to get things done, everyone packed up and loaded in silence. A few of the patrons wandered by to see if everything was all right, but Cameron didn't pay much attention to them, and they gradually drifted off. A few young ladies hung around by the door, but eventually they, too, drifted into the night, regretfully ensuring that the band would be spending the evening only in their own company. One more reason Cameron hated Frank.

Frank emerged from the office, and called for Cameron. The singer didn't acknowledge him, merely shaking his head and motioning for Evan to see what Frank wanted. Without saying a word, the roadie followed the drummer.

Evan returned a few minutes later with another envelope and a set of keys, which he handed to Cameron. Evan whispered in Cameron's ear, saying nothing to anyone else, and began loading his equipment into the truck. Finally, the Roadhouse Sons were done.

"You all know where the band house is?" Cameron asked. "If not, follow us. I'm tired and want to get some sleep."

"You're actually going to stay there?" Doug was surprised at his decision.

"I said I'm tired and I want to get some sleep. Now *drive*." With that, the roadie realized that there was no point in continuing the conversation. Cameron knew that there would likely be no rooms available in the hotels they'd pass, and that sleeping in a place familiar to Frank was dangerous. But with the newly established curfews in place, the Roadhouse Sons had to be off the road soon. Since they had initially planned on staying at the band house, they hadn't bothered to secure hotel rooms prior to the gig, and Cameron wasn't sure where any might be. He didn't know what choice they had, if any. Besides, he not only had a gun, but if he told the roadie that Frank's behavior cost them the additional time and wages, Doug would be ready to take Frank on. Cameron wasn't thrilled whatsoever at the thought of this, especially after appearing so victorious earlier.

You can't win them all.

Cameron appreciated having Doug's additional capabilities as an occasional bouncer and body guard, posts for which Doug was very well suited. Doug was able to dispatch these duties quickly and without question. Big and solid, with shaggy black hair under his ever-present trucker cap and heavy work boots, Doug projected an irrefutable air of solidity. He had once told the band that he had never played sports in school, and the guys were surprised by that admission. Quieter than the others, he did not associate much with most of the people that came to the shows, a trait which many mistook for arrogance. In reality, Doug's seeming arrogance was a sense of insecurity around other people. Never having completed his education, for reasons never revealed, he was very self-conscious of saying the wrong thing, or not comprehending a conversation. Isolation was his defense mechanism, and loyalty and devotion his tokens of gratitude for the acceptance the band gave him.

After we leave tomorrow I'll "remember" that I do have your pay after all.

The band pulled out of the parking lot and headed south on Route 7A. Cameron didn't speak, but just looked out the window at the houses they passed. In the rear-view mirror, Doug kept an eye on the headlights of the other car as they followed behind closely to make sure their small caravan wouldn't be separated. Suddenly, Doug noticed the flash of blue lights and realized that there was a police car approaching his rear at a high rate of speed. As soon as he noticed the first police car, Doug realized that there were more behind it.

"What the hell is this all about?" he muttered.

"Better pull off to the side," Cameron advised. "Let them pass."

Doug was already pulling off the road when he noticed that one of the police cars had stopped behind Evan's car, and another one was pulling up ahead of him. Two more police cars were pulling up alongside the truck, and Doug realized this was not a routine pullover. Two state troopers emerged from their vehicles with guns drawn to confirm it.

"Keep your hands where we can see them," one of the troopers shouted. "Exit your vehicle slowly."

Opening the door with his right hand, Doug made certain to keep his left hand in plain view. As he was stepping down from the cab, he noticed one of the troopers was going around the front of the truck, his gun drawn, and shouting the same commands to Cameron.

"Put your hands against the side of the truck," his trooper ordered. "Spread your legs."

"What the hell is this about?" Doug demanded, but received no response. As he was undergoing the pat-down, he saw Cameron come around the front of the truck, his hands clasped together on top of his head. A few paces behind him followed the police officer, his gun drawn. From all the shouting, Doug guessed that the others were going through the same procedure, and were none too happy about it.

Doug was ordered to turn around, and perform a field sobriety test. While he was doing it, he heard one of the troopers shout.

"I think I found it," the trooper cried, holding up a white envelope. Doug recognized it as the pay envelope from the club. He knew instantly that this had something to do with the confrontation with Frank earlier.

"Hey, that's mine," cried Cameron, who was instantly slammed back up against the truck.

"Move one more time, and you're getting cuffed!"

One of the troopers began emptying the contents of the envelope onto the hood of the cruiser. In the glare of the trooper's flashlight, the money could be seen, and, as it was counted, Doug noticed something else drop onto the hood.

"Well, what have we got here?" the trooper asked, holding up a small plastic bag. "I think we might have found a little contraband."

"Where the hell did that come from?" cried Cameron, who had been turned toward the road, and could now see the scene unfold. "That's not mine!"

"You just said it was, son."

"I know, but *that* isn't mine!"

"Well then, who's is it and how did it end up in your pocket?"

"I have no idea, but there is no way in hell that belongs to me!"

"You can tell that to a judge. Turn around and put your hands behind your back."

"What the hell for?"

"You're under arrest for robbery, assault and possession of narcotics."

"Are you out of your fucking minds? That was planted..." Cameron began, but was not able to finish. In mid-sentence he was thrown against the side of the truck. Seeing this, Doug began to protest and stepped toward the other officer, but the end of a service revolver behind his ear stopped him in his tracks.

"You're under arrest too, son," the officer warned. "Driving under the influence. And I'll add resisting arrest, if you make one more move that I don't tell you to make. Do you understand me?"

The five men were placed in the backs of the various police cars and taken to the nearby State Police barracks, where they were each booked and placed into custody in separate rooms. None of them had purchased or even used any illegal narcotics. With no sound reason for their arrests, they were left to contemplate their ominous, and respective, fates.

CHAPTER TWO

"Recruitment"

As Cameron sat in the austere interrogation room, he noticed that the clock on the wall had been removed. He had also been forced to turn over his watch and belongings when he was booked, and therefore had no idea of how long he had been in custody. In an attempt to occupy his mind, he studied the speckled pattern of the linoleum tiles on the floor, remarking to himself how it seemed to match the ceiling tiles. The halls were painted in a drab, military green and held no posters or notices, thus offering little to occupy his attention. Cameron began to stare at his hands, carefully examining the torn calluses on his fingertips, and replaying the evening events in his mind. The hard seat made his backside sore, adding to his irritation.

That asshole Frank did this. He must have! Couldn't get over the fact that he couldn't cheat us, so he decided to trump this shit up. When I get out of here, I'll sue his ass for the two cents its worth.

Cameron began to pace about the room. The sound of his boots against the linoleum of the floor echoed off the walls, increasing his feelings of abandonment and isolation. Cameron remembered what he had been charged with, and vaguely wondered if he should change his thoughts to *if* he got out of there. Then it dawned on him that he wasn't in a holding cell and no one had been brought in to provide a statement. He started to shout for one of the officers, but before he had a chance, the door opened and his arresting officer entered the stark room. Cameron felt a surge of relief as the sounds of the outer room floated in; he felt grateful for the trooper standing in the doorway because it meant that he was no longer alone. The trooper did not speak, but simply stood in the doorway. For a moment, Cameron thought the trooper was going to tell him that it was all a big mistake, and that Cameron was free to go. But something about the other man's demeanor crushed that hope.

"Your lawyer is here," the trooper said, holding the door open.

"What lawyer?" Cameron demanded. "I didn't call for a lawyer. You assholes haven't let me make my one phone call yet."

Another man stepped through the door before the trooper could respond. For a moment, Cameron wondered if the man was a public defender, but there was something vaguely familiar about the man, though Cameron couldn't quite place it.

"Thank you, Officer," the man smiled. "I'd like to confer with my client alone, if you don't mind."

"What client?" Cameron demanded. "I don't know you!"

The trooper nodded to the other man as if neither of them had heard a thing, and closed the door behind him as he left. Cameron stared at the closed door, no longer feeling abandoned, but still feeling anxious, and dubious about being left with this stranger. The stranger smiled at Cameron, and sat opposite him. The man was of average height, had dark hair and eyes, and looked to be in his mid-thirties, with a stocky build. There was a nagging familiarity to him that demanded Cameron's attention, but Cameron just could not recognize him. The man was dressed in a polyester dress shirt with no tie, with the top two buttons open. He wore tan slacks and tan dress boots with metal rings and leather straps. Cameron wondered why this man wore motorcycle boots, as he didn't look the type. He was clean-shaven and, from his smile, Cameron could see that he had fine teeth. His voice had a confident tone that made both Cameron relaxed, but on guard.

Who is this guy?

"Great show tonight," the man said with a smile. It was then that recognition dawned on Cameron. This man had been coming to the shows for the last month or so.

That couple I wanted to chat with...

Cameron spoke up. "OK, now I remember you. I've seen you at the gigs; you've been coming with a girl with sandy-brown hair and a nice smile. Kind of reminds me of Olivia Newton-John."

The other man settled into his seat, hands folded, on the table. He looked at Cameron, inspecting him. Cameron noticed a smile break across the man's face. Cameron dared to think that he had finally made a connection with someone, and nearly began to cry from the realization.

"You noticed her smile?" the man grinned. "I thought some of her other features might have been more ingrained in your memory."

Cameron gave him a knowing smirk and leaned back in his chair.

"OK, it's not the first thing that I remember when I think of her. No crime in that, is there?"

"None whatsoever."

"Is she your girlfriend?"

"No. She's my associate."

"Is she a lawyer, too?"

"No, not quite."

Before Cameron could ask him what he meant, the man continued.

"Mr. Walsh, I don't think I need to remind you that you are in serious trouble. Narcotics possession, assault, robbery, theft of government property, and, as if that weren't enough, possession of black market gas rations. Do you realize the gravity of this situation, Mr. Walsh?"

"Gravity nothing!" Cameron shouted. "Every charge you named is bogus, and I can prove it! Besides, exactly who did I supposedly assault and rob?"

"Frank Boucher, the owner of the Batten Kill Roadhouse. You do remember him, I assume?"

Cameron stared, dumbfounded.

"That's bullshit," he said at last. "I never touched him. He's twice my size! I never stole anything from him, either, and I've never used illegal rations, *ever*."

"Ever, Mr. Walsh? Ever is a big word and covers a broad range of time. Let's limit ourselves to tonight, specifically, the Mobil station just outside of Queeche. Your band truck was gassed up with unauthorized rations, and the car belonging to your associates was gassed up with similar rations at the same gas station immediately thereafter. That discounts your word "ever.""

Cameron found himself infuriated with the other man's condescending tone, but he realized that the man offered the best chance to deal with the potential nightmare of it all, so Cameron remained quiet.

"The police have corroborating witnesses that say you confronted Mr. Boucher in his office at the club tonight. Do you recall that situation?"

"Yeah, I confronted him. Boucher was trying to weasel out of paying us, so I went in to his office to get the rest of our money. That was it. I never laid a hand on him!"

"Did you, or did you not, take government-issue commodities from that establishment?"

"Hell no, I didn't," Cameron insisted, trying to keep the frustration and panic out of his voice, yet not confident that he was succeeding.

"Then how can you explain the canned meat, peanut butter, powdered eggs, and other government-issue foods in the back of your truck?"

"I don't know anything about them," Cameron said, feeling his mouth go dry. "Just because they were in the back of the truck doesn't mean they belong to me."

"The truck is registered to you; therefore, you are responsible for its contents."

Cameron eyed the man warily. Something was not right.

"For someone claiming to be my lawyer, you seem to be building quite a case for the prosecution."

The other man smiled and leaned forward.

"I'm not a lawyer."

Cameron sat back in his chair. He could not believe his ears. If the man wasn't a lawyer, what was he? Another cop? Was all of this a set up to gather more information from him? Cameron began to fear that he would never get out of there, and panic sprang up anew. He desperately wanted to escape.

"Then who the fuck are you?" Cameron demanded.

"I represent a company that is interested in your band, and possibly retaining its services."

"What the fuck did you say?" Cameron gasped. "Let me get this straight. I'm looking at spending the rest of my life in Windsor, and you want to book the band? What the fuck can you be thinking?"

"You won't be going to Windsor State Prison, Mr. Walsh. I can assure you of that."

Cameron, convinced that his future was over, felt his heart race as he talked to this stranger. To hear the man say those words, however, gave Cameron a feeling of hope that things weren't as bad as they seemed.

"Really?"

The man smiled and nodded, which made Cameron relax.

"Yes. These charges are federal offenses over which the federal government has jurisdiction. Under normal circumstances, you would be headed to a federal prison."

Cameron felt his stomach tighten.

"Normal circumstances?"

"The world is at war, Mr. Walsh. Tampering with ration books affects the war effort. You would be subject to a military tribunal and military prison."

"Fuck my life," Cameron moaned, putting his head in his hands. He thought of his parents, and of the gigs the band had to play. He thought of small, inconsequential things that suddenly seemed so important, now that he was faced with the prospect of not being able to do them.

"I can help," the man said, esoterically.

Cameron looked at him, the perpetually cryptic smile on the man's face; pleasant, warm, yet totally inscrutable.

"And just how do you propose to do that? You just said you're not a lawyer."

"True. As I said, I work for a company that is interested in you, and can help facilitate your release."

"What kind of company? None of the record companies can have that kind of pull."

The man smiled and leaned back in his chair, casually crossing his legs. The man no longer annoyed Cameron. Now, Cameron hated him.

"Record companies don't; my company does."

"What company?" Cameron insisted, impatiently.

"We will discuss that later. Right now, I have a proposal for you."

Cameron's mind was spinning. First, he was charged with a list of crimes a mile long, then he found himself approached by a man whom he was told is a lawyer, but isn't, and who is now offering to help Cameron out of his very serious predicament.

Cameron decided to take advantage of the situation as best as he could.

"The longer I sit here talking to you, the longer it'll be before I go to prison. Go ahead. Talk."

"Your band is very popular," the man said, opening his briefcase and removing a manila folder.

Cameron shrugged.

"You play all over New England. Isn't it true that you've received requests to play elsewhere?"

Cameron could not see where this conversation was going, but followed along anyway.

"We always get requests. The trick is having them develop into real gigs."

"Such as, the opportunities you had to play in New York? The Roseland Ballroom in Messina, Buzio's in Malone, and the Officers' Club in Plattsburg?"

As the man mentioned each venue, Cameron felt his blood run cold. He hadn't told anyone about those phone calls. The managers offered very sweet deals for the band to come and play, but, as is often the case, the leads turned out to be pipe dreams. Cameron was never willing to sacrifice confirmed show dates until he was certain new leads would actually work out.

"How did you know about those?" Cameron

"That isn't important right now. Your band has the talent and ability to return to its previous stature of shows, but has no means to take advantage of these opportunities. Is that a fair assessment?"

"Yeah, I suppose."

"What if I said we could help you with that? Would you be interested?"

"Not that it makes any difference under the circumstances, but, yeah; let's say that I was interested. What then?"

"We would make it possible for you, and perhaps present other possibilities as well."

"What kind of possibilities?"

"Let's not get ahead of ourselves, Mr. Walsh. Before we do anything at all, you must agree to cooperate with us."

"And if I don't agree?"

The man smiled. "Your only other option involves serving a prison sentence."

With that, the man rose from his chair and left the room. A trooper entered and, motioning for Cameron to get up, led him out into the hall. Cameron saw another officer leading Evan. Cameron called out to him, but was cut off by his handler.

"No talking," the trooper commanded. Cameron was in no mood to argue.

Cameron and Evan were brought into another room, where the other band members were waiting. Cameron could tell that, by the look on their faces, the band had been subjected to the same conversation as he had.

Possibly even with the same man, and no doubt they got the same offer, or rather, the same ultimatum.

Before he could confirm this with Evan, the door opened and the same gentleman entered, followed by another man, and a woman they had recognized from the club. Now, though, she was dressed far more professionally than the sweater and painted-on jeans she donned earlier in the evening. The other man was no one they recognized. He had short brown hair and dark eyes. Despite the fact that he wore a t-shirt and blue jeans, they could tell that he would have been more comfortable in a suit. The clothes were all too new, right down to the sneakers. It was obvious that this man was trying to look casual, and failing miserably. Entering the room, he ignored the rest of them and stared at Doug. The roadie returned his stare and Cameron noticed him tighten his jaw. Cameron suspected that this was the man that had talked with Doug. The others seemed to brighten when they saw the woman, but they did not relax.

"All right, gentlemen," Cameron's interrogator said. "My associates have spoken to you all, and presented to you an offer that will assist you with your current situation. We've given you enough time to think it over and discuss it amongst yourselves. Now, we want your decision."

"We need more information before we can give you that," Evan said. "Who do you work for? What do you want us to do? You've been pretty specific as far as the consequences of saying "no," but you haven't said much about what we'd be saying "yes" to."

The man considered that for a minute.

"You're right. I will lay the cards on the table. We are operatives with a government agency and are responsible for establishing a network of observers in this region. We feel that you would be suitable for the job."

"What kind of agency and what kind of observers, exactly?" demanded Rich.

"Spies."

The word hit the room like a bomb. The truth, once revealed, did nothing to make the band feel less uneasy. In fact, it made them feel much worse.

"Certainly, you know what a spy is, gentlemen?"

"Russian spies?"

"No, American."

"Why would America want to spy on her own people?" asked Clyde.

"Not all of her citizens are loyal to her cause," the man explained. "Sometimes people need to be watched."

"Isn't that what the KGB says, too?" Cameron muttered.

"Yes it is, in fact," the man smiled, unperturbed. "Motives and methods are quite similar on both sides of this business, though ideology may differ."

"What are you asking us to do?" Rich asked, and the others noticed that while he did not change his body language, his eyes displayed a great deal of interest, which surprised some of the others.

"Wherever there are people loyal to a cause, there are also people who are not. That is a concern to us, considering that we are actively involved in fighting the Soviets. Anything that potentially destabilizes the war effort is of great concern."

"But what does that have to do with us?" asked Cameron. "We don't get involved with politics. What the hell are we supposed to do about it?"

"One of the missions of any intelligence organization is to keep black marketers under surveillance, and uncover their plans."

"And?" snapped Cameron.

The band shifted impatiently, waiting for the man to get to his point.

"Many of the black market racketeers attend your shows."

"That's not our fault," insisted Cameron. "We have no way of monitoring or controlling our fans' political views!"

"We see no connection between them and you, except for their enjoyment of your type of music and their propensity to congregate at your shows. "

"So, we're supposed to switch our music," grumbled Rich. "You want us to start playing selections from Bread, or James Taylor, so you can hear what they're saying? Fuck you. Learn to read lips!"

The man leaned back in his chair and took a deep breath.

"We won't do either," the man replied. "We want you to keep doing what you're doing. Do not change a thing. You are perfect for what we need."

"How? What do *we* do that's so special?"

"Three months of observation at your every show, every battle of the bands, every acoustic set has given us the opportunity to see how you interact with the crowds and the venue staff. You have an advantage over the rest of the population; you are already infiltrated into the groups that we need to monitor. All we require is that you pay attention to what certain people are saying, and pass along to us anything that you hear."

"If you've been coming to the shows, how come you haven't made contact with them yourself?" asked Evan. "What do you need us for?"

"Attempts by our agents have yielded no results, Mr. Dixon," the man explained. "We noticed the attention that the racketeers pay to you, and we decided upon this as the best course of action."

"Getting us arrested?" asked Clyde.

"Enlisting your assistance," the man replied with a smile.

"How come you never talked to us about it before?" demanded Evan. "I noticed that you always left before the show was over."

"Your activity is chaotic following your shows. You are packing equipment and preparing to leave. There is no opportunity for substantial discussion then, or during your performances."

"Why didn't you just call us, or ask?" Cameron was losing patience with the situation and the tension showed in his voice.

"Recruitment is most successful when conducted in an environment that ensures cooperation."

"What do you mean?"

"We employ incentives to encourage cooperation. We are, therefore, more persuasive and successful in our recruitment attempts."

"That's a nice way of saying blackmail," grumbled Doug.

The man laughed. "Extortion is employed as necessary. Pictures or films of a compromising nature are particularly effective. Prominent individuals caught in flagrante delicto are far more willing to help us than, say, ordinary individuals going about their business."

"You've got embarrassing pictures of us?" cried Clyde.

"No, Mr. Poulin, that is not the direction we chose to take with you gentlemen."

"And why not, may I ask?" sneered Cameron.

"Mr. Walsh, even we realize that such photos would hardly embarrass you. Instead, we offer you something you can't refuse— assistance in avoiding time in prison."

"Wow... It was lucky for you we got arrested then, wasn't it?" asked Clyde.

"I don't think luck had a hell of a lot to do with it," muttered Doug. The man smiled knowingly.

"If you choose to cooperate, you stay out of prison. If you refuse to cooperate, there is no way we can help you."

"So, tell us again. What exactly happens if we say yes?" Rich asked.

"All of the charges against each of you disappear. You walk out of here and to new accommodations that we have reserved for you. You'll have warm, clean rooms, hot baths, and cold beer are at your fingertips."

"And, again, if we don't cooperate?" asked Clyde. The man chuckled and stretched.

"Mr. Poulin, a man of your build will have a very difficult time in prison."

"Can we have a few more minutes to think this over?" Evan asked.

"No," the man replied. "We gave you ample time to consider things already. What is your answer, gentlemen? Yes or no?"

"You can't expect us to just answer like that," Evan insisted. "What are the consequences of saying yes? What are the risks? What could happen to us? What if we change our minds?"

"Mr. Dixon, there are consequences to every decision one makes in life, and this is no different. The risks are great. You could be killed by one of the racketeers, but then again you could be killed while driving to your next performance. You could be caught while undercover, but every occupation has its hazards. Failure is the only real risk, but one risks in everything. If you fail, you could die and so could others. And changing your mind later is highly discouraged. Your answer, gentlemen?"

"Just a minute," blurted Rich. "How do we know that you're really Americans? What proof do you have that you're not Russians?"

"Russians would not use a Vermont police barracks to recruit spies."

"But how do we know that isn't what you want us to think?" asked Clyde. It was obvious to everyone that he was trying to buy time by dragging out the conversation.

"You don't, Mr. Poulin. Your time is up. You simply and ultimately have to trust us. Your answer!" the man commanded.

The Roadhouse Sons looked from one to the other.

"I don't want to go to prison, man," insisted Clyde.

"I don't want to die," declared Evan.

"Damned if we do, damned if we don't," muttered Cameron.

The woman, having been silent the whole time, startled the band when, at last, she finally spoke. "There is a way to avoid prison if you decide not to go along with us," she said, with an esoteric smile.

"Really?!" Cameron smiled back. "And what would that be?"

"Volunteer for the Alaskan Front."

The smile faded from Cameron's face, but not from hers.

"This is the last time I will ask, gentlemen," the man sighed. "Yes or no?"

"Yes," said Clyde.

"Sure," said Rich.

"What choice have we got?" muttered Evan. "Yes."

They all looked at Cameron. He leaned back in his chair with his hands clasped behind his head, staring at the ceiling.

"Have fun guys, I'll take my chances with the judge."

"Mr. Walsh, the offer is only good if all parties come to the same decision. You have thirty seconds."

Cameron shifted his gaze, but not his position. The other band members looked at him with pleading expressions. As he looked at them seated around the table, some corner of his mind wanted to see them as removed from him, as guys headed down a road that he didn't need to travel. However, he knew better. They had been together for a long time; he and Rich had gone to school together, and Clyde was the first person ever to audition for the band, and Evan came on board shortly thereafter. Even Doug had demonstrated loyalty to them by his constant willingness to stay with the band through all of their career ups and downs, even sleeping in hotels when it was possible, but in the band truck when it wasn't.

No. I can't do it to them.

At last, Cameron said, "Well then, we can't break up a set, can we? Besides, like the man says, with your long hair, Clyde, prison might not be the best place for you, and none of you like the cold, so I guess my answer's yes, then, isn't it?"

"That leaves you," the man said. All eyes turned on Doug.

The roadie shifted in his chair and stared at the wall, but made no response.

"Once again, I will remind you that you all go free as a group, or to jail as a group. Everyone's fate now rests in your hands, Mr. Courtland. Your decision?"

Doug put his head in his hands and stared at the floor for a few moments. Finally, he muttered something under his breath.

"I didn't hear you, Mr. Courtland," the man snapped, clearly losing patience.

"I said yes," Doug snapped back, still keeping his back to the rest of them.

"That settles it. My associates and I will gather your personal effects and take you to your accommodations. We have much to discuss. That can wait until the early morning."

Cameron could tolerate the situation no longer. "Now just a minute! Who the hell *are* you!?"

"I am Mr. Dwyer, and these are my associates, Miss McIntyre and Mr. D'Lorenzo. Miss McIntyre and I are your designated contacts. Mr. D'Lorenzo is here on a check ride, a refresher course, aren't you Don?"

The other man sat with his arms crossed, scowling and saying nothing.

He and Doug could pass for sulking bookends.

"Mr. D'Lorenzo, get the car. Miss McIntyre, please deliver this file to the sergeant." Dwyer handed her a folder from his briefcase, and Miss McIntyre left the room. Reaching into the briefcase again, Dwyer withdrew a battered white envelope. Cameron recognized it as the one from his own pocket. Mr. Dwyer tossed it toward him.

"Mr. Walsh, I believe this is yours. You will find that upon reflection, Mr. Boucher realized his serious error in judgment and decided to make certain that he paid you in full. There is also an additional thousand dollars. A bonus."

Cameron eyed Dwyer and reached for the envelope, quickly pocketing it.

"Your vehicles and equipment will be returned to you at a later date," Dwyer continued. "You will find everything intact."

As they were getting up to leave, Mr. Dwyer turned to Evan.

"Oh, Mr. Dixon, congratulations on your wife's promotion. I'm sure the pay increase will come in quite handy."

"What promotion?"

"The supervisor position for which she applied," Dwyer continued. "Upon reconsideration, her superiors felt that she was the best qualified for the position, after all. And there's another bit of good news. Jessica had an unexpected opening in her daycare, so your parents won't have to take care of the baby. Until tomorrow, gentlemen. Goodnight."

With that, Dwyer left the room. The guys looked from one to each other, a chill creeping over them.

"Man, they know about your family," murmured Clyde. "Who's Jessica?"

"She's a friend of Elaine's," Evan whispered. "She told me she'd talked to Jessica about putting the baby with her, but she was only licensed to have five kids, and didn't expect to have an opening for some time."

"So, what a coincidence that she just got an opening, eh?"

Evan looked at the keyboard player, his face pale.

"I just talked to her about that tonight, just before the show. I didn't even mention it to you guys."

"Oh, Christ," gasped Clyde, sinking into the chair.

"Don't be surprised," spat Doug. "They're like spiders. They have webs everywhere. Let's go." Before anyone could respond, he left the room.

In the hallway outside, none of the troopers noticed the band. The guys were each handed an envelope of their personal effects and they signed for the packages without saying a word.

"Your ride is waiting outside," said the dispatcher with a smile. "Have a nice evening."

Cameron went to the window, where he saw a Chevy Blazer sitting outside the front door. He couldn't see into the driver's seat to see who was driving, but he wondered if it was the mysterious Mr. Dwyer. The group looked at one another uneasily before heading outside.

"We can go out the back, guys," Clyde suggested. "We can disappear and they'll never find us."

"Do you think he was really congratulating me about my wife?" said Evan. "He wasn't making small talk, Clyde. He was letting me know they had information on my family, and I'm willing to bet that they've got something on each one of us, something that will make us behave if we think of resisting."

"You're probably right," agreed Rich. "Looks like there's nothing we can do about it, is there?"

"Nope," said Clyde. "There's no turning back now."

"Let's get this over with," muttered Cameron, pulling up the collar of his Navy pea coat against the cold, and climbing into the front seat. The others climbed into the back. It was then that they noticed who the driver was. It was Mr. D'Lorenzo.

"Where's your friend?" D'Lorenzo asked. "There are only four of you."

"Yeah. Where's Doug?" asked Clyde.

Just then they saw him emerging from the police barracks.

"You'll have to get into the far back," smiled D'Lorenzo. "All the other seats are taken."

"They're small," Doug answered in an undoubtedly authoritative tone. "They can slide over."

Before anyone could protest, the roadie climbed into the back seat and slammed the door, forcing the other three to push closer together.

"Always have to have it your way, don't you?" D'Lorenzo muttered, putting the Blazer into gear and pulling out into the night. They drove on in silence, no one daring to say anything. Eventually, they arrived in a parking lot surrounded by several darkened buildings.

"Wait here," instructed D'Lorenzo, putting the vehicle in park and getting out. A few moments later, he emerged from one of the buildings and motioned for them to follow him.

"There's a suite on the top floor," he told them, handing Cameron the keys. "There is enough room for all of you, so stay together. There is a stocked kitchen if you're hungry and want to eat. Don't leave the room for any reason. We'll contact you with instructions tomorrow. Don't talk to anyone, and leave the *Do Not Disturb* sign on the door like you usually do. That will help ensure privacy. Now, I see five of you here. We expect to see the same five of you tomorrow, so please don't try to reconsider our little arrangement. I think you realize that that would not be a good idea."

Without ceremony, D'Lorenzo left them at the front door of the building and, getting back into the Blazer, drove back toward town. Stepping through the front door, the guys found themselves in what appeared to be a lobby, but there was no one at the desk. It was then that they realized there were no cars in the parking lot. They wondered if there was anyone else at all in the building.

"Didn't he say it was on the top floor?" asked Cameron.

"Yeah."

"Well, let's find it. I'm beat."

As they went up the stairs, they noticed the usual nondescript paintings on the corridor walls, and the typical generic flower arrangements on the tables. Cameron felt one of the blossoms as he walked past, and noticed, with great surprise, that it was real. They continued down the hall. There were numbers on the rooms, but no sound came from anywhere. Reaching the top of the second flight of stairs, they realized that there was only one door. They hesitated for a moment, as that door didn't have any identifying markings on it. However, when Cameron inserted the key into the lock, he was able to open it.

The light was already on and they stood for a few moments, regarding the room, which was actually a small apartment. Proceeding into the space, they first walked into a small kitchen, constructed with a breakfast bar in lieu of a table. This opened onto a sunken living room with plush, white wall-to-wall carpet. A matching white leather sectional sofa occupied the center of the room, faced with a matching white leather recliner. In one corner of the room was a large television, and along the opposite wall was a state-of-the-art stereo system. Along the far wall, the upper platform of the living room floor opened into a hallway with three doors on the far side, and a door at each end of the hall.

"Where's the bathroom?" asked Rich.

"How should I know?" shrugged Cameron. "This is my first time here, too."

There were two doors in the kitchen. One proved to be a linen closet, with additional sheets, blankets and towels. The other was the door to a large marbled bathroom.

"Whoa," mumbled Rich. "I've only seen stuff like this in the movies."

"A James Bond movie, perhaps," mused Evan.

Forgetting their fatigue, they began to open the cupboards, searching the purportedly stocked cupboards for provisions. Milk, eggs, sugar, and butter were among the rationed items, along with bread, cheese and coffee.

"Real coffee!" cried Clyde, who had never acquired a taste for the grain substitutes. Various cereals, boxed meals, and canned goods were also stocked. Cameron noticed the recycling bin for the used cans.

Even spies have to support the war effort, I guess.

In the living room, one of the buttons on the remote control revealed a hidden liquor cabinet. Clyde went over to examine the contents of it and discovered a shaker.

"Martini," Rich said, doing a poor imitation of Sean Connery.

"Shaken, not stirred!" cried Evan and Clyde in unison.

Just then, one of them hit another button, which dimmed the lights and turned on the stereo.

"Oh, God," moaned Cameron. "That makes this place look like a cheap porn movie. The only thing missing is a disco light, and maybe a trapeze."

"Speaking of which," asked Clyde. "Do you think that Miss McIntyre is in one of these rooms?"

"Nah," said Cameron. "Too warm. I bet she's colder than the Alaskan Front she talked about."

"I don't know," smiled Rich. "I've seen her at the gigs. She seems like she can really cut loose when she wants to. I bet she'd be pretty wild."

"A spy specializes in deception," said Doug. "Don't accept anything they say or do at face value."

"You seem to know a lot about them," said Rich. "Or else you think you do. What makes you the expert?"

"I watch a lot of James Bond movies," Doug replied. "And on that note, I'm going to bed." Without waiting for any response, he entered one of the rooms and shut the door. Clyde watched him go.

"What's with him, do you suppose?"

"Who knows?" yawned Cameron. "He obviously had to spend his session with that D'Lorenzo guy. That would have gotten me sideways, too. Besides, he's as exhausted as the rest of us. I'll see you guys in the morning."

"It *is* morning, " Evan pointed out. "Look outside."

The sky was turning its ominous, predawn gray, which made Cameron and the guys feel even more tired and vulnerable than they were already.

CHAPTER THREE
"Training"

Cameron awoke to the smell of coffee and, at first, thought that one of the others was making breakfast. He soon realized that the smell was too strong to be emanating from the kitchen. Opening his eyes, he noticed a cup of coffee on his night table, and standing next to his bed was a woman. For a few clouded moments, he wondered who this one was, then realized that it was Miss McIntyre. Her hair, which the previous evening had been sandy brown, was now blonde.

"Good afternoon," she smiled. "If you don't mind, your presence is requested in the living room."

"Ten more minutes," he moaned wearily, rolling over.

"I'm afraid not. It's time to go to school."

"Don't want to," he muttered, pulling a pillow over his head. "Tell the teacher I'm sick, and write me a note."

"I'm afraid I have to insist. Now, please get up and join us in the living room."

Sitting up in bed, he rubbed his eyes and looked for the clock, finally realizing there wasn't one.

"What time is it?"

"Four-thirty in the afternoon, now get dressed. You don't want to be late on your first day."

"I guess last night wasn't a bad dream then, was it?"

She handed him the coffee and shook her head.

"No, it wasn't."

"Thanks for the coffee, by the way."

Pausing in the door, she turned and smiled.

"Well, I can't *always* be colder than the Alaskan Front, now, can I?"

Getting dressed, he wondered at her comment, but put it out of his mind. Draining the last of the coffee, he stepped out to the living room and saw the others sitting on the sofa. In the easy chair sat Mr. Dwyer. Of Mr. D'Lorenzo, there was no sign.

"Now that we're all here, I need to go over the rules of engagement with you," Mr. Dwyer began. "I know that Mr. D'Lorenzo instructed you not to leave this suite, nor to have any contact with anyone from the outside. I have to stress the importance of this. From this moment on, do not contact anyone. We will contact you. We will contact people for you. We will teach you a series of contact signals so that we are readily identifiable to you. You will be tested on this. Make no mistakes."

With that, Dwyer produced a large color photograph and handed it to Rich.

"Your first lesson will be in recognition," Dwyer explained. "You will have a set amount of time to study this picture. This will approximate the time one usually spends examining a room upon entering it. After that time is called, you will pass the photograph to the next person, so that they can study it and so on until you have all examined the photograph. You will then be tested on your recall."

Each one of the band members studied the photograph, which depicted a kitchen scene. On the table was a box of cereal, a bowl, a carton of milk, and salt and pepper shakers. On the counter sat a toaster, a jar of peanut butter, and a knife. There were two chairs at the table, and a refrigerator in the background. The floor was tiled in black and white. Dwyer began asking each one of them different questions about the scene. How many chairs are there and what is their placement? What color is the box of cereal? Is it facing them, or can they only see the back of the box? What is the brand of the peanut butter? Is the toast white or wheat? Is the handle of the knife pointing toward the table or away from it? What is the first color tile in the most forefront row of tiles? Is it black or white? Did any of the tiles deviate from the floor pattern?

After the Roadhouse Sons answered the questions, Dwyer handed them another photograph. At first glance, it appeared to be the same one. Upon closer examination, though, there were certain differences. Some were quite obvious, such as the different placement of, or absence of, objects. However, other differences were not so apparent, such as the brand of refrigerator or the design on the cereal bowl. With the first test, the guys had done quite well. Not so with the second.

"You must notice every detail," Dwyer insisted. "The slightest discrepancy could be vital. At the very least, it could indicate the presence of a listening device or the presence of a bomb. You did well, considering that this was your first attempt."

"What do you mean, a bomb?" asked Clyde, startled. "I thought we only had to observe, and report what we heard?"

"You don't think the people that you are observing and listening to won't resent that?" Dwyer allowed his point to sink in before he continued. "I am not an alarmist, but a realist. " Dwyer folded his arms across his chest. "One other thing, gentlemen. Who can tell me what month was displayed on the calendar in the picture?"

"Oh, it was August," answered Rich.

"Are you sure?" asked Evan. "I think it was May, wasn't it?"

"Yeah, it was May," agreed Clyde. "And there was a picture of a field of wildflowers."

"No, it was August," insisted Rich. "It was a beach scene, and there was a beach chair and umbrella with blue sky, white clouds and whitecaps on the waves. There were no people in the picture."

"There was no calendar." Doug's voice was flat, displaying no emotion.

"What the hell are you talking about, man?" demanded Clyde. "Of course there was a calendar. He wouldn't have asked us about it if there wasn't one."

"Are you confident there was no calendar, Mr. Courtland?" Dwyer stared at him intently.

"There was no calendar," Doug repeated.

"Your friends are insistent that there was a calendar. Are you sure you're correct?"

"I'm sure."

"Doug," said Evan, shaking his head. "I hate to disagree, but there was a calendar. It was on the wall behind the table. It was the foldout type, big picture on the top, page with the dates on the bottom. Someone had even marked off some of the dates with an X."

"There was no calendar."

"Yes, there was," insisted Rich. "It was just like Evan described, only it was August, not May. The month was in bold, black type and the year was in red; they had it on both sides of the month."

"They had it split," Clyde corrected him. "The nineteen was on one side of the page, and the seventy-eight was on the other."

"There, you see? Your friends are able to give a rather detailed description. Are you certain there was no calendar?"

"They're giving the description of a calendar, but that doesn't mean one was in the picture."

"You seem confident that you're correct. However, yours is the lone opinion. The rest of them all insist that there was a calendar. You're not telling them they're *all* wrong, are you?"

Doug hesitated for a moment, then answered.

"Yes, I guess I am."

Protests erupted from the others, with insistence and justifications offered as proof of their arguments. However, Doug was unmoved.

"Guys, I'm telling you there was no calendar in that picture!"

"You have no support for your position," Dwyer smiled. "Your friends are not backing you up in this at all. Wouldn't it be simple to just go along with the rest of them, to save yourself the hassle of fighting all alone? To just say "yes"?"

"No," Doug replied. "There was no calendar."

"What was the color of the cereal box?" Dwyer countered.

"Huh?"

"The cereal box, Mr. Courtland," he repeated. "The cereal box on the table. Weren't you paying attention? It was a simple exercise. Even you saw the cereal box on the table, didn't you? What color was it?"

"I, I don't remember..." Doug stammered.

"What? You don't remember? You were so insistent and sure of yourself about the calendar a minute ago. I was certain you would have noticed the cereal box on the counter."

"The cereal box was on the table," corrected Evan.

"Be quiet!" Dwyer shouted. "I am not talking to you. I am talking to Mr. Courtland." Turning back to Doug, Dwyer demanded. "Now, what color was the cereal bowl on the counter?"

"You asked about the cereal box?" Doug began.

"I am the one asking the questions here! Now, what was the color of the box?"

"You just told me you wanted to know about the bowl!"

Dwyer threw his folder down onto the coffee table and stood up facing Doug. "I will not tolerate anymore of this! I will not have my time wasted! For the last time, was there or was there not a calendar on the wall?"

Doug tried leaning back against the couch, but Dwyer just leaned in closer.

"I asked you a question, now give me an answer!"

"There wasn't a calendar."

The color drained from Dwyer's face as he stood in front of the roadie. Quivering with anger, he turned away from the group and gradually regained his composure.

"Gentlemen," he said, still standing with his back to them. "Open the folder and look at the photograph one more time. Is there a calendar, or isn't there?"

Grabbing the folder, Evan removed the photograph and examined it. There was no calendar on the wall.

"I could have sworn there was a calendar," Evan murmured, as the others agreed. They, too, had been convinced that there was a calendar in the photograph.

"That, my friends was a brief glimpse of psychological manipulation," Dwyer explained, reclaiming his seat. "It is nothing as thorough as what you would experience in our training facilities, but a good example nonetheless."

"What the hell was the purpose of that?" demanded Cameron.

"To show you how easy it is to get people to think the way you want them to."

"But Doug didn't think the way you wanted him to," Cameron said. "He never agreed that there was a calendar."

"He didn't," Dwyer explained. "But the others did. People trust whomever they feel is in a position of authority. Using that trust, I was able to instill in them a sense of having earned my approval by asking questions and acknowledging their correct responses. From there, it was easy to get them to believe there was a calendar in the photograph. You are still unsure of your situation, and of me. You are isolated from familiar surroundings, and in a comfort and style to which you are not accustomed, but still isolated, nonetheless. You recognize in me a means of connection with your regular life and do not want to risk breaking that connection. Therefore, your subconscious mind urges you to avoid doing anything that might possibly jeopardize your association to me. I had already asked questions about things of which you were certain. When I asked about something in the photograph which might not be present, your mind was unable to recall the image, and so created one."

"Then why did you try beating the shit out of me with your questions?" demanded Doug.

"Your mind demonstrated resistance. You did not recall a calendar, but instead of creating one from your subconscious, you simply said there was no calendar. Interrogators try to break resistance, and thus break you. By making you doubt yourself, by giving you the sense of isolation from the rest of your associates and by keeping you guessing, then I can break your resistance. You almost broke at the end, didn't you?"

"Yeah," Doug agreed. "I guess I did."

"Most people do," Dwyer assured him. "That is why I want you to be aware of how this manipulation works. You might have to use these techniques yourself one day, or, worse, you might very well have them used on you."

For the next several hours, Dwyer and Miss McIntyre drilled the guys on recognition. Sending each of them to their room to rest, the two agents arranged items in the living room or the kitchen, or sometimes both, and had the guys return, one by one, to test their recognition ability. Some changes were obvious and the guys scored well; however, some changes were very subtle, and by seven o'clock, the band had had enough.

"I can't do this anymore, man," insisted Clyde. "My brain is totally fried."

"All right. Let's take a break for dinner," agreed Dwyer.

As they were finishing their meal of pepper steak with real mashed potatoes, Dwyer asked Rich if he had noticed anything different about the living room when he first came out after his nap.

"No. Why?" Rich answered, topping his potatoes with a welcome dab of real butter.

"Did you, Mr. Dixon?"

"I don't think so."

"Not good enough," Dwyer stated. "If I ask a *yes or no* question, I expect a *yes or no* answer. Now, once again, did you notice anything different about the living room when you got up?"

"No, I didn't."

"And yet, each of you utilized the difference."

"What are you talking about?"

"Both of you came out and had a cigarette with your coffee. Yet, neither of you stopped to think about where the coffee came from, or why there were ashtrays this morning but not last night."

"I thought you made the coffee," Evan told Rich.

"I thought one of you had gotten up and done it."

"Wait a minute," Evan said. "How did you know what we did this morning? You weren't here."

"We watched you," said Miss McIntyre. She settled herself into the recliner in the living room and put her feet up.

"You mean you've got cameras in here?"

"Yes," she agreed. Picking up the remote, she pushed some of the buttons and, once again, the lights dimmed and music began playing softly.

"I have to agree with you, Cameron," she said. "It does make it look like a cheap porn movie."

"You've got it wired for sound, too, I see." Cameron smiled sheepishly. "I should have known when you quoted me earlier."

"You mean you have the entire living room wired?" asked Clyde.

"No," Dwyer said, lighting his cigarette. "We have the entire suite wired. Both video and voice."

"You're watching everything we say and do?" Clyde's face became flushed.

"No," Dwyer said. "We randomly select different things in different rooms."

An uneasy silence fell over the room, eventually broken by Dwyer once again asking questions about the photographs they had seen earlier. The answers were suddenly not as assured as they had been earlier.

"You must learn to focus, and retain things in your memory," Dwyer insisted. "You will be thrust into situations where you will hear or see something of significance and not be able to report on it until much later, such as at one of your shows. After an exhausting performance and copious libations, you would still have to make a report. You can't expect to write it down on a pad by the phone, can you? I realize you are upset about the surveillance, but you have to learn how to work and operate under any circumstances."

Dwyer then took the guys through another series of exercises, once again challenging their recollections and forcing them to focus intently on their answers. He asked them about their morning routines, down to the details of one another's activities. The guys were surprised at their recall of minutiae. Doug was immune from this battery of questioning. Dwyer periodically asked him broad, routine questions, and then turn his attention back to the others.

"We'll review a few items and then let you gentlemen get some rest," Dwyer said. "For the time being, you will continue being sequestered. Again, you will contact no one. Your only contacts will be Miss McIntyre and myself."

"What about our families?" asked Evan, though everyone knew he was mostly concerned about his own.

"We are going to have you call them with exciting news, Mr. Dixon. You will tell your spouse that the Roadhouse Sons have just been hired to perform backup for a recording artist in need of a band, and that the artist in question is a bit eccentric and is trying to keep the project quiet, so you will not be able to tell her who the artist is. You will give her the name of the business office. Should she need to contact you, she is to call that number. If anyone is concerned because they haven't heard from you for an extended period of time, you will explain that the artist is having creative differences with the producer, causing a delay with the production. Ultimately, the diva will be too difficult to work with and the record will never be made. You will tell your spouse, though, that fortunately, you will still be paid."

"How long will we be here?" Evan asked again.

"As long as it takes," Dwyer said.

"OK, now this is going too far," Rich shouted. He began pacing back and forth in the living room, running his fingers through his hair. "I can't stay cooped up here forever, or even for whatever seems like forever. I have to know when I'll be leaving, and when I'll be getting back to normal."

"You will leave when we decide that you have learned enough in your training. The training you are undergoing now is of far shorter duration than the amount of time you would normally spend at the agency. Put the concept of "normal" out of your mind. Normal is not only a relative term, but also a thing of your past."

The Roadhouse Sons stared at Dwyer, stymied. No one spoke or moved. Only the cigarette smoke, languidly drifting to the ceiling, displayed any motion.

"When we contact you, either by phone or at the door, we will signal by ringing or knocking once, then silence, then three rings or knocks. After that, we will hang up, or stop knocking. The next ring or knock will be your signal to pick up the phone or open the door. Until you hear otherwise from us, do not respond to *any* other signal."

As Dwyer and Miss McIntyre were leaving, Cameron stopped them.

"Wait a minute," he said. "What about groceries. I mean, we'll need more milk and stuff. How do we get that?"

"Right now, you let us know what you need," said Miss McIntyre. "We'll make certain you get it. Good night."

As the door shut behind them, Rich stormed into the kitchen, hurling a coffee cup at the door.

"What the hell are you doing?" demanded Cameron.

"This is bullshit, man," he cried. "What the hell did we do to deserve this?"

Then, turning toward Cameron, Rich became belligerent.

"This is all your fault," he snarled, pushing his front man into the refrigerator.

"What the fuck do you mean, my fault? I didn't have anything to do with this!"

"If you hadn't gotten into that fight with the club manager, none of this would have happened!"

"You are so full of shit your eyes are brown!"

With that, Cameron lunged at his bass player and knocked him into the counter. The two of them grappled for several minutes before the others were able to separate them.

"Knock it off, you two," shouted Doug. "This is what they want!"

"What are you talking about?" demanded Cameron. "Get your hands off of me!"

"When you isolate a group of people, you watch to see how they react, who cracks, who freaks out. This is what they're doing. They watch everything and evaluate it."

"How do you know all this?" Evan moved Doug away from the group. Now, everyone was facing him.

"From watching *Manchurian Candidate* on the late show about a hundred times," Doug replied, taking another step back. "Besides, didn't Dwyer say that we were subconsciously trying to respond to being isolated from familiar things? This is just cabin fever, that's all."

The others didn't pay much attention to him. Settling down, Cameron took a beer out of the refrigerator, and the others either went back into the living room, or to their own rooms. The television remained silent, since they had recently discovered that it was disconnected. The stereo did not receive any radio stations, and only played cassettes and records, most of which were in a cheesy assortment left for the guys when they were forced to move in. The Roadhouse Sons' isolation was indeed complete, and listening to The Captain and Tenille, Fifth Dimension, Tavares and The Bee Gees could only add insult to injury.

They finally went to bed, leaving Cameron in the living room by himself. He took in the silence, felt the isolation, but somehow did not feel threatened by it. He looked out the window and examined the parking lot below. There were still no cars, nor did he notice many lights in the buildings nearby. There was no traffic on the street, which meant that they were obviously not in a residential area. Studying the view from the living room during the day did not help Cameron, either, as he was not familiar with Rutland, if that is where they really were. Since these were the only windows in the suite, it was even harder for Cameron to get his bearings. The sun didn't shine directly through the windows, but the light moved from the right to the left, which meant that the house faced south.

Christ. I'm already starting to think like them.

He got another beer from the refrigerator and sat on the couch. Lighting a cigarette, he replayed the day's events in his mind, making mental notes of things that Dwyer had said, until gradually weariness took over. Stubbing out the cigarette, he put his feet up to relax while he finished his beer. Gradually, sleep overtook Cameron.

The ringing of the phone suddenly woke him. Without thinking, he reached over and answered it.

"Hello," he yawned. He recoiled at the sound of a gunshot on the other end of the line., followed by Dwyer's voice.

"Remember the signal, Mr. Walsh. The next time you hear a gunshot, it might not be a recording."

Chapter Four
"Field Trip"

Dwyer and Miss McIntyre came dutifully each day, training the Roadhouse Sons on the different aspects of espionage, and testing the guys' comprehension. Every other day they brought more groceries or supplies. Miss McIntyre appreciated that everyone who smoked used the same brand of cigarettes, and she also noticed that they all liked the same assortment of beer, be it Rolling Rock, Budweiser or Genesee.

"I don't use either," she said. "So it's easy to remember one brand for each of your vices." Regardless of her personal habits, the guys loved it when Miss McIntyre showed up. She was the more human element in the band's dubious situation.

After nearly two weeks, Dwyer arrived, alone, but with an announcement.

"Congratulations, gentlemen, "Dwyer said, sardonically. "You've earned yourselves a field trip."

"Where?"

"Outside," Dwyer said with a smile. "But not all of you at once. I'll be training you one at a time. Mr. Dixon, will you get your coat, please?"

"Where are we going?"

"I told you. Outside. Hurry. We have a lot of work to do."

The two men left, leaving the others to contemplate what was going on. As time wore on, the guys became more anxious about their companions. There were no clocks in the suite and they had turned over their watches, so the only way that they could judge the time was by the progression of sunlight on the floor. Finally, the door opened and Evan walked in, cheeks red from the cold, and with a smile on his face. Dwyer was right behind him.

"Mr. Poulin, will you please join me outside?" Dwyer commanded.

This activity continued for the remainder of the day, each band member comparing notes from their own experience, until finally, Cameron was the only one that hadn't gone out with Dwyer. Anticipating that it would be his turn next, Cameron had his coat waiting in the kitchen. When the door opened, he began putting it on. Dwyer regarded Cameron silently, and then motioned with his head for him to follow.

They descended the stairs, saying nothing. Cameron noticed that there were different flowers on the tables, and there was still no one else around. He realized that this was obviously what he had heard Dwyer refer to as a "safe house," a place to hide agents or run base operations. Cameron's eyes adjusted to the light when they stepped outside, but he put on his sunglasses anyway.

Dwyer spoke first. "I was saving you for last, Mr. Walsh, because in addition to what I want to show you, I have something I wish to discuss with you. This way."

Dwyer led him east on the street in front of the hotel. Casually, Cameron looked over his shoulder to see if there were any identifying features to the building; oddly, there were none.

What the fuck? This place doesn't look like a hotel.

The building was a two-and-a-half story with an el, and the aluminum siding was a nondescript shade of blue. The trim around the windows was white and the overall feeling of the place was that it had been around long enough not to be remarkable. There was no sign out front, nor any street number on the building, nothing to give it a reference point. There were three cars parked in the large parking lot, but not together. Instead, they were parked in seemingly various random places around the lot. He wondered if they belonged to people in the surrounding buildings.

I don't like the looks of this.

They started walking and Cameron noticed the old warehouses that lined both sides of the street. Some of them had windows broken out, but others had lights on inside.

"What's in these?" he asked, his shoulders hunched against the cold.

"We're not exactly sure," Dwyer replied. "We believe they're machine shops."

"For someone who stresses knowing your environment, you're a bit ignorant about your neighbors, aren't you?"

Instead of taking offence, Dwyer laughed.

"Maybe if I have clay feet, it will be easier for you to fill my shoes?"

"I don't know about that."

"Why? Don't you think you could do what I do?"

"Fuck no, excuse my Russian. I just want to do my music."

"Why do you think you can only do one?"

"Because both of them are things that require your full attention. I don't know how long I could carry that off."

"You do realize that you will have to do it for some time, don't you?"

"I think about it every day."

"Does it bother you?"

"Like I said, I think about it every day."

"And what is your conclusion?"

"We need to do what we've been asked to do; complete it, and get out of here."

"What if it doesn't work out that way?"

"I'm trying not to think about that part."

"Smart man," Dwyer said, sardonically.

They continued on down the street, eventually turning north along a more traveled street. There were cars parked on both sides of the street, a few spaces left open. Cameron checked to see if there was anything he could recognize, but there wasn't. He had played Rutland several times before, and while he wasn't entirely familiar with the city, he did have a working knowledge of it. However, if they were still in Rutland, they were no place that he had been before. Nor were there any street signs or traffic lights.

The next neighborhood they entered was much more residential. Several yards were fenced, and many open. Some had heavily entwined plastic or burlap bags covering yard structures. Cameron figured that they were either birdbaths or religious statues, a la Mary on the Half Shell, he called them, or, Our Lady of the Bathtub.

The two men trundled on in silence for several blocks. They passed side streets, none of which were major intersections. Eventually, Cameron noticed a small convenience store ahead, and had an overwhelming urge to run in to it. The need to connect with other people seized him, shook him and wouldn't let him go. He hungered to find out what was going on in the world, to possibly find a way out of *this* world. He fought back tears when Dwyer motioned for him to enter the convenience store.

Cameron's sunglasses began to mist before he had a chance to reposition them on his head; he used that as an excuse to stand in the aisle and take in the experience of existing in something that he deemed to feel normal. The smell of the imitation coffee and government-issued cigarettes assailed him, as well as the smell of old bologna and stale sliced meats. The meat counter held little else. The Roadhouse Sons managed to escape the rationing, and Cameron never took it upon himself to contemplate the reasons why. Looking over the top of one shelf, he could see that there was also a deli counter along the far side of the establishment.

The store itself was cramped, the only three aisles barely big enough for one person to travel, which helped to make the amount of sparse merchandise on the shelves—as such due to the war effort—appear more abundant. The center aisle held condiments, cereal and boxed meals. From what Cameron could see, the household cleaners were along the short shelves on the far wall, while bread and chips were along the aisle he faced. Behind the counter were several shelves of basic pharmacy items such as aspirin and a few brands of cough syrups. There was a large container over the counter, and he guessed that this was where the all-precious cigarettes were kept. On the wall next to the door were coolers that held beer, soda and milk.

Cameron followed Dwyer down the side aisle to the coffee machine. The glass coffee pot held only hot water, and a jar of coffee substitute, a jar of sugar and one of non-dairy creamer sat next to it. A box of individually wrapped doughnuts was there as well, and he noticed there were only three left. Realizing how long they must have been sitting there, Cameron decided he'd leave the doughnuts for someone else. He continued surveying the store while Dwyer paid for their coffee. Cameron noticed the other patrons in the store. One man stood at the register, counting out money for his purchase. He was of medium height, with wavy, sandy brown hair and was dressed in a worn, brown jacket that was heavily discolored with grease, as were his pants. His hands were blackened as well, suggesting to Cameron that he worked in a garage. The man made a few jokes about politics and the government to the shopkeeper and, grabbing his bag, he turned and left the store. He made brief eye contact with Cameron and nodded politely, then continued out the door without saying a word.

The other man waiting his turn at the counter was dressed in blue jeans and wore a dirty hooded jacket and red knit cap. As he approached the counter, Cameron noticed well-worn and patched denims, battered Herman Survivor work boots, and a serious looking hunting knife on his right side. He sported a five o'clock shadow with a heavy, black mustache. His eyes were also dark, and shocks of black hair showed from underneath his toque. He said very little as he paid for his six-pack of beer, and left without having it bagged. This man said nothing to anyone, nor did he make any eye contact.

The only other people that were in the store were an old man and an old woman behind the counter, whom Cameron assumed were the owners. The man was a large fellow, with a big belly and a bald head framed with white hair. He wore wire-rimmed glasses, a flannel shirt and suspenders. The shopkeeper's wife was a white-haired, pigeon-breasted woman. She wore a floral print dress and a pink sweater. She also donned wire-rimmed glasses, and spent most of her time focused on her knitting.

"Shall we?" Dwyer asked, heading toward the door. Cameron followed, sipping his coffee. Outside, they continued down the street the way they had come.

"Do you notice anything about these cars, Mr. Walsh?"

"Such as what?"

Dwyer raised his eyebrows slightly, and thought for a moment.

"Have any of them changed position, or are any of them different from those we saw when we arrived at the store?"

Cameron didn't answer right away, nor did he appear obvious as he scanned the street. One block down, he noticed a car that seemed somehow brighter than the others. There didn't seem to be anything specifically different about it, yet it did attract his attention. He noticed that there was someone sitting in the driver's seat.

"The yellow caddy in front of the green house," Cameron said quietly, sipping his coffee.

"Have you seen it anywhere else?" Dwyer asked, continuing down the street.

Cameron was momentarily caught off guard. Had he seen it before? Searching through his memory, he couldn't honestly recall having ever seen it. Stalling for time, he continued to sip on his coffee. Then it dawned on him.

"In the parking lot outside that place that you're trying to pass off as a hotel, or should I call it a safe house?" Cameron said, keeping his voice in a normal tone and keeping his movements calm and unsuspicious. "It was off to the side, looked like it belonged to one of the warehouses next door. That's why I noticed it; it looked strange to see that fancy a car there."

"You've done this before," chuckled Dwyer.

Cameron shrugged.

"I watch a lot of cop shows," he said. "You know, *Mod Squad*, *Kojak*, *Starsky and Hutch*, that sort of thing. You really do pick up things from TV, I guess."

Dwyer rolled his eyes, undetected by Cameron. "Some of your friends were a bit more awkward. They drew too much attention to themselves."

"Well, perhaps we might not be what you were looking for after all," Cameron suggested with a smile. "Cut your losses and send us home before it's too late."

"We won't do that, Mr. Walsh," Dwyer assured him. "Your friends will improve with time. Meanwhile, there are three others that showed quite an aptitude for this type of work."

"Really? Who are they, if you don't mind my asking?"

"Mr. Dixon, your roadie, and yourself. *You* display a cooler manner than the others do."

"Really?"

"Yes, but they are not without flaws. Mr. Poulin had difficulty focusing on individual concepts. Mr. Webster, at this juncture, is incapable of providing complete descriptions of *anything*. Mr. Dixon's short-term memory inhibits his recollection process, yet he is very careful and methodical, too much so, in fact."

"What about Doug?"

Dwyer sighed. "He gave accurate descriptions, but it was obvious that he resents being dragged through this. By behaving so petulantly, he drew attention to himself and made people nervous. No one in the store could keep their eyes off of him, but he didn't seem to care."

"That's Dougie," Cameron chuckled. "Don't take it personally. He's always like that. Being that way at the shows keeps some of the rowdier patrons away from the stage. Being that way offstage keeps the jealous boyfriends away from us. It's just how he is."

Dwyer seemed to consider what the singer said.

"Interesting."

Cameron noticed they were now in a different neighborhood than the one they had come through earlier.

"There is something else I would like to discuss with you, Mr. Walsh."

"Fantastic. I'm all ears."

"This team is going to need a leader," he explained. "I had made up my mind who I was going to ask before I approached you and your friends, but I was not entirely certain at first. Now, I am."

"Yes?"

"You."

Cameron didn't say anything, but continued walking, finishing the last of his coffee.

"Why, may I ask?"

"You are the spokesman for the band, as well as the front man. You set the pace on stage and there is inherent respect in that."

"And you think that talent can carry over into this? This is literally apples and oranges."

"It can carry very well from there to here, Mr. Walsh. You don't need to try and inspire a large crowd at this level; you simply need to motivate and guide your team. Your talent will serve you very well. You also possess persuasive charm. You have a unique ability to gain the confidence of people, and with little effort."

"I think you're exaggerating."

Dwyer paused, sipped his coffee, then spoke quietly.

"Do you ever get the feeling that you're being watched?"

Cameron did not immediately turn around to check; instead, he reached into his pocket and removed his cigarettes.

"Since I met you, all the time," he muttered. Turning around to have his back to the wind, he lit his cigarette. Taking advantage of the fact that his sunglasses hid his eyes, he scanned the street behind him. Appearing to struggle with his lighter and cupping the flame, he studied each vehicle, and then the few pedestrians on both sides of the street. Taking a drag, he focused on possible likely suspects.

"Service van facing us, this side of the street," Cameron said, resuming his walk down the sidewalk. "One person in the van, assistant working on the outside of the house they are parked in front of."

"Why do you suspect them?"

"Windshield pointed this direction, no cars immediately in front of it. Able to provide unobstructed visual surveillance from both inside and outside the van."

"Anything else?"

"Man walking his dog, opposite side. He 's been following us since we left the store."

"Why is that suspicious?"

"He hasn't gone into any of the houses. That suggests he's not from this neighborhood. Casual walkers will usually move *with* the flow of traffic, not against."

"You have remarkable recall, Mr. Walsh. We discussed this well over a week ago, and only once."

"How did I do?"

"Mixed results," Dwyer conceded. "The service van would be an ideal surveillance set up, for the reasons you cited, and in fact, it is. The man walking his dog isn't."

"But a couple of weeks ago, you said…"

"I said they usually walk that way, Mr. Walsh. If people will usually do something, then they sometimes won't. Sometimes a cigar is just a cigar."

"How can you be sure?"

"You can't. In the store, where was the sugar kept?"

Cameron hated these topic jumps of Dwyer's, but said nothing. Recalling the layout of the store, Cameron reconstructed the coffee counter, and for a moment couldn't remember, but then had a quick flash of memory.

"There was a sugar pourer next to the coffee cups."

"Are you certain? Sugar is rationed, and even coffee shops and restaurants have to comply."

"That's how I remembered it," Cameron explained. "It was so unusual."

"One of the people whom we encountered was another operative. Have you any idea whom it was?"

This caught Cameron by surprise. Who could it be? He hadn't spoken to anyone, nor anyone to him.

"Guy with greasy brown jacket," Cameron said at last. "He nodded at me when he left."

"He probably liked the look of you, but it was not he."

"I have no idea, then."

"Mr. Walsh, this isn't a game. You need to be able to recognize situations when other operatives are attempting to make contact with you. Someone's life may depend on it, and it will likely be yours. Now think; the clue they gave was obvious."

"I have no idea, I swear."

Dwyer gave him an angry look.

"Have you noticed anything out of the ordinary on this walk?"

"Man, I've kind of forgotten what the fuck ordinary is like these days. Just give me a hint."

"You didn't put it in your coffee."

It took Cameron a few moments to process Dwyer's hint.

"The sugar. The man behind the counter was the operative?"

"Yes, the sugar was the indication. Blatant disregard for Office of Price Control ration regulations is designed to attract attention. For regular people frustrated with the government, it would appear that the shopkeeper was making a political statement. For those who are searching for suspicious signs and indicators, it would put them on their guard. If you had been given a password or phrase, you would have used it when paying for your coffee. If it was the correct word or phrase, the shopkeeper would have given you designated information, or you would have relayed information to him."

"And if it wasn't the correct one?"

"You would likely be dead by now, Mr. Walsh."

Dwyer's repeated use of the word mister and his constant distant, condescending tone had been wearing on Cameron for some time, and he decided that now was the moment to get it off his chest.

"Knock it off with the *mister* shit, will you?" Cameron snapped, flicking his cigarette into the street. "You aren't all that older than me, and it sounds ridiculous. I mean, is that policy or something? Are *we* going to have to start doing that? You refer to all of us and to your own as mister or miss. Use my fucking name, damn it!"

Dwyer crumpled his coffee cup and tossed it into an open trashcan by the curb. Sticking his hands into his coat pockets, he continued on in silence for a few moments before answering.

"It isn't company policy, Mr. Walsh. It is mine. Whether or not you adopt the practice is entirely up to you."

"And why do you act so holier-than-thou?" Cameron demanded. Once he had begun to voice his grievances, he discovered that he'd been damming a deluge. "You act like some fancy professor or some father figure out of a stupid fifties television show. You might have gone to some fancy finishing school or college, but I'll bet that you aren't any different from the rest of us. You sure as hell aren't any better than we are."

"Keep your voice down, Mr. Walsh," Dwyer said. He kept his gaze on the horizon, and Cameron noticed a distinct edge to Dwyer's voice. "I am sorry that my manners are so offensive to you. It can't be helped."

"What the sweet hell is that supposed to mean?"

"At some point, depending on how long one is used, one discovers one's self developing personal and protective safety measures. For some, it is drugs; for others, it is alcohol, and for some, it is promiscuity. There are also the power junkies who immerse themselves in this business wholeheartedly. For me, however, my measure of choice is detachment. I form no personal connections. I keep myself aloof from everything. I impart strict rules for my own comportment and conduct. I adhere to those rules as religiously as I maintain the directives of my agency."

"And that helps? I'd think you'd need to have some human contact in this, something to keep you from going stir crazy."

"To have a connection is to invite someone to have power over you. That is something you cannot afford."

"That's such bullshit," Cameron scoffed. "You can't expect me to believe that!"

"Ask Mr. Evans if it is bullshit, Mr. Walsh. I would be interested to hear his response."

Cameron remembered the parting remarks Dwyer had made at the police barracks, congratulating Evan on his wife's promotion and informing him about the babysitter.

Subtle threats; nothing said, everything implied. Cameron felt nauseous.

"Don't be naïve, Mr. Walsh. This profession is built upon deception and on using people. We are not a fraternity or a lodge. The longstanding relationships are not as numerous as one would think, especially at our level. Upper management might be another story, but not we agents. We will be together as long as we are required to be, and then we go our separate ways. We may work together some other time, or we may never see each other again. There will never be any reunions, any office parties or weekend barbeques. We are individual islands, Mr. Walsh, in a foggy, foggy sea."

"You're wrong," Cameron insisted. "I've known the guys in my band for years. Hell, I went to school with some of them. We've got a bond that can't be broken!"

'"Commendable and enviable, Mr. Walsh. Yet unfortunate."

"Will you stop speaking in riddles, for Christ's sakes? What are you talking about?"

"You have already set yourself up for devastation."

"What the hell are you going to do?" Cameron snarled, turning to face Dwyer.

"Me? Nothing, I assure you. However, fate is not a lady much of the time."

"What do you mean?"

Dwyer sighed and shook his head.

"Discussing this subject will make no difference, Mr. Walsh. Everyone either adopts your attitude or mine, initially, or at least attempts to. However, fate forces resolution, and one's character and temperament dictate how one deals with it all. One could crumble entirely, become hardened, become resolved, or simply walk away. I can explain it in as many ways as I wish, but it simply must be learned through personal experience."

Cameron considered what Dwyer was saying, and realized that he spoke from personal experience. Dwyer must have lost a colleague at some point. That would explain why he kept hammering at the danger aspect of this work. Before Cameron could comment, Dwyer resumed his walk and began discussing the reason behind the alternate route they'd taken back to the safe house.

"It makes it easier to detect a tail," Dwyer explained. "If you use the same route out of habit, it is logical to assume that others will do the same. Altering a habit announces suspicious activity," Dwyer emphasized. "However, if one constantly alternates one's patterns, it is difficult for any habits to be detected in the first place."

"If not impossible."

"Mr. Walsh, nothing is impossible to the truly persistent."

They arrived back at the safe house, and Dwyer led Cameron to the door.

"Goodnight, Mr. Walsh," he said. Cameron noticed that Dwyer did not extend his hand.

"See you in the morning?" Cameron hated the thought of leaving things on a bad note, and hoped to repair whatever damage he might have done earlier.

"Perhaps. Good night, Mr. Walsh."

Though nothing was said, Cameron realized that he was expected to go into the safe house and not witness Dwyer's departure. Stepping through the front door, Cameron was instantly struck by the stillness.

"Honey, I'm home!" he cried out, as much as to hear the sound of a voice as to see if anyone else was there. There was no answer, for which he was both disappointed and relieved. He wasn't certain what he would have done if someone had responded. Heading up the stairs, the only sound was his steps on the carpet. No noise came from the band's suite.

Must be soundproofed.

Cameron paused in the hallway before ascending to the next landing. He wondered what was in the other rooms, and was tempted to knock on a strange door or two, but decided against it. He was stuck with a sudden sense of isolation as he went up the stairs.

"We're individual islands, Mr. Walsh," Cameron recalled Dwyer saying. "In a foggy, foggy, sea."

And he was truly feeling adrift.

CHAPTER FIVE
"Internship"

Following the field trip, Dwyer and Miss McIntyre spent a great deal of time instructing the Roadhouse Sons in the art of surveillance. Using nothing but their own eyes and ears, the band members were shown how to conduct surveillance on foot, and how to perform undercover directives from an automobile while following a suspect in a car. They were hardly impressed.

"I thought we'd get cool shit like they have in the Bond movies," Clyde complained. "Or maybe one of those shoe phones like on *Get Smart*."

"Told you," Miss McIntyre said, winking at Dwyer. "Dinner is on you."

"What?" asked Clyde, suddenly blushing as he realized that he had once again said something embarrassing, but had no concept of what it was.

"Miss McIntyre and I had a wager, gentlemen," Dwyer explained. "She was convinced that, at some point, at least one of you would mention the legendary and mythical shoe phone. I was confident that you would wait until your training was complete. She was convinced you were dying to know about it now. As much as I hate to disappoint you, we do not have shoe phones."

Despite his efforts, Clyde could not hide a hint of disappointment.

"Nor, for that matter, do we have a 'Q' to create interesting inventions for Sean Connery's or Roger Moore's rescue from their various predicaments. While there are interesting intelligence devices, like the rest of us, you will predominantly rely on your own innate talents to accomplish your assigned tasks. There will be no screenwriters to propel the plot smoothly or to ensure your appearance in the next movie, nor are there any special effects providing your rescue from dangerous situations. This is reality, gentlemen. A dangerous reality."

Clyde and Rich shifted uncomfortably in their chairs, and Evan hurried into the kitchen for more coffee. Cameron looked away, surprised at Dwyer's breach from his own declared impersonal comportment, and pretended to look out the window. Doug maintained his typical, stony silence.

Sensing their angst, Dwyer continued, his tone slightly more reassuring. "Give yourselves credit. You will discover that you are much more up to the task than you think."

"Actually, I'm only interested in one bunch of gadgets," Cameron said. "I want my guitars."

Dwyer cocked his head inquiringly.

"Our guitars," Cameron repeated. "Our instruments. We need to start playing them."

"Mr. Walsh, you have enough to keep you occupied for the foreseeable future."

"I don't care," Cameron retorted. Getting up from the chair, Cameron strode across the room to face Dwyer. There was no belligerence in his attitude; rather, he conveyed a strong sense of determination.

"I want those guitars and the amps for them," Cameron repeated. "And I want them now, tonight."

"Now see here," Dwyer began, his jaw clenched.

"I'll see nothing," Cameron snapped. "The guitars, here, tonight. End of discussion."

"What possible good would that do?" insisted Dwyer. "You can't play them in here."

"Why can't we?" Cameron demanded. "Guitar, amps, and we can practice at least. Evan can set up his kit over there in the corner. Clyde doesn't need that much room for his guitar or the keyboard. I'm not talking about all the lights, and the entire PA, just the basics. I'm telling you, we need to practice!"

"Practice? For what?"

"You had us tell everyone that we were going to be working in a recording studio, did you not?"

"I did," Dwyer hissed.

"You said we could be expected to be doing that for quite some time, did you not?"

"Yes." Dwyer hedged slightly, clearly affronted.

Cameron held up his hands, showing Dwyer his palms.

"Look at my fingertips," he said. "What do you see?"

"Nothing," Dwyer snapped. "What am I supposed to see?"

"Calluses," Cameron explained. "There should be calluses here from the guitar strings, but there're aren't; they've mostly healed."

Dwyer, enervated by the irrelevancy of the discussion, sighed. "Is that not good?"

"No, it most certainly is not good. It is bad, very bad. My fingers should be toughened up. If we were to do a show right now, my fingertips would look like hamburger. No one who hears that we're in a recording studio would believe it. If we got into a club and stumbled over our sets it would be obvious that we hadn't been rehearsing in some time. What would that do to your cover story? Even some drunken groupie would see through that."

Dwyer waved dismissively. "That cover story was only used with your families. No one else knows about it."

"I am willing to bet you another dinner that our families have all received at least twenty phone calls each wondering where we are. They will obviously repeat what they've been told, especially since you had us tell them not to. If we were to go into a club after all of that and I couldn't get through a set because of my fingers, or our timing was off in some of our songs, they would know something was up. Do you want to subject us all to unnecessary scrutiny?"

Dwyer squinted, studying Cameron's face for a few moments. Cameron could tell that he'd won Dwyer over.

"I hadn't considered that aspect," Dwyer agreed. "I think you might be right. Very well, we'll bring them over first thing in the morning."

"Tonight."

"First thing in the morning," Dwyer averred.

"You mean it?"

"Yes."

"Good, because I'd have hated to use my second argument to get them."

"Which is?"

"That I am going so crazy in here, I'm gonna start talking to myself and pissing in the corners."

Dwyer regarded him intently, but Cameron did not look away.

You can learn from us, too, asshole!

The two men locked their gazes, and the others in the room began to feel uncomfortable.

Dwyer spoke first. "Mr. Walsh, sometimes I can't be certain when you are being serious, facetious, crude or a combination of all three."

"Don't feel bad," Cameron replied with a sardonic smile. "Sometimes, neither can I."

Dwyer tried, unsuccessfully, to suppress a shudder. He cleared his throat, shuffled his papers, and resumed his tutorial, this time on how to conduct audio surveillance from a stationary vehicle.

Miss McIntyre, who had silently observed the previous interactions and verbal altercation, employed the newly discovered dynamics in clarifying directives to the band when Dwyer appeared obtuse or spoke too technically. The band began asking questions, and suggested possible fallback scenarios, and Cameron felt a huge sense of relief. He was not at all certain what situations they would encounter, but he did know that they would find themselves in circumstances where they would have to be entirely dependent and reliant upon one another. He had worked for many years with most of the boys in the band, and he knew their abilities in that arena. He was much less distressed now, as he watched them transform from a bunch of wild and talented musicians into a team that would handle life-or-death situations.

Maybe, after all is said and done, we will get through this in one piece.

Dwyer spoke on and switched to on-foot street surveillance, while Miss McIntyre occasionally interjected and provided additional handouts. Rich examined one diagram that she had scribbled, and made some suggestions.

"Wouldn't it be better to have one person here, here and here?" Rich said, indicating several different places on the diagram. "If you have them in a couple of different spots, rather than having one set of them in one spot and another there, it would seem less obvious to me to have a bunch of people wandering around, like maybe one or two friends bumping into each other, rather than sets of them being more conspicuous."

"If you do that too often, that would raise more flags than doing it the other way," Miss McIntyre explained. "The best way is to have one main person follow the target, have someone tagging them from the other side of the street, and to have someone farther down the street surveilling the whole scenario from that vantage point."

"I'm not saying that," Rich told her. "I'm saying if there is one person here," he pointed with a pencil to one area on the diagram, "...then maybe one here," he indicated another location, "...the main person is following, a secondary person is wandering down the other side of the street, they meet up with a friend possibly coming out of a shop, and the two of them wander down the street together. It would look to the subject like they were having a casual conversation, but they could still observe, then the first guy hands off the surveillance to another one of us on his side of the street. That way, you've had at least four sets of eyes watching whoever it is."

Miss McIntyre considered this carefully, glancing over to Dwyer for his assessment.

"You do have a point. It would seem less obvious to have more random selections," she agreed. "However, you need to remember one thing. The more things are spread out, the easier it is for things to go wrong. You could lose contact with your subject, or you could miss your contact with the other people with whom you're working. Whenever you're planning, always make certain that you keep things as simple as you can."

They discussed and debated several approach scenarios, and eventually the conversation began to go in a circle.

"This is all academic," Clyde grumbled. "We aren't going to be following anybody, are we?"

"One can never be certain," Dwyer said. "As a matter of fact, you will be conducting surveillance very soon."

"On who?" asked Clyde.

"We have our eye on an individual," Dwyer explained. "We have reason to believe that they are active with a black market trade group here in Rutland."

"How will we know who it is?" Evan asked. "Do we have to try and find out ourselves, or are you going to tell us?"

"We've identified them," Dwyer said. "You will watch them and note their actions, where they go, with whom they talk, and so on. We feel that this case is a good way to break you in."

"Then we can expect to finally get on with whatever the hell it is you want us to do?" Cameron tried disguising his impatience, but was unable to sound convincing.

"Patience, Mr. Walsh," Dwyer smiled. "When you actually begin your assignment, you will feel it is all too soon."

Cameron shook his head. *Never soon enough.*

The meeting continued on for several hours, with Dwyer and Miss McIntyre further outlining their expectations.

"Don't worry," Miss McIntyre said with an esoteric smile toward Dwyer. "We won't leave you babes in the woods. We'll have people working with you."

"How do we start this?" Cameron asked. "Do you give us pictures, a description? What do we work with?"

"Everything starts tomorrow," Miss McIntyre explained. "You make contact with your contact, you start watching what they do, you report it back to us."

"Doesn't sound very complicated," mused Cameron. "Nice and simple, just like you said. I like it."

"Simple things can sometimes be very complicated," Miss McIntyre explained. "Don't ever let that deceive you."

Doug tried to suppress a laugh, and went to the kitchen for more coffee. Cameron watched Dwyer, curious for his reaction. Dwyer shot a quick glance to Miss McIntyre, unaware that Cameron noticed. No one said anything, and the awkward silence spawned tension. From the kitchen, Doug was the one to break the silence.

"Just where are we supposed to conduct this little operation, if you don't mind my asking?"

"You will be working here in town," Dwyer answered. "Your contact will give you a photograph and some basic information. You will evaluate this person, learn this individual's routines as much as possible, and begin to plan your surveillance around the information you gather."

Doug laughed aloud, this time not holding back. "Well, in case you haven't noticed, Rutland is pretty much a working class town and, with the exception of me, the rest of these guys don't actually blend in to a working class community. Cameron here could probably pass, since he's got some regular clothes and his hair isn't too wild. So could Evan, as he helps out in his dad's hardware store from time to time, so he has to keep himself a bit straight. These other two, though, they'll stick out like flamingos in a flock of penguins. They'd be spotted in a minute hanging around anyplace other than of one of our clubs. Do we become masters of disguise, or are you just going to hope for the best? Trust me, that approach won't work."

Dwyer regarded Doug closely. Cameron noticed that Dwyer bristled at Doug's remark and wondered if Dwyer's carefully cultivated reserve would finally break. At the last moment, though, Dwyer retained his usual composure.

"You are not expected to do anything but that which you are told, Mr. Courtland. We realize that long hair and biker boots will not keep you from being conspicuous, however, a few simple changes will correct that. Before your attitude perpetuates, do not assume that my managerial style is lenient. Are we clear on that particular point?"

"Clear as mud," Doug sneered.

"Perhaps you have something you wish to address?" Dwyer inquired, the icy edge returning to his voice. "Would you prefer to speak in private, or would you like to discuss it openly?"

"I don't have anything more to say," Doug said. "You tell me you've got things under control. Why wouldn't I believe you?"

Dwyer began to speak again, when Miss McIntyre cut him off.

"I think Doug here has raised a point," she said. She turned to Doug. "We should review basic ways to change your appearance quickly in the event that you need to."

Reluctantly, Dwyer agreed and the two of them demonstrated several manners of camouflage, such as dressing in removable layers, tucking long hair into caps, adding a pebble to one shoe to affect a limp, using newspapers to stuff their shoulders in order to appear taller, and using a burnt cork to affect razor stubble.

"Though, when you are burning your cork, make certain you have it wedged into a door frame to hold it," Miss McIntyre said. "Otherwise, you'll end up burning your fingers. Trust me on this."

Cameron noticed that this evening her hair was raven black, and realized that she must practice what she preached. As usual, the training sessions lasted late into the night, covering new ground, reiterating previous training, and reviewing various possible encounters.

"Who is our contact, anyway?" Rich asked. He had been silent for the rest of the evening, contributing nothing to the discussion after his initial diagram discussion with Miss McIntyre.

"The storekeeper," Dwyer explained. "One of you will go there tomorrow and retrieve the information."

"Do we just walk in and ask for it?"

"Absolutely not," Dwyer said emphatically. "You will have a password to which they will give you a designated response. You will then provide a reply with another predetermined password, and then you will receive the information."

"What's the word?"

"It's more correctly a phrase, Mr. Dixon," Dwyer explained. "It is "Sure do wish I could get some good beef." Make certain you pause before saying the word beef."

"What's the response?"

Dwyer responded. "I'd settle for some good hamburger."

"Hamburger *is* beef," said Clyde.

"Don't be literal," sighed Dwyer. "Your response is "Then I guess I'll have to settle for peanut butter." Do you understand?"

The band assured him that they got it, and Dwyer made each one of them repeat it to him, all the while making corrections to their passwords and responses until he was certain that they all had memorized it correctly.

"You and Doug shouldn't go tomorrow," Miss McIntyre said to Evan. "You'll be too conspicuous."

"What do you mean?" Evan demanded. "Didn't you just say that he and I would best be able to fit in?"

"Yes, but that's also the reason you wouldn't fit in now," she explained. "You both look more working class than the others do, so why wouldn't you be working instead of hanging around a neighborhood store? Unemployment isn't that bad here, and everyone has at least day jobs. Longhaired guys with rock and roll t-shirts would not raise too much suspicion then. Contempt, yes, but not suspicion."

"Gee, thanks," muttered Rich. "I love these morale boosts."

"Sorry," she smiled. "But it's true."

"Quite true," Dwyer agreed. "Now, here's your last instruction. You need to ascertain with certainty that your contact has your information. They will signal to you that they are ready to make a drop. The signal that we use is the color orange."

"Oh, Agent Orange," laughed Clyde.

"Another dinner," Miss McIntyre said to Dwyer. "And ten dollars on top of it. If this keeps up, I won't have to use my ration books at all this month."

"What's she talking about?" asked Evan.

"Never mind," grumbled Dwyer. "Pay attention! The color orange is your indicator that your contact has information for you. When you walk in the door, there is a bulletin board right there on the wall to your right. Check it carefully. There might be a business card or a notice on orange paper stock, or there might be something written in orange. If your contact has important information about which they can't be obvious, they might even simply use the word *orange*. If there's nothing on the board, check by the counter for a box of oranges. If you see nothing, simply buy a cup of coffee and say "See you later." Return every hour or so, alternating personnel. Do not go before nine o'clock AM; they wouldn't expect you to be early risers. Mr. Dixon and Mr. Courtland should go there only after four o'clock PM as, by then, most men are coming home from work. If you do see something orange, purchase a jar of peanut butter and take it to the counter. Use the passwords and phrases we taught you, and your contact will make the drop."

They reviewed the instructions again, until both Dwyer and Miss McIntyre were confident that the band members knew what to do. They began to ask more questions, but Dwyer cut them off.

"Gentlemen, we must be going," he said. Both he and Miss McIntyre had put on their coats and were standing by the door. Cameron looked at her and studied her profile. She possessed a proud chin, high cheekbones and fine features. His heart dropped at the thought of her walking out the door. He knew that the usual lines he used to attract the attention of "club women" would be scoffed at or go unnoticed, so he decided to abandon all of the clichés and simply be himself.

"Let me walk you to the door," Cameron said, giving Miss McIntyre a smile. She returned his smile, and he realized that she saw through his efforts.

So what? This is how I am. What are you going to do about it?

He opened the door for her and Dwyer, and made brief conversation with them both. He made sure that he gave her a special smile and nod, which he was pleased to noticed that she returned again, giving him plenty to think about as he closed the door. Cameron pondered pleasant images much worthier of entertaining than whatever it was that Rich, who had suddenly appeared at his elbow, wanted to discuss.

"I don't know what you're smiling about," the bass player demanded. "This shit is getting serious."

"Don't worry about it," Cameron yawned.

Please don't bring this up now. I'm begging you. Don't bring this up now.

"Don't worry about it? Are you serious? They're expecting us to start tailing someone and showing how much we know!"

"What, you've never done an apprenticeship before?"

"Be serious! This isn't anything like that and you know it. Lives will be at stake here. Actual lives! And more than anything else, it'll be ours!"

The pleasant image of Miss McIntyre's dimpled smile disappeared, only to be replaced by Rich's scowling face.

"I'll say this once," Cameron warned. "Step back, and get out of my face."

"Don't you have any clue what is going on here? We're kept in here against our will, and now we're going to be expected to start spying on people?! We've got to get out of here. We've got to do something!"

"What?" shouted Cameron. "Do what? Everyone is demanding we do something, but no one has any suggestions! Do you want me to call the cops? How? No phone, remember? Why don't we write letters to our congressmen? That should be a big help, wouldn't you think? Especially since none of you jackasses even knows who they are! You want to know what I'm going to do? I'm going to do what they fucking ask me to do, and hope the hell I do it right and make it through this in one fucking piece. That's what I suggest the rest of you assholes do!"

No one said a word. No one wanted to admit it, but they all realized that Cameron was right; their only hope of getting out of this sudden situation was to give in. That realization only made things worse.

"If I get out of this shit, I'll never use another black market ration coupon again," stated Clyde. "They'll never have the opportunity to use that over me ever again, I swear to God."

"Oh, great, he's getting religion," muttered Cameron. Grabbing a beer from the fridge, he went back into the living room.

"No, I'm not," Clyde insisted. "But don't you think we should be careful of what we do from now on?"

"Yeah, as a matter of fact I do," agreed Cameron. "But not so I can make certain they can never do anything to me again, because that's bullshit. I'll do it because I don't want to get killed."

"Why do you say it's bullshit?" asked Evan.

"Because we don't need to worry if they might do something to us in the future. They've got us by the balls already."

"You seem to be getting pretty adjusted to this," Evan noted.

"If you've got someone by the balls, their hearts and minds usually follow," Cameron retorted.

There was an uneasy silence among them. They all knew that no matter how much they might insist otherwise, Cameron was right.

"What the hell do we do, then?" Evan demanded.

"We do what we need to do and get it done," Rich said. He had not moved from the recliner all evening. He simply sat there and stared at the ceiling.

"As simple as that?" demanded Evan.

"As simple as that," Rich agreed.

"The simplest things can be the most complicated," Clyde sighed.

"That they can," Rich agreed once more.

Again, the uneasy silence filled the room. The novelty and the comfort of their accommodations had long ago worn off. Over the last few weeks it seemed that the walls had been gradually closing in. Now, realizing that in a few short hours they would be heading down an unfamiliar road from which there was no return—no longer in theory, but in actual fact—they felt like the room was pushing them out, and they longed for the consolation that their sequestering had previously offered.

"Nothing to do but get rested up then, is there?" asked Evan. No one answered. What was there to say? Bidding goodnight, they each retired. After the others headed for their rooms, Cameron cornered Doug.

"Do you mind telling me what went on tonight?"

"I don't know what you're talking about," Doug said.

"I think you do," Cameron told him. "I notice you get on the high hog whenever Dwyer and the others talk to you and I want to know why."

Doug shrugged him off.

"There's nothing," he insisted. He paused as though searching for words. "I just think sometimes he forgets that all this shit is second nature to him, and the rest of us haven't left this place since he recruited us."

"That's it?"

"Yeah, that's it."

Cameron considered the roadie's answers, and they did make sense, but only to a point. However, there were still other incidents and remarks that had been traded back and forth between Doug and Dwyer that were not so easily explained away.

"Would you be pissed if I didn't believe you?"

"You've got to do what you've got to do. Would you be pissed if I didn't care?"

"No," Cameron assured him. "But I don't believe you."

"Fair enough, because I don't care," the roadie said after a long pause. They eyed each other intently. Cameron reflected on the last few years that they'd worked together. He knew Doug to be a hard worker, appreciative of getting a job when so many others were in bread lines. Doug was not always easy to work with; he was the youngest among them all and prone to stubbornness but, following any trouble, he could easily be brought around to reason. He took his orders and, after several difficult episodes relating to his behavior at shows, learned to anticipate how he would be expected to behave, and he did his best to behave accordingly. That did not eliminate the fact that Doug always projected a sense of someone with a past. Cameron had never seriously wondered about it, until tonight. Now he wondered if Doug's past could catch up to him.

Or us?

CHAPTER SIX
"Agent Orange"

Clyde made his way to the store after the Roadhouse Sons had drawn straws to decide who would be the first one to go out on surveillance. Clyde wondered if he was the lucky one, or not; he still wasn't sure. As he left the safe house at nine o'clock AM and walked down the sidewalk, he cast glances at each person he passed, wondering if one of them might be the person he was supposed to watch. He looked at the houses, studied the sky, and made note of the cars that passed. He sniffed the air and tried to identify the smells. There were more colored houses than white ones, he noticed. He tried to focus his mind, but dozens of thoughts and images pervaded him, and he was unable to settle on any one thing.

As he crossed the street and made his way to the store, Clyde briefly considered simply passing by and continuing on his way. He could call his brother from a pay phone and make arrangements to go home; he only lived in Pennsylvania, after all. That was a big state, far from Vermont and an easy place to hide. Almost as soon as he thought it, though, he forced the idea out of his mind. He knew that running away simply wouldn't work.

Clyde felt his stomach tighten as he moved closer to the door of the shop. He knew that this was it. There was no turning back now.

Stepping inside and remembering Dwyer's instructions, he noted the appearance of the bulletin board. He studied it, scrutinizing every inch for anything to do with the color orange. At first glance, there was nothing noticeable. There was no orange paper, nor anything with orange writing. He tried looking for the word "orange," but there were so many notices and cards posted that it was hard to take it all in at first. He must have been standing there for some time when one of the customers spoke up.

"You've been staring at that thing for a long time. You taking root?"

Clyde turned toward the male voice. The man was short, stocky, and with close-cropped blonde hair. Piercing hazel eyes stared out beneath thick blonde eyebrows. The man's face was in a sneer.

"Just seeing what they've got up there," Clyde answered. "No harm in that, is there?"

"Why don't you get a hair cut?" the man demanded. Clyde's inner defenses automatically kicked in; he had heard this from so many others before, he learned to ignore it. He wanted to make a sharp retort, but knew that would only escalate the situation. Clyde did not want to draw any attention to himself, so against his will, he reconsidered his response.

"I might have to," Clyde replied. "Especially if I have a chance to get a job."

"Should have thought of that before," the man grumbled, pushing his way past Clyde and rambling out of the store. Clyde tripped on the black carpet runner by the door, and was about to forget his original idea and go after the man when he noticed something out of the corner of his eye. There on the counter was a small basket of oranges. The contact was present and had the information!

Adjusting his coat, Clyde began searching for the peanut butter and noticed that there was only one jar left on the shelf. For a moment, he wondered if that really was the last jar, or if they had put just one on the shelf for him. It really didn't matter, he decided. It was there.

"Will that be all?" the old storekeeper asked, as Clyde set the jar down on the counter. Clyde felt his mouth go dry, and for a moment wondered if he would actually be able to continue.

"I, uhm," Clyde stammered. The old man stared at him curiously.

"Sure do wish I could get some good..." he took a deep breath before continuing. "...beef."

The old man shook his head, but didn't say anything. Clyde began to panic. Did he say the wrong pass phrase? Did he overlook something? Did he make a mistake? Clyde did not know what to do, but for a moment considered simply running out of the store and taking his chances. Before he could do anything, the old man spoke up.

"I'd settle for some good hamburger," the old man said, chuckling and nodding his head toward the meat counter. Clyde glanced over to where the old man indicated, and noticed the graying mound of ground beef behind the glass. At first glance it did look like hamburger, but there was something different about it, and Clyde suddenly felt the urge to become a vegetarian.

"Then I guess I'll have to settle for peanut butter," Clyde said, amazed at the sincerity in his voice. The storekeeper picked up the jar to place it in the paper sack, and then carefully examined it.

"I'm sorry, young fellow," he said. "This jar seems to have a crack in it. No telling how long it had that. Let me get you another one from the back. I haven't put the new delivery out on the shelves yet."

Before Clyde could protest, the old man disappeared through a door behind the counter. The room on the other side was dark, but Clyde noticed stacks of boxes in there, so he assumed that it was a storeroom. Almost as quickly as he had left, the old man returned with another jar of peanut butter, which he set on the counter and rang up on the register. Clyde counted out his money, realizing that he had just barely enough. As Clyde handed over the money, the storekeeper's wife spoke to him.

"What's the weather like outside?" she asked, looking up from her knitting. "Is it getting cold out?"

"Not too bad," Clyde smiled. He was never good at making small talk, but he knew he had to be polite. "A bit of a cool breeze, but nothing bad." She smiled, and went back to her knitting.

"Here you go, young man," the storekeeper said, pushing the bag toward him. "You have a nice day."

Clyde nodded with a smile and turned to leave. He didn't look in the bag, or say anything. He just wanted to get out of there. Hurrying through the door, he stepped into a cold blast of wind and shuddered. That provided him with the perfect excuse to pick up his pace. He briefly wondered about taking a separate route home but decided against it. He was trying to give the impression of someone nearly broke and looking for work. If all he could afford was a jar of peanut butter, then why would he be wandering all over town? Besides, he just wanted to get back to the safe house as quickly as possible. As he made his way back, he did look over his shoulder several times, as instructed by Dwyer and Miss McIntyre, but he didn't notice anyone following him, either by foot or by car. But he didn't relax, either.

Back at the safe house, Clyde set the bag on the counter and got himself a beer. Everyone noticed his hands shake as he struggled to open it.

"If this is how you are getting peanut butter, remind me never to send you out for pizza," said Cameron.

"Fuck you," said Clyde, who then gulped down the entire bottle. Cameron emptied the bag on the counter.

"Hey, what's the idea?" he demanded. "Why did you get cigarettes? Dwyer specifically said only buy the peanut butter and only take enough for that!"

"I didn't get any smokes," insisted Clyde. "All I got was the peanut butter."

Cameron didn't answer, just held up the package of Marlboros for Clyde to see.

"I didn't get those," Clyde said. "I never saw them before."

"You must have," said Cameron. "They've been opened. How many did you have on the way here?"

"None," snapped Clyde, removing another pack of Marlboros from his pocket. "Here's *my* pack right here."

"Can we forget about those things for a second?" demanded Evan. "They obviously got put in the bag by mistake. We've got to figure out what he was trying to tell us."

The band members opened the jar of peanut butter, and noticed that there was nothing under the lid, nor was the peanut butter itself disturbed. They peeled off the label and held it up to the light. There was nothing written on the back, nor was there anything on the jar itself. Taking turns, they each examined the label carefully, but could not determine if there was any code. Holding a lighter to it did not reveal any invisible ink, either.

"This is another one of Dwyer's mind fucking tricks," snapped Rich. "There was no information and there was nothing to find. The bastard just wanted to see what we'd do!"

Clyde threw his bottle into the sink, his anger increasing when the bottle didn't break.

"Fucking lab rats, that's what we are," he bellowed. "And I don't care if the cocksucker hears me!" He stuck his middle fingers toward the ceiling. The others didn't say anything, but no one hurried to correct his impression.

"Tell me exactly what happened," asked Cameron. Slowly and carefully, Clyde recounted the events of the morning. Cameron listened intently, but said nothing.

"So, he gave you the correct responses and you did, too," Cameron mused. "Something's not right."

"Oh, are you just noticing this now?!" yelled Clyde. "What gave you the clue? The kidnapping by supposed secret agents, the sequestering, or all the bullshit we go through every day?"

Cameron didn't respond. He simply stared at the items on the counter. He picked up the jar, then the lid, then the label, and carefully reexamined each item. Again, he found nothing. He reached for the pack of cigarettes. That was when he noticed something.

"What the hell is this?" Cameron cried, removing a small slip of paper from the pack. It was a bit of torn typing paper carefully folded around a small photograph that itself had been folded in half to fit inside the pack. Resting behind the cigarettes, one would never have noticed it unless one reached into the pack.

The photo was of a man that Cameron recognized.

The silent man in the store when I went with Dwyer.

On the back of the photograph was a name, Louis Barre.

"What the hell is going on?" demanded Clyde. "I never put the smokes in the bag, I swear!"

"Then how did they get in there? Didn't you see the old man put them in?" asked Evan.

"No! I swear to God!" Clyde responded. "I watched him the whole time!"

"The whole time," asked Rich. "You must have looked somewhere else sometime, because how else could they have gotten in there?"

"Well, there was the time his wife spoke to me. She asked me how cold it was out there and I told her. He must have put smokes in the bag when I was talking to her."

"Yeah, he must have," muttered Cameron, lighting the cigarette he had removed. "Next time, let's remember to share all of the details, not just shit we might think is important."

They each studied the photograph carefully, as if examining a piece of a puzzle. How might this piece fit with the next one? It was a task made more difficult by the fact there were no other pieces at the moment.

"All right, what do we do now?" asked Rich. "We know his name, and what he looks like, but that's it. Where do we go from here?"

Cameron continued studying the photograph.

"Well, we know he frequents that store," he said. "We could hang out around there and watch for him."

"That wouldn't work," said Evan. "The place isn't that busy, and no one hangs around there, not even over the coffee machine. That would be too conspicuous."

"We could ask Dwyer for what he's got on him," suggested Clyde. "He must have some information, or else they wouldn't have asked us to do this."

"No, I don't think that would work," said Cameron. "I think he wants to see what we'd do on our own. That's why he wanted us to gather the information, not wait for him to provide it. No, *we've* got to figure this out."

They each studied the photograph again, hoping to find some clue to suggest their next step.

"If we at least knew where this picture was taken," said Evan, "then we might be able to get an idea."

"Let me see that again," said Doug. "It almost looks like one of these warehouses."

"But which one?"

"That I can't say," Doug replied.

"Well, that's a start at least," sighed Rich. "How do we narrow this down? There has to be a dozen of these places. Is there any reflection of a street sign or anything?"

"Nothing," said Cameron. "Not even a shadow to suggest the time of day."

"Well, then. I guess we stake them out," said Clyde. "That's all there is to it."

"You've got to start sniffing some better glue, man," Doug said. "Didn't you hear what Rich said? There are a dozen of them! What the fuck are we going to do? Stand outside each one?"

Clyde glared at the roadie, but didn't say anything.

"I think he has a point," said Evan. "We can divide ourselves up and each watch a couple of the warehouses."

"How are we supposed to do that?" demanded Doug. "If we hang around outside, we'll attract too much attention. Isn't that what we're supposed to avoid?"

"We wouldn't have to hang around," said Rich. "We could just watch them in the mornings when people are heading into work, and keep our eyes open for this guy. Once we find where he's employed, we can find the times he's in that building and we work with that."

"What if he was just walking in front of one of these buildings, though?" asked Clyde. "Maybe he doesn't work here, or maybe it isn't one of these places."

"No. It would be one of these places," said Cameron. "Remember, I saw him in that store when I was there. So, we know he's around here. But you're right; he might not work in one of those warehouses."

"So, what do we do?" asked Doug. Everyone noticed the irritation in his voice.

"We calm down, first of all," warned Cameron. "Then we take Clyde's suggestion and watch the places."

"All of them?" demanded Doug.

Cameron considered that for a minute before answering.

"No," he said at last. "This picture was taken during the day. There aren't any shadows, so that would suggest it was around noon. I saw him during the day, late afternoon. So, that would suggest that if he works at all, then he is either a part-time worker, or he works third shift."

"Which one of these places has a third shift, though?" asked Evan.

"That is what we're going to find out," Cameron said, smiling.

They discussed how best to divide the locations among them, and decided to wait until evening to put their plan into action. During all this, the familiar knock at the door signaled that their handlers had returned.

Cameron opened the door to find Dwyer and D'Lorenzo standing there.

"Good morning, gentlemen," Dwyer said. "Get your coats and come with me."

"Why?" Doug demanded.

Disgusted with Doug's constantly challenging attitude, Dwyer, despite himself, again broke form from his usual comportment. "Mr. Courtland, my sole experience with musical instruments is limited to the sandpaper blocks that we were issued in elementary school. Far from promoting any musical aptitude, they merely allowed me to give Ernie McGuire the mother of all Indian burns.

After months of attending your shows, I am aware that a guitar has strings and that chords issue from them to large black boxes. However, that is where my knowledge of such matters ends. Since your colleagues wish to have their instruments, I need you all to go with Mr. D'Lorenzo to retrieve them."

Doug stood there, mouth agape and stunned. The rest of the Roadhouse Sons didn't even react to Dwyer; they were ecstatic, and couldn't get out the door fast enough. As they left to get their coats, Dwyer motioned to Cameron.

"Except you, Mr. Walsh. I need to speak with you privately."

"But what about my stuff?" Cameron demanded. "I want my gear, too!"

"Mr. Courtland will retrieve your equipment and return it to you."

Reluctantly, Cameron told Doug and Rich what to take out of the truck. He plopped down in one of the kitchen chairs, waiting impatiently. Dwyer waited silently until the door was closed. When Cameron began to speak, Dwyer held up his hand to call for silence. Placing his ear to the door, Dwyer listened for a moment before speaking.

"You gentlemen successfully retrieved the information," Dwyer said, nodding to the items on the counter.

"Clyde was the one that actually went and got it."

"Congratulate him for me. You've all done rather well. Have you devised a surveillance plan yet?"

"Yeah, we were just working on it when you arrived." Cameron described what the band members had discussed about Clyde's adventure, and what they thought would be the next best course of action.

"That's good starter strategy. Well thought out," Dwyer replied, though something in his voice told Cameron that he was not thinking about their assignment. Dwyer had a distant look in his eyes, as though concentrating on a remote problem. His manner was distracted, only half hearing what Cameron said, and giving merely noncommittal nods. This began to unsettle Cameron, who was used to Dwyer's careful manner and hawk-like conscientiousness. For a fleeting moment, Cameron wondered if this might be another one of Dwyer's tests, but soon realized it was not.

"Mr. Walsh, promise me you that you will tell *no one* of your plans other than me. Do not speak of them to anyone else, not Miss McIntyre, not Mr. D'Lorenzo, not anyone."

"Why the hell not?"

"Mr. Walsh, it is imperative that you give me your assurance and agree to speak with no one but me, and then only vis-à-vis. Never speak of this over the phone, and do not speak of this aloud, even again in here."

"What the hell is going on?"

Dwyer paused for a moment before answering. Cameron noticed how Dwyer examined his hands before he spoke.

"Do you know what a mole is, Mr. Walsh?"

Cameron just stared at him, waiting.

"A mole is someone who burrows into an organization and attempts to destroy it at the roots."

Cameron felt his stomach tighten, despite Dwyer's uncharacteristically clumsy metaphor. He was not certain to what Dwyer was referring, but judging from his actions and words, Cameron knew that it was a matter of great concern and no levity.

"What are you getting at?"

"We have a mole amongst us, Mr. Walsh. Our network has been infiltrated."

"By who?"

Dwyer stared at Cameron for a moment, visibly irritated.

"If we knew, would I warn you to be cautious?" Dwyer seethed, unable to hold his usual composure.

"Well you don't need to bite my fucking head off!"

Dwyer sighed. "Forgive my familiarity. Today, in particular, I must remind myself that we have only been working together for two months."

"Is that how long it's been?" Cameron sighed.

Dwyer nodded, then began, almost absent-mindedly picking up and studying the items on the counter. Cameron watched Dwyer closely, sensing that there was something more that Dwyer needed to say. Cameron broke the silence, hoping to prod more details from Dwyer.

"So, how did you find this out?"

"This," Dwyer replied, holding up the jar of peanut butter. "Mr. Poulin was the second person to ask for it."

"Holy shit," Cameron whispered.

"Fortunately, the other party did not have the correct counter response, so they did not get the information. When they gave the wrong answer, the storekeeper mentioned that the jar appeared cracked and took it in the back room and replaced it with an ordinary one."

"Clyde said the storekeeper did the same thing with him."

"Yes," Dwyer nodded. "The storekeeper realized that something was wrong and removed the information from the jar, and placed it in a pack of cigarettes in the back room. The rules of engagement are that if the storekeeper receives the incorrect pass phrase, whomever requests the information receives the regular peanut butter jar. If the storekeeper gets the correct response, then the information is released."

"Do you know who the person was that tried to get it?"

"I'm afraid we don't. The storekeeper gave us a description, but it was no one with whom we have had any contact. I doubt we will find them, or, if we do, they will not be in any position to be interrogated."

Cameron did not ask what Dwyer meant by that; he didn't need to. Looking down, Cameron noticed his own hands were shaking slightly. Before this conversation, Cameron had been apprehensive about what they all were doing. Now, though, he was scared, much more scared than he had been in the interrogation room when all this began.

"Do you have any clues at all as to who might be behind it?" Cameron implored.

"At this point, none whatsoever, I'm afraid," Dwyer admitted. "However, I do know that it must be someone at my level."

"Why's that?" Cameron was surprised.

"As we were driving over here last night, I changed the counter response that you were required to give. The other individual gave the incorrect one, the old one."

"Do you remember who you talked to about it before?"

"My superiors, and the ones in my network, Miss McIntyre and Mr. D'Lorenzo."

"Do you think it's one of them? You don't really think it could be Miss McIntyre?" Cameron asked. The image of her bringing him coffee that morning flashed through his mind, and he silently prayed that it was not his divine Miss McIntyre.

Dwyer eyed Cameron curiously for just a moment. "I am not entirely certain, Mr. Walsh. Mr. D'Lorenzo has not had any direct involvement with planning an operation. He is more of an assistant at the moment. It would be logical to rule out Miss McIntyre. She was with me last night when I decided to change the pass phrase. She would have had to pass the information along before the attempt, or called it off entirely. Neither was done."

"Unless she didn't want to tip her hand."

Dwyer continued to study Cameron, his eyes squinted.

"Congratulations, Mr. Walsh. You're beginning to think like me."

Cameron shifted uncomfortably, wondering why that didn't feel like a compliment at all.

"An assistant has access to everything you do, so D'Lorenzo isn't entirely ruled out," Cameron suggested.

Dwyer gave a little nod at that assessment.

"Was that what tipped you off?" Cameron asked. "Changing things last night, I mean?"

"No," Dwyer sighed. "I had suspicions before. Other operations went wrong, but never anything very serious, nothing to raise any alarms, just events that could be ascribed to human error or chance. 'Snowflakes,' as my mentor would describe them."

"Snowflakes?"

"Snowflakes. By itself, a snowflake is of no consequence. It drifts about and falls on the ground to either sit or melt. However, enough snowflakes impede one's movements, or render one snowbound. To be trapped by the snow is to risk death from exposure."

"So, there were a lot of these snowflakes?"

"Enough to make me suspicious, but not enough to give me reason to take any action. Last night was a method to simply test my hypothesis. Sadly, the results are what I had suspected."

"So what do we do now? Call everything off?" Cameron hoped that Dwyer would concur. For a moment, Cameron saw a door to freedom opening, and the chance to put all of this behind him, only to be recounted during drunken nights hanging out with friends once he was back to normal. Dwyer slammed that door shut in his face.

"No, Mr. Walsh. That would be the worst course of action to employ. By doing so, the mole will be aware that we know they are in operation, and that would send them further undercover, making it difficult for us to discover their identity. We have no other course of action but to see this operation through."

"Then how the hell do we keep it quiet?"

"By doing what I told you before. Speak to no one but me about this, not even Miss McIntyre nor Mr. D'Lorenzo. Be careful of how you discuss it amongst yourselves. I suspect that the mole has been monitoring some of our surveillance tapes from this very suite."

Cameron felt the air go out of him.

"Then what the fuck are we talking about this for? They've probably heard everything we've just said!"

"They will if you don't keep your voice down," Dwyer snapped. Pausing, exasperated, Dwyer said, "I've disconnect the audio surveillance system here for the time being. However, I can't do that indefinitely without raising suspicion."

"Then what the hell are we supposed to do? How are we going to set everything up? How are we going to communicate with you? How the fuck are we going to get out of this alive?"

"Communicate with one another by writing it down, and folding the paper over until the one for whom it is intended reads it. Basic and complicated, but certainly effective for now."

"No, that wouldn't work. The mole could see what we were writing."

"Mr. Walsh, you try my patience. Have you a better idea?"

"I think so," Cameron replied.

"Then, let's review it."

"Doug's sister is deaf and mute," Cameron explained. "She had to go to a special school to learn how to talk with her hands so she could communicate."

"American Sign Language. How is that a solution any more than writing things down? If you fear detection while writing, then sign language would be more detectable."

"I figured you'd say that," said Cameron. "But Doug and his sister developed their own signs so they could talk about things they didn't want their folks in on. He taught some of it to us so we could communicate to him when we were on stage. We can simply use that."

"Is it adequate to employ in this situation?"

"It would help us quite a bit. We can use that writing idea you mentioned earlier, and have regular conversations about other shit while with the secret sign language, and we should be OK."

Dwyer considered this for a moment, and then nodded his assent.

"Mr. Walsh, I made a wise choice in selecting you."

"That doesn't make me feel better."

"It shouldn't."

"Can I ask you something?" Cameron pressed. "What's so important about this guy? You and I saw him in the store that day. If you needed to know something about him, why didn't you just have the same people you had trailing me trail *him*?"

"At the time, we were not aware of his involvement in our interests. He had only recently arrived in this area, and wasn't rumored to have been involved in black market operations. We now have reason to suspect that he is a contact for an organization that we are surveilling."

"Suspect? You mean you're not sure, right?"

"Correct," Dwyer admitted freely. "He has appeared at various times with various other people we have under surveillance, but nothing gelled. Now, he is here. We are not certain if he is just a mere messenger, or if he is deeply involved."

"Then why pass this shit off on us?" Cameron grew impatient.

"At this juncture, all we want to ascertain is where he goes and what he does. We have no reason to believe that his level of importance requires our full attention. This is a minor task perfect for a novice team such as yours. You gain experience, and we gain intelligence."

"What if it turns out to be bigger than you thought? What if he is important?"

"Should we make that discovery, you and your colleagues will find yourselves safely removed from the situation, and more experienced personnel will take over. Does that reassure you, Mr. Walsh?"

"No, not really."

"Good."

CHAPTER SEVEN
"The First Mission"

It was hard for Cameron to motivate the band to embark upon the Louis Barre surveillance. Everyone was anxious to get back to their instruments, since they hadn't played in so long. Cameron's conversation with Dwyer escalated his own anxiety, especially because he would eventually have to tell the others about it. After much deliberation, it was decided that, the following day, Doug would go out at six o'clock AM for the first check, and the others would go out later. They reasoned that it would be less conspicuous for Doug to leave the safe house when most people would be leaving for work. That way, his movements would be less noticeable, since most people walked to work these days, or took car pools. The occasional meanderer could go undisturbed. Doug could wander with the crowds and locate a local watering hole, and then come back through to see what businesses, if any, were open day or night.

At dawn the next day, Doug was ready. "I'm just anxious to be outside for awhile," he told himself.

Stepping outside, Doug felt a sense of release. The air was invigorating, with the smell of winter coming on. Looking toward the hills, he noticed that many of the trees which, just a few weeks ago, were blazing with color, were now muted umber, dry and about to shed all of their foliage. Doug surmised that it was probably the middle of October by now. He made a mental note to grab a newspaper while he was out. He thought that, at the very least, it would be nice to know what month it is.

Knowing that there were several businesses just down the street, Doug moved in that direction, and as he made his way down the sidewalk, he cut across the parking lot. There were more cars there than before. Doug saw people exiting from the safe house, some toward the cars and some toward the sidewalk. A quick glance toward the parking lot showed him that the guy he was looking for was not there, so he headed around the building.

Six or so people were walking down the sidewalk, but no one seemed to resemble the photograph of Louis Barre, which showed a man of average height and build, with dark hair. The men Doug now saw fit every description but that. Doug made his way along the street and noted other places where people had gathered. Quick inspections of those faces were likewise unsuccessful in locating Louis, so Doug kept going. He walked rapidly down a narrow side street, noticing the people who took this same shortcut, and still didn't see anyone. Frustration began to mount, until he reminded himself that he was not actually here to find the guy, but only to get a lay of the land, as Cameron had described it. With that, at least, he was successful.

Rounding the corner, Doug saw the small convenience store. He struggled for a moment to decide if he should go inside or not. Hadn't Cameron noticed Louis Barre there before? It might be a long shot, but if Louis frequented the store, he might be there now. Doug figured his thirst was a good excuse to stop in and buy a Coke.

Quickening his pace, he made his way inside and, as the band members had been told to do, he glanced at the bulletin board for anything remotely related to the color orange. He didn't expect to find anything, but saw a notice for a yard sale, part of which had been written in orange marker. Doug chalked this up to coincidence, and made his way toward the cooler, when he heard someone come in behind him. Glancing over his shoulder, Doug hoped for an incredible break, that there would be Louis Barre himself, framed in the doorway. Much to Doug's chagrin, he was wrong. Instead of Louis Barre, there was a heavyset woman, a look of irritation on her worn and flushed face, waiting for him to move aside.

"Excuse me," Doug muttered, and stepped out of the woman's way. She said nothing as she barreled past him toward the coolers, from which she removed a small carton of milk. Since the soda coolers were next to the dairy coolers, Doug decided to wait before moving past her again. Instead, he headed toward the coffee machine to examine the stack of newspapers there.

Doug poured hot water into a cup, and added enough coffee substitute to give it some flavor. His eyes scanned the front page of the *Rutland Herald*, and he noticed the usual stories of war in bold print. There were reports of more attacks by Soviet subs on shipping lanes, NATO forces still pushing into Austria, and the wavering of the German front. There was no definite word on what was going on in Alaska. There were also items dealing with other goings-on in the world, as if those headlines would divert the minds of the populace from the horrors of war.

"I need to put something on a slip," the heavyset woman declared for all the store to hear.

"I'm sorry, ma'am, but we don't issue credit to anyone anymore."

"You gave my husband credit the other day," she shouted. "He came home with a six pack of beer. He didn't have any money for it, and I never gave it to him! He said he put it on a slip. If he can do that with beer, than I can do that with a gallon of milk."

"Buying alcohol on credit is against the law in Vermont," the man insisted. "If your husband got it that way, I assure you, he did not get it here!"

"Well, we don't shop anywhere else! This is the only store in walking distance of the house, and we can't get to the big stores since Louie lost his car."

Doug, upon hearing this, dropped his coffee cup and, scrambling, grabbed a bunch of napkins and wiped the counter, thankful that no one noticed him. There was a very good chance that the "Louie" to whom the fat woman referred, and the Louis in the photograph, were the same man. Doug wanted to get more out of this mission than a headache, figurative or otherwise, but one was literally building; whether it was from the horrible coffee substitute, or the screaming of that irate woman, he couldn't be certain.

"I told you already, ma'am, your husband did not get any such service here! Now, I will thank you to either purchase something legitimately, or leave."

The woman slammed her palm down on the counter and leaned into the storekeeper's face.

"You'll give me some milk or I'll go to the police!"

"If you want this milk, you'll produce your ration coupon, or *I* will be calling the police!"

"I haven't got any coupons, I've used them up already!" she ranted.

"Then you better get the instant milk and make do 'til next month. And before you ask, I won't be giving you that on credit, either!"

The woman began to tremble, and for a moment Doug wondered if she was going to become violent, but then she began to cry.

"Its not fair," she sobbed. "He gets everything and I get nothing. He told you not to help me, didn't he?"

"I have no idea what you're talking about, ma'am. Now, please. Either make a purchase, or leave."

"It's not fair," she said, the words choking out. Doug could tell that she was on the verge of tears, and he could tell that the tears were genuine, born out of frustration and despair. Dealing with the band's myriad groupies had taught Doug the difference between crocodile tears and dime store sorrow, and the brokenhearted anguish of someone who honestly believed that something special had happened. The former were used by groupies who just wanted to bag another conquest; the latter was a symptom of a heart too new to be jaded. The first he could simply ignore; for the other, he could offer a few kind words and call them a cab home. This woman was somewhere in between.

"He says he goes to work, but he doesn't," she stammered. "He's gone all day and comes home like he used to. He thinks I don't know, but I do. When I asked him last night where his check was, he said they were holding it 'til accounts came in. I called the office today and they said he quit weeks ago! He comes home with beer and when I ask where he got the money, he says he put it on a slip 'til his pay comes in. All I want is some milk for the kids."

"Ma'am, some men are born liars," the old man said. "There is nothing I can do about their nature or your situation. I have never given anyone credit and will not start now. Is there anything else I can do for you?"

The woman did not answer. For a moment, she stood glaring into the old man's face. Her lip began to tremble and her face became flushed. Doug feared that she would give in to her emotions and things would become even more awkward. Instead, she grabbed her purse and stormed away, once again gruffly brushing past Doug. He stepped up to the counter and placed his coffee cup down.

"Will that be all, young man?" the storekeeper muttered. He did not look at Doug, nor did he make any reference to what had transpired. Instead, the old man waved his finger over the cash register, as though he were seeking out the appropriate keys to press. Doug took the unspoken hint and made no reference to the woman, either.

"Yes, thank you," Doug replied.

"Twenty-five cents, then."

Doug reached into his pocket, and counted out the amount in nickels and pennies. The mention of the name "Louie" gave Doug an idea, and he had been working on it in his mind while they had their exchange. Tossing his empty cup in the trash, he headed back out to the street. He lit a cigarette and leaned against the side of the building and let his mind wander.

Doug thought back to his life after dropping out of school. He had moved out of his parents' house and, after staying with one of his buddies, hooked up with a waitress from Montpelier. They moved in together and things seemed fine. Then, one day, he lost his job. He didn't know how to tell her the news, so he left every day at the same time. Instead of going to work, he went to the unemployment office or checked out other job leads. When he wasn't doing that, he hung out at one of the bars near his old workplace. She never caught on. Doug was willing to bet that "Louie" was doing the exact same thing, except, maybe unbeknownst to him, *his* woman was on to him.

Doug allowed his mind to return to the present. He had previously walked down the streets near the store and hadn't noticed anything that resembled a bar. Looking toward the left, he saw more houses, and what appeared to be a residential area. Toward the right, it appeared less residential, and more promising, so he headed that way.

Several blocks from the store, he was surprised to discover a small bar. "Pete's Tavern" was written in peeling paint on the front of the building. Half-lit neon signs glared out at passersby, making it difficult to see inside. However, there was an "Open" sign in the corner of one of the windows, and so Doug ventured inside.

The first thing to hit him was the familiar smell of every bar. It reeked of spilled beer, stale cigarette smoke, and sweat. He was never certain if the beer stench was from the patrons spilling their drinks, or from the drain beneath the beer taps. To Doug, it wasn't an offensive smell, but one that suggested the familiarity of belonging to places in which he had spent so much of his time. He was actually quite grateful to be there. He took a few deep breaths, which gave his eyes the chance to adjust to the lack of light in the place.

Doug performed a headcount. "Pete's" currently had three patrons and a bartender. The latter, a rather grizzled man with a severe scowl, had an assistant that looked as though he were expecting a beating at any moment. Doug wondered what it must be like to work for the bartender, but didn't worry about it for too long. He examined the patrons next. Lo, and behold. There sat Doug's quarry. At the corner of the bar was Louis Barre, who glanced at Doug briefly. Doug sat down two stools away from Barre.

"What'll you have?" demanded the bartender.

"Bud," Doug answered. "Bottle, and open it here, please."

Experience had taught Doug to order a bottled beer, and have it opened in front of him. These days, in order to save metal for the war effort, cans were no longer used. The only choice was bottled beer or draft. It wasn't unheard of for bars to mix partially consumed beers, and either put them into kegs, or into other bottles. At least if he saw the bartender open it, Doug knew he had a good chance of getting a real brew. Bartenders understood that concern, and the more reputable ones were happy to accommodate, but others were not so obliging. Doug soon realized in which camp he found himself.

"Then you show me the money," the bartender snapped. "Extra two bits for the bottled stuff."

Doug produced the money and smacked it on the counter without comment, staring steadily at the bartender.

"Would you like a glass with that?" the man sneered, turning away without waiting for an answer.

Doug studied the bar as he sipped his beer. Dark lighting hid most of the wear and tear. Even in the murky twilight, he could see the cracks in the floor tiles and the dark spots where corners had broken off and bar grunge made a home for itself. White specks along the walls revealed dents and scratches, and bits of streamers from holidays and celebrations long past still were taped in the cobwebbed corners. The vinyl stools were patched in several places with duct tape. In the far end of the place, better lit than where Doug sat, was a pool table. In addition to the main door, Doug noticed a sign at the far end of the bar, and suspected that there had to be another door over there.

Louis Barre sat three stools away from Doug. Barre was studying his beer bottle, and Doug noticed that it was still covered with condensation. That indicated clearly that Barre hadn't been there for very long.

Several stools to Barre's right sat two other men, deep in conversation. Both men were older, and could have passed for any senior patrons of bars anywhere in the world. Each of them drank from rocks glasses, and several cocktail napkins were piled near them. Doug was willing to bet that they had been there for some time.

Barre glanced at Doug occasionally, then cast a glance over his shoulder to the door. At all other times, Barre's concentration seemed to be on the bottle in front of him. Doug suspected that Barre was going to be there for a good long time, but he was wrong. Five minutes later, Barre finished his beer and left without saying anything to anyone. Doug had just ordered a second beer. He took a few sips of it and stepped outside, feeling a flash of resentment for the man who made him waste the second beer. Doug figured that a return trip would redeem the unfinished beer.

He found Barre heading in the direction of the store and, for a moment, wondered if the man would head home. The memory of the heavyset woman who had been asking for Barre flashed through Doug's mind, and Doug realized that the man would likely avoid going home to her.

Barre continued past the store and down the block, eventually turning left onto an unmarked street. Doug hesitated at the entrance to the street, realizing that if he were caught, there was no way he could invent an excuse for why he was there. He had no knowledge of Rutland, so he couldn't claim using the street as a shortcut. He knew no one in the area, and therefore couldn't claim that he was paying a visit to anyone. Finally, Doug realized there was no other choice; he had to follow Barre.

Hurrying down the street, he realized that it was actually a driveway between two houses. Each side of the driveway was lined with trashcans, and the properties' back yards were fully visible to one another. There was no one around, and Doug didn't see anyone looking out of any windows.

Doug paused when he reached the end of the driveway. There was no place for him to find cover, so he acted as though he had nothing to hide and stepped out onto the sidewalk. There was no sign of Barre. Angrily, Doug returned to the safe house.

When he reached the suite, Cameron was in the living room playing his guitar, eyes closed and fingers carefully drawing out each note from the strings over which they danced. Over time, Doug discovered that, when the band rehearsed, they did not always play a song through. Instead, they would work on parts that needed attention, and would repeat the music until they were confident that they knew it and could play it the way they wanted. Doug had also discovered that they would do the same thing when they were simply jamming with one another, only then they would sometimes skip from song to song, playing parts they liked, or suggesting other songs to see if one another knew them. The band would either attempt the song or move on to something else. To one not musically inclined, it was not always easy to take.

The sudden slam of the door caused Cameron to jump, and Doug avoided looking at him, knowing instinctively the angry glare that was directed at him.

"What's up with you?" Cameron called out. Doug related the events of the morning, and expected his boss to commiserate with him about the frustrations of losing one's quarry. He was in for a rude surprise.

"Where did you say he was sitting?" asked Cameron, leaning in, looking at Doug a little too closely.

"At the end of the bar."

"Near the door?"

"Yeah, near the door. What difference does it make?"

"And you say he didn't stay long after you got there?"

"No, I had just finished my beer and ordered another one when he left."

"Had he finished his drink?"

"I don't know. What difference does it make?"

"Think," Cameron urged. "Had he finished it or not?"

"No, I don't think so."

"Are you sure?"

"Yeah, pretty sure, I guess."

Cameron rested his head in his hands and for several minutes stared at the floor.

"How long did he wait after you got your drink before he left?" Cameron asked.

"I'd just had the second beer set in front of me, and he left. Why?"

"You said he darted down an alley and that was when you lost him?"

"Yeah, that's right."

Doug watched as Cameron got up and paced the room. He knew from Cameron's deep breaths that his boss was contemplating a difficult subject.

"What's with all the questions, anyway?" demanded Doug. "What difference does it make?"

"It makes a lot of difference," muttered Cameron.

"How?"

"It means he suspected someone was following him."

"How do you know?"

"First, he sat near the door," Cameron explained. "That way, he could watch who came in and out. If he's a regular there, and he probably is, he would have noticed any new person coming in."

Doug began to feel nauseous.

"Which means?"

"Which means you stuck out like a shit stain on a wedding dress," Cameron yelled.

"How the hell do you know that?"

Cameron sat on the ottoman and looked Doug in the eye.

"Because he waited until you made yourself comfortable before he left, and he didn't even finish his beer. Guys don't usually do that, and they certainly don't do it if they haven't got any money to spend on it. That is, not without a very, very good reason. Second, he waited to see if you were following him and took a route that would force you to reveal yourself if you were following him. I'm willing to bet he was in one of those houses, watching you."

Doug sat there stunned, silently considering everything Cameron had said.

"Did you turn around and retrace your steps by any chance?"

Doug shook his head. "No," he replied. "I kept going like I had intended to do that all along. I went back a few blocks and cut over to the store and made my way back here."

Cameron seemed relieved to hear that. Perhaps it removed some of the suspicion that Louis Barre might have had about Doug.

I sure as hell hope so.

"That was good," Cameron assured him. "Smart move there."

Before Doug could say anything, Cameron called out to the others to join them.

"I've got some news," he told them. "We found Louis Barre, but he also might have found us."

He related Doug's account of the morning, and waited for their responses.

"Good move, asshole," Clyde grumbled. "You blow everything before we even start!"

"Screw you," Doug snarled. "Can you tell me you'd have done anything different?"

"Yeah, I wouldn't have gotten caught, for one thing!"

"Only because you wouldn't have found the bastard in the first place!"

Doug and Clyde rose up from their chairs and continued to hurl insults and barbs at one another, with Evan and Rich standing between them. They all fell silent when Cameron slammed a beer bottle against the table.

"This isn't accomplishing anything," he said. "Now sit your asses down and lets figure this out."

They each sat down with the exception of Doug, who went into the kitchen to get something to drink. Cameron watched him, recognizing the small act of insubordination, but realizing that now was not the time to say anything.

"It might not be a total loss," Cameron said. "I think I have an idea. We know what time Doug was at the bar, and we know this guy had at least one drink, because the bottle was still cool. His wife had been looking for him before then, so we know he wasn't home. I think what we should try to do now is get an idea of where he comes from and what time he reaches his destination."

"That's just as open-ended as before," said Evan. "We've got to try something new."

"No, we've actually got a bit to go on," insisted Cameron. "We know that he at least lives near the bar and the store, possibly even down by where Doug followed him. For starters, we figure he must have been at the bar at least half an hour before Doug found him, so we'll stake out the store a little earlier than that."

"How do we know that will work?" asked Rich.

"Do you have a better idea?"

No one spoke up.

"OK, so tomorrow morning we'll head to the store," continued Cameron. "One of us, then a little bit later two of us, then one more."

"That's only four guys, though," said Rich. "There are five of us."

"Doug needs to stay away. He shouldn't be seen hanging around there too often, especially now."

"Yeah," said Clyde. "We don't want him fucking things up more than he has already."

"It's not as fucked up as you'll be if you don't get off my ass!"

"Enough, you two!" snapped Cameron. "I've got another job for Doug, anyhow."

"What?" the roadie asked. Doug was still standing, jaw clenched, and Cameron knew that he had to get Doug to relax.

"You have to go for a walk," Cameron explained. "You have to be seen in other places, doing other things. That way, people will begin to relax around you; you won't be considered a stranger. Go look for a job or something."

"You're firing me now?"

"No," Cameron sighed. "But you need to look like you belong around here, not like you're scouting for someone. We can salvage this if we don't lose our shit. Do you understand?"

Doug nodded, but he still did not sit down.

"Might as well leave now," he muttered, but then paused. "Unless you're not done."

"No, go ahead," Cameron assured him. "We'll work on our stuff."

Doug grabbed his coat. He left without looking at anyone. Cameron and the others sat in silence for a moment. Cameron broke the ice by discussing the most effective ways to surveil the convenience store and the surrounding neighborhood.

"Act natural," he reminded them. "If we do anything else, we'll just draw attention to ourselves."

They deliberated over other details, then each went back to what they had been doing before the upheaval over Doug. Cameron lit a cigarette and watched the smoke drift languorously toward the ceiling. He wondered if it had been pure chance that Louis Barre had acted the way he did, or if he was more experienced at all this than they were. While Cameron had to admit that Barre's prowess was a real possibility, he could not escape the feeling that the mole may have tipped Barre off. As he pondered the idea, Cameron realized that, forgetting Dwyer's instructions, they had discussed aloud and in detail, all of their plans.

Did I just tip them off, too?

CHAPTER EIGHT
"Redemption"

It took almost a week, but the band's plan and persistence paid off and they were able to establish a routine for watching Louis Barre. Even Doug was able to redeem himself for having jeopardized the initial surveillance by developing, with Evan, a series of layered disguises for Doug's use, and later, for use by each of the others.

By using trucker caps to hide their long hair, extra shirts to put on or take off as needed, and burnt cork to affect dirt or razor stubble, they were each able to alter their appearance significantly, and constantly. On at least one occasion, Doug even went so far as to place rocks in his boot to affect a limp, removing them later when he changed his disguise. Eventually, the band members were able to blend into the neighborhood and surrounding area and move around unnoticed.

On one occasion, though, Louis Barre suspected that he was being followed, and lured his tracker by dashing down an alley similar to the one in Doug's initial experience following Barre. But this time, Louis (as he was now referred to by the band) was being followed by Clyde, who realized what Louis was up to. Previous reconnaissance had taught Clyde another way around that area and he continued past the alleyway. One block up the street, there was another passage that ran parallel and, quickly turning down that, Clyde removed his cap and extra shirt. Rolling the hat up into the shirt and tucking it into a paper bag in his pocket, Clyde casually stepped out onto the street and behind an unsuspecting Louis Barre.

Clyde returned to the house to report his efforts to Cameron. Based on Clyde's recount of the exercise, Cameron hoped that Louis really didn't notice Clyde trailing him. In the back of his mind, Cameron still wondered if he hadn't revealed the entire plan to the mole while talking aloud the previous day. Could their adversary simply going along quietly in an attempt to draw the band out into the open?

Or to draw us into a trap?

Cameron's thoughts were interrupted by the sound of the front door opening. He expected one of the others to be there, and was shocked to see that it was Dwyer standing in the kitchen.

"Did you forget the secret knock?"

"I did not," Dwyer replied. "I am anxious to speak with you, if you have a moment."

Cameron eyed Dwyer, who would usually be more commanding while requesting a sit-down. Cameron shrugged nonetheless and Dwyer motioned him to the table. Dwyer produced a yellow legal pad from his briefcase and began writing. Cameron watched him, and was once again reminded of the band's serious breach of protocol. He couldn't assuage his own guilt and his own stupidity tortured him. Since the time that he had informed the guys of Dwyer's instructions, they had unquestioningly obeyed Cameron, and used the written system. Now, though, with Cameron unable to forgive himself for the breach, was it all just a case of locking the barn after the horse has escaped? That thought, and the realization that he had not yet told Dwyer what he'd done, tormented Cameron further.

Dwyer continued penning his questions on his legal pad. Cameron picked up the pad and read what Dwyer had written. Dwyer's phraseology was unequivocal and strict, demanding to know the progress the band was making on their assignment.

"You've had Barre under surveillance for over one month. We need to cite specific results. We do not have much time. You must increase your efforts."

Cameron nodded, and wrote his response.

"Yes. We think we have his movements tracked and have noticed some routines. This is in our case notes."

Dwyer smiled, and began to write. Cameron could stand it no longer. He had to confess his breach to Dwyer, and, clearing his throat to attract Dwyer's attention, he motioned for the pad, whereupon he wrote his confession.

This time, Dwyer did not smile when he read, nor did he look at Cameron. He did not react at all, but simply slid the pad to the side and hung his head. Eventually, Dwyer looked at Cameron, who, by this time, was genuinely unnerved. Finally, Dwyer spoke.

"Is this true?" Dwyer asked quietly. Cameron simply nodded.

"Do not trouble yourself over it."

"What?"

"There is nothing that can be done about the past, Mr. Walsh."

"Is that supposed to be some sort of Zen philosophy? How can you tell me not to worry about it?"

"Again, there is nothing you can do about it. The fact is, yours was the correct decision."

Cameron was shocked. "How the hell can you say that?"

"Mr. Walsh, " Dwyer explained. "As I explained to you that evening, I suspect that we are being monitored. To begin the new routine that I had suggested would have immediately alerted the mole that we were aware of them. They would either have become more secretive, or made a move to interrupt the operation. Remember, Mr. Walsh, the sudden change of regular routine draws attention. You did not alter your pattern suddenly, and likely did not attract interest."

"But what about the fact that we changed later?"

"You are all novices in this field, Mr. Walsh. I am aware of it, my colleagues are aware of it, and my superiors are aware of it. I am certain that whoever is attempting to spy on us is aware of it."

"What does that have to do with anything?"

"You would obviously attempt to experiment with different techniques and methods of secrecy."

"So it really doesn't matter that I blabbed?"

Dwyer sighed. "It would have been better if you hadn't; however the fact remains that you did."

"Well, you sure as hell seemed insistent on it at the time!"

"We take precautions, Mr. Walsh. They do not come with guarantees."

Still feeling no divine absolution, Cameron continued to voice his concerns about being led into a trap, now that the mole may know their plans.

"That is a possibility," Dwyer conceded. "Over-analysis will immobilize you completely."

"But what do we do?" Cameron demanded. The strain of the mission was getting to him, and it Dwyer could hear it in Cameron's voice.

"We compose ourselves," Dwyer replied. Dwyer spoke in the same maddening monotone that had annoyed Cameron from the very moment they met. "Panic solves nothing. You are doing what you have been instructed to do. There is nothing else that you can do.

There is no indication that things are compromised or that anyone is in any danger."

Cameron fidgeted in his chair. He began to speak, but stopped himself.

"You are over-analyzing," Dwyer observed. "Not surprising."

"What the hell is that supposed to mean?"

"We try to ensure that our actions will be one hundred percent perfect and that we will give our adversaries no weaknesses to exploit. If that actually occurs, then neither side would be able to function. We exist entirely on the mistakes that others make, as they do on ours."

So what's the point of it all, then?

Dwyer peered at Cameron, as though reading his thoughts. "Mr. Walsh, we must be certain that we exploit the other side's mistakes to the utmost, while making certain that they do not exploit ours. To paraphrase General Patton, it is not so much making sure that we die for our country as it is making sure that they die for theirs."

Cameron scowled. "I can't say as I'm happy about the word die, in either case."

"Unavoidable. One accepts facts since there is no way to change them."

"It's all cut and dried for you, isn't it?"

"Hardly, Mr. Walsh. Remember the defense mechanisms we discussed once before. This is simply another manifestation of them."

Cameron felt as though the room was reeling. Ever since the band began this particular operation, he had felt a sense of foreboding, as if his mistake would have drastic and disastrous consequences. He had allowed himself to think of the remote possibility that his mistake held no dire consequences, and that more knowledgeable and experienced people could correct it. He now realized that it wasn't that way at all. If anything, rather than being good for the soul, confession had made him feel much worse.

Imploring Dwyer, he asked, "So, what do we do?"

"Nothing, for the moment."

"Nothing?"

Dwyer explained. "Do nothing out of the ordinary. We will continue with our plans as usual, then determine our next step based upon evaluation of outcomes."

"You mean you don't know." Cameron slumped in his seat, deflated.

"I mean that you and your team will not concern yourselves with it."

"But I thought you wanted us to monitor Barre."

"I did, and you performed in a thoroughly commendable fashion. Your involvement is now finished. It is up to us to make the next move."

"So, all we were was a bunch of babysitters?"

Dwyer was weary. "Mr. Walsh, your training and the situations in which you have found yourselves have given you ideas that you are now master spies. You are *our* agents. You provide *us* with information. You will *not* find yourselves in the exotic locales of Monte Carlo, Rio or San Moritz. We will use you to gather intelligence and we will act upon the intelligence provided. Are there any questions?"

"Are we done, then?" Cameron was angry and exhausted, and made no attempts to hide it.

"In regards to this conversation, or your mission as a whole?"

"Well... both."

"What do you think, Mr. Walsh?"

Cameron studied the other man carefully. There was nothing to be read in either Dwyer's expression or his body language to indicate what his feelings were.

A sense of abandonment swept over Cameron.

"Yeah, I guess we're done, then."

"Very well," Dwyer conjured a smile. "I will collect your case notes and be on my way. Good evening, Mr. Walsh."

Cameron retrieved the rough notes on Louis Barre's surveillance, jammed them in a manila folder and handed them to Dwyer. Without a word, Dwyer put the folder in his briefcase and left the apartment, leaving Cameron to ponder their thorough, albeit very unsettling, discussion. He did not have time to consider it for very long. The door burst open and the band rushed in.

"What the fuck is going on?" demanded Rich.

"What are you talking about?" Cameron yelled back.

"Dwyer just stopped us on the stairs and said we were done, and to hang out here and wait for instructions. We weren't to leave the building at all until he contacted us."

"He decided we had enough information for them to do something with," Cameron explained. "We're done."

"Just like that?" Clyde exclaimed. "All that work and we don't get to see it through?"

"That's the size of it," sighed Cameron.

"Why!?" Clyde was not letting up.

Cameron told his fellow band members about his talk with Dwyer. He explained that their roles were played out and that senior agents would now step in. Cameron could see that none of this sat well with the guys. He understood exactly how they felt.

It doesn't sit well with me, either.

The guys grabbed beers and sat around the table, complaining loudly about being involved in a detective story and not finding out the "Who done it."

"This reminds me of when I was a kid," Doug said. "One winter we had spent the evenings putting together this humongous puzzle, a late autumn scene with a harvested corn field, trees missing a lot of leaves, all sorts of little bits. It was a real pain, but everyone got involved in it, my folks, my sisters, my grandparents, everyone. We got so that we looked forward to working on it every night. Then we got set to finish it, and it all went to hell."

"What could possibly have happened?" asked Evan. "It was a puzzle, for Christ's sake."

"The last piece was missing," grumbled Doug. "And not some small bit off to the side, or hidden in the complicated scenery where you wouldn't notice it, either. It was right smack in the middle of the fucking blue sky!"

"What the hell does that have to do with this?" Clyde asked, with more than a grain of ridicule in his voice.

"We did all this work finding out about this guy, his movements, his habits, all that shit, and we don't get to have anything to do with what happens next. That one fucking piece of sky is missing!"

Cameron noticed the other guys exchanging glances and smirking. Doug wasn't the emotional type and they found his story to be an amusing distraction from the matter at hand. Cameron, however, still drained from his meeting with Dwyer, continued to wilt with fatigue, and this discourse with the guys was not helping.

"Did you ever find the missing piece?" Cameron asked.

"No," Doug said. "It wouldn't have mattered anyway."

"Why not?"

"My mom lost her shit so bad, she kicked the table over and the whole damn thing flew apart. We were finding the pieces for years after."

Evan laughed aloud. Doug glared him down.

"Well, don't kick the table over tonight," mumbled Cameron, as he made his way to his room. Clyde called out to him, but Cameron pretended not to hear. He wanted to go to his room and be alone. He recalled all of Dwyer's reassurances, but none of them made Cameron feel any better. He began to wonder if they really had gathered all of the necessary information on Louis Barre.

Are we sidelined because of my screw-up?

It was going to be a long night.

You're over-analyzing. Knock it off, or you won't be able to function at all.

If they all screwed up bad enough, would they be turned loose? Cameron wondered. As tempting a thought as it was, Cameron knew that freedom was unlikely. Collapsing onto his bed, he had another troubling thought. Cameron was concerned about having failed the mission in its entirety. Was his perspective changing about who he was? Until now, if anyone asked him how he would describe himself, there was no question that he would answer, "A musician."

That's what I love. That's what I do best.

But now, having potentially blown the cover on fieldwork for a seemingly inconsequential task, he was suddenly concerned that, for the first time in his life, he didn't do his best. Full of self-doubt, he realized that he was over-analyzing this, as well.

Knock it off!

Cameron needed to rest. He needed to clear his head. He switched on the stereo next to his bed, and drifted off into a troubled, fitful sleep.

CHAPTER NINE
"Cold Reality"

"Start collecting your belongings, gentlemen," Dwyer told them. "You're leaving."

The Roadhouse Sons did not know how to react. They had awaited release from their enforced seclusion since the day that they arrived. On several occasions, they had even considered attempting a run for it, but changed their minds, realizing that an escape attempt would render them fugitives. Now, they were told that they were leaving, and, much to their surprise, this dream-come-true was not fulfilling at all. In fact, it made them quite nervous.

"Where are we going?" Evan asked. Dwyer noticed that Evan's knuckles were white, he was gripping the kitchen chair so tightly.

"You are going back where you belong, Mr. Dixon," Dwyer replied. Although Dwyer did not consider himself a cruel man, he chose to let the tension permeate the room.

"Oh, man, you mean we're going home?" Clyde could barely contain his excitement.

"Hardly, Mr. Poulin," he smiled. "I mean that the Roadhouse Sons are leaving this safe house and going back onstage." The disappointment on Clyde's face reminded Dwyer of that on the face of a small child dropping his ice cream.

"You mean we're done here? You don't need us anymore?"

"You are done, here, Mr. Dixon. However, we are far from done with you. The Louis Barre surveillance was an exercise to determine your ability to act as instructed, and perform basic operations. Further training depended on those outcomes. Now, it is time for you to begin the operations for which you were chosen."

"So, I guess we did a pretty good job?" asked Rich.

"You all did an adequate job, Mr. Webster. You achieved the objective, albeit clumsily. There is still room for much improvement."

"Where are we going?" Cameron asked. He was horribly ill at ease with his mistake, and wondered if this was really an attempt to get them out of here and away from danger.

"At this moment, you do not need to know. Go to your rooms and gather your belongings," Dwyer commanded.

"Bullshit we don't need to know," snapped Doug, knocking over his chair as he jumped up. "You've played enough games with us! There's nothing that you need us to do that justifies all this cloak-and-dagger crap, and all of the mind-fucking you've been doing since we got here! Now you won't even tell us what the fuck we're supposed to do next? Screw you. I'm done with this shit!"

Dwyer registered no reaction to the roadie's outburst, and continued to stand in the center of the kitchen, his comportment calm and serene. A look of bemusement spread across Dwyer's face as he regarded the menacing figure before him. For a moment, everyone thought that Dwyer might begin to laugh. However, when he finally spoke, his icy tone was palpable.

"I grow weary of your attitude, Mr. Courtland," Dwyer said. His voice, though composed, did not hide the fact that each word landed on Doug as if fired from a pistol, a vague foreshadowing of what could follow.

"Let me make this perfectly clear: I am under no obligations to explain my motives or my methods. From this moment on, Mr. Courtland, you are on probation."

Before Doug could respond, Dwyer spoke again, his voice louder and harsher.

"Do not make your situation worse, Mr. Courtland. My sympathies and understanding are exhausted. From this moment on, you will do exactly as you are instructed. You will behave exactly as expected of you. You will control your petulance and outbursts. Is that clear?"

Doug glared, his body rigid, his fists clenched.

"*Is that clear?*" Dwyer repeated, jaw taut. His voice, almost a whisper, had lost none of its bite. Doug did not answer. The two men continued to stare at one another. Cameron was about to speak when Doug broke the silence.

"What if I say no?" Doug sneered. "You're going to say I don't have much of a choice, aren't you?"

"Your attitude, Mr. Courtland..." Dwyer replied.

Doug took a deep breath; the others held theirs, knowing their roadie had a reputation for trying to get in the last word in every argument, even if he had already lost. They also knew that Doug did not take orders from anyone that he did not like, and since the beginning of this ordeal, he had never attempted to conceal his dislike of Dwyer. By observation, the band learned early on just how violent arguments between roadies and stage managers could be, be they over the handling of equipment or the loading of trucks. Those grapples did not compare to a battle of wills with a spy.

"Don't repeat mistakes of your past, Mr. Courtland. You will not live to regret it."

"Oh, really?" Doug challenged. "Is there a squad of your goons watching and listening, waiting to burst in on me if things don't go your fucking way?"

"I have a Colt Model 1911 .45 caliber pistol aimed at your heart, Mr. Courtland. I need no other assistance."

If Doug believed Dwyer, he displayed no sign of it. The others noticed that both of Dwyer's hands were in his coat pockets. Was he telling the truth, or was this simply another one of his tricks? There was no way for them to know for certain.

"Man, back off," Evan whispered to Doug. Everyone noticed the muscles in Doug's neck tighten as he clenched his teeth; he made no other move, but gave no indication that he was changing his mind.

"I will ask you again, Mr. Courtland. Are we clear on this?"

"Yes," Doug said at last. He did not relax his stance, nor did he redirect his gaze. Neither did Dwyer.

"I will overlook this episode. However, Mr. Courtland, this will be the last occasion that I do so. Do not test my sufferance again."

Facing the others, Dwyer removed his hands from his pocket, his steely expression unchanged.

"As for the rest of you, gather your belongings as I have instructed. We will be leaving this evening and I want everything out of here."

With that, Dwyer suddenly stormed out of the suite, leaving the group nonplussed, and pondering what might be in store.

"Man, what were you fucking thinking?" demanded Rich. "He was going to shoot you! Why do you have to push people's buttons so frigging much?"

Doug said nothing. He opened the refrigerator to select a beer, but there were none. Some milk and a pitcher of powdered drink were the only beverages in there, and neither of them appealed to Doug at the moment. Slamming the refrigerator door, Doug stomped toward his room.

"Don't you walk off," shouted Rich. "I'm talking to you!"

Doug continued down the hallway, ignoring Rich, who started after him.

"I don't know what the fuck is going on, but you're not putting us in any jeopardy with them, do you hear me? Get back here or you're out of the band!"

Doug returned to the living room, coat in hand and a look of contempt on his face.

"You're going to fire me," he laughed. "You poor dumb fuck, you think you can get rid of me, or that any of you can quit? We are now carved in stone! Nothing changes without their say-so. I don't leave and you don't leave. I have the best fucking job security in the world because I serve their purpose by being here, just like the rest of you sons of bitches! So don't give me your fucking attitude anymore; I was never impressed with it before, and I sure as hell am not impressed with it now!"

With that, Doug forced his way past the dumbstruck band members and left the suite, slamming the door behind him.

"What the hell is going on here?" gasped Clyde. "He's never gone that apeshit before, and what was Dwyer talking about, having a gun aimed at his chest?"

They all began talking at once, shouting questions and jumping to conclusions.

"Just shut it for a goddamned minute," Cameron hollered. "I don't know any more than you guys know. Do I think that Dwyer had a gun aimed at Doug? Hell, yes I do! I wouldn't put it past Dwyer to be ready to bump any one of us off if he thought he had to! Do I know what he was talking about with all that other stuff that he was saying? Hell, no I don't. But I'm going to find out."

Cameron grabbed his coat and headed out the door. He didn't find the roadie in the hallway or in the foyer at the bottom of the stairs. Stepping outside into the autumn afternoon, he saw no sign of

Doug there either. Pausing to light a cigarette, Cameron performed a mental run-down of the list of Doug's possible whereabouts. While Doug could have conceivably gone anywhere, Cameron realized that Doug was not one to meander aimlessly; he would have a destination in mind. That knowledge provided Cameron with two options. Doug went to either the bar or the store. Fortunately, the shortest distance to one would lead Cameron past the other, so he hurried in that direction.

As he made his way down the street, Cameron saw no sign of Doug and, for a moment, wondered if he might have miscalculated the likelihood of Doug's actions. In the distance, Cameron heard the sound of a siren, followed by another. He came to an alley that he knew to be a shortcut to the store, and headed into it. He realized that if he did encounter Doug, the roadie would be onto him, and Cameron knew that it would be a waste of time coming up with a cover story about why he was out in the field. In fact, Cameron knew that lying to Doug would inevitably make matters worse. Doug, who had not finished school like the rest of the band members, carried sensitivities and paranoia about being made fun of, and was constantly on the lookout for any sign of possible sport. As Cameron struggled to conjure some type of explanation for Doug, he heard more sirens, this time much closer.

Must have happened nearby. From the sounds of it, must be pretty bad.

Stepping out at the other end of the alley, Cameron realized that he was right on both counts.

The street in front of the store was a sea of activity. An ambulance, fire truck and several police cars were there, as well as dozens of onlookers. Cameron noticed Doug standing on the far edge of the crowd, and began walking toward him. The roadie noticed Cameron approaching, and started to retreat, then stopped. Two ambulance attendants emerged from the doorway of the store, pushing a gurney on which was a body covered by a sheet. While Doug paused to watch the attendants load the gurney into the ambulance, Cameron was able to sidle up to him.

"What happened?" Cameron prodded, realizing as he did so that he wasn't certain if he was asking about the commotion here, or the one back at the safe house. An answer to either question would do, at this point.

"They shot them," said an elderly woman standing nearby. "Those poor, poor people, shot dead!"

"Who, the storekeepers?" Cameron asked.

"Yes," the woman said, bursting into tears. "Shot in their own store in broad daylight! Twenty years they've been here without a problem. They were both veterans, too."

"Was it a robbery?" The woman shook her head.

"I don't know," she sobbed, making her way back toward her house. Cameron remembered that he had seen the old woman once, raking in her yard. She lived two houses down from the store.

Doug stared at the scene before him, his face registering no emotion.

"I need to talk to you," Cameron whispered.

Doug ignored him and turned away. Cameron grabbed Doug by the elbow and tried to pull him back, only to have Doug shake off his grip and walk away. Cameron followed Doug and grabbed him again. This time, Doug paused.

"What the hell is going on?" Cameron demanded, his voice a low whisper. They had separated from the crowd and he knew that no one could hear them. Cameron wanted the roadie to understand that he was genuinely interested.

"I don't know what you're talking about," Doug insisted, attempting to wrest his arm away. Undaunted, Cameron gripped Doug's arm even tighter.

"You've had a hard-on for Dwyer and his people ever since this started," Cameron insisted. "More than the rest of us. Today was totally over the top, even for you. Something's going on, and not just the general resentment we all feel. Now tell me, what the hell is it?"

Doug studied Cameron's face. Cameron sensed the struggle going on inside Doug's head. Several seconds passed, and finally Doug spoke.

"Dwyer isn't the only one that has need-to-know information," Doug grumbled. "And right now, you don't need to know."

"Fuck you I don't," Cameron snapped, amazed at his own response. "They put me in charge of this group, and if you've got something that makes them draw a gun on you, then I have a need to know. Now what the fuck is it?"

"Nothing," Doug repeated. "Nothing at all. Nothing that will fuck anything up for you or anyone else."

Cameron released his grip on the roadie's arm. Cameron knew that nothing would come of pulling rank on Doug. That said, Doug's answer was far from satisfactory.

"We had this discussion once before," Cameron reminded him. "Would you be pissed if I didn't believe you?"

"I remember," Doug smiled. "I asked if you'd be pissed if I didn't care. Would you?"

"Then, no," Cameron replied. "Now, things are obviously very different. So yes, I would be pissed, really pissed."

Doug stepped back. Cameron wondered if Doug would try to make a break for it, but he didn't. Instead, Doug leaned in and whispered into Cameron's ear.

"Not here," he said, motioning with his head for the two of them to continue down the street. Cameron followed, wondering how this would play out, and deciding to trust his roadie not to lead him on. After they walked a few blocks, Doug paused. By this time, the commotion at the store was a distant buzz, and there was no one else on the sidewalk with them. Cameron looked up and down the street, self-consciously wondering if there were any surveillance vehicles. He noticed that there were several empty cars parked in the street. With a sense of satisfaction, he noticed that Doug was doing the same thing.

"Yeah, I've got a beef with them," the roadie admitted. "I hate the way they've done things, even doing these things in the first place. It pisses me off that now I'm just a minion. I don't have any say in anything. I can't even go home. I can't call anyone, I can't do anything without their permission. Fuck, I'm surprised Dwyer doesn't make me get permission to wipe my ass! The rest of you don't seem to mind it, but I do. Now I'm on probation. Fuck all of it!"

"Don't get all high and mighty with me," Cameron insisted. "You don't have it one bit worse than the rest of us! Everything you have to do, we have to do. Don't you forget that. But you don't see us making it worse by provoking them every chance we get, do you?"

"So you'd rather be sheep, is that it?"

Cameron felt himself flush at the roadie's remarks.

No, I wouldn't rather be a sheep, you fucker. You damn well know that.

"I don't even know what to say to that," Cameron replied. "I don't even know how to deal with that bullshit. You better tell me what I'm supposed to do if you want this to work out."

"Aren't you the leader? Figure it out yourself!"

"What the hell am I supposed to figure out?" Cameron demanded. "I'm not a fucking mind reader!"

The roadie didn't reply, he only glared, and Cameron relaxed a little. To others, Doug's glare was taken as a threat. Cameron knew, though, that Doug was considering Cameron's question. Cameron was also acutely aware that he had a very small window of opportunity.

"Look, I wish I had my life back too," he said, his voice lower and calmer. "I wish I was surrounded by groupies right now in some hotel in New York or LA, but I'm not. I'm in a situation I never would have dreamed up on my own, and one I want to get out of as soon as I can. Just like you, and just like the rest of them."

Doug shoved his hands in his pockets. Cameron noticed Doug's weight shift and his shoulders relax.

"Yeah, they made me the leader of all this," Cameron continued. "I didn't ask for it and don't want it. I want to sing and play my guitar, and get laid once in awhile. I don't want any of this spook shit, but apparently I don't have a choice right now."

"So, what are you going to do about it?"

"I'm going to do whatever I can to make sure that we all get out of this in one piece, and that includes you, but I need you to help."

"What the hell am I supposed to do?"

"Stop pushing everyone's fucking buttons and work with us."

"You sold out awfully fast."

"Fuck you I did. We only get through this together, not alone."

"Do you work for Dwyer now?"

"Hell, no," Cameron insisted. "I work for this band, and I only care about this band, and the only way we're going to do anything is with this band. That includes you, too, asshole."

"I'll ask again. What the hell do you need me to do?"

"I need you to be someone I can count on."

"What about Dwyer and his crew. Aren't they the experts?"

"Fuck them," Cameron spat. "Dwyer tries to stay as far away from us as he can, and McIntyre shows up with a different hairstyle and color every time we see her, and D'Lorenzo couldn't find his balls in the dark with both hands and a roadmap. If we're going to accomplish whatever it is they want us to, then *we're* going to have to be the ones to do it. You guys are the only, and I do mean *only*, ones that I can count on."

Doug said nothing, and Cameron noticed Doug's tension easing.

Ah! Progress!

"Man, I'm not conning you," Cameron insisted. "When we're on stage I relax when I see you standing there watching everything. I know that if anyone starts shit, you'll be between them and us before the bouncers move. You make sure equipment works, you watch everything we can't watch. We need you to do that same thing for us now. I've got to have someone watching my back. You've never let me down before."

Doug shook out a cigarette, offering one to Cameron. He lit it, took a deep drag and stared off into the distance. Cameron didn't press for an answer. The roadie was coming to his own conclusion, and getting on Doug's case would only cause him to balk more.

"I always did my best by you," Doug said at last.

"I know you did." Cameron took another deep drag from his cigarette, and glanced at the sky.

"You've taken good care of me," the roadie continued. Cameron was relieved that Doug was talking, but a little concerned that he wasn't looking Cameron in the eye as he did so.

"But this is different," Doug said. "This is already out of everyone's control. It was that night it all started. It won't end good, for anyone."

"You're probably right," Cameron agreed. "But we'll stand a better chance of getting through it together than alone, won't we?"

"I suppose," Doug sighed. "The farther and faster we get them away from us, the better off we'll be, trust me on that one."

"I've already come to that conclusion," Cameron assured him. "But there isn't much I can do about it. The only way we'll keep our sanity or our lives is to stick together. I go into every gig counting on you to take care of everything and keep it all working. Can I still keep counting on you?"

"I'll always make sure the shows go on, you know that," Doug muttered.

"That's not what I'm talking about."

Doug didn't answer, instead pretending to watch the activity down the street. Cameron watched as the ambulance drove away, lights flashing and windows drawn, but no siren blaring. There was no emergency anymore, not for the elderly couple the ambulance carried away. For a moment, Cameron wondered if the storekeepers weren't the lucky ones.

"You've got some shit you're not talking about," Cameron said. "I've noticed it for a long time. I just never said anything. You've been holding it close since the very first night, and it isn't just because you resent what's going on. It's way more than that."

The roadie made no reply, other than turning his collar against the cold. The wind picked up, blowing dirty scraps of paper and dried leaves down the sidewalk.

"Man, I need to know what's going on," Cameron insisted.

"Do you believe in coincidences?" Doug asked.

"Yeah, I guess so. Why?"

"Well, the night all this shit began, I had quite a coincidence."

"What was it?"

"D'Lorenzo," Doug mumbled.

"You knew that guy already?"

"Sort of," Doug concurred. "He used to work with a buddy of mine, and was supposed to be some kind of engineer who wanted my friend to help his company design some stuff for the Navy."

"I thought there was some shit between you two," Cameron agreed. "I take it things didn't work out with D'Lorenzo and your buddy?"

"No, not really," Doug said, his voice becoming soft.

"What happened?"

"My buddy was onboard the Mustang."

Cameron was stunned. The Mustang was one of the first ships sunk in the war. It was a small experimental nuclear submarine placed on patrol in the Arctic when the events in Eastern Europe exacerbated the Cold War. There had been talk that the sub may have been monitoring Soviet activities, but shortly after the Mustang was destroyed, the Soviets launched their invasion of Alaska and Canada and the media had many other things to discuss. The Mustang situation took a fast backseat to goings-on in Alaska and Canada.

Cameron's heart tightened in his chest as he realized what Doug was inferring. Cameron recalled his talk with Dwyer.

Mole.

"You think D'Lorenzo had something to do with that?" he asked Doug.

"How the fuck should I know?" Doug shrugged. "All I know is that a good buddy of mine was mixed up with D'Lorenzo and now my buddy's dead. Then D'Lorenzo shows up again, and I'm not only supposed to forget about the whole Mustang situation, I'm also supposed to play along, too, and play *nice*. It doesn't work like that."

No platitudes existed that would entice Doug to listen to Cameron, and Cameron didn't insult Doug's sensibilities by pretending otherwise. Nevertheless, he needed to convince Doug to work with the rest of them.

"I bet that is one of the reasons Dwyer keeps him on a short leash," Cameron said. "He's a fuckup."

"Twenty men are dead, and D'Lorenzo's in the corner 'til he learns his lesson? Fuck that."

"I know what you're saying," Cameron sympathized. "I know, now, how you feel about him, and everything else. But you know how he works. Do you honestly think that he'd have been able to set up something like that? I bet he was just a recruiter. I know that doesn't change the fact that your buddy's dead, but it might help you be less angry at him."

"Why the hell shouldn't I be angry at him? If it wasn't for D'Lorenzo, my buddy would still be alive."

"Possibly," agreed Cameron. "But staying angry at him will just make it harder for you to do your job."

"Which is what, exactly?"

"Making sure none of us end up the same way."

Progress. Come back to the safe house.

"Now let me ask you something. Can you think of any way out?"

The roadie shook his head. Cameron figured that Doug had been looking for a way out from the very beginning.

"I don't want to see any more people killed because of D'Lorenzo's mistakes," Doug muttered.

"We don't really know that he had anything to do with the Mustang," Cameron said. "I don't like the guy anymore than you do, but you can't blame him for what happened."

"If it weren't for him, my friend wouldn't have been on that sub," Doug insisted. "He got my buddy to reenlist, got him that assignment. I sat at the table when they talked about it over cards."

"They talked about a mission over a game of cards?" Cameron couldn't hide his shock. He had been convinced that D'Lorenzo, for all of his faults, was more professional than that.

"He never said anything about a secret mission, or what they would have been doing," Doug said. "He just knew that Gus had been great at radar and electronics and had helped work on some prototype of something they wanted to use on the Mustang. He thought Gus'd be a great help working on developing it further. He laid on a lot of beer and a lot of soft soap."

"Did he recognize you when we met at the police station?"

"Yeah," Doug spat. "He recognized me and acted like it was meeting an old friend again. Like he was glad to see me and I should be glad to see him. He asked me about Gus and if I had heard from him lately. I threw a fucking chair at him."

"What happened then?"

"The cops came in and we had a little altercation. They handcuffed me and left me there. He took off out of the room and I didn't see anyone else 'til Dwyer came in to talk to me."

"What did you two talk about? Was it the same conversation he'd had with the rest of us?"

"I don't know," Doug shrugged. "He asked how I'd known D'Lorenzo previously and I told him. That changed his tune a bit, and he insisted they take the cuffs off me and leave us alone to talk. He said it was unfortunate that things had turned out the way they did. He insisted that D'Lorenzo was ignorant of Gus's death and I told him he was full of shit."

"How's that?"

"It was all over the news, for crying out loud! Dwyer knew D'Lorenzo recruited Gus for that, and even a dumb bastard like him should know that "all hands lost" means no one survived."

"Maybe he didn't follow what went on after your buddy got recruited. He might not have known Gus was actually on the Mustang."

"Then they're all an even bigger bunch of assholes than I thought. We're just meat. They'll send us out and forget about us."

Cameron didn't reply. He simply didn't know what to say. He fought a conflict of emotions. On one hand, he was convincing himself that Doug was wrong, that Doug's bitterness was just an emotional reaction to a friend's death. On the other hand, Cameron had to wonder if Doug wasn't right. Behind all this was the added anxiety that the mole Dwyer had warned him about might have been active for a lot longer than he thought. And what about D'Lorenzo? What *was* his involvement in all of this? Cameron realized that he couldn't think about all of this now. They had to get back to the safe house and get ready to move out. This time, Doug was willing to go with him.

"Was that the only thing you and Dwyer talked about that night?"

Doug shook his head.

"No. He made a pitch about how I was up shit's creek without a paddle, and how they could get me out of it if I cooperated with them. That didn't get him very far."

"Oh?"

"I've been locked up before. This wouldn't be the first time."

"That's fucking news to me!" Doug stunned Cameron for the second time today.

The roadie shrugged. "You never asked if I'd ever been in any trouble before, so I never said anything. I didn't hide anything from you. I just didn't volunteer anything."

"What the fuck were you in for, if you don't mind my asking?"

"They dropped it to simple assault."

"Dropped it, so obviously "it" started out a hell of a lot more seriously."

Doug nodded

"From what?"

"Are you sure you want to know?"

"No, not really. But I do want to know how Dwyer was able to convince you to go along with this."

"He said I could consider this mission as getting revenge for Gus."

"Do you?"

The roadie shrugged once more and turned, heading down the sidewalk. They walked back to the safe house. Neither of them spoke. When they arrived, they realized how busy everyone else had been. Nearly all of their belongings were out of the apartment. There was no sign of the other band members, nor of the instruments and equipment, but Dwyer was sitting in the living room, facing the door.

"I was hoping you gentlemen would be returning soon," he said. As usual, his voice betrayed no emotion. It was impossible to tell Dwyer's mood from his expression. He could have been annoyed, enraged or in the throes of an orgasm, for all Cameron knew.

"There was some excitement at the store..." Cameron began.

"The deaths of the Laverdiers," Dwyer interrupted. "We are aware."

"You don't seem to be too upset about it!" Cameron snapped.

"My emotions regarding that are of no concern to anyone but myself," Dwyer said, pulling his hand out of his coat pocket. Cameron remembered Dwyer's threat to Doug earlier, and he shuddered at Dwyer's choice of seating. Dwyer was facing the door and had the gun aimed at it. He was waiting for someone.

"Get your belongings. Do not delay. We are pressed for time."

Doug caught Cameron's eye, and the singer nodded for Doug to leave the room. When they were alone, Cameron turned to Dwyer.

"I take it that it wasn't a robbery gone bad?"

"No, Mr. Walsh, it was not. The storekeepers were bound and gagged, each with a single shot to the back of the head."

"By who?"

"The principal responsible for the act neglected to leave a business card, unfortunately. A fact that would make matters difficult for the local police to investigate were they in charge of the case, which they are not."

Dwyer's uncharacteristic sarcasm revealed to Cameron that something was very wrong.

"Why not?" Cameron asked.

"The situation would be subject to unnecessary scrutiny, Mr. Walsh, should the local authorities become involved. The government will handle that investigation. In the event of any arrests, the local authorities will then receive the credit."

"Why do you care?"

"The Laverdiers were members of our network, Mr. Walsh, as you are well aware. The manner of their deaths, and the fact that it occurred so soon after the demise of Louis Barre, suggests either a coincidence or a connection. I do not believe in coincidence."

"Barre is dead?!" Cameron gasped. "I didn't know you even got him yet."

"Need-to-know basis, Mr. Walsh. Remember that. Once you are removed from a situation, it no longer concerns you. Mr. Barre attempted to escape while being questioned, during which he stole a firearm and was subsequently shot. We thought that Barre's death could be kept secret for the time being, until we could make it appear to be unconnected to us. The execution of the Laverdiers suggests that we did not have that opportunity."

Dwyer's words were too big for Cameron to process. How could an elderly couple in Rutland be executed? These things didn't happen here.

"Mr. Walsh, you cannot be in a sheltered environment any longer, a fact dictated by fate and not by me. Now gather your belongings. This safe house is no longer safe."

"What do you mean?"

Without saying a word, Dwyer led him to the front door and opening it, pointed to the lock on the door. Cameron examined it and noticed signs of scratching around the keyhole. That in and of itself wasn't cause for alarm; people often scuff keyholes trying to work the lock. What Cameron noticed, though, was the damage to the lock itself. While most marks could be easily dismissed, this damage to the keyhole itself was obvious. Someone had tried to pick the lock.

Beware

of war

Chapter Ten
"Get to Work"

Dwyer situated the Roadhouse Sons in a series of rooms at the Grand Isle House in Burlington. The move was smooth, for the most part, and as far as Dwyer was concerned, thankfully complete. Clyde and Rich stayed in one room, with Evan in a connecting room. Cameron had a small suite to himself, with shared party walls to Doug's room. Cameron examined his new surroundings with a fine-tooth comb. Although it wasn't as fancy as the safe house, it was better than some of the other hotels, and far surpassed band houses in which he'd played and been forced to stay.

Initially, and not entirely unexpectedly, there were complaints from certain band members about shared room assignments.

"Mr. Dixon is married," Dwyer explained. I'm sure he would like the opportunity for conjugal visits with his wife. Mr. Walsh is in his own room so that I can brief him, in private, as needed. Mr. Courtland is in a double room, as are the rest of you. The other bed in his room is available, should a need for an extra bed arise."

"What if the rest of us want to have conjugal visits?" asked Clyde.

Dwyer arched one eyebrow at this. "Mr. Poulin, your sense of modesty has never prevented you from expressing your primal instincts in the presence of others, nor is it an impediment to the various women that congregate near the stage entrance." Clyde did not reply; the rise of color to his cheeks and the smirks on the faces of the others said it all. "Before you raise a protest, Mr. Poulin" Dwyer continued, "I should inform you that I attended the Odyssey Club following your show in Boston."

The rooming arrangement remained intact.

Cameron was grateful for the privacy. He loved his friends and enjoyed working with them, but there were times when he just wanted to shut it all out, to let the sounds of the shows fade away, to disregard everything, especially now. The band had not started their new assignment, and for that Cameron was grateful. He needed to prepare himself mentally for what lay ahead. This time, the territory would be a familiar one; the initiation mission in Rutland had traumatized all of them.

"You will play a series of engagements here in the Champlain Valley," Dwyer revealed. "This safe house is your base, and you will travel to your booked venues. The schedule engages you for several nights a week in each town, with designated rest days prior to performances at the next venue."

This plan, Dwyer explained, rendered the band self-supporting, and not reliant solely on income from sporadic gigs. The rooms were already paid for via an account established by Dwyer. The band was more the than surprised when Dwyer revealed that, unbeknownst to them until this very moment, *he* was now operating as their Business Manager. Cameron balked.

No shit...

He kept his sentiments to himself. Dwyer continued explaining that he himself would collect receipts from the band's gigs, the funds of which would be attributed to the band's daily expenses, as well as to their strictly enforced gas rations.

"You are no more reliant upon black market ration coupons," Dwyer warned. "You all receive sufficient rations. As ironic as it may seem, in this line of work you are expected to be honest and law abiding citizens. Blatantly illegal activities will not be tolerated."

Several of them shifted uncomfortably, but said nothing. Dwyer sighed wearily.

"None of you are eligible for sainthood. Some of you prefer recreational substances. Perhaps you recall a gentleman by the name of Archer who attended your show in Manchester, New Hampshire, roughly eight months ago? Mr. Poulin?"

No one replied. Clyde was reminded of the time, back in high school, when the health teacher asked if anyone had smoked in the restroom. Clyde wasn't certain if it was a rhetorical question, or one that would incriminate him. Recalling the Manchester gig, Clyde could see Archer's face in his mind's eye. Archer, a rather seedy, swarthy individual, was nonetheless able to provide Clyde with some decent marijuana. Had Archer been arrested, or was he simply being monitored?

"*I* was Archer, Mr. Poulin," Dwyer explained. Clyde's face flushed bright red, and his eyes moved around the room, as though Dwyer's words were an equation in need of some esoteric calculation. "You can still enjoy that activity, as long as it is kept to a minimum, Mr. Poulin. Does that ease your rattled mind?"

"You were Archer!" Clyde exclaimed. "Man, I never would have made the connection! He was so laid back and you're such a…"

Dwyer gazed at Clyde, unblinking and expressionless.

Clyde blushed once again, saying nary another word. Doug laughed silently, but heaving shoulders caught Dwyer's attention.

"Mr. Courtland, that brings us to you." No one was immune. Dwyer parked his steady gaze on the roadie. "I appreciate the fact that the powdered substance you use is not done to excess. Observation has shown that your use of it has been for the purposes of staying awake while driving between venues. Your past behavior reveals that such is not always the case. That behavior will not be repeated."

Doug looked away, but said nothing. Dwyer looked at each band member, saying nothing. Suddenly he yawned and stretched, closing his eyes and folding his arms behind his head. The band members stared at Dwyer, expectantly. Cameron examined Dwyer's expression, but could read nothing from it.

What an odd guy.

"Gentlemen, I am not naïve." Dwyer broke the silence as suddenly as he'd stopped talking before. "I know that you are rock stars. Your antics are not as notorious as the ones chronicled in the magazines, but your ways have not gone unnoticed. That's a fact driven home by the difficulty I've had in booking your rooms."

The Roadhouse Sons looked at one another, their collective minds recalling incidents from their respective pasts. Televisions had been thrown through windows, corners of hotel rooms used as urinals, the rooms themselves set on fire, bumper car tournaments in parking lots of music halls, and myriad other nonsensical, drunk-addled idiocies. No one said a thing. Finally, Dwyer spoke.

"As your manager, I will have to field constant phone calls from the police, and, no doubt, answer questions about you with apologies. Keep your behavior in check. Is that clear?"

The band members nodded, but did not respond otherwise. Dwyer considered his point made, and resumed his earlier course of conversation.

"Very well. Gentlemen, since you will be traveling to your venues, you will need vehicles in which to do so. I'm afraid your previous automobiles are hardly suitable."

"What do you mean?" Evan cried. "I still owed money on that car!"

"Relax, Mr. Dixon," Dwyer said. "That is taken care of. Your car loan was paid off. Both the car and the title have been sent to your wife. In its place, you will have a new car. In addition, there is also a new band truck for your equipment."

"Ok! I'm liking the sound of this!" Doug said, a wide grin spreading across his face..

"The rest of you will also have new cars," Dwyer continued. "You have the reputation of an up-and-coming band to maintain. Follow me. I will present your new toys."

The band followed Dwyer down to the parking lot, talking excitedly, wondering what kind of car awaited each of them. Stepping outside, they were dismayed to find three used cars and a used Ryder truck in the parking lot.

"I thought you said they were new," Rich demanded. "These aren't new, that one's a '75, and that one's a '76. What gives?"

"A case of semantics," said Dwyer. "You are aware that the government has stopped the production of new cars to preserve metal for the war effort. If the White House is unable to procure a new Presidential limousine then I'm afraid we are unable to procure new cars for you. However, you will find that these are all low mileage and perfectly acceptable."

Their collective disappointment eased somewhat when they realized that the registrations were provided for them, and in their own names. Cameron did not share the band's distress. He was quite happy with his car, a 1970 Mustang Grande, yellow and with thin black stripes down the side. The roof was also black, in a simulated alligator skin vinyl, coming down in a straight back, giving its short and wide body a 'cut off' appearance. It had a standard transmission with bucket seats, wide back tires and wire rims. It was a dream come true.

"How come I don't get one?" demanded Clyde.

"In order to drive an automobile in the State of Vermont, or anywhere else for that matter, one must first be in possession of a valid driver's license issued by that state. The license that you have in your possession cites you as a resident of California. We both know that you actually purchased the license in Portland, Maine from an individual who has never left that state. The terms of that man's probation indicate that, for the foreseeable future, he isn't likely to."

"Does he work for you, too?" Clyde sneered.

"Not at the moment," Dwyer replied. "As soon as the paperwork can be done, I hope to correct that. Other than the occasional misspelling, he actually does excellent work."

Cameron smiled. He realized that he and Dwyer shared a mutual difficulty. It was impossible to tell whether or not either one of them was being facetious to the other.

"Test drive your vehicles gentlemen," Dwyer said. "Enjoy the afternoon. We must establish your presence here in Burlington. Locals seeing you drive around town is a good start. You will frequently perform at the Civic Center. There is a bar and restaurant located near there, The Catamount. It is an excellent location for you to establish as your primary watering hole. Meet me there at 6:00PM for dinner. Until then!"

Without waiting for a response, Dwyer abruptly turned and left, disappearing around the corner of the hotel. Clyde and Rich drove off in Rich's car, while Evan followed. Cameron and Doug remained behind to look over the new equipment truck.

Chafing at the bit, Doug was first to open the rear roll-up door of the vehicle. He and Cameron were amazed to find brand new equipment, along with their old instruments and speakers. Climbing in, they carefully moved the stacks and opened the new cases. New lights, mixers, speakers and amps were carefully set in place.

"I'll have to repack this after the first show," Doug observed. "Whoever packed this truck had good spatial relations and got everything to fit, but they obviously don't know how to pack a band truck."

"Do you know which windows are our new rooms?" Cameron asked.

"It's on the other side," Doug told him. "I already thought of that. I noticed there was a lamppost in the parking lot outside my room. I'll park the truck there when we're not using it, and grab a padlock for this door, too."

"Look around. I wouldn't be surprised if they left a lock here for you."

Hopping out, Cameron pulled the door down behind him. Doug made his way to the cab and opened the driver's side and, with a yell, held up a padlock. Triumphantly, he locked the rear, securing the equipment inside.

Cameron was circling around the truck. "When we get to the first gig, you and I'll get there early and go through all of this stuff and decide what we want to use, and what we want to keep as a spare," Cameron said. "I don't know if Dwyer has any sound tech experience or has someone on standby who does, but he did a fucking good job of getting stuff for us. We could blow the roof off of Madison Square Garden with this!"

Doug wasn't listening. His full attention was on the Cameron's new wheels, and the expression on his face spoke volumes, but Cameron couldn't discern about what.

"What's the matter?" he asked.

"It's a Mustang," Doug muttered. "Do you think it's an omen?"

"I hope the hell not," Cameron attempted a smile, but it was wan at best. The two men stood staring at the car, the silence becoming palpable.

"Want to go for a ride?" Cameron asked, twirling the keys on his finger.

"Can I drive?"

"Hell, no."

"Just thought I'd ask," Doug laughed.

"Man, on second thought, do you mind if I take off by myself?" Cameron asked. The roadie gave him a puzzled look, but shook his head.

"No," Doug answered. "Not at all."

"Nothing personal, man. I just need some time to myself before shit starts going down."

"Now that you mention it, I was kind of hoping to do the same thing. I can still see those gurneys coming out of that store. I don't know what the fuck we'll be doing on this next leg of things, but I don't want to end up like that."

"You and me both." Cameron attempted a smile. "Go relax. I'm sure this place has a bar in it, if there isn't another one nearby."

"I'm going to start going through the truck and the equipment," Doug said.

"Hell, there's time enough for that later," Cameron insisted. The roadie shook his head.

"I need to be with something I'm familiar with, something that I have some control over. I don't know what the hell else is going on, but I do know our equipment, and I need to know the new shit. This is relaxing for me."

Cameron reluctantly agreed with Doug's decision, and agreed to pick him up later for dinner with the rest of the band. As he pulled out of the parking lot, Cameron found himself pondering what Doug had said. Cameron, too, wanted to be in some place that was familiar and that was easy for him to control. He couldn't systematically go through the gear and equipment like the roadie could, but he felt his hands almost itch to hold his guitar, to have his fingers plucking out the chords from the strings, moving along the frets. He wanted to feel the sound come out of his Marshall stacks, the power of sound reverberating his insides. Cameron drove along Battery Park, idly tuning the radio as he sought something, anything, to help him relax. Failing that, he finally switched the radio off and let himself sink into the leather seat of the Mustang. The sun was lower in the sky, and he considered heading back to pick up Doug. He wished there was a way to delay the planned dinner meeting and just enjoy the quiet a bit longer.

I only hope it isn't the quiet before the storm.

The lights of the city were blinking on one by one, but Cameron paid no attention to them. He didn't even want to think. Not thinking, he reasoned, could starve out the feeling of anxiety overtaking him. He felt an impending sense of doom about the immediate future. He didn't need a crystal ball, though; he knew that the meeting with Dwyer would push the band forward into their next mission. What, exactly, would this one entail? Would it be any different than the job they had already done? Could anything be fiercer, really? There were already at least three people dead.

That I know of.

With that thought, his anxiety intensified.

Pausing at a traffic light, Cameron noticed snowflakes drifting through the early evening air. Today in particular, this brought him a sense of peace. The approach of winter reminded him of their usual gigs at the ski resorts around Vermont and New Hampshire. The memories of past shows, and the crowds and parties afterward, helped him to relax. Cameron's tension ebbed as he reminded himself that the band was about to perform in new venues, and he'd be thusly distracted. He found himself suddenly and strangely at peace. Perhaps he had finally resigned himself to his fate and the realization that there was truly no way out of this. Cameron was actually looking forward to it, and sensed that there was something more in all of this, although he couldn't define what that could be.

He didn't have much time to indulge in his epiphany. As he pulled up in front of the hotel, he found his roadie waiting on the curb, a sardonic smile on his face.

"Guess what?" Doug snarled, as he climbed into the passenger side. "I've got a roomie!"

Cameron was nonplussed. Who could it be? Clyde and Rich got along well enough with each other, and he knew Evan had his own room and wouldn't want to share unless he absolutely had to. Regardless, Doug and Evan got along well. Something was obviously wrong.

"Who?"

"That fucking D'Lorenzo," Doug said, slamming the door. "Can you believe it? Can you fucking believe that shit!"

"Don't slam my doors," Cameron said, his voice surprisingly calm.

"What?"

"I said don't slam my doors. I know you're upset and I don't blame you, but don't start beating on the new wheels just because you're mad. I didn't have anything to do with it. I don't like him any more than you do."

"Sorry," Doug mumbled, staring out the window.

"When did that happen?"

"After you left, I stayed in the truck and did an inventory of all the new stuff to make sure we have everything we need for the next show."

"Do we?" Cameron asked, as he started the car. As curious as he was about what had transpired, ultimately, he was a musician and was anxious about his performances.

"Oh, hell yeah," Doug smiled. "Everything and then some!"

They briefly sidetracked into a discussion about the new equipment and its capabilities. Finally, Cameron guided the conversation back to the other important issue at hand.

"What the fuck is D'Lorenzo doing rooming with you? Is he trying to make amends with you, or what?"

"I have no idea. All I know is that they showed up while I was working in the truck, and told me that he'd be staying. "

"No reasons, no explanations? None at all."

"None at all, and believe me, I demanded one!"

I have no doubt about that.

Cameron and Doug arrived at the restaurant and noticed Miss McIntyre heading inside. Once they stepped into the lobby, they spotted the band gathered at a table in the far corner. With them sat Dwyer, Miss McIntyre and D'Lorenzo. Clyde noticed Cameron and Doug standing in the doorway and waved to get their attention.

"I trust you had an enjoyable ride," Dwyer asked as the two men sat down.

"Yes, it's a nice car. My compliments to whoever picked it out," Cameron said.

"Mr. Courtland informed you of your new equipment?"

"Yes, he did," Cameron smiled, warming up to the conversation. "Where do you expect us to play, Madison Square Garden?"

Dwyer shook his head. "We need you at your best. All the talent in the world will do you no good if the people can't hear it. Therefore, new equipment and bookings in mid-sized venues."

"Hmm," muttered Cameron.

"I've taken the liberty of ordering drinks for each of you. I'm sure you don't mind," Dwyer said.

Cameron shook his head. Doug studied the menu.

"When exactly do we start performing?" asked Evan.

"Your first show is in two weeks," Dwyer replied, as the waitress arrived with the drinks. "That should give you all enough time to develop your set lists, rehearse, and become acquainted with your new equipment. Mr. Courtland will appreciate the opportunity to break in the new equipment."

Doug smiled and nodded, but said nothing, nor did he look up from the list of entrees.

"You'll be playing the civic center first," Dwyer continued. "You have four shows there, and three in Barre the following week. You have one week off and then return to this area, though in Shelburne before playing the Civic Center once again. This is the first time in a long while that you've had such steady work."

"In a little bit," Cameron agreed. "Once the war hit, things became difficult all around, as I'm sure you're aware."

Dwyer chuckled and nodded his head.

"Only too well, I'm afraid."

At that moment, the waitress returned for their orders.

"I didn't tell you fellows the specials," she said with a smile. "If you're looking for just a soup and sandwich, we've got some excellent vegetable soup, and we're lucky to have real bologna for a change!"

"I'll have the soup and sandwich special," Doug smiled, handing her the menu. "But I think I'll have the tuna instead."

"You don't want the bologna?" she asked, taken aback. "We haven't had the good stuff for awhile. We were lucky to get this in!"

"I'll pass," he smiled. "I've had enough baloney for awhile."

The waitress shook her head as she wrote Doug's order, and continued with the others'. Cameron elicited no reaction to his friend's double entendre, nor did he notice recognition from anyone else. He doubted that the other guys knew about Doug's rooming arrangement, but obviously Dwyer and D'Lorenzo did. No one said a word.

The meal proceeded without incident. Dwyer spent much of the time discussing business, but this time it was *band* business. He asked questions about the band's song selections and discussed the various merits of different styles of music.

"I must confess that I have a fondness for the blues," Dwyer said, pushing his plate away. "There is nothing better in the world than B. B. King or Sonny Boy Williams."

"Oh, I like the Stones and David Bowie myself," smiled Miss McIntyre, to which many of the others agreed.

"I like Led Zeppelin," smirked D'Lorenzo. "I'll take good, classic rock over anything else any day."

It was hard to ignore D'Lorenzo's air of imagined superiority as he attempted to clearly distance himself from each of their preferences. Dwyer and Miss McIntyre cast disapproving glances at D'Lorenzo. The band members, though, said nothing. They had long ago adopted the perception of D'Lorenzo as the "dreaded relative." He was the type that shows up at every family gathering and does something to embarrass everyone. D'Lorenzo reiterated two more times his love of Led Zeppelin.

"Really, " Doug smiled, showing a sudden interest. "No shit, so do I! What's your favorite song?"

D'Lorenzo smiled, enjoying the admiration.

"Well, you know, I like them all really," he replied, giving a nonchalant shrug.

"Seriously, man," insisted Doug. "What's your favorite out of all of them?"

"Well, you have to admit that *Stairway to Heaven* is pretty cool."

"Oh, no doubt," smiled the roadie. "But *Immigrant Song* blows me away, and I just dig the Beast's drum solo in *Moby Dick*."

"Who?" D'Lorenzo asked, a look of bewilderment on his face.

"The drummer," replied Doug. "C'mon, you've heard of the Beast!"

"Oh, yeah," said D'Lorenzo quickly. "I just never heard him called that. Yeah, Jimmy Plant has got to be the best drummer ever."

Casting a quick glance to Evan, D'Lorenzo began to blush.

"Present company excluded, of course," he added. "No offence, man."

"Oh, trust me," assured the drummer with a knowing smile. "None was taken."

Holy shit! This guy is undercover with us and he doesn't even know the members of Led Zeppelin?

Before anyone could say anything else, Cameron spoke up.

"Well, I'm glad to see the new addition to our crew is an expert on rock bands."

"What new addition?" Clyde demanded. "When the hell did he become a member of this crew?"

"When the hell did he become an expert on rock bands?" giggled Rich.

Dwyer took a sip of his coffee substitute and cleared his throat before answering.

"Mr. D'Lorenzo will be working with you as a member of your road crew. Even to an untrained layman such as myself, I realize that the additional equipment is far too much for Mr. Courtland to handle alone. To bring in someone from the outside was out of the question. We assigned Mr. D'Lorenzo to the road crew."

"Without discussing anything with the rest of us?" demanded Rich, his amusement now past.

"There is a need, and, as your business manager, it is my duty to see that it is filled. Added concerns limited my personnel selection. I see no problem here."

"You don't?" Rich, leaned over the table, his face in Dwyer's. "Well, I sure as hell do!"

"Guys, let me handle this," said Cameron, as he reached out to put a hand on his bass player's arm. "Dwyer and I need to talk alone."

"No fucking way," said Rich, shaking off Cameron's hand. "There's been too much of this cloak and dagger shit already. Some we have to put up with, some we don't!"

"I know that," insisted Cameron. "But you've got to let me handle this."

Rich turned and faced him, and that was when Cameron saw how truly angry Rich was, not just displaying mild irritation at an arbitrary decision, or the usual resentment for their undercover work. Cameron knew exactly how Rich felt because Cameron felt the same way.

"Brother, trust me on this one," urged Cameron, meeting his friend's gaze. "Trust me."

"I've been asked to trust too fucking much lately!"

"I know that," Cameron said, sympathy evident in his voice. "But I really need you to trust me on this. Just me. Haven't I always tried to do my best in the past?"

Rich paused for a minute and studied Cameron's face, considering what he was saying.

"This is bullshit," Rich spat. "Fine! You handle it. I'm going back to the fucking hotel."

As Rich stormed off, Clyde and Evan both got up to follow him, muttering quick goodbyes and nodding to Cameron. Doug remained behind. Finally Cameron nodded toward the door.

"You better go with them," Cameron insisted. "Dwyer and I need to talk alone."

Doug didn't answer, nor did he make any moves to leave; he looked from Dwyer to the others and shifted in his chair.

"That wasn't a suggestion, man," said Cameron. "I said I wanted to talk to Dwyer alone."

Giving Dwyer a warning look, Cameron added, "And I do mean *alone.*"

Dwyer donned his icy gaze and replied coolly, "Very well. We shall talk alone."

D'Lorenzo and Miss McIntyre arose and left the table, followed, at last, by Doug. Cameron waited for all of them to step into the front entryway of the restaurant. He waited until he saw them exit the building, and was about to speak, but was instantly cut off by Dwyer.

"We are in a public place, and a heavily populated one at that," he said, his voice low and menacing. "Do not air our dirty laundry for all to hear."

"You don't need to worry about me," assured Cameron, the same icy tone in his voice. "But I do think we need to clarify a few things."

"*What* things, Mr. Walsh?"

"First off, I don't care what this band has been hired to do, and I don't care that you are our manager. If there anything to be done that affects this band, then it is discussed with this band. Do you understand me?"

"I have no intention of performing my duties by committee, Mr. Walsh. Do you understand *me?*"

Cameron took a deep breath. He couldn't lose his composure. Slowly, he sipped at his coffee substitute, buying time to calm himself.

"I'm not talking about doing it that way," he said, his irritation showing nonetheless. "But I want to make something perfectly clear."

Dwyer raised his eyebrows inquiringly, his visage still stony.

"You might be good at what you do," snapped Cameron. "But, by God we're good at what we do! If you want us to perform and make a big impression on the crowds, not to mention anything else you'll force us do, then let *us* do it. We can't perform with you springing decisions that affect the band."

"To what are you referring, Mr. Walsh?"

"Like changing the dynamic of the band."

"Meaning?"

Cameron leaned into Dwyer. The seriousness of his expression set Dwyer aback, and Dwyer, realizing he'd reacted, countered by leaning into Cameron. Cameron, however, held his own stance.

"When you introduce anyone new into this group, even if it's just a roadie, or God forbid, someone who'll play with us, then you change the dynamic. We've all been together for a long time. Hell, some of us have been around since the very beginning. Doug might be new, but he's earned his place with us and that clown, D'Lorenzo, hasn't. Sticking him with us and in the way you did it is pure bullshit!"

Dwyer maintained his posture and spoke in almost a whisper.

"When a decision affecting this team needs to be made, I will be the one to make it." At this, Cameron bristled.

"When that kind of decision needs to be made, *I* will be the one to make it. I have enough to fucking worry about without the added concern of wondering what byzantine bullshit you're pulling in the background."

Dwyer let out a hearty laugh.

"Mr. Walsh, I hardly think adding an additional member to your road crew is considered byzantine, even by your standards."

"If you are trying to do my job, I can guarantee you've doomed the entire mission to failure. We're not a pack of pawns you get to move around. You don't get to make all the decisions for us and then expect us to go along, meek as sheep!"

Dwyer listened patiently, his gaze softening from its previous icy carapace.

Cameron continued. "We need to get something straight right now. If you want me to be the leader of this group, than trust me on something."

"On what?"

"On being able to gauge the feeling of this band. I've been the front man for years, and they all trust me. You even remarked on it when we started our arrangement."

"Your point, Mr. Walsh?"

"My point is this. If something needs to be done, then you and I discuss it together and agree on a plan. You keep talking about trust, and insisting that we trust you. This is a two-way street. The band trusts me. You have to trust me, too."

Dwyer considered Cameron's mandate. He gazed into his coffee cup, as if trying to divine an answer in the residue that ringed the edge. At last Dwyer spoke.

"Agreed, Mr. Walsh. I am not accustomed to dealing with people who are willing to cooperate with me."

Cameron nodded.

"Do you mind telling me the real reason you hired D'Lorenzo?"

"I already informed you," Dwyer insisted. "Mr. Courtland is, no doubt, capable of doing the usual heavy work, but even he cannot be expected to handle the extra load with all the venues you'll be playing."

"That's a job that I could have filled with a phone call. There's no need to hire anyone that could be a drawback or a complication to us, and you know it."

Dwyer was quiet. Instead of staring into his cup, though, he stared at Cameron. Finally, Dwyer motioned for Cameron to move to the seat next to him.

"Very well," Dwyer said, his voice low again. "There was another reason."

"Which is?"

"If two people have to be monitored, who better to monitor them than each other?"

"What the fuck do you mean?"

"Both Mr. Courtland and Mr. D'Lorenzo have a past connection to one another, one about which I have unresolved questions."

"Such as?"

"We cannot discuss it here."

Before Cameron could answer, the waitress had returned to their table with a pot of hot water and a jar of coffee substitute.

"Would you gentlemen like any more coffee?" she asked with a smile.

"No thank you," replied Dwyer with a smile. "May we have the check please?"

The waitress hesitated for a moment, a bit too long, Cameron thought, before heading back to the counter.

Oh, Christ, I'm thinking like a spook.

"There are less ears in a cornfield," muttered Dwyer.

I was right.

The waitress returned to the table and tried engaging the men in small talk, but met with no success. She appeared to be sizing them up, but then Cameron caught sight of the band's advance poster on a post near the door of the restaurant. Dwyer had obviously given it to the manager. Cameron realized that she probably recognized him from the poster.

Maybe she's just a potential groupie.

A wave of relief washed over him, but he still wasn't fully relaxed.

At last, the waitress gathered up Dwyer's money and returned to the register. The two men headed outside. Once out on the sidewalk, Dwyer eased.

"I do not believe in coincidences, Mr. Walsh," Dwyer informed him. "D'Lorenzo is the agent who recruited Gus Kalbe, the late friend of Mr. Courtland. Now we are all here together. Don't you find that odd?"

"Hell, yeah," agreed Cameron. "But why does that mean that they have to keep an eye on each other?"

"After I learned about Mr. Courtland's previous encounter with Mr. D'Lorenzo, I researched the Kalbe case. According to the file reports, just before the Mustang sailed, Mr. Kalbe discovered something that caused him great concern. He tried to inform us."

"And you think that Doug might know something about it?"

"I'm not certain. I know that they were in contact before Mr. Kalbe deployed, and he never followed through with us. I've wondered if Mr. Courtland received information from Mr. Kalbe without even knowing it."

"You mean in a code or a hidden message, or something?"

"Mr. Walsh, I haven't speculated. I have no idea if any information was passed on, or in what form it may have been."

"So why put the two of them together?"

"I am hoping that they can resolve their mutual animosity and perhaps reveal something useful to us."

"If they don't kill each other first."

Dwyer chuckled. "There is that distinct possibility."

Cameron lit a cigarette and turned his collar to the wind.

"So, why did you make them roommates, though? Wouldn't just working together be enough?"

"Your road crew usually shares living space, correct?"

"Yeah, it cuts down on expenses. They work out who sleeps where themselves, especially if there are more people than beds."

Dwyer smiled. "Precisely. Even though we have certain sponsorship, we must still behave economically. I seriously considered giving D'Lorenzo his own room, but decided that would raise more questions than is worth the trouble."

Cameron was about to ask him something when Dwyer interrupted him.

"And I also considered having him stay with me, but I realized that, too, wouldn't' work."

"Why not?"

"For several reasons. First, why would a member of the road crew stay with the business manager instead of the road manager?"

"True, and the second reason?"

"I really don't like him all the much, either."

Cameron laughed aloud. "That makes sense," Cameron conceded. "But I think that you're taking a hell of a risk, considering those two."

"Mr. Walsh, we are willing to take the risk that they are at least able to put their feelings aside. We surmise that they'll remain professional enough to accomplish the mission."

"Ok, I buy that, but one thing is still bothering me. You think Doug might have some idea of what Kalbe was talking about, so that explains why you've got D'Lorenzo watching Doug. Why do you have Doug watching D'Lorenzo?"

"Because, Mr. Walsh, I'm convinced that we're not the only ones searching for that information."

CHAPTER ELEVEN
"Sound Check"

Over the next few days, the Roadhouse Sons concentrated on readying for their debut. While they put together set lists and organized rehearsals, Dwyer surprised them by demonstrating that he actually knew what to do as their manager. Newspapers and radio stations called for interviews, and the guys were enjoying a notoriety they'd never known before. As their focus shifted to the shows and their own performances, the band members found themselves becoming much more relaxed and comfortable. Appetites returned to normal, and the boys were getting hungry. It was time to break for lunch.

Cameron stayed behind with Dwyer in the room Dwyer had reserved for business meetings. He wanted to discuss details for a scheduled publicity shoot. Cameron mentioned that, lately, he needed to remind himself of their real mission.

"Precisely what I want to hear," Dwyer told Cameron.

"Why?"

"It means, Mr. Walsh, that I am doing my job correctly."

"How's is that?"

"If you are not thinking about the actual nature of our relationship, you are instinctively concentrating on what is supposed to be. The fact that you are relating to all of us in this capacity suggests that you are finally accepting your new role as second nature."

"Well, we're back in our element," Cameron explained. "I've got my guitar back in my hand, the mic's in front of me, the lights are flashing, the kick pedal board, all of it. This is *my* world."

"Yes, it is," Dwyer smiled. "I know you'll be able to handle this. You truly are in your element."

Cameron lit a cigarette. He took a deep drag, temporarily lost in thought. Finally, he spoke, as though searching for the right way to ask his question.

"Do you have any ideas about how we go on to the next step?"

"The best way is the way you always do it. Be friendly to all of the fans, make sure you throw the after-parties, invite people from the shows, get them to know you and spend time with you. You will pick up information that way."

"None of that other shit you taught us?"

"I wouldn't concern myself with that at this point, Mr. Walsh. Those methods would only serve to confuse the situation."

Cameron leaned into Dwyer, consternation in his face. The memories of their months sequestered away were racing through his mind. He was angry.

"What the hell do you mean?" Cameron demanded. "You put us through all of that shit and you want us to forget it now?"

"Mr. Walsh..." Dwyer spoke calmly. "I don't want you to think laboriously. Now, we rely solely on your natural talents and abilities."

"Then what the fuck was the rest of that shit about?"

"We needed to be sure that you could learn new behaviors and impart them instinctively, Mr. Walsh. You will indeed find yourselves in situations that require you to draw on that training. That said, to ask you to sacrifice your innate ability to charm crowds and impress people is pure folly." Dwyer smiled for emphasis.

Cameron considered Dwyer's words. Was Dwyer actually saying that he trusted them, or, at the very least, Cameron himself? Cameron refrained from asking the question, deciding that it was a subject best left untouched.

"Again, I would encourage you not to dwell on this. Remember: to overanalyze is to paralyze. Be yourself, Mr. Walsh. That is the only requirement."

As if to underscore that statement, Dwyer redirected the conversation toward matters concerning equipment, gas rations for the band's vehicles, and the set-up for the upcoming show.

"Doug has all of that under control," Cameron assured him. "He even seems to work well with D'Lorenzo, at least for the most part. Some days, he doesn't' even call D'Lorenzo names. To his face, anyway."

"That surprised me," Dwyer chuckled. "I surmise that Mr. Courtland was anxious to be in his element as well."

"Or, he likes the fact that D'Lorenzo has to take orders from him. The band equipment is his kingdom, and he can run it with an iron fist if he has to."

"So I've heard," Dwyer said. "Perhaps you can convince him to place that iron fist in a velvet glove? At least, once in a while?"

"I'll see what I can do," laughed Cameron. "But no promises. Even I don't mess with that area of things unless it's necessary."

Cameron left Dwyer in the business room and went outside to his car. He took a breath of fresh air, and realized that he was instinctively looking around, watching out for anything unusual.

Dwyer was right.

Cameron got into his car. He was finally hungry, too, and wanted to get a bite to eat before the day's schedule flew into full throttle. For the past week, he had been stopping in at one of the local bars to enjoy a few drinks between rehearsals. Finding a place that was able to provide non-black market liquor was a challenge, but he was able to do it.

Hart's Tavern was a small establishment near the waterfront, almost a literal hole in the wall. A modest painted sign lit by a few spotlights, as opposed to the more conventional neon lights, was the only indication that the brick building was a tavern. There were no windows; even the glass on the door was painted. There was no parking for the tavern, either, except for a few spots on the street. Nonetheless, Cameron noticed that, every time he'd gone there, the place was always crowded. He took that as a good sign, and was glad that he had followed his instinct to check out the place.

Cameron had, over time, made the acquaintance of some of the regulars. They were interested in hearing about his career as a musician. The bartenders had even posted the promotional material for the band's shows, and a few people had asked Cameron for his autograph. He made a mental note to have Dwyer issue some passes for him to give out.

It was always a good idea to be in good graces with the locals, especially if one of the locals happened to be an attractive bartender.

Bambi, as her friends called her, was Cameron's age. She, though, looked younger, having been spared the wear and tear of road years, unlike Cameron. Bambi had sandy brown hair, dark brown eyes, a ready smile and an athletic build that, she'd once told Cameron, was a result of many years' attempts to become a professional dancer. All of these physical attributes made her a very striking young woman, but none of them compared to her warm personality. Cameron was very attracted to Bambi from the moment he met her. At first, getting to know her proved to be a bit difficult.

Despite her inherent warmth, she was quite guarded and reserved when Cameron tried to move past her pleasant professionalism. Her comportment went beyond just someone trying to keep their distance from a bar patron. Gradually, though, Cameron made her feel relaxed, and Bambi became more forthcoming with him. But it had not been easy.

He had begun to worry that he might never make any progress with her, until he noticed that his drinks were arriving with more and more alcohol and less and less mixer in them. And, he noticed that his area of the bar was being cleaned more frequently than the others.

"I was wondering if I was going to see you today," she said, as he sat down. Before he asked, a fresh drink was placed in front of him.

"But you were obviously confident I'd be here," he teased. "I might have to start adjusting my routine if I'm becoming that predictable."

"You do whatever you want," she said with a toss of her hair, as she made her way to the opposite end of the bar. Cameron sipped his drink, watching the television over the bar, and espying her from the corner of his eye. He noticed that she was watching him as well, but he knew enough not to appear obvious or overly confident. When their eyes chanced to meet, he simply smiled. She returned his smile, gradually making her way back to him, another glass in hand.

"Are you ready for another one?" she asked. Cameron detected a slight giggle to her voice.

Caught you!

"Yeah, I think I am." He smiled, then drained his glass.

"I thought you said you had to do some extra rehearsals this week," she said. She was suddenly quite serious. Her tone was direct and non-committal and her posture very straight. "Isn't your show coming up?"

Cameron nodded, sipping his drink and eyeing her.

"Next week," he smiled. "Can't wait, either."

"Then shouldn't you be back with your band and not hanging around here?"

"Sounds like you're trying to get rid of me," he said, just as serious.

"No," Bambi replied, her Cupid's bow mouth curving up into a small grin.

"All work and no play makes Jack a dull boy," Cameron said with a wink.

"I don't want you to be slacking off hanging out here when you've got a show," she said, still serious.

"Are you my agent now?"

"No," she pouted. For a moment, Cameron thought he detected a look of wounded remorse in her eyes, and he immediately regretted his remark.

"Sure sounds like you're trying to get rid of me," he said with a slight smile, hoping to redeem himself and make her feel at ease.

"No," she insisted, planting her hands on her hips. "It's just that I've been telling a lot of people about it and they're going to your show. I don't want to look foolish."

"And just why would you look foolish?" He didn't flash his usual grin. He wanted her to think that he was really interested in her reasons. To his surprise, he really was.

"I've been talking you up to my friends, that's all," Bambi said. It was she that flashed a reassuring smile. "I want you to be at your best when they come see you."

"Oh, you've been talking me up, eh?" Cameron laughed. "Have I been that convincing?"

Bambi gave a characteristic toss of her head and began to clean the bar.

"Don't flatter yourself," she sniffed. "I form my own conclusions, thank you very much."

"Except in this case."

She stopped cleaning and looked him in the eye.

"Are you sure about that?"

"Yeah," he smiled. "We haven't had the show yet."

"Not here," she smiled back.

After thinking this through for a moment, it dawned on Cameron what she was getting at, and his look of amazement made her laugh.

"I saw you about a year ago in Stowe," she said. "Some of my girlfriends and I were up there on a ski vacation, and we caught you at one of the clubs. I don't remember which one."

"Oh, wow," he said, nodding.

"And just what is that supposed to mean?"

"Nothing much," he said with a shrug. "Just that of all the ways I'd pictured you, I had never thought of you as a snow bunny."

"A woman likes her mystery," she said, heading back to the other end of the bar.

Cameron watched her go, noticing how her jeans were practically painted onto her frame. Her sweater flattered, rather than hid, her figure. Other than small, delicately ornate earrings, Bambi wore no jewelry. Cameron couldn't figure out if she was, for the most part, unadorned due to modesty or economy. She also wore very little makeup, which was just as well. Hers was a natural beauty.

Cameron, distracted by his thoughts of Bambi, happened to glance at the clock. He realized that it was time for the daily band meeting at the hotel. He quickly drained his glass. Catching Bambi's eye, he indicated that he was for his tab. Reaching for his wallet, he suddenly had an idea.

"So, since you said you'd been talking us up, I suppose that means *you're* coming to the show?"

A slight flush of color came to her cheeks and she looked away, giving Cameron a feeling of concern.

"I really don't know yet," she said briskly, focusing on the register. From her abrupt response, Cameron knew that she didn't want to discuss it, though he was anxious to know the reason. He knew that pressing the issue would only serve to satisfy his curiosity.

"OK, then," he said, attempting to sound casually sensitive. "Well, I hope to see you there."

"You never know," she said, trying to sound cheerful. Cameron could see that her smile was more than slightly forced. Returning a far less forced one, he left the tavern and went to his car. All the way back to the hotel, he debated a course of action.

Back at the hotel, Cameron had difficulty concentrating on the various discussions.

Thank God, I don't really have to, anyhow.

Dwyer had instituted the daily briefings as a means to checklist all of the band's needs prior to their shows. At first, everyone was convinced that meeting would just be a nuisance. Over time, though, the band realized that the meetings made life a lot easier. Dwyer had ample time to deal with Doug's and the band's equipment, and they all had more time to prepare for their scheduled interviews and appearances. Dwyer's meetings eliminated surprises, and for that, the band was thankful. In the beginning, the meetings could drag on for hours. Now, it was rare if they spent more than thirty minutes together. As the meeting was breaking up, Cameron took Dwyer aside.

"I need a couple of passes for the show," he said.

"How many?" Dwyer asked cautiously. As a business manager, Dwyer took his role very seriously, and he hated giving out free tickets. The band members were always in the position of having to convince Dwyer, and several vehement arguments ensued. From the band's perspective, giving free tickets to the radio stations and newspapers plugging the shows was actually an investment in advertising, not "throwing them away," as Dwyer called it. The media used the tickets in promotional contests, which helped to boost their own exposure. Dwyer had to be persuaded over and over again that it was actually a mutually beneficial relationship. He countered every time, making it clear that he had to consider the box office, and that issuing free tickets must be kept to an absolute bare minimum.

"Just a couple," Cameron assured him.

"Your definition of a couple, or mine?"

"Yours," Cameron insisted. "I only need two."

Reluctantly, Dwyer opened his ever-present briefcase and removed two of the yellow passes, hesitating for a moment before handing them over.

"Why do you need them?"

"I'm bringing a guest," Cameron said, making no effort to hide the irritation in his voice.

"Then why do you need two?"

"Let me explain something to you, again," Cameron grumbled. "We give out these passes and people get interested in coming to the shows. They tell their friends, and their friends get excited and want to come, too. They don't have enough free passes, so their friends have to buy tickets. That is why we give them out. Promotional expenses."

"I'm not entirely convinced of your arguments, Mr. Walsh, but very well. You may have them."

"Thank you," Cameron said, insincerity dripping in his tone. "By the way, I need a couple of back stage passes as well."

Before Dwyer could raise a protest, Cameron cut him off.

"Do you or do you not want us to fraternize with the locals? It would be a lot easier to do it backstage and at the hotel, than hollering it out from the mic, don't you agree? Of course you do. Thank you for seeing my point."

Dwyer stared, dumbstruck, as Cameron held out his hand for the requested passes.

"Once again, Mr. Walsh, I am unable to determine if you are being serious or facetious."

"Once again, neither am I," Cameron smiled, his hand still outstretched. Dwyer shook his head, and, opening his case, removed two laminated backstage passes.

"This is it, Mr. Walsh," Dwyer insisted. "No more free passes, for *any* of you. That was the last of them. I have to print more. Promotional resources or not, we still need to cover our expenses, and this little venture needs to be self-supporting. Am I making myself clear?"

"Absolutely," Cameron said solemnly. Cameron slipped the tickets and passes into his shirt pocket.

Your bottom line is the last thing I care about. Nope, a far more desirable bottom is what I'm...

"Good day, Mr. Walsh," he heard Dwyer say officiously. As they left the office and headed to the parking lot, Cameron decided to go to the Civic Center. He wanted to put in some extra time on his guitar.

We'll see whose up for their best performance.

He smiled to himself, considering the personal performance he'd do onstage for Bambi. It was then that he realized that he'd forgotten to ask Dwyer for the keys. He was about to call out to him, but remembered that Doug was headed to the Civic Center for another sound and lights check.

No need to harass the old boy more than necessary.

Besides that, as show dates approached, tensions mounted higher. He thought it best to "casually" stop by the Civic Center, as there had already been a huge argument between Doug and one of the stagehands that worked at the hall. The Civic Center had offered the use of their house lights, and Doug quickly rejected the offer, insisting that the band would use their own system. This caused the union workers to threaten a walk-off, and tempers began to flare.

Dwyer was unwilling to entertain any unpleasantries, and insisted that Doug give in, which predictably served to render Doug even more determined to maintain his stance. At first, Cameron had sided with Doug, and with good reason. There was no way of counting the number of times that venue staff attempted to force the band to use house lights, only to discover that the lights were hardly adequate. Experience had taught Doug that there was no reason to suspect otherwise here. However, upon inspection of this venue,

Cameron was surprised to discover a very professional lighting system that far exceeded the band's. The lights here were fairly new, having been either installed just before the war started, or purchased on the black market. Cameron decided that he didn't care which; it was a good system.

Together, he and Dwyer were able to convince Doug that the Civic Center's lighting was acceptable. The roadie was not entirely confident in their judgments, and insisted on examining the system with them. Cameron and Dwyer conceded, and Doug toured them through each and every light and cable.

Not a bad idea to see how it's working.

The Civic Center was an ambitious construction project taken on by the city of Burlington prior to the war. Designed to hold three thousand people, it had partitions that could be used to close off portions of the building and stage. This allowed the accommodation of multiple events and performances on the same date. State-of-the-art lighting and sound systems ensured that the Civic Center was an attractive venue for acts traveling from Boston or New York to Montreal. This arena was in a small city and provided an easy payday for the bands, offering the performers appreciative audiences packed with eager fans. Promoters of the project were able to use that description to win arguments with and sell the project to city officials. Several big-name bands had tentatively lined up for premier performances. The Civic Center was guaranteed to be a moneymaker for the city. Then the war broke out and everything changed.

The popular English bands were unable to make it to the United States, and the popular bands in the U.S. were forced to charge more than the Civic Center could pay, due to the ever-increasing restrictions placed upon non-essential travel. This was a blessing and a curse for the local bands. On one hand, venues opened up that would ordinarily be closed to them. On the other hand, promoters were often cash-strapped, and not always able to pay the asking price for the talent. Necessity forced all parties to be accommodating and creative in their dealings.

Cameron didn't know all the details of Dwyer's deal with the Civic Center. Whatever they were, it was good enough for the band to secure multiple performances. At first, Cameron thought it odd that the band would play this venue so often. After all, how many times can the good people of Burlington be expected to shell out hard cash to see the same show, even if the band's set lists are changed night to night? Cameron then realized the scheduled multiple performances coincided with the rationing schedules in the surrounding areas. New York restricted non-essential travel to certain dates, as did Vermont. Fortunately, those dates were staggered. People from all over, therefore, would be able to catch any of the band's performances without difficulty.

What do you know? I guess Dwyer knows what he's doing, after all.

Cameron arrived at the Civic Center. Pulling into the rear parking lot, he noticed that there were few cars parked. The band's new truck was there, and Cameron noted a few more cars, which he assumed belonged to employees. One car, though, parked next to the band truck, stuck out like a sore thumb. It was a blue 1977 Chevy Nova that Cameron knew belonged to D'Lorenzo. Cameron laughed aloud. Doug had refused to let D'Lorenzo ride in the band truck.

"I have to room with the son of a bitch," Doug had bellowed at a staff meeting. "I have to work with him, but I refuse to spend every goddamn waking minute with him!"

Threats and pleading were totally ineffectual as bargaining tools with the roadie, and Dwyer was forced to give in. D'Lorenzo was provided with his own means of transportation.

Stepping inside, Cameron heard Doug's voice, and half expected the roadie to be quibbling in another dispute. Instead, he soon discovered that Doug was helping the venue staff adjust a new spotlight.

"A little bit more this way," Doug shouted, motioning to his right. "Right...there! Perfect. How's the other one? Did you get that bulb replaced?"

"It wasn't the bulb. It was the wiring," called down a disembodied voice from the rafters. "Something must have rubbed against it and cut part of it. "

"How the hell did that happen?" Doug called back.

"No idea," replied the voice. "Probably somebody slacking off when they installed it. We had some problems with those guys, got rid of them. I swear none of them knew how to screw in a light bulb, much less do this shit."

"It was brand new, though, wasn't it?"

"We ordered it about ten months back," the stagehand shouted. "Hard time getting the shit. They only came in a few weeks ago. Rush job. They must be pretty backlogged, so that's why they hired those monkeys."

"Well it's fixed now, though, right?"

"Yeah."

As Cameron approached, he made certain to cough, as well as step heavily. The roadie was not one for being startled or surprised, something the band had learned to accept long ago, but a bone of contention with Dwyer and his colleagues.

"What's up?" Cameron asked, giving another cough.

"Just getting the last few bugs out," Doug replied. His attention was focused on the scaffolding above, and he didn't turn to look at the singer. "Couple of bad lights, but we've got everything fixed now."

"Was that the only problem?"

"Lucky for us, yeah," yawned Doug, arching his back.

"Rough night?"

The roadie rolled his eyes and shook his head.

"Not just for me, it seems."

"What happened now?"

Doug took out a cigarette and offered one to Cameron.

"Guess my roommate had a little too much black market booze or bad food last night," he said, taking a long drag from his cigarette. "Spent most of the night ralphing into the can or moaning in his bed. I was about to put a pillow over his face, again."

"You two have got to get along," Cameron insisted, more than a trace of annoyance in his voice. He could understand that Doug thought the man was "an absolute asshole," but they had to work together. Anything else would make a difficult situation intolerable. "We're all going to be working together for sometime. Fighting it is just going to make it harder on you."

Doug shrugged his shoulders.

"He's not so bad, I guess," he agreed. "As long as he keeps his mouth shut."

"What, he talks a lot?"

Cameron made no effort to hide the sarcasm in his voice. D'Lorenzo liked to portray himself as an expert on nearly every topic mentioned. Even if he had never heard of it before, he proffered it for discussion. That fact that he was wrong as often as he was right didn't deter him for a moment; he would persist in prattling on, to the point of annoying everyone around him.

"No, I've broken him of that habit," Doug said. "When we get back to the room, if he doesn't have to talk to me, he isn't allowed to."

Cameron smiled knowingly at Doug, yet recalling that one of the reasons that Doug and D'Lorenzo were housed together was the hope that Dwyer's people could gather information on Kalbe. That wouldn't happen with the silent treatment.

"Man, just try to get along with him, OK?"

Doug nodded. "Yeah, I know," he agreed. "Its not really all that bad now. Sometimes we do get along. That wasn't what I was talking about. It's his singing."

Cameron gave the roadie an incredulous stare. He had great difficulty picturing D'Lorenzo singing.

"You're kidding me, right?"

"Oh, fuck, I wish I was," Doug moaned, wearily shaking his head.

Cameron repressed a laugh.

"Is he any good?" he chuckled. "We might book him."

Doug shuddered.

"It's not his voice so much," he grumbled. "It's his selection. I doubt if he'll fit in our format."

This is getting better and better.

"What does he sing?"

Doug hesitated. Cameron noticed that the roadie's cheeks were turning pink. His curiosity was piqued.

Oh, shit! This has to be good!

"C'mon, man!" Cameron begged. "You have to tell me!"

Doug closed his eyes and took a deep breath, as if standing at the edge of a cliff before taking a dive into deep water. Finally, he spoke.

"If he knows I'm hanging around, he sings pop songs," Doug sneered. "If he doesn't think I'm around, like when he's in the shower or working in the truck, he sings his favorite song, over and over."

"Which is?"

Doug turned and faced him, his face pleading.

"Don't make me say it, not out loud!"

"Nobody's listening," Cameron insisted, but to accommodate his friend, he stepped in closer and lowered his voice.

"Come on," he insisted. "I can't stand it. You've got to tell me!"

Dough hesitated for a moment, then leaned closer to Cameron's ear.

"*Sugar, Sugar.*"

Cameron's jaw dropped. He was completely at a loss trying to picture a big, muscular man like D'Lorenzo singing, whistling or even humming a selection from the The Archies. A cartoon band! One look at Doug's face, however, convinced Cameron that Doug was telling the truth.

"Oh, you poor bastard!" Cameron collapsed in a fit of laughter.

CHAPTER TWELVE
"Show Time"

Cameron felt the heat of the lights on his face and the weight of his guitar forcing the strap against the back of his neck. The instrument itself was pulsing and vibrating, as much from its own desire to once again come alive in the musician's hands as from the power coursing through it from the amp. Cameron's body seemed to quiver in response. This is what he lived for, what he had felt so bereft of for so long. But now he was back. He was in the spotlight.

I'm home.

"Hello Burlington!" he cried out to the crowd. "Are you ready to rock?"

The last part was as much a challenge as it was a question, and the thunderous response told him that the audience was more than ready, and *more* than up to the challenge.

Cameron strummed his fingers across the strings of his guitar, the theater coming alive with a blast of sound and lights so sharp and sudden that it startled even him for a moment. He surrendered to it. The beat of the drums, the chords from his and the others' guitars, all of it blasted him from without through the amps and speakers, and from within by melding with the beat of his own breathing, his own heart. Cameron realized, as he became one with it, how deeply he had missed his music.

The stage lights beat in time to the music, shifting from red to white to blue, and occasionally to amber and green. Small spotlights gradually swept the audience, illuminating a sea of smiles. As a light settled on one section, Cameron carefully scanned the seating area, looking for familiar faces, albeit one in particular. Several times he thought that he had seen someone he knew, but couldn't be certain.

Doug and the others had told him that some of "The Girls" had shown up. The Girls were groupies that, before the war, followed the band to nearly every show, no matter how far away the performance. With the war and subsequent rationing, The Girls were somewhat inconvenienced, but hardly deterred. When pressed, groupies could be the embodiment of ingenuity.

As the lights flashed through the front of the stage, Cameron caught sight of several of The Girls and, for a few moments, he directed his attention toward them. There was no way he could make direct eye contact, but he would make them feel like he could. That was part of being the performer, of doing his best to make every person in the audience feel as if he were focusing all of his attention solely on them.

By doing so, Cameron was not only able to engage the audience, but he was also able to search the crowd for Bambi's face. Several times he thought that he had seen her, but the flashing lights made it impossible to be sure. He knew that, as difficult as it might be, his attention needed to be on the music, not on her. He played the next chord with more effort and flourish, bringing his attention back to the show.

The thrill of the moment filled him, pushing everything but the song he was playing out of his mind. He moved in time with the music. His fingers, as if by a will of their own, moved flawlessly along the strings and frets. Turning to look at the rest of the band, he saw their faces glowing, more from an inner light than the houselights.

This is where we belong.

Rich focused entirely on his guitar, as though it were an old friend with whom he was finally reunited. Clyde sang his vocals as if he had been waiting his entire life for this very moment, bound and determined to make the most of it. Evan's face was a picture of elation, with each beat of the drum being pounded out as though it was able to make this moment infinitely better than the one before. Looking to his right, Cameron noticed Doug standing just offstage. The roadie's attention seemed to be on everything at once—the lights, the band, and the crowd. Cameron noticed that Doug's hand lightly tapped his leg in time with the music. Doug was caught in the moment, as well.

Beside Doug stood D'Lorenzo, his attention entirely on the band and nothing else.

Amateur...

No matter. If D'Lorenzo missed anything he was supposed to do, Doug would correct him, no question about it. Movement in the shadows distracted Cameron for a moment, but when he saw Doug turn only slightly without reacting, Cameron realized that it must be either Dwyer or Miss McIntyre, or someone from the Civic Center. The roadie did not move from his position, so Cameron knew that all was well. He went back to his music.

At the end of the first song, the lights halted for a moment, allowing everyone's eyes to adjust. In response, the audience cheered and clapped, and the band took a moment to acknowledge the applause. Scanning the crowd, Cameron spotted Bambi sitting in the middle section, almost directly at eye level to him. She wore a yellow sweater and a white scarf. Was that to make her stand out in the crowd? He gave her a smile and a wave that every woman in the crowd thought was their own.

Go ahead. I know who it's for.

As the applause grew louder, Cameron turned to the Roadhouse Sons. As one, the band struck the chords for the next song. The cheers from the audience thundered through the arena. So did the music.

The band made their way through each song of the first set. After the first few numbers, people from the crowd got up and danced in the aisles and at the stage front. At some shows, The Girls would climb up on the stage with the band, but tonight, they would have no such luck. The only access to the band during this performance was through the backstage area, and the management had closed it off.

For now, anyway.

After all, what rule had Cameron ever encountered that he didn't challenge?

It was toward the end of set one that Cameron experienced his first sign of trouble. After a quick twist and turn during one of the songs, Cameron felt his jeans tear along the seam of his crotch. He panicked for a moment as the cool air revealed exactly where the tear occurred, but being an accomplished rock star, his panic diffused quickly. This was not the first time this had happened. He knew the band had only one song left in the set. He would simply be careful of how he moved, so as not to make the tear worse. And he would have to keep his guitar strategically placed. His panic returned, though, when he realized that he couldn't remember if he had a spare set of clothes in the dressing room.

The last song of the set seemed to go on forever, each solo a performance unto itself. Cameron was getting more anxious by the moment. After what felt like an eternity, the song and the first set ended.

The band members gave a slight bow to the crowd, but Cameron gave a big wave and a smile, turning his head, in lieu of his body, to the various sections of the audience. Moving sideways while watching his step out of the corner of his eye, he made his way offstage, still smiling and waving to the cheers of the crowd. Handing his guitar to Doug, he rushed to the small dressing room. He knew that the jeans he had worn before the show would be there. They were white, but that didn't matter. Something else to wear from the waist down was all that concerned him. He found the white jeans. As he was about to put them on, his heart sank. There, clearly visible on the front, was a large grease stain. That was why he had changed out of them in the first place. He'd accidentally smeared them up while helping Doug backstage before the show.

Now what?!

An idea occurred to him. Going to the door, Cameron called for someone to send Doug to his dressing room. When the roadie appeared, he showed Doug the torn jeans.

"Can you run back to the hotel and get me another pair from my room?"

"No way, man," the roadie replied. "I'd never have time to get back before you go back on."

"Well what the fuck am I going to do?"

The roadie shook his head and shrugged, then smiled.

"Wait here," he said, hurrying out of the room. "I know what we can do!"

A few moments later, Doug returned with a young blonde. Cameron nearly cried with relief. The guys called her Flannel Annie. She always wore flannel as part of her outfits, be it flannel shirts, flannel skirts or flannel shawls. Somehow, Annie always fashioned flannel into her ensemble. While she was not one of the band's regular groupies, she was one of the most popular. Annie's mother was seamstress by trade, and Annie worked for her, often making for the band customized shirts and vests, one of which Cameron was wearing at the moment. Annie recognized her work and smiled, but her smile was short lived. She realized that Cameron was standing there in his shirtsleeves, another shirt hastily pulled around his waist. With a gasp, she covered her eyes as her cheeks turned crimson.

"Sweetheart, please don't freak out on me," he begged, taking her by the arm with one hand and sitting her down, all while gripping the shirtsleeves with his other hand. Showing her both the torn jeans and the stained ones, he explained his predicament.

"Please tell me you brought your sewing kit," he begged.

"Of course I did," she said with a nervous giggle. "But I don't think I'll have anything strong enough to mend them with, or have time to do it before you go back on."

Cameron sat down and put his head in his hands. He'd been anticipating this night for months. This gig had kept him going, had kept him sane, and now it was going to be undone all because of a pair of ripped jeans.

"But I do think I can figure something out so you can get through the show," Annie giggled. "Just don't jump around too much out there."

Cameron felt so grateful that, once again, he nearly wept.

"Oh, my God, I love you!"

Calling for Clyde, Cameron explained what was going on, and told Clyde that they might not be able to start the set exactly on time.

"No sweat, man," the guitarist assured him. "Rich and I can do a little jamming till you can get out there."

After his friend left, Cameron heard other voices outside the door, and realized that Doug was probably explaining to Dwyer and the others what had happened.

Annie snapped Cameron back to attention. "I need Doug to get me some of that black tape he uses to tape down the mic cords," she said, turning the jeans inside out.

"What the hell do you need gaffer's tape for?"

"Don't argue, silly," she smiled. "Just trust me on this one!"

Opening the door slightly, Cameron called out to his road manager. Doug came in and Cameron told him to get the gaffer's tape from the toolbox. Doug nodded and left immediately.

"And a roll of duct tape, too," Annie added. Cameron called out those instructions as well, slamming the door to avoid the curious looks from the backstage onlookers.

"Holy crap," she muttered. "Was something trying to get in, or get out?"

Cameron blushed, and gave her a stern look.

"There's a war on in case you didn't know," he muttered. "You make things stretch."

"You've stretched these so far they're snapping back,!" Annie giggled unabashedly. "You're not giving me much to work with." She grinned, eyeing Cameron slyly. "Well, not here anyway." Cameron blushed once again.

He was rescued from having to reply by a knock at the door. Opening the door carefully, he saw Doug standing there holding the black gaffer's tape and a roll of silver duct tape. Cameron didn't remember ever looking at tape and feeling Heaven, but he did now. With a hurried "Thanks," he slammed the door shut and tossed the rolls of tape to his favorite seamstress.

Moving quickly, Annie turned the torn pants inside out and laid them on a table in front of her, carefully smoothing them. Ripping off a section of duct tape, she laid it over the tear, adding more tape overlapping the first section on both sides. Turning the pants back out, she took the black gaffer's tape and laid sections of that over the outside.

"Why are you doing it like that?"

"The black tape blends in with your jeans better," she explained, carefully smoothing out any bumps. "The duct tape will hold everything together well enough, but this will help to make it less noticeable."

She handed the jeans to Cameron, who thanked her and turned away to pull on his pants.

"But wouldn't it be cool to have the silver stuff on the outside?" he joked. His back was to her, but he could tell from the tiny gasp that she was blushing.

"I mean, think about it," he continued. "It would be pretty cool having the lights reflect off it. Don't you agree?"

Turning to face her, he winked and faked a leer. Annie drew herself up with her back pin-straight, trying to give him the look of a proper lady.

"Perhaps," she said, tossing her head. "But I thought you didn't want people talking about *that* performance until after your performance on stage."

"Oh, get out of here, you brat!" he laughed, then leaned over and gave her a kiss on the cheek. "And thank you so much!"

Smiling, Annie kissed him back, but on the lips. She pointed to his pants.

"That should get you through the show, but I wouldn't get too carried away out there. If you want, I can come back and get them and fix them up for you. I've got tickets for the Barre show next week and can get them back to you then."

"That would be cool, sweetheart. Thanks!"

"You better hurry up and get out there," she smiled, grabbing her purse and heading toward the door. She paused there and blew him a kiss before leaving. Cameron waited a few minutes himself before rushing back to the stage. He grabbed his guitar from Doug and stepped onstage to loud applause. Soaking it in for a few seconds, he flawlessly joined the Roadhouse Sons' jam.

Just like we know what we're doing.

Cameron smiled to himself. Looking out into the crowd, he saw Annie, back in her seat and smiling contentedly. Sitting directly behind her was Bambi. He gave a smile and a wave toward them, and blew a kiss. The ladies in that section clapped and cheered, waving back. Bambi seemed slightly uncomfortable, but gave a quick wave and a shy smile. Cameron saw Bambi talk to the woman beside her. He had no idea who that woman was, and he had never seen her in Hart's Tavern. The man seated next to the woman leaned forward to say something to her and Bambi. The man looked familiar, but Cameron couldn't figure out why.

Probably someone I saw at the bar.

The rest of the show proceeded without incident. The guys were relaxed, occasionally veering from their set list to jam, and improvise their chords and lyrics. If the audience minded, there was no way to tell. The space in front of the stage was filled with people dancing. The first three rows of seats emptied as people jumped to their feet. Cameron noticed that hardly anyone was heading to the beer taps. He didn't mind, but he knew the managers would be complaining to Dwyer later on.

Not my problem.

Catching sight of Annie once more, Cameron decided to have a little fun. While Rich was doing a solo, Cameron swung his guitar way out to the side and imitated Elvis, complete with pelvic thrust. Annie covered her face with her hands, anticipating disaster. Cautiously, she peeked between her fingers to make sure that her mending held up. Fortunately, it did. Cameron let out a big laugh and continued playing, savoring the anxiety written all over Annie's face. Just to make up for his bad behavior, Cameron smiled and blew her another kiss. He noticed that Bambi was also laughing, and he was happy that she was enjoying herself.

The second set came to an end, and the crowd called out for more. Cameron and Evan each called out songs, and the band did an encore of three more numbers. After the encore, the crowd called for still more. Acknowledging the calls of the crowd, the Roadhouse Sons waved and smiled, leaving the stage one by one.

Doug held back the curtain, ready to take their instruments. He gave D'Lorenzo orders about disconnecting the amps and mics. Cameron wandered by them, exhausted, and felt a pat on his shoulder. It was Doug, passing him with a reassuring nod, acknowledging their performance.

Dwyer was waiting in the wings, along with Miss McIntyre. Both of them were smiling, so Cameron assumed they were happy. He recalled that the pair had been regulars at the guys' shows before. Of course, Dwyer and McIntyre would be happy to see them perform again. He knew they probably wanted to talk, but he was so tired that all he wanted to do was collapse somewhere, anywhere. Nodding to Dwyer and Miss McIntyre, Cameron made his way into the dressing room and flopped into a well-worn easy chair.

They might have spent a mint on the sound system, but they got damn cheap when it came to furnishing the place.

A cooler full of ice and beer sat by the sofa on the other side of the room. He was still too exhausted to get up, and wished that there was someone who would bring it to him. As if on cue, he heard a knock at the door.

"Who is it?" he called out, eyes closed.

"It's me," came Annie's voice. Cameron smiled and got up, moving toward the door. He appreciated Annie's creativity in solving his dilemma. The duct tape, however, was beginning to irritate a rather sensitive part of his anatomy. He welcomed Annie with a big hug and kiss.

"Thanks again," he said, closing the door. "I honestly couldn't have done it without you!"

"Oh, you're smart," she said, blushing slightly. "You'd have figured it out for yourself, eventually."

"Yeah, but not before giving the folks in the front row an eyeful more than they were expecting!"

"You have to keep your audience happy, don't you?"

"Brat!" he yelled, tossing a towel at her.

She caught the towel in midair. "I've got to get going," she laughed. "Montpelier is starting a curfew. If I leave soon, I might just make it home, so hurry up and give me those pants!"

Cameron began removing his jeans when, suddenly, the door burst open and D'Lorenzo stepped into the room, startling them both.

"Don't you ever fucking knock!?" Cameron shouted, quickly covering himself with his pants.

"Oh, man, I'm sorry," stammered D'Lorenzo. "There's someone out here that was looking for you."

"Ah, busy?" Cameron snarled. "Tell them to wait!"

"Yeah, right," D'Lorenzo replied, his face red. Cameron heard a lady scream. D'Lorenzo quickly backed out of the room and slammed the door behind him.

"Sorry, lady," Cameron heard him say. "You'll have to wait your turn. He's got someone else in there right now."

"Aw, fuck!" moaned Cameron. "What the hell is he saying?"

Cameron grabbed his grease-stained jeans and pulled them on. He felt a rush of nausea. Was D'Lorenzo talking to Bambi?

"Here you go, sweetheart," Cameron said to Annie while handing her his torn jeans. "I hate to rush you, but I've got to get out there and make sure he doesn't do something stupid!"

"Who was that?"

"Living proof that Darwin got it wrong," he said, giving her a kiss. "Again, thanks for saving my ass tonight!"

"The tear didn't go back *that* far," she smiled. "*That* part wasn't in any danger!"

Cameron shook his head and wagged his finger at Annie, then dashed out the door to find D'Lorenzo.

"D'Lorenzo,!" he called out. "Who was looking for me?"

The ad hoc roadie stopped what he was doing and shrugged.

"I don't know," he said. "Some woman was looking for you. I told her you were busy."

"Yeah, I heard what you said, asshole!" bellowed Cameron, moving toward D'Lorenzo. "You don't ever say shit like that again, do you hear me? I don't "take turns" with anyone. Do you fucking understand me?"

"Hey, it was just a joke," said D'Lorenzo, stepping back. "I thought that was the image you guys wanted."

"I'll worry about my fucking image, you dumb shit! You keep your mouth shut! Now, who was looking for me?"

"Some girl, like I said…"

"Well, did she have a name?"

"I, I didn't ask…"

"Why the hell not, you dumb fuck? Is she still here?"

D'Lorenzo shook his head.

"No. She got kind of upset and left with her friends."

Cameron had a nagging, sinking feeling in his gut.

"What did she look like?"

"I don't know," D'Lorenzo stammered. "Average height, brown hair…"

Brown hair?

"Dark brown or light brown?"

D'Lorenzo gave him a quizzical look and shrugged. Cameron felt his anger brewing, and fought the urge to grab D'Lorenzo by the collar. For all of Dwyer's tutelage and insistence about noticing and remembering details, Cameron was frustrated by how bad a job D'Lorenzo was doing at those very things.

"Just brown," D'Lorenzo muttered. "What's the big deal?"

"What was she wearing?" Cameron yelled, as he lunged toward D'Lorenzo with fists clenched.

Keep calm. Get it together.

D'Lorenzo shrugged again, this time backing away from Cameron.

"I didn't really pay attention," he muttered.

"Was it yellow? White? Was it green? Was it a sweater or a blouse? What the fuck was she wearing, you worthless goddamn idiot?"

By now, the shouting had attracted the attention of everyone backstage. In some distance corner of his mind, Cameron was aware of people gathering around them. By now, he was beyond caring, focused only on his rage. He tried to recall the image of Bambi sitting in the crowd, but to no avail. He was so incensed with D'Lorenzo, that he couldn't see Bambi in his mind's eye; all he could see was D'Lorenzo standing in that doorway, a woman screaming behind him. Cameron couldn't hide his fury.

"I think it was a sweater, I'm not sure," D'Lorenzo said, but before he could continue Cameron grabbed him by the collar.

"Why don't you keep your fucking mouth shut from now on?" Cameron shouted, his beet red face mere inches from D'Lorenzo's. "You don't know what you're talking about, and you don't have any business commenting on *anything* about me. Do you understand?" He grabbed D'Lorenzo tighter, and shook him.

"Get your fucking hands off me!" yelled D'Lorenzo. He brought his arm up to take a swing at the singer, but a rapid response from Doug hooked D'Lorenzo's arm, preventing D'Lorenzo's fist from connecting with Cameron's face. With his attention now directed away from Cameron, D'Lorenzo and Doug locked eyes in a steely gaze and, for a moment, Cameron thought the situation would burst totally out of control. Just then, Dwyer stepped right into their midst and ordered Doug to release his grip on D'Lorenzo.

"Take Mr. Walsh back to his dressing room."

Nobody argued.

"Come on, man," said Doug, escorting Cameron back to the dressing room. Cameron kicked at the door. It swung inward with such force that it knocked a picture off the wall, glass shattering to the floor. Cameron grabbed a beer and pounded his fist against the cooler lid.

"What was that asshole thinking?" he snarled.

"What the fuck happened?" asked Doug, bewildered. He began to pick up the broken glass.

"Yes. Tell me exactly what did happen out there," demanded Dwyer, entering the room and slamming the door behind him.

"Your associate decided to take it upon himself to pretend he was either my social secretary or my fucking pimp! Either way, he managed to ruin something I have been trying to put together for a good long time!"

Starting with the torn pants, Cameron told Dwyer about the events of the evening, and how he learned that someone had been looking for him, only to be caught with his pants down.

"Literally," Cameron snapped. "Then, D'Lorenzo decided to improvise things from then on, and now it's all a delightful little cluster fuck!"

Dwyer ran his hand through his hair and began to pace about the room. Neither Cameron nor Doug had ever seen Dwyer, the picture of grace under fire, so agitated.

"I can't believe this," Dwyer muttered. "*That's* what this was all about? What the hell."

With that, Dwyer stormed out of the room, leaving the door wide open. Doug saw Dwyer head down the hallway, away from the backstage area. Rich and the others were watching from their rooms. They filed in quickly after Dwyer left.

"You all right?" asked Evan. Cameron nodded, and guzzled his beer.

"Did anyone think to bring any tequila?" he asked. Doug disappeared through the door and Cameron knew that was a "yes."

"What happened?"

Once again, Cameron related the story to them. When he finished, he grabbed another beer.

"Dude, I didn't see anyone in a yellow sweater," said Rich.

"Then who the hell was asking for me?"

Rich shrugged. For a moment, Cameron began to doubt if perhaps it was Bambi after all, but the uncertainty brought back his anxiety full throttle.

"Do you want me to go check and see if she's here?" offered Clyde.

"Do you know what she looks like?" asked Cameron, as he reached for another beer.

"No," his friend muttered. "But you said she was wearing a yellow sweater. How many could there be out there?"

Cameron reclined in his chair and tilted his head back, eyes closed. He took a deep breath and slowly exhaled.

"Clyde, it is the middle of November in northern Vermont. We're two farts and a sneeze away from Lake Champlain. There is a fuel shortage, so everyone is reducing the heat. This arena held three thousand people, and damn near all of the seats were full. Would you like to take a guess at how many people wore sweaters? Yellow, or otherwise?"

Clyde seemed downcast, and Cameron regretted snapping at his friend.

"Sorry, man. I know you're just trying to help."

"Not that many would be able to get backstage," Clyde offered. "You need passes to get here."

It was then that Cameron remembered he had given Bambi backstage passes with her free tickets. Clyde was right. One could not come backstage without one of those! Without saying a word, Cameron leapt from his chair and raced out of the room. The backstage area was filled with people, hardly any of whom Cameron knew or recognized. No doubt, they were people that Dwyer had invited. Many of them smiled and nodded to Cameron, who greeted each person. A few people regarded him curiously and moved away, as though afraid of him.

Guess I treated you to more than one performance tonight, didn't I?

But even to those people, he smiled and nodded, all the while mindful of any sign of Bambi.

Opening the stage door, he was not surprised to find a small crowd of people gathered there, too. There were fans looking for autographs, young guys looking to get a break in the music business, and of course, the infamous groupies. These weren't the ones that followed the band from one show to another year after year. These girls simply hung around the back door of the Civic Center, regardless of what event was taking place. Some of the men with whom Cameron had worked looked down on these girls, but he often felt sorry for them. More often than not, they were young girls looking for an escape from the boredom and monotony of their lives, convinced that some big star would notice them and sweep them off their feet, making all of their dreams come true. Cameron knew that their "future" would likely be one wild night with cab fare home in the morning.

He waved and greeted them all, signing autographs for those who asked for one. Seeing no sign of Bambi, he hurried back inside. Dejected, he returned to his dressing room and found Doug there with the bottle of tequila.

"Thanks, man," he said, taking a drink from it.

"You need anything else?" asked Doug. Cameron noticed the concern in his friend's voice and shook his head.

"No," he sighed. "I'm going to gather my shit and head back to the hotel. I'm done here tonight."

Doug offered to help, but Cameron waved him off. He wanted to be alone. He put his guitar in its case for the drive take back to his room, and collected his clothes, except for the jeans he'd given to Annie.

The ones that started this whole mess.

He made his way to the stage door, passing people and giving a polite smile or a brief nod. He was just about to step out into the night when he heard Dwyer call out for him.

"Hold it right there!" Dwyer yelled, and Cameron heard the sound of Dwyer's footsteps hurrying up the hallway. He didn't bother to turn around and face Dwyer. For a moment, Cameron considered walking away and letting the door slam in Dwyer's face, but he knew that it was not a wise idea.

"You still have some work to do," Dwyer reminded him didactically.

"Now isn't the best time," Cameron muttered. "Later. I'm tired and I want to go home."

"You and I need to talk," Dwyer said, moving in closer so that no one else could hear them. "This is important."

"I don't need a bitching out over what happened tonight, OK?" whispered Cameron. "Just let me go home, all right?"

Dwyer stepped closer.

"No. You and I need to talk. Now! This is important."

Cameron was about to protest, but hesitated. There was something curious about Dwyer's manner. This wasn't about what had happened earlier. Reluctantly, Cameron stepped back into the building and followed his manager into the room they used as an office.

"Close that door," Dwyer said, without turning around.

Cameron did as he was told. "Listen," he said. "If you're going to get on my ass about what happened earlier..."

"I could not care less," interjected Dwyer. "We've got something much more important on our hands."

With that, he gave Cameron a piece of paper. It was twice folded in half. Cameron unfolded the paper. It was a note written in block letters and unsigned.

"There are no accidents!" was written across the front.

"What the fuck is this?" Cameron demanded. He could not see for the life of him how this scrap of paper with its cryptic message could justify Dwyer's grave concern. "It's a piece of paper and a lousy fortune cookie quote. You called me back in here for this? What the fuck?"

"Do you notice anything special about it?"

Cameron was about to throw it back and tell Dwyer to stop wasting his time, when he suddenly realized that, indeed, there was something special about this note. It was orange.

CHAPTER THIRTEEN
"From Out of Nowhere"

Doug stumbled toward his room. As drunk as he was, he knew that he was feeling taxed beyond the usual effects of drinking. Each step was more and more difficult, his legs like bars of lead. Finally, he reached his door and, heaving his body against the wall, was able to steady himself. As he attempted to fish the key from his pocket, he noticed with surreal detachment that his hands would not cooperate. For a moment, he could have sworn the keyhole was moving to avoid being unlocked. Eventually, after much struggle and frustration, Doug was able to open the door and tumble inside.

With what seemed to be gargantuan effort, Doug located the light switch and flicked it on. He instantly regretted it. The sudden blast from the lights caused him to wince; the very contraction of his irises sent pulses of pain through his head. Steadying himself against the door, he closed his eyes until he felt sure that they were accustomed to the brightness. Gradually, he opened them. The room undulated and, feeling a sudden rush of nausea, Doug clamped his eyes shut once again, hoping to stave off the sickness that was gripping him. Once his nausea passed, he made his way to the bathroom, eyes squinted, and splashed cold water on his face. He could not remember, for the life of him, being this drunk before. Despite his foggy state, he reasoned that his inebriation must be due to the fact that, for the longest time, he'd really not had a lot to drink on any one occasion. So what made tonight different? He concentrated as much as his mind would allow, as if recalling a distant memory. Some thoughts, though seemingly random glimpses, brought him clarity. He was aware that several people at tonight's after-party brought their own homemade blends of booze, and he wondered if a bad batch of that was the culprit for his current state. He couldn't dwell on that thought or anything else, though. Thinking took too much effort right now. Bracing himself on the toilet tank, Doug plopped onto the edge of the bathtub, waiting for his head to clear. Within fifteen minutes, he grew more aware of his surroundings. Half of his brain knew that he was in his bathroom; the other half couldn't piece together exactly where he had been all night, and how he ended up at the hotel.

After the show, he performed the usual tasks of securing the band's instruments and storing the equipment, a job made easier by the fact that he had used a lot of the venue's sound and lighting implements. After that, and as usual, he joined the band backstage as they entertained friends and guests. Doug noticed that Cameron was absent and made an effort to find him. Doug had seen the lead singer heading into Dwyer's office after the show, and figured that they had business to discuss. After a half hour or so, he saw both men leave. Doug pondered going after Cameron, but thought better of it, figuring that Cameron was probably just tired and heading back to the hotel to unwind.

Best to leave him alone.

Doug remembered going back to the party and seeing some of the regular groupies, and he recalled spending time with them. The regular girls didn't bother him very much. They had traveled with the Roadhouse Sons for some time and they knew the boys quite well. They no longer relied on Doug to be their liaison. Oftentimes, they shared major events in the band member's lives, both good and bad, and the girls provided a sense of security for the guys. It was nice to know that wherever they played, the band would see the familiar faces of girls that were there to "support the Sons."

Doug didn't always care for the new faces. These were groupies that didn't even bother to show respect for the band, or for themselves. They thought that the more suggestive and outrageous their behavior, the better their chances of being snagged by the band. These girls thought nothing of creating scenes in public, or lasciviously plying the guys with lewd suggestions. None of that ever worked, and only served to embarrass the band members. Some of the smarter girls realized that their behavior was self-defeating. Others, though, weren't so smart, and inadvertently rendered themselves as outcasts forever.

The nature of Doug's job meant that *he* was the one who had the most involvement with the groupies and hangers-on. As road manager, he was the person with whom the public had the most direct access. It was through Doug that people tried to meet the band, both those with legitimate interests, such as reporters, and the groupies that were dying to be part of the band's inner circle. Most of the time, Doug didn't mind this additional role. Occasionally, though, he hated it. He had no patience for dealing with phonies but, at times, he had no choice but to grin and bear it. Cameron never allowed Doug to toss anyone out, so he was forced to merely fantasize about it.

Tonight, however, it was like a whole new experience. People that hadn't seen the guys in a long time were anxious to know what the band had been up to. The rumors explaining the band's absence had taken root, and, all night long, Doug fielded gossip about the band's purported new record. He simply shrugged and said it "didn't work out," and that the person for whom the band was working was too temperamental and "everything just fell apart." Doug told anyone who asked that, to make up for it, the record company put together this tour under the condition that no one was allowed to divulge any details. Doug's story seemed to work. Friends of the band didn't ask for details, but instead proposed their own theories as to why the record deal fell through. Doug just smiled and poured himself another drink, and allowed everyone their suppositions.

Doug met a lot of new people that evening. Some were connected to the Civic Center, and some were the local groupies. Still suffering from inebriation now, he recalled thinking at the party that some of the groupies seemed vaguely familiar to him, but after a while, the faces all blended together. The girls introduced themselves, as if he should know who they were, but Doug was lousy with names. He also suddenly remembered that Dwyer questioned him about something, but Doug couldn't remember what it was.

Doug continued to recount the night's events. He remembered that Rich and Clyde jammed with their guitars in accompaniment to the radio or the record player. He ran through his mind the assortment of liquor at the party. Regular liquor and beer had been provided, and, yes, many people brought their own, both bootleg and black market. As the evening wore on, the party drifted back to the hotel rooms and, yes, Doug realized that the liquor seemed to be hitting him a bit harder than usual. Giving Rich a quick goodbye, yes, Doug had left the party and headed back to his room. Even though it was just a short trip down the hall, Doug wondered a few times if he would make it to his room.

Yes. It all matches up.

As if in protest to recalling the night's events, another wave of nausea swept over him. Doug instinctively put his head in his lap. After a few moments, the nausea subsided, and he slowly stood up. Leaning over the sink to avoid falling, Doug looked in the mirror. He did not like what he saw.

His face, usually ruddy, was extremely pale. His pupils were dilated and his long black hair and scruffy beard drew his face downward, making him appear even more pallid. The dark circles under his eyes certainly did not help.

I need to go lay down.

He staggered out to his bed. He was able to kick off his boots and lay back for a moment to relax. The pounding in his head was fierce, but somehow, as soon as he hit the pillow, he fell fast asleep.

His was not a restful slumber. Frantic images invaded Doug's dreams, dark images with no form or substance, suggesting danger, but to whom, he could not tell. Several times, Doug felt as if someone was reaching out to grab him, but he was too paralyzed to move. Was he still dreaming? Doug awoke suddenly to a loud bang. His head still clouded by sleep, he tried to determine if he heard an actual sound or simply dreamed it. Adjusting his eyes to the light, he soon realized that he had a more immediate concern. In the center of the room stood D'Lorenzo, stark naked.

"Oh, shit," muttered Doug. "D'Lorenzo, what the fuck is wrong with you?"

D'Lorenzo gave no response, nor did he even acknowledge having heard Doug. D'Lorenzo just stood there, staring blankly at the far wall, his hair disheveled, his body covered in sweat and his breathing belabored. He attempted to utter something, but to Doug, it was unintelligible.

"What?" Doug asked. Ignoring his pounding head and weakened state, Doug tried to pull himself up from the bed.

"What the hell are you saying?"

D'Lorenzo continued to mutter incoherently. Doug, suffering his own afflictions, paid no attention until the stricken D'Lorenzo grabbed the front of Doug's shirt and began repeating several words. "Radio," "pickles," "tan," and "mustard" were the only words that Doug could understand. All demands for an explanation or repetition went unanswered, as D'Lorenzo slumped in Doug's arms, exhausted from overexertion. Forcing himself to stand up, Doug took a closer look at

D'Lorenzo and noticed that there was bruising on his arm and scratches on his calf. Doug also noticed that the D'Lorenzo seemed to be swaying, but a sense of dizziness made him wonder if it wasn't he that was unsteady. Suddenly, a new concern confronted Doug.

D'Lorenzo began swatting at the air, as if fighting off bugs. His face became twisted in terror. He began to make a high-pitched squeal and dropped to the floor in a fetal position. Doug tried to focus, but found it difficult to concentrate. He had seen many people have bad trips before, but something told him that this was different. D'Lorenzo began to sob and tremble, rapidly repeating words, rendering it impossible for Doug to understand what he was saying. As Doug leaned over the man in an attempt to talk with him, Doug heard D'Lorenzo retch. Doug feared that D'Lorenzo was about to be sick, and headed D'Lorenzo toward the bathroom.

This proved to be much more difficult than Doug could have imagined. D'Lorenzo was roughly Doug's size, and muscular with a medium build. However, his present inability to stand on his own made him dead weight and that, combined with his profuse sweating, made it almost impossible for Doug to lift him up off the floor. Slinging D'Lorenzo's arm about Doug's neck just made the man struggle more. Finally, Doug was able to prop D'Lorenzo up on his knees. Grabbing D'Lorenzo under the arms, Doug dragged him across the floor to the bathroom. D'Lorenzo kicked his legs into the air, struggling to get free.

Doug tried leaning him over the toilet, but D'Lorenzo would not stay upright. After several attempts, Doug finally propped the man against the tub, figuring that he'd at least be sick on the floor and not the rug. At that moment, D'Lorenzo began to twitch, and Doug feared that the man was having a seizure. Doug knew that he could not deal with this on his own and decided to go for help. Racing out into the hallway, he paused at Cameron's door for a moment, but realized that his boss was probably in the same state he was. Doug forced himself to focus. The person he really needed was Dwyer. "He never does any shit," Doug thought to himself.

Hurrying down the hallway, Doug arrived at Dwyer's door and pounded on it. The moments dragged on, and Doug fended off a feeling of despair that Dwyer might not be home. Doug pounded harder. He feared that he might wake up everyone on the floor, but decided that he didn't care. After what felt like an eternity, the door opened and there stood Dwyer in a tee-shirt and boxer shorts.

"There better be a fucking reason for this," Dwyer snapped, his characteristic reserve absent.

"D'Lorenzo's all fucked up," Doug slurred pathetically, imploring Dwyer to accompany him. Without waiting to see if Dwyer would follow, Doug trundled back up the hallway.

Doug arrived at his room and tried opening the door, only to realize that it was locked. He began pounding on the door.

"What are you doing?" demanded Dwyer, grabbing Doug's wrist.

"He fucking locked me out!" snapped Doug. "That fucking asshole locked me out!"

"No he didn't," Dwyer explained. "These doors lock automatically. Don't you have your key?"

Doug stared at Dwyer for a moment, trying to comprehend what Dwyer was telling him. He was about to ask how they could get into the room, when he remembered that he was still wearing his clothes from earlier, and that his key should therefore be in his pocket. It was. Doug stared at it, as though not sure if it was the correct key. He attempted to fit they key into the lock, and struggled. Doug seemed stupefied and just stood there, again staring at the key. In frustration, Dwyer grabbed it away from him and unlocked the door. They rushed inside.

Doug pointed to D'Lorenzo, who was still sprawled out on the bathroom floor. Dwyer hurried over and knelt next to him. D'Lorenzo began muttering. Dwyer putting his ear next to D'Lorenzo's mouth to listen, jerking away when D'Lorenzo began gagging.

"Is he all right?" Doug asked, leaning against the doorway for support. Dwyer made no response. Doug was about to ask again when D'Lorenzo began sobbing and shaking his head back and forth.

"What's the matter?" Doug asked once more, but Dwyer's attention was on his associate, not the roadie. Dwyer leaned in further, whispering into D'Lorenzo's ear. This had no effect upon the stricken man. Doug was becoming more anxious by the second. Suddenly, D'Lorenzo began to shudder. Doug thought the man was having a seizure, but Dwyer reached over to grab the wastebasket. Dumping out the contents onto the floor, Dwyer placed the bucket under the D'Lorenzo's chin and leaned back as D'Lorenzo quickly filled it with the contents of his stomach. Doug fought back his own gag reflex as the stench filled the room. As Dwyer carefully set the bucket into the bathtub, Doug, now even more unsteady on his feet, stepped forward to grab it.

"Leave it," Dwyer ordered. "I want to take a look at it."

"It's puke, man!" Doug gagged.

"Leave it!"

Doug noticed the stern look on Dwyer's face and stepped back, relieved that he did not have to deal with the contents of the bucket. D'Lorenzo shuddered again, and Dwyer quickly placed the container back under the man's chin. This went on a few more times until D'Lorenzo seemed to fall asleep.

"Help me get him up," Dwyer ordered, motioning for Doug.

The two of them struggled to get D'Lorenzo off the floor. Doug followed Dwyer's lead as best he could as they moved D'Lorenzo to the bed. Doug was going to lay D'Lorenzo down, when Dwyer ordered him to wait so that the covers could be pulled back. Doug observed, detached, as though he was watching television through someone's window. He suddenly became aware of D'Lorenzo lying in the bed, and of Dwyer standing right up in his face.

"What did you give him?" demanded Dwyer.

Doug just stood there, struggling to understand what Dwyer was asking of him. Dwyer grabbed Doug by the shoulders and shook him.

"What did you give him?" Dwyer demanded again.

"Nothing, man," Doug muttered. "I didn't see him all night."

Dwyer demanded that Doug explain everything that he'd done that evening. The roadie sat down on the edge of his bed, but missed and landed on the floor. Rather than trying to rise, Doug drew his knees up to his chest, and rested his head on them. Thoughts raced in his mind, but in no cohesive order, and certainly in no way that he could relate to or explain. Doug attempted to answer, but trailed off, rambling indistinctly. Dwyer sat on the bed opposite Doug.

"What did you do right after the show?" Dwyer asked, his voice loud and didactic. Dwyer realized that Doug was not capable of forming complex sentences, nor could he provide detailed explanations. Dwyer would have to keep his inquiry simple if he wanted any answers.

"I hung out backstage," Doug told him. Vague images fleeted through Doug's mind, images of people from the party, but the winds of thought dispersed them almost as soon as appeared. "I had a few beers with some of the guys."

"The band?"

Doug nodded at first, but then shook his head.

"Yeah, but no," he muttered. "Stage guys, too."

"Did you meet with anyone else?"

"Yeah," Doug yawned, suddenly very tired. "Groupies."

"Were these people that you recognized?"

"Yeah…" Doug said. He started to say more, but was unable to conjure the right words.

"Were there any new people backstage?"

Doug looked at Dwyer, who seemed to be traveling rapidly down a dark narrow tunnel, and boomeranging back toward Doug's face. Doug lost himself in pondering the process of it, when he suddenly heard Dwyer's voice, louder and more insistent.

"Were there any new people backstage?" Dwyer demanded.

Doug nodded.

"Were they with you. A*ny* of you?"

"Yeah," Doug mumbled. "They wanted to hang out with us, meet the band. Same shit, different day."

Dwyer grabbed Doug's head and turned his face toward Dwyer's.

"Did they meet any of you? Did you introduce them to anyone?"

"I think so," Doug mumbled. "Rich, Evan…"

Dwyer considered this for a moment, then spoke softly.

"Do you remember who they were? Any of them?"

Doug stared into Dwyer's face, marveling at how a mouth could move so oddly and actually produce words. He wanted Dwyer to speak again, but was snapped back to reality by a hard shake hard from Dwyer.

"Listen to me!" Dwyer demanded. "This is very important. Do… you… remember… any… of… them?"

"No, man," Doug sighed. "Didn't want to hang out with them. They wanted to see the band."

"What did you do when you left the Civic Center?"

Doug stared at Dwyer. He had no idea what had happened between the parties backstage and how he got to the hotel. Disparate images continued to through his mind like random leaves in the wind, but there was nothing upon which Doug could focus.

"Where did you go?" Dwyer continued, his patience evaporating.

"Party in one of their rooms."

"Here in this hotel?"

Doug recalled walking in a building. He must have been in this hotel, as, yes, he remembered staggering up the hallway. He didn't remember a room number, though, or even passing through the lobby to his floor.

"Was it here?" Dwyer demanded, shaking Doug once again.

"Yeah."

"Which room. Do you remember it?"

Doug put his head on his knees. His felt as though his very brain ached, and his nausea returned.

"No," he moaned.

"Do you remember if it was on this floor?"

Doug shook his head.

"It was this way and that way," he said, leaning first one way and then the other. "Didn't want to stay, felt funny."

"Do you feel alright now?" asked Dwyer, solicitously.

"No, feel sick."

Dwyer helped Doug to his feet, and maneuvered him to the bathroom, and sat him on the edge of the tub. Dwyer hurried to retrieve another wastebasket. Fresh waves of nausea swept over Doug and the room began to spin. Shaking uncontrollably, he began to vomit as soon as Dwyer returned. As his stomach emptied with every retch, Doug realized that he couldn't breath. Panic set in and Doug was afraid that he would die. At last, he was able to stop vomiting. He took a deep breath and tried to push himself up, but his hand slipped and he fell, striking his head against the side of the tub. Surprisingly, the pain caused him to become momentarily alert and, as he tried to push himself up from the floor, he caught the sound of Dwyer's voice coming from the other room. He couldn't hear or discern everything that was said, but as he closed his eyes, he heard one thing very distinctly... the word "Naomi."

CHAPTER FOURTEEN

"Opportunity"

Cameron lay in bed long after he awoke. He had no desire to get out of bed and face the day. The effort to merely roll over onto his back was more than he wanted to attempt, and he pulled a pillow over his head. It was no hangover that made him feel that way, though there was enough of that around the edges of his consciousness. Instead, he was fighting off the memories of the night before, the humiliation of his torn pants, the argument with D'Lorenzo, and the solitary return to his room when everything was all said and done.

Cameron knew that the reason he kept replaying those events in his head was not to dwell on them, but because they served as a makeshift ward against the things he wanted to push out of his mind—the absence of Bambi, and the presence of an orange note. However, his defenses were paper-thin against the thoughts that demanded his attention. At last, he rolled over on his back and allowed himself to address the inevitable.

Bambi. The orange note.

The glass and the bottle on the bedside table were empty. There was no way to get any coffee without going downstairs to the restaurant next door, so Cameron lit his first cigarette of the day with a sense of resignation. He lay back on the pillows.

Don't want to think about it.

What was the meaning of the orange note? Was it a warning or a threat? Dwyer appeared to have no knowledge of the note at all, and despite the agent's usual calm, cool and collected manner, Cameron could see that Dwyer was equally as concerned about that piece of paper. But, no. "Concerned" wasn't the word that Cameron was looking for.

Unnerved is more like it.

The thought chilled Cameron to his core. If something was bad enough to rattle Dwyer, it was something very serious, indeed. *There are no accidents* was how the note read, but what did that mean? What about the significance of the color of the note itself?

Orange... who knows about that, other than us and our contacts? Probably coincidence...

Cameron watched the cigarette smoke drift up to the ceiling. He knew that he was kidding himself. This was no coincidence. If the message had meaning, then the color had meaning, as well. Someone was trying to tell them something, and Cameron was almost certain it wasn't someone on their side. If it was, the delivery would have occurred in a way that would have left no doubts in Dwyer's mind. Dwyer wouldn't be left to guess its source and its meaning. The fact that Dwyer was confused proved the sender was someone that Dwyer didn't know. The fact that the note was delivered in the manner that it was offered firm proof that the sender was someone who *didn't* want Dwyer to recognize them.

Either because he would have recognized them, or because they might still have something else planned.

The fact that Cameron was able to put things into that, or any, perspective did not comfort him. It only confirmed that his thought processes proved to him that he was firmly entrenched in all of this cloak-and-dagger mess. He had no answers to any of these questions, and he hated himself for that lingering lack of ability.

Did the arrival of the note have anything to do with the mole?

It must...

Cameron surmised that Dwyer was so rattled because now they both knew that *someone* had discovered their communication system. Cameron dismissed that thought.

No, it couldn't be that.

The whole system existed solely for practice runs, Cameron figured.

It's way too simple to use for real.

It was also possible that Dwyer was simply agitated, thinking that someone had played a practical joke. Or, in Cameron's favorite assessment of things, the famous *Door Number 3* hypothesis—it could have been a mere coincidence. Cameron certainly had no way of knowing for sure, and Dwyer didn't seem to have had any more information than he'd initially shared in the office, and clearly had drawn no concrete conclusions.

Shit! Coming up with decisions without all the answers sucks.

Cameron hated ambiguity with a passion, but suspected that he'd have to accept it as a necessary evil, at least in this line of work, anyway. Hopefully by now, Dwyer would have more answers.

Cameron sank back into his pillows and groaned. He realized that, having thought through the situation with the note, he was now left with no defense against thinking through the next item on the list: Bambi.

Had she tried to come see him after the show? Was it Bambi that screamed when D'Lorenzo opened the door?

That fucking idiot!

If she wasn't upset, why did she just leave? She had her backstage passes, and there should have been enough for her and her friends. Then Cameron remembered that there was that man sitting next to Bambi. Did he come to the show with Bambi, or with someone else? The man looked vaguely familiar, but Cameron couldn't remember why.

It was possible that I saw him in the bar one of those times, I guess.

But Cameron couldn't be sure. This was just another worrisome question to which Cameron had answer.

Fuck that!

It was bad enough that Cameron simply didn't like where this line of reasoning would take him, but now he had the unfortunate luxury of imagining the absolute unthinkable. Was Bambi already seeing someone?

That would definitely explain her hot and cold attitude toward him, her "just polite enough" demeanor that rendered him a repeat customer at the tavern. Cameron tossed the pillow from his face and considered getting dressed and heading to the bar. Maybe Bambi was working and he could get *some* answers today. As usual, he had slept late enough in the day that the bar would be open. Once he kicked off the covers, though, he thought better of it.

Why *should* he go? Why look desperate? Then again, why go through this at all? It wasn't as if there was any shortage of women at the show, and practically all of them were interested in him. But there was something he liked about Bambi, something that was nice. Perhaps that was it.

After all the shit I have to deal with, I found something nice. It's like an oasis for me in this shit desert.

The heat of his desert showed no sign of letting up. Cameron was not going to give up this one bright spot without any effort.

Hell, not without a fight.

Maybe that guy was Bambi's boyfriend. Cameron accepted that she had to be flirtatious with the customers to keep them coming back. Maybe that guy was just a friend who came to the show with her so she wouldn't be out during curfew alone. Maybe he was just someone sitting next to her that resembled someone Cameron had seen. That idea, which seemed perfectly logical, relaxed Cameron. He settled back onto his bed with a wave of welcome relief.

Guess Door Number 3 isn't so bad after all.

The only way to find out for certain, when dealing with anything, is to simply ask the question. Cameron had enough questions—unanswered and unanswerable—in his midst. He could, and would, deal with something as tangible as this, he decided. Unfortunately, in order to deal with it, he would have to get out of bed. Reluctantly, he did so.

A quick shower did little to cheer or energize Cameron, in large part due to the patriotism of the hotel owners who decided to reduce the temperature of the hot water in an effort to conserve energy. The lukewarm shower over with, he donned the cleanest dirty clothes that he had, and set out on his mission. In the hallway, he noticed an absence of activity. Usually after a show, the guys were going from one room to another comparing notes on the prior evening's activities, either onstage or backstage. Sometimes, someone would be sneaking in or sneaking out, or the more desperate hangers-on would be lying on the floor, waiting to meet the band. Today, however, it was oddly still.

Cameron decided not to chance the elevator, in the event that someone would stop him to talk or assign him work, and therefore derail his plans. He wondered if he hadn't timed it just right when he heard the elevator doors opening just as the stairwell door closed. Cameron hurried down the stairs to the lobby, lest whoever it was might notice him. Pulling on his suede coat as he stepped out into the hall, he was halfway to the front door when he heard someone call his name.

Fuck!

Cameron turned around and found himself face-to-face with Bambi.

"Hey there!" he smiled, genuinely glad to see her. "What a surprise. I was thinking of popping over to grab a drink or two."

"I had today off," she smiled, twisting her handkerchief. Cameron noted that she was diverting her gaze away from him, casting her eyes downward and then glancing up at him through her long eyelashes, her shy smile and soft laugh ever present. If she had been upset by anything last night, she certainly wasn't showing it now.

"Did you enjoy the show?" he asked, smiling back at her. "I saw you in the crowd. I waved, but wasn't sure you knew I was waving at you." He gently tapped the end of her bobbed nose with his forefinger. Bambi giggled.

"Yes, I enjoyed it a lot," she said, her smile growing wider and her eyes finally fixed upon him. "I did notice you wave, but never thought it was just for me."

"Of course it was," he laughed. "Why wouldn't it be?"

"There were so many other people there!" Bambi blushed. "Why would I think you had singled me out of all of them?"

"Oh, I don't know. Maybe because you were someone that I really hoped would be there?"

This time, Bambi did not blush, nor did she look away. Her smile broadened. Cameron felt a bit of encouragement.

"Would you like to go somewhere for a cup of coffee?" he asked. "Maybe grab some lunch?"

"Some coffee would be nice." Bambi, still smiling, leaned in closer and whispered in Cameron's ear. "I know a place nearby that has some of the real stuff."

"Oh, well then, lead on!"

Outside, snowflakes fell from steel-grey skies into the bitter cold air. Turning up his collar against the wind, Cameron cast a glance toward Bambi. He understood now why she bundled up in layers; she didn't seem to be affected by the cold like he was. Bambi pulled up the collar of her turtleneck sweater and leaned into the wind. Wrapping her scarf around her neck and over her head gave her the appearance of a Bedouin, and Cameron smiled at the thought of her in an oasis, peeling grapes and dropping them into his mouth.

They walked for a few blocks, ending up at the restaurant that he and the band usually inhabited with Dwyer.

"I love this place," he said, opening the door for Bambi.

"You come here often?" she asked, surprised at his response.

"Sometimes," he said. "For business. Our manager likes it here."

"One of the few places that still sells real coffee."

"I think that was the selling point with him."

Entering the restaurant, the hostess greeted them with a smile, and said a few words to Bambi before waving them inside. Initially, Cameron thought this strange, but realized that Bambi, too, was a waitress and a bartender, and had probably worked with the woman, either here or somewhere else. Bambi continued into the dining room and selected a table some distance from the doorway.

Cameron pulled out Bambi's chair and helped her with her coat, studying her as she sat down. She seemed more relaxed and at ease here than when he saw her in the bar.

Perhaps that's because she's not at work and can be herself, finally.

He caught the scent of her hair as he sat opposite her. He couldn't place it, but it was a light, floral essence. Cameron imagined it to be an expensive cologne that she used sparingly. The subtle touch seemed to suit her. He settled in and turned to face her. She smiled at him once again. Her smile was always warm and friendly, but now, without the bar between them, it was almost inviting. Cameron was about to say something when the waitress came over. Before he had a chance to speak, Bambi ordered coffee for them. Cameron sensed a familiarity about the waitress, but couldn't discern from where. Using the opportunity to ask the waitress about the day's specials, he studied the woman carefully. Finally, he remembered where he'd seen her. She was the woman who had conspicuously hung around him and Dwyer the first time they ate there. Her easy manner with Bambi now suggested that the ladies knew each other well, and Cameron realized that this was easily possible. They were both waitresses and Burlington wasn't that large a town.

His curiosity momentarily satisfied, he decided not to order anything other than the coffee, and watched the waitress as she walked away. There was still something he couldn't place about her.

"I really liked the show," Bambi said, drawing Cameron's attention back to the table. Bambi's expression was eager, as though she genuinely wanted him to know how she felt and that her feelings were indeed sincere. Looking into her eyes, Cameron remembered the beautiful, happy smile on her face the night before, and he wanted to reiterate that he had played just for her. The other reasons ran through his mind, those being the fact that performing was his job, that he loved to do it, and that he'd needed to do it to save his own sanity. All of these were true in their own right, but the fact that he had seen *her* there, looking at him almost as expectantly as she was now, made him want to do his best, and just for her. Other people might have appreciated the band, but he appreciated her.

"I'm so glad to hear that," he said, coyly glancing downward. "It's been a while since we've performed in front of a crowd. I didn't know how it would come off!"

"You did great," she insisted. "But I thought you played all the time?"

A moment of panic seized Cameron as he tried to remember his cover story.

Why haven't we been seen lately? Shit!

He faked a cough in an effort to stall for time, then remembered their record deal story.

"We usually do," he explained. "But we got the chance to work on a record and have been off the circuit for a bit. Studio work is a hell of a lot different than playing a live show. Sometimes you spend hours working on just one song or one section, or stuff like that. You're always trying to do something different to make everything sound just right. When you do a show, you have one shot and one shot only. Everything and everyone has to be ready."

Bambi looked at him in amazement, her eyes fixed on him, taking in his every word. She waited for a moment before speaking herself, to see if Cameron had anything more to say.

"A chance to do a record!" she gasped. "You got signed! Oh, my God! That's great!"

Cameron blushed, partly because he felt horrible about lying to her, but also because he realized that modesty would, to Bambi, be a worthy virtue.

"Well, we didn't get signed, unfortunately," he smiled. "We were working for someone else. We hoped that it would lead to something for us, but it didn't quite work out that way. The person we were working for drove the producers crazy and so the label decided to cut the project."

Cameron felt a kick in his gut as he saw her face fall.

"Oh, no," she sighed. "I'm so sorry!"

He shrugged his shoulders and looked away, not able to accept the disappointment in her eyes.

"Well, it wasn't such a bad thing," he explained. "We might not have gotten a record or a contract out of it, but we did get a tour, so I suppose things do work out in the end, don't they?"

He tried smiling, hoping he could distract her from the topic. Cameron was torn between enjoying her interest in him, and that fact that he had to lie.

"Who were you recording for, if you don't mind me asking?"

Cameron sighed. There was no easy way out of this. He knew the answer he was supposed to give; in fact, he'd given it a hundred times at last night's show, but to people with whom he didn't have a connection like he did with Bambi. Or rather, like he hoped he could have with her.

"Sorry…" Cameron smiled weakly, as much because he had no stomach for continuing this ruse as he did to discuss it. "We had to sign a nondisclosure agreement. One of the reasons the record company was willing to spring for our tour is because we promised not to say anything about it. I think the company is still hoping to do stuff with the people we were working for, and they don't want to burn any bridges."

"Still, that's a pretty generous package, wouldn't you agree?" she asked, just as the coffee arrived.

"Cheaper than getting their attorneys involved, I guess," Cameron shrugged.

"What attorneys?" the waitress asked Bambi. Cameron was shocked by the woman's impudence, and offended by her intrusive questioning. He was about to say something when Bambi spoke up.

"Oh, nothing. Just a question about a company he worked for," she said, giving the waitress a warm, but very fixed smile. The waitress blushed slightly and hurried away.

"Some people!" Bambi said, turning back to Cameron. "Oh well. Never mind that. How long are you guys going to be out on tour?"

Cameron recited the basic tour dates, at least as many as he could remember.

"That's just here in Burlington," he said. "Our manager has the other dates, and most of the rest of the schedule. He's great at that and I suck at it. You could say he's the brains of the outfit."

Bambi gave him a quizzical look.

"But I thought you were the front man?"

"I am," he said. "But when you've got someone who's better at doing things than you are, you let them do it. I sing, I play guitar; he does everything else."

"I take it he's been with you for quite a while then?"

Cameron hesitated before answering, taking a sip of coffee to buy himself a few moments. He was unsure of how to respond. Cameron knew that it was a bad idea to divulge any information about the band's special relationship with Dwyer and his colleagues. At the same time, though, Cameron was seriously interested in Bambi, and hated that he was starting their relationship with lies. Ultimately, he knew there was really no way around it.

"Well, we hired him when we realized the record deal was going to hell," he said with a shrug. "We wanted to make the most of the offer in front of us, and he seemed right for the job."

"Does he do a good job?"

"So far, he has," Cameron said with a smile, attempting to hide his discomfort. "So, what's with all the questions about the band? I didn't know you were that interested in the business end of it."

"Oh, I was just trying to show an interest," Bambi said. "I didn't mean to talk shop."

"No problem," he laughed. "I just didn't want to mistake the chance to have a cup of real coffee for an interview."

Bambi laughed in agreement. Thankfully, the conversation turned to other topics. She asked Cameron about himself, where he grew up and what his interests were. She asked about his favorite foods and music, and the work he'd done prior to becoming a musician. Cameron asked Bambi questions in return. She answered some of them with a blush and giggle, but it was hard for him to get any straight answers from her.

"What are you being so shy for?" he teased, flashing her a smile. "Seriously; I'm interested."

"Oh, you can't be that interested," she insisted. "I'm not that interesting. I just work in my father's bar. I've done it for almost a year."

"So, there you go," insisted Cameron. "You've been there less than a year, so that means you must have done something else before, right? So, what was it?"

Bambi laughed loudly, and as she tossed her head back, Cameron noticed her creamy white, smooth neck. He knew, from brushing his hands across hers, how cool and soft her skin was, and he leaned in closer, once again catching the subtle scent of her perfume.

"What's so funny now?" he smiled.

"What if I told you I worked in another bar someplace else? Would that still be interesting?"

"Sure it would," he smiled, resting his chin in his hand. "I'd learn a little bit more about you."

Bambi smiled and shook her head, sipping her coffee.

"I'll bet you actually worked in that ski lodge you said you saw me in," Cameron ventured.

At that, Bambi stopped laughing and looked at him, a puzzled expression on her face.

"What ski lodge?" she said. "I never saw you in a ski lodge before."

Cameron gave her a knowing look.

"Yes, you did," he chuckled. "When you were talking about bringing friends to the show, you said you'd been talking me up based on having seen my show before, and I teased you about being a snow bunny."

"I think you might have misunderstood me. I'd heard about you from a friend of mine who saw you in Stowe. That was what I based my opinion on."

Cameron looked at her carefully. He didn't want to argue the point, but he clearly remembered her saying something about seeing the band at a ski lodge. Nothing would be gained by pressing the issue, so he dropped the subject.

"So, did you like the show last night?" he asked, taking a sip of his coffee.

"I thought it was great," she smiled, leaning in toward him. "I really needed a night out like that. Even though that isn't really my type of music, I had a lot of fun."

Cameron jolted, scrutinizing her expression to see if she was joking. Her smile had not changed, and she still seemed to be interested in him, but he knew that she was serious. His heart sunk, as he replayed her words in his mind. After a few moments of awkward silence, Cameron spoke.

"Really?" he said. "Why didn't you say something? I'd never have pushed the tickets on you then."

"Oh, I didn't mean that I hate rock. I do like it somewhat, and I actually liked what you did. It was the same songs that I hear on the radio, but somehow you do them differently. I liked yours better, to be honest."

Well, that's a relief.

"What is your favorite music, if you don't mind my asking?"

She hesitated a moment before answering.

She's going to say hymns or Gospel music, you just watch...

"Well, I do like some jazz," she said, slowly.

"Any particular singer?"

She shook her head, and then blushed.

"What's the matter?" he asked with a smile.

"I was thinking of some other songs I like, that's all."

Oh, shit! Here it comes.

"Like what?"

"Well, I've always liked songs from the fifties and sixties, but not the kind you usually hear on the radio these days. My mother had a collection of Cadillac Record artists, and one of my favorites is Etta James."

"My folks loved to dance to *At Last*," Cameron smiled. "That's nothing to be embarrassed about. That all came from the blues, and that's where rock comes from. Listen to the Stones, Led Zeppelin, all of them. That's great that you appreciate jazz."

"I know, but it isn't very cool to like it these days."

"I like classical guitar and blues myself," Cameron said. "Its nice to rock out and feel the strength of the music and all, but sometimes I just like to feel the music move through me, like a slow river, or something like that. I want to lose myself in it, but not be lost. Does that make any sense?"

"Have you ever heard of Andre Segovia?" she asked.

"Oh, hell, yeah!"

Cameron and Bambi spent the greater part of the next hour talking about music. Finally, the conversation returned to the previous night's show.

"Sorry I missed you backstage," Cameron said, hoping that he didn't appear too eager. "It was a bit crazy back there after the show."

Bambi's smile seemed to fade slightly. For a moment, he was afraid that her seemingly diminished enthusiasm was somehow a result of last night's situation with D'Lorenzo. Cameron was about to begin his carefully rehearsed explanation when she cut him off.

"We couldn't really stay," Bambi said. "My friends had to get home. They live in Winooski and they have a stricter curfew that we do. Their town pass only allows them to be out until a certain time.

We did stay after for a little while and met some of the people in the band, but I didn't have time to find you."

Cameron felt both relieved and concerned. No one in the band had mentioned that they'd talked to her.

"Oh, sorry I missed you," he said, secretly hoping the relief in his voice wasn't too obvious. "Who did you meet?"

I want to know, so I can kick their asses.

"Oh, I don't remember their names," she smiled. "I remember meeting some of the guys that work at the Civic Center. I recognized them from the tavern. I noticed your band members, but didn't dare introduce myself."

"Why on earth not?" Cameron exclaimed.

"I didn't want them to get the wrong idea about me," she whispered, leaning in toward him. "I didn't know if you had said that I was coming, and didn't want them to think I was like some of the other girls I saw there."

"You mean the groupies?" Cameron already knew the answer. He even suspected that he knew the women to whom she was referring.

"There were some girls there that made a point of acting like they were rather familiar with all of you, though we didn't quite believe them."

"Oh, we are familiar with them," Cameron admitted. He regretted his phraseology as soon as he saw the disheartened expression on her face.

"Not familiar in that way," he quickly added. "They come to the shows all the time and are some are our most faithful fans. Yes, some of them are problem children and take appreciation and friendship to rather dangerous extremes in their fantasies about the band, but there are certainly no serious relationships going on between any of them and *any* of us."

Bambi said nothing, silently considering his words. He could tell by the way she avoided his gaze that she was having a hard time believing him. She took another sip of coffee, holding the mug with both hands. The silence became uncomfortably palpable, and Cameron was tempted to break it. At last, though, Bambi spoke.

"I hear a lot of stories," she said.

"About me?"

"About musicians in general."

"There are a lot of stories to be told, I won't deny that," Cameron stated, looking her in the eyes. "Some of them are even true."

"Do you have any stories?" she asked, after another long pause. Cameron pondered his answer. On one hand, he didn't feel that he needed to explain himself, even to someone in whom he was developing an interest. On the other hand, since she was also developing an interest in him, Cameron felt that he should just be honest.

But is honesty always the best policy?

Cameron took a deep breath. "I do have a past," he said. "I won't deny that. I won't go into sordid details or lurid descriptions. I haven't done anything I'm ashamed of, but I'm no angel and no saint."

"Why not go into lurid descriptions?" Bambi asked. It seemed more like a demand. "Isn't that what being a rock star is all about?"

Cameron was amazed that he wasn't put off by her tone. After all, she had no reason to be offended by anything that he had done in his past, since theirs was merely a casual acquaintance at this point.

"Maybe for some," he replied. "I prefer an approach with a bit more substance. But just so you know, I'm not going into any details because I don't see the need to embarrass either of us."

"How would that embarrass me?"

"You strike me as a person that doesn't like to openly discuss details that are, shall we say, intimate, and I don't feel the need to offend you. I don't need to discuss any conquests just to stroke my ego. Therefore, not a topic for discussion."

Cameron felt relieved that she seemed to accept his answer. He didn't press the issue any further.

"You aren't what I expected to find," Bambi admitted.

"What were you expecting?"

"I expected to find all of the things that I'd read about," she admitted. "I had heard stories about bands destroying hotel rooms and assaulting the girls that came to their shows. I'd heard of stories of wild parties with lots of drugs and alcohol, where young girls would be drugged and violated. But you're different from that image. Very different. I expected to find a pig, not a gentleman."

Before Cameron could answer, he noticed Miss McIntyre bursting through the doorway. She paused briefly, trying to locate him, and then hurried over to his table.

"Walsh!"

Cameron laughed. "McIntyre!" he said, half jokingly.

"I'm glad I finally found you," she said, flushed and out of breath. Bambi, clearly startled, stared hard at this interloper who had suddenly appeared and situated herself amongst them. Cameron saw what he took for confusion and hurt in Bambi's eyes, and instantly felt the urge to tell McIntyre to go to hell. But then he saw the look in McIntyre's eyes. Her visage and posture were composed, but Cameron had realized long ago that this woman would never make it as a poker player. The expression in her eyes would always give her away, just as it was doing now. The look was not irritation at having had to hunt him down, but one of genuine concern. Something was definitely wrong. Cameron knew that McIntyre had an issue, but he also had to prevent Bambi from becoming one.

"Bambi, I would like you to meet McIntyre, uh, Miss McIntyre," he said. "She's the assistant to our Manager, Mr. Dwyer." Looking right into McIntyre's eyes, Cameron gestured with a flourish. "I would like *you* to meet Bambi."

McIntyre turned, feigning that she'd not seen Bambi, but not a good enough actress to pull it off. Cameron knew for a fact that McIntyre didn't miss much.

"Oh, I'm so sorry," McIntyre gasped, flushing even more and placing her hand to her mouth. She leaned forward in a slight bow, and offered Bambi her hand. "I didn't even see you there!"

Before Bambi had a chance to respond, the busybody waitress hurried over.

"Will you be joining them?" she asked McIntyre. Cameron thought that waitress's request was a bit hurried, but realized that she'd been avoiding their table for over an hour, probably due to a reprimand from her boss.

"No, I won't be staying," replied McIntyre. "I just need to talk to Cameron."

"Well, then, have a seat," he said. "Bambi and I were just having coffee and getting acquainted."

"I'd really love to," McIntyre answered. "But we've got to get back to the office and finish up some details about the show."

Cameron caught an edge in McIntyre's voice, one not usually present. He had to leave, he knew, but he was immensely enjoying Bambi's company, if only in a casual way at this point. He was not about to throw himself back into the isolation that had driven him so crazy of late. Not without a good explanation, that is.

"You guys can discuss gate receipts and lighting problems without me," Cameron said, trying to control his irritation. "I'll be over later."

"No," McIntyre insisted. "We need you there and we need to get going."

The waitress leaned down to fill Cameron's cup, and accidentally knocked it over, spilling coffee across the tablecloth. Bambi let out a cry and pushed her chair back. Cameron was about to say something when McIntyre grabbed him by the arm, giving it a slight squeeze. Looking McIntyre in the eyes, he could tell that she wasn't admonishing him for lack of control of his temper. She needed his help.

"I'm awful sorry," the waitress gushed, making feeble attempts to blot at the spill with a napkin. "Let me get you guys a fresh tablecloth and some more coffee."

"No. We're leaving," replied McIntyre. She looked at Cameron, then headed toward the door. Cameron arose to follow her. Before leaving, he paused next to Bambi.

"I'd really like to see you again," he told her, holding out his hand to help her up. "Are you free sometime this week?"

Bambi hesitated before speaking, looking nervously between Cameron and McIntyre, who was waiting impatiently at the door.

"I'm free... on Thursday," she said, hesitantly.

"Excellent!" Cameron beamed. "Would you like to meet at, say, six?"

Bambi nodded in agreement. Cameron leaned over to give her a kiss on the cheek. He paused for a moment to study her face, and gave her a warm smile. She smiled back, still holding his hand in hers. He kissed her on the hand and walked away toward McIntyre. Out on the street, he confronted her.

"This had better be fucking good," Cameron snarled. "If you dragged me out of there for another one of his fucking business meetings, then you two damn well better be packing!"

McIntyre stepped in closer to Cameron.

"Get out of my face," he warned.

"I'm not getting in your face," McIntyre said in a low voice. "I just don't want anyone else to hear. We've got a problem. A serious one."

"I can just imagine," Cameron sneered. "What? Dwyer can't get someone to do a radio interview? Does he want to make sure the lights will still be in the exact same spot for the second set as they were last night? Is he trying to set up another interview with the newspaper? What the fuck could be so important?"

"It's D'Lorenzo and Doug," she said. "We've got a problem with them."

Cameron felt his muscles tense. It finally happened. His roadie had finally reached his limit and snapped.

"What's the matter?" Cameron asked, no longer shouting. "What the fuck did they do now?"

"They've been poisoned."

CHAPTER FIFTEEN

"NAOMI"

Rich and Clyde were waiting in the hotel lobby for Cameron and McIntyre. Cameron thought it odd that the guys weren't really nervous or upset.

"Hey, man! I was wondering if they'd find you," Clyde laughed. "Dwyer's been rounding us all up, says he's got something to tell us."

"Man," said Cameron, "She said they'd been…"

"I think we should get upstairs." McIntyre cut Cameron off. "No need to air dirty laundry in public."

"Oh, come on," snapped Clyde. "So things got a little out of hand at the party last night! It's no big deal. It's not like it hadn't happened before or won't happen again!"

"I said, let's get upstairs." The tone of McIntyre's voice was irrefutable; she was not in the mood to argue either point. Rich and Clyde considered the merits of pressing the issue, but, deciding that it was not worth the hassle, followed McIntyre to the elevators. To everyone's surprise, she did not lead them to Dwyer's room, but went straight to Doug's room instead. Once inside, they found Dwyer sitting in one of the armchairs, his feet up on another. His face showed that he'd had little, if any, sleep the night before, and he did not get up or acknowledge them in any way. The two occupants of the room were both sleeping in their beds. Doug was lying on top of his bed, and would periodically toss and turn, occasionally eliciting a low moan. His hair was matted, and his shirt and pillow were soaked with sweat. D'Lorenzo was a different matter.

From what the guys could see, he was bare from the chest up and glistening with sweat. He lay flat on his back, his breathing labored and his color ashen. He appeared to be talking, but none of them could discern what he was saying. His eyes were open, staring at the ceiling. Neither D'Lorenzo nor Doug acknowledged that the others were there.

The band members observed Doug and D'Lorenzo, knowing that their respective conditions were not related to a simple case of sleeping off a good party, or of fending off a bad trip. The guys had seen such cases many times, and those situations bore little, if any, resemblance to what was going on right before their eyes.

"What the fuck happened to them?" whispered Clyde. As if to answer, Doug began to shudder as though suddenly submerged into freezing water.

"Mr. Dixon, please hurry," said Dwyer, rushing to the roadie's side. Evan came rushing out of the bathroom with a wastebasket and placed it next to Doug's head as Dwyer turned him over. Doug made a whimpering sound and began to vomit into the basket. Despite the fact that he expelled a clear liquid, the room stunk of burnt garlic.

"Oh, man," gagged Rich. "Open a window!"

"They're both open, Mr. Webster," replied Dwyer, wiping Doug's face with a damp cloth. "I can't open them much more without making it too cold in here for these two."

"Are they going to be all right?" asked Clyde.

"Shouldn't we call a doctor?!" Evan shouted, imploringly.

Dwyer disregarded Evan, and answered Clyde. "I certainly hope so, Mr. Poulin. Much depends on answers provided by you, gentlemen."

"Us?" said Cameron. "What the hell do we know about this? We barely saw them last night after the show."

Dwyer rolled Doug onto his back and faced the other band members.

"Yes, but you did see them at some point. That is the key. Did you notice what they were doing, or with whom they were talking?"

"I saw Doug talking with some of the stage guys," said Rich. "I stopped to talk to them a bit, but nothing much. They were talking about the lights and the sound system. Doug seemed pretty high when I was there."

"High?" said Dwyer. "What time? Was this immediately after the show, or later in the evening? When was it? Have you any idea what he might have taken?"

"He means that Doug was happy," corrected Clyde. "High means that he was in a good mood and pretty pleased with how things went, especially after all the fussing and arguing they had done.

When I was talking to him, he seemed to be in a good mood. Other than that, he seemed pretty straight. I don't think he even had more than a few beers by then. That was right after we put our guitars away in our room."

Dwyer contemplated this, his brow furrowed. Turning his attention to D'Lorenzo, Dwyer placed a damp cloth on the man's forehead. D'Lorenzo continued with his obscure murmurs while staring at the ceiling, eyes only half open. Cameron wondered if there was any risk that D'Lorenzo's eyes would dry out.

"Did any of you see Mr. D'Lorenzo during the course of the evening?" Dwyer asked, to no one in particular.

"I saw him right after the show, around the same time that I saw Doug," answered Clyde. "He was talking to some of the groupies. It was pretty funny, actually."

"I don't find anything humorous about this whatsoever," said Dwyer, his voice calm and even. "Please elaborate."

"I mean, he was trying to impress them with being part of the band and being so knowledgeable about us, and some of the groupies were leading him on, getting him to make a fool of himself."

"What do you mean, exactly?" Dwyer stared hard at Clyde, his voice still maintaining that calm, even tone that made them all nervous. Cameron found Dwyer's comportment especially irritating. He felt that, one day, Dwyer would blow a gasket, unable to keep his temper fettered.

Clyde eyed Dwyer. "They were asking him how long he had known us, and what our favorite things were and silly stuff. Nothing important."

"I will be the arbiter of what is and is not important, Mr. Poulin. Exactly what silly stuff?"

"They asked him about how we rehearse, where we like to eat, what we like to drink, if we have steady girlfriends, that sort of shit."

Dwyer stared at Clyde, saying nothing.

"And you found this "amazing, humorous"?"

"Well, yeah, I guess."

Dwyer took a step toward Clyde, but McIntyre intervened.

"You've had a long evening and little rest," she said to Dwyer. "This isn't going to get us anywhere." McIntyre turned to Clyde.

"Did you recognize these women at all?"

"Yeah, they were our regulars," he insisted. "Porky, Tits, and some other girl."

"Who!?" demanded Dwyer, his patience evaporating. "This is no time for humor!"

"Those were some of the girls that were hanging around backstage," Clyde murmured, sheepishly.

"Do you know their real names?"

"I think so," he answered. "Porky's name is Marguerite Swanson. We call her porky because…"

"Never mind that," snapped Evan. "I'm sure her Bohemian lifestyle doesn't interest him."

"Right," said Clyde. "Tits is Barbara Boobier. That's how she got the name "Tits," 'cause her last name sounds like *booby*."

"What about the other girl you mentioned?" asked McIntyre, visibly annoyed with them. "Do you know her at all?"

"No," Clyde said, after a moment's thought. "But she kind of looked familiar, and she looked a little like Tits, so I thought they might be related."

"But you were never introduced?" McIntyre asked incredulously. "She didn't introduce herself? You didn't think to ask her name? You just let a stranger wander around backstage?"

"What difference does that make?" Evan asked. "We've known those girls for years. They've been hanging out with us almost from the beginning. They wouldn't have done anything like this." Evan gestured toward Doug and D'Lorenzo.

"It makes a big difference," McIntyre insisted. "You had an unknown individual asking specific questions about you, and you didn't bother give it another thought?"

"No," said Cameron, who had been quietly observing the heated discourse from the corner of the room. "That shit happens all the time. Girls are always doing reconnaissance before they try to make a move. They ask questions, they hang out by the hotel, and they hang out by the stage door. They find out stuff about you so they can impress you and do stuff to get your attention so you'll choose them over someone else. It happens all the time."

Then he gave McIntyre a wicked grin.

"In fact," Cameron continued, smiling lasciviously, "If I'm not mistaken, there used to be this woman that would hang around the door during load-out. Her hair style resembled your curly, brown wig. She was about your build and your age, I think. Might have your eye color, too, but she wore tinted glasses, so I can't be sure. Besides, you told us to do things exactly the way we'd always done them, so why should we have changed last night? How were we supposed to know this shit would happen?"

McIntyre glared at Cameron, but for a moment, he felt sure that he detected a slight flush in her cheeks. McIntyre resumed the questioning.

"I still can't believe that not one of you at least *tried* to find out about that strange woman," she said. "Despite how you've done things in the past, you still can't let your guard down now."

"You're probably right, but that creates trouble," Rich said. "You start asking one girl about another, you run the risk of starting shit if the girl you asked already has an interest in you. If you start marking favorites, you set off rivalries and tensions that turn into feuds, and before you know it, you've got people fighting backstage. The best way to handle it is to let the girls come to you when they're ready. We learned that shit the hard way."

"You'll have to reconsider that approach," Dwyer said. "At the very least, you should maintain a casual awareness of *everyone* that comes in contact with you *from now on.*"

"But why?" insisted Rich. "We've done it this way forever. We know these people."

"After awhile, you learn not to trust anyone, or take anything for granted," McIntyre said. "Think about it. Why would someone be asking those questions?"

"Probably to teach D'Lorenzo a little humility," Cameron said. "He spends all his time strutting around acting like he's the expert on us, when he doesn't know a damn thing about us, or about anything we're doing. They probably wanted to bring him down a few pegs, leading him on to get him to make a mistake."

"Who was the other woman?" asked Dwyer.

"What?"

"Mr. Poulin identified two of them, but not the third. I am still curious to know who she was."

Everyone looked at Clyde, waiting for his answer. He began to fidget under their collective gaze.

"I think she came with one of them," he stammered. "I hadn't seen her before, but she was hanging out with them all night. I told you that I just assumed she'd come with them."

"Did anyone make any introductions?" asked Dwyer. Suddenly, D'Lorenzo began to moan again.

"No, not to me," Clyde said. "But I don't hang around with them much. They get too clingy and pushy."

"Did D'Lorenzo give any correct responses to their questions?"

"From what I heard, yeah. But he said some other shit that I can't say if it was true or not."

"Such as what?" McIntyre asked.

"Well, they asked him about himself, too. They seemed to take an interest in him."

"Really?" she said, her curiosity further piqued. "What did they ask him about?"

"Well, the same things, really. His favorite shit, stuff about him."

"Do you mean the girls you know, or the one you don't?"

"All of them, I guess."

"No, you don't guess! You remember, and you tell me who the hell it was!" Dwyer snapped, as he shoved his face, dark with anger, within a few inches of the guitar player's face.

"What are you getting so upset about?" Clyde asked, visibly shaken by his manager's uncharacteristic display of emotion. "It was just a couple of groupies! No big deal!"

"Look at them," Dwyer demanded, pointing to the men on the beds. "Look at them and tell me it wasn't any big deal!"

"I think you're all overreacting," Cameron said, and then turned to the others. "Did any of you see either of them drinking, especially beer?"

"Yeah, I did," said Rich. "Someone had a bottle of rye whiskey and offered some to Doug, but he turned it down. He said he wanted to stay straight tonight. He was sticking to beer, from what I saw."

"Yeah," said Evan. "D'Lorenzo said the same thing. I spoke to him a little bit here and there, but he seemed fine then."

"But they were drinking, though, right?" demanded Cameron. The other guys all agreed.

"There, you see?" Cameron said, triumphantly. "I bet they were dosed. Someone must have slipped something into their drinks during the party. Unfortunate, but not uncommon."

Dwyer began to nod, but then shook his head. He didn't believe that the poisoning of two men was a mere coincidence.

"Have you ever seen a reaction that resembles this?" Dwyer asked the group.

"No," Cameron conceded. "But that doesn't necessarily mean anything. People are making homemade booze. You can't tell me they're not making homemade drugs, too. God alone knows what they're putting in it."

Dwyer seemed to accept this argument, and nodded his head, this time in agreement.

"I won't deny that," he said. "But I'm afraid that it doesn't apply in this case, though the argument you made is one they'd hoped we would consider."

"How can you be so fucking sure?" Cameron snapped. "Do you know something we don't know?"

"How closely do you gentlemen follow the news?" Dwyer asked. They shrugged in response. No one said anything, and Dwyer had his answer.

"Do any of you recall hearing coverage of a substance called MK-ULTRA?"

"I think so," Rich said. "Wasn't that something about secret tests or some shit?"

"That's the gist of it," Dwyer sighed. "It referred to a series of tests of ambiguous legality that were officially, though secretly, conducted many years ago. Reports leaked out about some of the tests, and Congress had a field day with it. That program was known as MK-ULTRA."

"We were trying to determine the effects of certain drugs on specific demographics," continued McIntyre. "We wanted to know how to recognize if any of our people or political figures had been drugged, and how the drugs could be most efficaciously administered."

The band members stared at her, slack-jawed. It was Rich that spoke up.

"And how they'd be if you administered them to someone else, too, right?"

McIntyre nodded, her face bare of emotion.

"The ULTRA program that caused a huge fuss was simply the successor to other programs that were officially dropped."

"You say "officially" like it doesn't matter," said Cameron. "You mean they went on with the programs, don't you?"

"Yes," Dwyer nodded. "One of them was MKNAOMI. That was the most promising program. It led to ULTRA and another, even more secret, program, MKSPECTER."

"I never heard anything about them," said Cameron.

"You wouldn't have," said Dwyer. "The first program was discontinued long before any of the hearings took place. The second program was kept so secret that only a dozen or so people knew about it. That is the one that most concerns me now."

"Why?"

"Because some of the project leaders of NAOMI and ULTRA were frustrated by the results of several test drugs administered, and they wanted us to develop our own versions. We conducted research and attempted to develop a substance similar to a combination of LSD and sodium pentothal."

"I know what LSD is," said Clyde. "But I've never heard of that other shit."

"You've probably heard it called by another name," Dwyer explained. "They call it truth serum."

"You mean it makes you tell the truth?"

"Not really," he said. "I mean that it makes it more difficult for one to lie. It relaxes inhibitions and causes confusion so that a person is more likely to disclose what they know and what they are thinking, instead of trying to create or recall a cover story. In the right dosage, it can be somewhat effective. However, it is not completely reliable. Therefore, the program heads wanted something more potent and easier to control, so they began developing a substance of their own, called Spectorol. At first, they thought that it was the answer they were looking for."

"But I take it that wasn't it?" asked Clyde.

"Not at all," said Dwyer. "It proved to be even more unpredictable than the other substances. The results were less reliable, and the side effects even worse."

"What were they?" Cameron asked, lighting a cigarette..

"Hallucinations, reduced heart rate, nausea, respiratory depression, emergence delirium, and sometimes death."

"You know an awful lot about this," accused Cameron.

"I worked on MKSPECTOR."

No wonder you didn't want us to call a doctor.

An uneasy silence hung over the room. The guys understood that Dwyer, and the others, were secret agents, and had made peace with that a long time ago. However, now Dwyer was admitting to involvement with undercover projects performed against their own fellow Americans. *That* was difficult to overlook.

"Are Doug and D'Lorenzo going to die?" demanded Cameron. Dwyer shook his head.

"I have no way of knowing," he said, turning back to the beds. "The effects depend upon so many variables—weight, body fat, preexisting conditions, solid and liquid consumption before the drug is administered, and so on."

"So you think one of the groupies did it?" asked Evan, returning once again from rinsing the wastebasket.

"I think the party provided someone with the cover they needed," Dwyer replied.

"That doesn't make any sense," said Rich. "We aren't doing anything. You said all we were supposed to be doing was listening for stuff and reporting on that. How would they have known, and why would they have done something like this? Wouldn't it have been easier for them to simply not hang around here and not say anything?"

"Yes, it would," agreed Dwyer. "However, I believe the game has changed. I think they were after a specific target."

"Who. Us?"

"No," replied Dwyer. "I think they were after Mr. D'Lorenzo."

"Why would they go after him?" snickered Clyde. "What's so special about him?"

Dwyer stood, his back to them, pensive. Finally, he answered.

"Mr. D'Lorenzo and Mr. Courtland have a bit of history together, Mr. Poulin," he explained. "I believe it has something to do with that."

"What kind of history?" Clyde laughed. "Those two couldn't stand one another!"

"And you think that people simply like or dislike without prior provocation?" asked Dwyer.

"You didn't know Dougie," Clyde smiled. "He made up his mind just by looking at you, and precious little would get him to change it, either. It's either like or hate with him and nothing in between, only varying degrees of either one."

"You are no doubt correct," Dwyer conceded. "However, not in this case. Mr. Courtland and Mr. D'Lorenzo once had a mutual acquaintance, one Gus Kalbe. Mr. Kalbe was a researcher who had worked with a team that was developing a new system of radar, a system of interest to the Pentagon. Mr. D'Lorenzo was the one that convinced Mr. Kalbe to return to work on the project."

"What does that have to do with Doug?"

"Mr. Courtland was a roommate of Mr. Kalbe's, as well as a former classmate and close friend. Mr. Courtland made the acquaintance with Mr. D'Lorenzo during that time, and he knew of D'Lorenzo's efforts to get his roommate to join the crew on the U.S.S. Mustang."

"The one that blew up at the North Pole?" asked Clyde.

"Hardly the north pole, Mr. Poulin," Dwyer explained. "But it was above the Arctic Circle."

"But didn't the Mustang sink?"

"No. It blew up," replied McIntyre. "At first they thought that it was a Soviet strike, but we now suspect that it was sabotage."

"Why do you think that?"

"That really isn't important now," interrupted Dwyer. "Before D'Lorenzo had been given that assignment, he worked on SPECTER. I know because I was working on it with him."

"What did you guys do?" asked Rich.

"I can assure you, Mr. Webster, you do not want to know."

"But what the fuck does that have to do with all of this?" Cameron asked. He, for one, was growing short of patience.

Dwyer ignored Cameron and continued. "From what I have been able to gather from both Mr. D'Lorenzo's rantings and Mr. Courtland's report before he lost consciousness, it has everything to do with it."

"How so?" McIntyre asked.

"Mr. Courtland said that when he helped Mr. D'Lorenzo into the bathroom, he kept mumbling certain words over and over again. To him, they seemed nonsensical, but that is only to be expected, considering he was not only aroused from sleep, but apparently also under the effect of that drug as well."

"What did he say, exactly?" McIntyre asked again.

"He said he couldn't make out everything, but he caught the words *pickles, radio, mustard,* and *tan.*"

"And that shit is supposed to connect this together?" cried Cameron. "The bastard mumbles how he wants a sandwich and you've uncovered some plot? Oh, my fucking word! I don't believe what the hell I am hearing!"

"If you are quite through, Mr. Walsh I will explain why I have come to these conclusions," said Dwyer. Except for a slight narrowing of his eyes, his features and voice displayed no irritation. The rest of them knew what lay beneath the surface.

"Then go ahead," snapped Cameron. "I'm all fucking ears!"

"Captain Pickering was the captain of the Mustang," said Dwyer. "The Mustang was a special mobile radar station. Pickering can sound like "pickles," radar resembles "radio," and so on."

"I have to admit, that sounds incredibly farfetched to me, too," said McIntyre. "Are you positive you're not grasping at straws?"

"Not entirely, no," Dwyer admitted. "But considering how insistent he was, I stand by my assumption."

"I think it's just a guilty conscience coming out," grumbled Cameron. "He knew the reason Doug hated his fucking guts was because he got his friend to sign on with the Mustang. That's been the source of all the tension between them this whole time. That was the reason you wanted to stick them together, hoping one of them would let something slip. Well, now it's fucking happened! Your man is actually feeling guilty!"

"I think your conclusion is as farfetched as Dwyer's," said McIntyre.

"She's right," said Rich. "I think he was just talking through his hat. The booze and whatever he took must have addled him, and he was just rambling."

"That is a possibility, I grant you," said Dwyer.

"But you're not convinced, are you?" asked McIntyre.

"No, I'm afraid I'm not," he replied. Dwyer sat back down on the edge of D'Lorenzo's bed, the other man giving no indication that he was aware of his supervisor's presence.

"Why do you think this had anything to do with that other project you were working on?" asked Evan.

"Before Mr. D'Lorenzo lost consciousness, he tried to communicate something to me. I was unable to discern most of what he was saying, but I very clearly heard the word, "Naomi." After that, he passed out."

"Naomi could have been the name of that other girl," insisted Cameron, still irritable. "I think you're just jumping to a lot of conclusions!"

"Perhaps I am, Mr. Walsh," Dwyer agreed. "But don't you think that there are too many coincidences here?"

"Perhaps he was just rambling then, too," offered Evan. "We really don't have any reason to suspect anything else."

Dwyer nodded, resting his chin in his hands. He stared at the floor.

"There are just a few things that are puzzling me," Dwyer said at last. "First of all, did any of you see either Mr. D'Lorenzo or Mr. Courtland leave after the show?"

They all answered in the negative.

"That's unusual," muttered Dwyer to McIntyre. Looking back at the guys, he said, "That he could leave and not be noticed by any of you?"

"Not that unusual," said Cameron. "Once he's done his work, he's free to do whatever he wants. Sometimes he sticks around, sometimes he takes off with some of the girls."

"That is what he did last night," said Dwyer. "He said that there were some girls that were trying to hang out with him, but he didn't like them. He said they only wanted to meet the band, and they kept asking him questions. He felt uncomfortable and tried to get away from them. I wonder what they were asking?"

"That's not such a big mystery," said Evan. "Doug gets very touchy about his position. He thinks people look down on him since he's a roadie, and when he thinks he's just being used to get close to us, then he gets defensive. There's been a lot of times when groupies, club owners, reporters, and so on, have come on very strong and really turned him off. We've told him he has to be nice to them, but he doesn't have to hang out with them."

"Has that ever prevented you from having contact with those people?" asked Dwyer, seeming to consider what Evan was saying.

"No," he replied. "For all of his faults, he's professional, and unless he has a really good reason, he won't try to stand in the way of someone meeting us."

"Did he make any introductions last night with *any* of you?"

They each shook their heads, and explained that they had been elsewhere. Clyde and Rich had been talking to some of their old friends, and Evan turned in early to talk to his family. Cameron had been with Dwyer most of the night before returning to his room, alone.

"Are any of the women who came to the show last night booked here in this hotel?" McIntyre pressed.

"I doubt it," said Evan.

"We have to find out," McIntyre asked Dwyer.

Dwyer agreed. "I will check with the front desk and see who registered recently, and has not checked out today. If they came in for the concert, they will not be able to travel on weekends due to the enforced travel restrictions. We will compare that list of names against the groupies with whom you are familiar. We will contact the names you don't recognize. I suggest a call telling them that one of their peers misplaced an item and is looking for it."

"One of who?" asked Cameron, visibly confused.

"It is likely that both men were at a party last night," Dwyer explained. "We need to find out with whom, and where."

"That would be an impossibility," insisted Cameron. "Doug hates D'Lorenzo. He would never have gone to any party that D'Lorenzo was attending, no matter how badly he wanted to."

"Is it likely that there was more than one function after the show?"

"Oh, I'm sure," said Evan. "Some of the groupies like hanging around with each other as much as they do with us, especially if they were new people that didn't know the others that well."

Dwyer bit his lower lip, his brow knitted in concentration.

"We will stick to the plan. We will call the ones you know, and use the "lost item" excuse," Dwyer said. "That way, we can narrow down information on their whereabouts. Do any of you recall seeing *any*one that appears to be staying at this hotel that was also at the show or was with us backstage?"

The guys shook their heads.

Dwyer seemed perplexed. He shook his head.

"Why not?" Rich asked. "What difference does it make?"

"Mr. Courtland insisted that he attended a party here at the hotel with some of the new people that he had met after the concert."

"Wait a minute," Cameron said. "Did you say that Doug told you he attended a party with people he didn't know?"

"That's correct," said Dwyer. "He met them after the show and came back here and went to their room. He said he left later on when he began to feel ill. Why do you ask?"

Cameron sat on the edge of Doug's bed and nodded at Dwyer.

"Ok, man," he said. "I think you've finally convinced me that there is some freaky shit going on."

Dwyer raised one eyebrow in inquiry. Cameron continued.

"Well, for one thing, you said that Doug told you before that he did not like the new people he met. Now you say he was in their room at a party. That's not possible. If Doug doesn't like you, he doesn't hang out with you, period. Remember what we told you about him. There is no half way in his attitude toward you. We've known him for years and he has never changed. If he suddenly did last night, there was a reason for it, and I bet it wasn't his decision."

Dwyer nodded.

"I think you need to tell me a little more about that NAOMI thing, too," Cameron pressed.

Dwyer looked at him, saying nothing.

Cameron told Dwyer about Doug's complaint that D'Lorenzo had been ill several times lately, after going out for the evening.

"Doug thought that he had been getting some bad food, or some bad booze. I thought so, too, when he told me."

"I take it you don't agree with that conclusion?" asked Dwyer.

"No, I don't," said Cameron. "Not after last night. I also don't think this was sudden, either. I think it's been building up."

Dwyer studied him, but did not speak. Cameron parked a direct gaze on Dwyer.

"How is this shit given to someone?" he asked.

"It was designed to be delivered several ways," Dwyer answered. "It could be dissolved in liquid, swallowed in capsule form, or administered intravenously."

"You mentioned that one of the side effects was nausea, right?"

"That's correct," agreed Dwyer. He spoke slowly, analyzing the new information, ultimately reaching Cameron's conclusions. "I checked the contents of the wastebaskets when Mr. Courtland and Mr. D'Lorenzo vomited, but was unable to find any capsules, pills or remnants thereof."

"I'm willing to bet that he was being drugged all along, and they were trying to work out the correct dosage," said Cameron. "They didn't do it right the first few times and decided to do it big time this time around. Before, they just made him sick. This time they fucked him up."

"That is something to consider," agreed Dwyer.

"Yeah," Cameron said. "You said D'Lorenzo came back here stark naked, right?"

"That's correct," said Dwyer. "Mr. Courtland said that he awoke to find Mr. D'Lorenzo standing in the middle of the room, completely nude."

"Where are his clothes?" asked Cameron. "I don't see them anywhere."

"We were unable to find them," conceded Dwyer. "When we make the phone calls, we have more than one valid reason to inquire about missing property. I can only assume that he left his personal effects in someone's room."

"That's what worries me."

"Why?"

"These doors lock when you shut them," he said. "D'Lorenzo was buck-assed naked when Doug woke up and saw him, right?"

"That is correct."

"Then how did he get into the room?"

Chapter Sixteen
"On Guard"

Cameron was lying on his bed, watching the smoke from his cigarette drift toward the ceiling, replaying in his mind the events of the day. He felt that there was something being overlooked, but he couldn't figure out what.

Shit. They're the forensic experts. Let them figure it out.

But they weren't figuring it out; at least, not fast enough for him.

The Roadhouse Sons had stayed with Doug, D'Lorenzo, Dwyer and McIntyre for the greater part of the day when things took an interesting turn. Doug suddenly tossed and turned a great deal more than he had been. He was also steadily muttering in his sleep. Gradually, the words were clearer and Doug became semi-awake and more lucid. However, he had no awareness of his surroundings, and was near hysteria as he was waking up.

"Emergence delirium," Dwyer explained. "But I've never seen it like this before!"

It took several of them to hold Doug to the bed, his arms and legs flailing wildly about.

"Where's my hat?" he cried, to no one in particular. "Where's my hat?"

Doug resisted any efforts to calm him, ignoring their soothing words and giving no indication that he was aware of their identities, let alone their very presence. Cameron was concerned. He knew people who had dropped acid, causing irreparable damage to themselves, and he feared that Doug might have done the same thing. As the roadie's cries became manic, Cameron's fear and frustration grew. In an effort to calm the man down, he searched the room for his friend's cap, finding it, at last, under the bed.

Giving Doug his hat was like tossing a preserver to a drowning man. As Doug turned the hat over in his hands, his agitation subsided. Eventually, he collapsed back onto the bed. His cries gave way to mumbles, and he clutched his hat to his breast.

"What the fuck was so important about that stupid thing?" wondered Clyde.

Cameron agreed. Doug's hat was a typical trucker cap, with a black front panel and visor and a mesh background that, at one point, had been white but now was a dirty grey. The plastic size adjuster tab was broken now held in place by a section of gaffer's tape, the color of which matched the front. The visor was worn and tattered, with scattered spots revealing the cardboard underneath the cloth. After so much use, the visor had long ago lost its gentle curve, and was creased and peaked. It had neither writing nor symbols on its front, but it appeared that Doug had written on the inside of it, the inscription now faded. There was certainly nothing to give this hat the importance that Doug attached to it in his current state of delirium.

Eventually, Doug attempted to sit up and he was finally able to acknowledge their presence. He responded to questions, recognizing his inquisitors and identifying his surroundings. He was still quite weak. He had asked for a glass of water, but vomited as soon as he consumed it.

"You need to sip it," McIntyre told Doug, wiping his face with a towel.

"Did you work on that project too?" Cameron asked. He wouldn't have been surprised if she had.

"No, but I did used to work in a hospital," she said without looking at him. "This isn't all that different from certain effects of anesthesia, which it can make you sick for a while."

"How long is he going to be like that?" Evan asked.

"The effects can sometimes last as long as thirty-six hours," said Dwyer. "In some cases, even more."

Cameron watched his friend closely. There was no mistaking that Doug was completely out of it, but he was gradually coming down from whatever substance he'd been fed. Cameron looked over D'Lorenzo, who showed little improvement.

"What the fuck happened?" Doug moaned. As best they could, Dwyer and the others explained the situation, and inquired about the previous night. Did he, in fact, go to a party with any of the new people he'd met at the show? Did he go to a party at all? If so, where was it held and how did he get back to his room? Doug couldn't answer any of their questions. He was unable to focus directly on anything and, therefore, provided no information of any substance. His vague, partial recollections of the previous evening did nothing to bring the group any closer to understanding who could drug these two men, or why.

Eventually, Dwyer and McIntyre concluded that they had done as much as possible for the time being. They insisted that Doug get some rest, and, for once, Doug didn't argue with his fellow human beings. He fell back onto the bed, his hat still clutched tightly in his hand.

"For the rest of you, try and contact as many of the people known to have attended the concert last night. We must locate as many of these individuals as is possible," said Dwyer. "Most importantly, we must ascertain whether those people made contact with any of the local crowds, or the new faces."

"That's a hell of a long shot," said Cameron.

"Do you have a better suggestion?" Dwyer retorted.

Cameron had to admit that he didn't. Dwyer issued a warning before he left.

"I don't need to tell you that things have changed, considerably," he said. "From now on, we play by the Game Rules."

The guys knew that they would have no choice but to utilize all of Dwyer's and McIntyre's counter-surveillance techniques. This time, the guys did not argue.

While Cameron, Clyde, Evan and Rich returned to their rooms to make the phone calls, Dwyer went to the front desk to inquire about any parties or unusual activity on the previous night. McIntyre stayed in Doug's room to monitor him and D'Lorenzo.

Before he left, Clyde pulled McIntyre aside. "This stuff isn't deadly, is it? I mean, it just gives you one hell of a trip, right?"

"In sufficient dosage, anything can be lethal," she said. "Even alcohol. However, neither of them were given enough of the drug to cause permanent harm, or else they'd be dead by now."

Cameron hung back, listening to their conversation. He decided that McIntyre's words made him feel better, but only a little. Cameron checked on Doug and D'Lorenzo one last time before leaving. Doug was rubbing his eyes, as though that very action would force him into focus. D'Lorenzo was sleeping now, his breathing steady and even, no longer shallow and labored.

Maybe they will get through this.

Cameron, his mind still unsettled, returned to his room to make the phone calls. He wasn't feeling any better as he conversed with various friends about the night before.

Everyone wanted to talk either about the show and the after-party, or catching up since the last time they'd all seen one another. Cameron was distracted. He was having difficulty focusing on the purpose of the calls. However, he was grateful that he had listened to Evan's advice.

"Listen, we have to decide on a cover story and stick to it," Evan had counseled. "And we need to make it not only something they'll buy, but also something we'll remember. I think I've got an idea what to say. We tell them that Doug lost a set of keys to the band truck and we need to find them before we have to do the Barre show next week. The only thing he remembers is that he was at a party with some of the groupies after the show. Did they see him anywhere and do they know where his keys are? That's what we ask."

The band agreed that Evan's was the best story, as it was totally plausible; everyone loses keys, and anyone who knew the band would know that Doug rarely talked to anyone other than the guys. It wouldn't raise any suspicion if the guys called instead of Doug.

Cameron found himself caught up in other conversations, as well. Oftentimes, he had to suddenly switch gears to bring the conversation back to the reason for his call.

Goddamn! It's a good thing we kept this simple.

His mind drifted, too, as he was not only worried about Doug and D'Lorenzo, but about the three shows coming up that week, on Wednesday, Friday and Saturday.

And Bambi on Thursday...

Cameron smiled, grateful for the ray of sunshine in these longer than momentary clouds. Just then, there was a knock at his door. For a moment, Cameron considered being completely still to see if whoever it was would go away. He desperately needed some rest. There was too much happening too fast, and he needed time to process it all. As if to contradict his thoughts, the knocking became louder and more insistent. He realized that whoever it was knew he was in there, and had no intention of leaving him alone. It took Herculean effort to get up off the bed, and Cameron knew that his fatigue was not merely a result of the long night before. He also knew that there wasn't a hell of a lot he could do about it.

Cameron suddenly hesitated as he was about to open the door. Something in his gut told him not to turn the knob. The knocking resumed, louder, but with no more urgency. Cameron wondered if the housekeeping staff was outside, but remembered that he had placed the "Do Not Disturb" sign on the door. It could be one of the guys, but he doubted that. They would have said something. He also ruled out Dwyer and McIntyre; neither of them would give in to such a sense of urgency, even if bombs were falling on Washington. D'Lorenzo was probably still out cold, and even if he were somewhat better, he wouldn't be able to get out of bed, let alone stumble down the hall to knock on Cameron's door. Nor would Doug, who was probably not much better off than his roommate.

So, who the fuck are you?

Cameron crept closer to the door, silently looking through the peephole into the hallway.

Who the fuck ARE you?

In the hallway stood a woman whom he'd never before seen. She was dressed in torn jeans, worn suede boots, and an oversized down jacket that had clearly seen better days. A wide scarf was wrapped around her neck, and she wore a pair of large, rose tinted glasses. Her hair was dark brown and wavy and hung loose about her shoulders. She looked up and down the hallway, shifting her weight from one leg to the other, hiking her large, heavy purse farther up her arm. Her movements suggested impatience.

Are you nervous?

Cameron opened the door slowly.

"Hey there," he smiled, trying to be pleasant. "Can I help you?"

"Oh, my God," the woman gasped. "It really is you, isn't it?"

"I think so," laughed Cameron. "But I'll be honest. I haven't been feeling quite myself lately, so anything's possible."

The woman laughed at his bon mot, a little too eagerly, Cameron thought. He instantly pegged her as a groupie.

"Can I come in?" she asked, and began to blush. "Oh, my God, I am so sorry!" she cried, putting her hand over her mouth. "I didn't mean to be so forward."

The hell you didn't.

"Oh, no problem," assured Cameron. "What did you say your name was?"

The woman stepped back, a look of surprise on her face.

"Oh, I didn't introduce myself, did I?"

Cameron shook his head, smiling.

"Oh, my name is..." The woman hesitated before answering. "Ruby. Ruby Martin."

"Well, Ruby Martin, it is nice to meet you," Cameron said, stepping aside so she could enter his room. As she did so, he glanced quickly up and down the corridor to see who else was there, but noticed no one, except for the cleaning lady a few doors down. Ruby stood in the center of the room, clutching her purse under one arm, the other hand grabbing onto the strap as though it were a lifeline. She seemed to be trembling a bit as she looked at him.

"To what do I owe this surprise?" Cameron asked, still smiling in an attempt to put the woman at ease. It certainly wasn't unusual to have strange women mysteriously show up at his door, and this situation gave Cameron a comforting sense of familiarity. Regardless, recent events dictated that he employ caution.

Ruby's voice was what one would call "smoky, " imparting a slight rasp.

"Oh, I've been trying to meet you," she said, taking a step toward Cameron, then halting.

"Well, this is your lucky day," he smiled.

She smiled nervously, tilting her head back to get a better look at him. Cameron began to suspect that she wore a disguise, perhaps to hide from a boyfriend or even a husband. He didn't feel like pressing the issue, knowing that he probably wouldn't like the answer.

"Would you like to sit down?" he asked. She gave no indication that she had actually heard him. Now, Cameron was becoming nervous.

"It was a great show last night," Ruby said, the words firing rapidly, as if not to change her mind.

"Well, thank you," he said. "I'm glad you enjoyed it. Have you been to one of our gigs before?" She shook her head in response. Her hair suggested a lion's mane as it moved. Realizing that this awkward dance of words was getting him nowhere quickly, Cameron decided to begin directing the situation.

"I'd offer you a drink," he apologized. "But I'm afraid I don't have anything at the moment." He wanted to know if she was here for a particular purpose, or if she was just a typical fan.

"Oh," she said, with little attempt to conceal her disappointment. "That's all right, I guess."

"Would you like to sit down?"

"Oh, right. Thank you."

Cameron was about to offer her a chair, when Ruby sat herself down on the edge of the bed. Looking at him, she smiled, but still clutched her purse, almost as though it was a shield. Something about her manner set Cameron on guard. He sat in the chair himself, but straddled it with its back turned out, as though it was a shield of his own. He was about to say something, when there was another knock at the door. The knocking stopped, then started again.

Shit, the signal!

Not wanting Ruby to learn it and possibly try it later, Cameron quickly made his way to the door. Looking through the peephole, he saw that it was McIntyre. He flung the door open wide, an exaggerated smile on his face. McIntyre stood awkwardly at the threshold, her hand in position to finish the secret knock. The woman on the bed let out a shriek and dashed into the bathroom, slamming the door behind her.

"Am I interrupting something?" McIntyre asked, still standing in the doorway.

"I honestly have no fucking idea," Cameron whispered.

"Um, who was that?"

"Ruby, somebody or other. I don't remember her last name."

"That memorable, eh?"

Cameron just shook his head.

"She just got here. Hasn't said a full sentence and just sits there. But she is giving me the royal fucking creeps, to be honest."

McIntyre motioned for him to step out into the hall.

"Dwyer wants to meet us," she whispered. "He thinks he's found something."

"What?"

"He wouldn't say over the phone. He said to bring only you, and he wants to see us now."

"What about the other guys?"

"Evan and Clyde are staying with the Doug and D'Lorenzo, and Rich is getting some soup from one of the diners for them. Doug is coming around pretty quickly and D'Lorenzo is showing a lot of improvement."

Cameron made no attempt to hide his relief.

"But what do we do about old Ruby?" he asked.

"Leave her to me," McIntyre smiled. Stepping into the room, she began to knock on the bathroom door.

"Ruby, honey," she said. "I need to get in there, please. Cammy and I have to go out and I need to freshen my makeup."

At first, the door remained closed and there was no indication that anyone was actually in the bathroom. McIntyre rapped more forcefully on the door. This had the desired result, and the door opened. Ruby stood, framed by the bathroom door, her hand over her mouth. She then pushed past McIntyre to the door of the room. Pausing there, she noticed that McIntyre was not heading into the bathroom, but was standing there staring at her.

"Oh, I'm so sorry," Ruby gasped, still holding her hand over her mouth. She dashed down the hallway before anyone could speak.

"Close the door," McIntyre said quietly.

"That was a little strange," Cameron said, but was waved into silence by McIntyre. He watched as she carefully made her way around the bathroom, inspecting every square foot. She moved slowly and methodically, absorbing everything she saw.

"What are you..." but she motioned for Cameron to be quiet. Cautiously, McIntyre moved her hand around the doorframe and the window frame, finally testing the window itself. It yielded under her touch, and slid partially open. Cameron was about to tell McIntyre that the window was supposed to be locked, but a furtive glance from her reminded him to remain silent. The opening of the window was just wide enough for McIntyre to poke her head through it. She seemed to be observing something outside. McIntyre pulled her head back in. Slowly, she shut the window and resumed her search of the bathroom. Satisfied that there was nothing of any importance there, she went back into the main room.

"What the fuck was that all about?" Cameron demanded.

"Even you had to notice that she was wearing a crappy disguise," McIntyre replied. "First of all, crows don't have hair that black. Second of all, she had to tilt her head back so that she could see out of her glasses, plus an oversized coat and a scarf? Come *on*! She was obviously trying to hide."

"I don't mean to sound egotistical, but she could have been trying to go unrecognized by someone that would rat her out to a husband or boyfriend."

"That does sound egotistical."

"But not unheard of, and not something that hasn't happened to me before."

"I don't doubt that," McIntyre agreed. "Under normal circumstances, I would even agree with you, but I don't think being a possible paramour was why she was here, or why she was hiding."

"How do you know that?"

"The window was unlocked," she explained. "You always keep it locked. She was in here long enough to dispose of something, and the only means that she had was to toss it out the window. When I looked, I noticed that there were bushes right below and she was just coming around the corner heading toward them. She started to look for something and ran off when a car approached. I think we need to check out the area when we go to see Dwyer."

"What do you think she dropped?"

"I don't know, but it's worth a look."

As they rode down in the elevator, Cameron laughed to himself.

"What's so funny?" McIntyre asked.

"'Cammy'?"

"If I have to clean up your messes, I get to call you whatever I want," she said with a smug grin.

Outside, Cameron and McIntyre went around the corner of the building toward the parking lot. Looking up at the windows, McIntyre oriented herself by comparing different locations in the parking lot. Eventually, she located the bushes under Cameron's window. The two of them looked in and around the bushes, but Cameron didn't feel like he was helping very much.

"What are we looking for?"

"Something small. Something that doesn't belong here," McIntyre replied.

"That's a big fucking help, by the way."

"That's really my criteria," she shrugged. "Do you see anything over there?"

"Bottle caps, cigarette butts, wrappers. That's about it."

"Check the bottle caps," she said. "Do any of them look funny?"

"No, not really," he said. "Wait, this one's just plain."

"Give it to me!"

Cameron reached down and grabbed what he thought was a bottle cap. He quickly discovered that this was no bottle cap. It was half the size of one, and he knew that it would never cover the opening of a bottle. He examined it closely. He didn't recognize it as anything with which he was familiar. He handed it to McIntyre, who examined it herself.

"What is it?"

"A bug," she said.

Cameron stared at the small device, which he'd mistaken for a piece of trash.

"How do you know she dropped it here?"

"I only suspected that she'd dropped something. I wasn't sure what it was, but she certainly acted like she had something to hide."

Cameron was dumbfounded.

"What the hell was she going to do with that?"

"Obviously, she was going to bug someone's room. No doubt yours."

"What the fuck would she want to do that for?"

"Think about it," McIntyre said. "The guys being drugged. This. Obviously our little network isn't as secret as we'd thought."

"Who's doing it?"

McIntyre shook her head.

"I don't think it's my place to say," she explained. "Dwyer has been working with some new information, trying to track some possible leads. I think that's why he wants to see us now. Is your car here?"

Cameron led her around to the other side of the building. They climbed into Cameron's Mustang and left the parking lot.

"Where to?" he asked. McIntyre gave him directions to a place a few blocks away from the Civic Center.

"Park up there and we'll walk down."

"Why not just park there at the Center?"

"We don't want to draw attention to what we're doing, or tip anyone off, in case the building's being watched, which we're pretty certain it is. We park up above it and walk down toward it. If the coast is clear, Dwyer said he'd leave a signal for us. If there's a signal, we go in and take a look around."

"And if not?"

"We go back to the hotel and wait for him to contact us."

To their right, the Civic Center loomed as they approached. As instructed, Cameron continued past it for three blocks. He pulled into a parking space just off the street.

"Are you ready for the real stuff?" she asked him.

"What do you mean?"

"No more practicing in the safe house," McIntyre explained. "And no more just listening to see what information you can overhear. Now, you start hunting and you get them before they get you."

"Pardon me, but it seems like they've already gotten us."

"Any casualties so far?"

"Pretty fucking close," Cameron snapped, thinking of Doug and D'Lorenzo.

"Close only counts in horseshoes."

"And hand grenades."

"Oh, I hope it isn't going to get to that."

"Promise?"

"I wish," McIntyre sighed, getting out of the car.

Cameron zipped up his coat as they headed down the street toward the Civic Center. He had a thousand questions running through his mind, but he realized that there was no way to ask them here. The sidewalk was filled with people.

McIntyre slipped her arm through his.

"Just act casual," she said in a low voice, smiling up at him. "A couple out window shopping is less likely to draw attention."

He smiled back, going along with her suggestion. As they made their way down the street, they paused from time to time, pointing at landmarks or reading posters. To the world around them, they appeared to be a couple out for a pleasant afternoon. Eventually, they made their way to the Civic Center. With McIntyre reassuring Cameron that they weren't being watched, they made their way to the stage entrance at the back of the building. Once there, McIntyre carefully checked the wall around the door.

"What are you looking for?" asked Cameron.

"Dwyer leaves a certain mark when he's trying to get a message to us," she explained. "I'll try to find it. You keep your eyes open for anyone hanging around or coming our way."

"What kind of symbol?" Cameron asked, watching the parking area closest to them. It was empty, but he realized that this lot was often used as a shortcut from one street to the other, so there was bound to be someone coming eventually.

"A straight line if it isn't safe," she said. "And a slash if it is."

"That doesn't seem too easy to spot."

"That's the idea, remember? You only want the person you chose to find it, not everyone else."

"Find anything yet?"

"Am I still looking?"

"Just asking," Cameron laughed. "No need to be sarcastic."

"One of the problems with him is he's so damn good, you can't always spot it right away."

"So, what do we do?" Cameron asked again. "Because here comes some kid on a skateboard."

Without saying a word, she turned and grabbed him in a tight embrace, locking him in a passionate kiss.

"What the hell was that for?" he gasped when she finally released him.

"I didn't want to raise suspicion by having us just hang around. If the kid thought that we were just trying to find a place to make out, we wouldn't seem so conspicuous to him."

"Did you find anything?"

"You tell me," she smiled, stepping back.

Cameron inwardly cursed McIntyre for turning this into another lesson, but he accepted the fact that he needed to know how to perform this part of a mission. Glancing around the door, he didn't notice anything but the bare brick. He had difficulty distinguishing any marks, since the area was covered with scratches already. Cameron nodded at the brilliance the idea. It was perfect because the symbol could be hidden in plain sight. Examining the scratches more carefully, he spotted one on the left side of the door, just below eye level, and noticeable to someone reaching for the handle. It was just a casual slash mark, a "/," but something about it set it apart from the others. Cameron was about to point to the symbol when McIntyre took his hand.

"Good boy," she smiled. "No need to broadcast, though."

"So, are we going in?" he asked. "Just what did he find?"

"Not here," she said, rummaging through her purse. "He said he found something of interest in one of the buildings next door."

"Which one, for Christ's sake? In case you haven't noticed, we're not in the middle of a field!"

"Keep your voice down! I know where to go."

Pretending to drop something, McIntyre bent down, noting that the parking area was free of passers-by. She led Cameron to one of the buildings directly across from the stage door. It was a rundown structure, most likely used only for storage, Cameron surmised. There was an old painted placard on the building, its lettering so faded that the sign was impossible to read. The windows on the ground floor were all boarded up, while some of the windows on the upper stories were missing entire panes of glass. Some windows remained unbroken. This building hadn't been occupied for some time. They went to the back door, and McIntyre looked for a corresponding symbol. She located it then jiggled the handle, relieved to discover that the door was unlocked.

They stepped into the building, allowing their eyes to adjust to the gloom. Shards of light seared through the gaps in the boards covering the windows.

"What are we looking for in here?" Cameron asked, brushing off dirt drifting down from the rafters.

McIntyre paused as though listening for something. She leaned closer to Cameron so that she wouldn't have to raise her voice.

"I don't know," she whispered. "He didn't want to say it over the phone in case the line was bugged. He said we were to meet him here."

"I don't think we're going to," Cameron muttered.

"What are you talking about?"

Cameron didn't reply. He just pointed to an area in the corner. There lay Dwyer, his coat and shirt bunched up under his arms. He lay in an awkward position, his arms and legs splayed at odd angles, but Cameron didn't think Dwyer would've complained about that. The bullet hole in his chest would be of greater concern.

CHAPTER SEVENTEEN
"Bring it"

Cameron sat, his gaze fixated at a spot on the floor. He wouldn't look at the others. To an outsider, it would seem as though he was studying the smoldering tip of his cigarette, but as the cylinder of ash grew longer, it was obvious that he was even oblivious to that. Eventually, the ash dropped to the floor, remaining unattended there, as it was before it fell. Neither Cameron, nor anyone else in the room, would clean it up. Of all the things within their focus, dust and ash were not high on the list.

Cameron was still nonplussed about today's events, and was anxiously trying to digest what he'd seen—the body, the aftermath, all of it. After discovering Dwyer's body, McIntyre told Cameron to stand. As he stood there, panicked and unable to move, McIntyre quickly examined the body and the surrounding area. When he was finally allowed to move, McIntyre pulled him close beside her, as she tutored him on how to properly examine the scene.

"If two of us home in on this, it will help with recall later," she explained. "I can't do anything until the police arrive, but I want to get a good idea of what's here before it gets trampled underfoot. If we can figure out the *what, when, where,* and *how* clues, the police have a better chance figuring out the *who* and the *why.* "

"But wouldn't the police take care of all of this?" Cameron felt nauseous.

"They might, but you never know about their crime scene technicians. It isn't unusual for evidence to be lost through carelessness. I can't take that chance here."

"What do you want me to do?" Cameron asked, fighting the urge to be sick.

"Keep your eyes open. He's still slightly warm, no rigor mortis yet. Whoever did it couldn't have gotten far. Dwyer hasn't been dead that long."

There was little blood around the body itself, and the blood around the wound appeared sticky, but not dried. Trash was spread all over the floor. There were old papers, beer cans, cigarette butts and empty packs, but no clear prints were discernable, nor was McIntyre able to find any gun shells. There was nothing there but a body.

Dead. That was the word that she used to describe someone that Cameron had known, that he had talked to just hours before. This was a person with whom Cameron spent time, in and out of the performance world. But that person was alive then. Memories stormed through Cameron's mind, unconnected by anything other than the fact that they involved Dwyer. Random memories, like walking to the store from the safe house, talking to Dwyer in the interrogation room, laughing over some joke during their training, images of Dwyer from gigs before they had met, private meetings after he'd been appointed as the group's leader... It was this last image of Dwyer that brought Cameron back to the present, the image that weighed on Cameron so heavily.

Was there anything I could have done?

McIntyre maneuvered Cameron out of the warehouse as quickly as she could, and without attracting attention. There was no indication that they had been seen, but she still chose an indirect route back to the hotel, just in case there had been anyone watching them. McIntyre had to drive, as Cameron was in shock upon discovering Dwyer's body. Once in the car, his questions were ceaseless. Why were they were doing what they were doing? What should they be doing? What were they going to do? McIntyre was meager with her answers, simply telling Cameron that the entire matter was out of their hands.

"You're just going to leave him there?" Cameron cried in disbelief. She drove in silence, weaving around a slower car and moving into the other lane.

"No," McIntyre said, without emotion in her voice. "I'm not."

"Then we need to call someone, like, right fucking now!"

"When we get back to the hotel," she said. "I need to make another call first."

"To who?"

McIntyre didn't respond, and Cameron was incensed. She just stared straight ahead, oblivious to anything that he said. Cameron knew instinctively that his state of acute anxiety was a result of this situation, one with which he had absolutely no experience. But McIntyre did. For his own comfort, Cameron desperately needed her to explain to him what was going on, and give him a modicum of direction. However, McIntyre wasn't offering any of that. She wouldn't even look at him. Instead of feeling sympathetic, Cameron was getting downright pissed.

"I said, *to who?*" he demanded. "Who the fuck do you need to call, other than the fucking cops!?"

"Our contact," McIntyre muttered, still avoiding eye contact with him.

"Who the hell is *that?*" he yelled.

"I know that you've heard us use the phrase "need to know'," at least once during all this," she said, finally facing him. "It's best that you do not know."

"Maybe if you bastards didn't play fucking games, he wouldn't have been shot!"

"Or maybe *you* would have," McIntyre said. Her voice was disturbingly calm and even. "Believe it or not, we don't always keep things from you because we don't trust you. We actually want to protect you as much as we can. We know what we're doing, and we knew that, initially, you didn't. We don't want to expect more of you than what you're capable of doing."

"Well, all of his fucking experience didn't help *him*, did it?"

McIntyre didn't reply, aggravating Cameron even further.

"Answer me!"

"He knew who did it," she said, her visage a mask of resolution. Cameron felt the air go out of him. A single word flashed through his mind.

Mole.

"You're shitting me, right?"

McIntyre shook her head, almost imperceptibly.

"How do you fucking know?" Cameron demanded. "Did he tell you, "Oh, you guys come meet me at the warehouse. Gotta go now, have to get shot in a few minutes."?"

"Of course not, you *asshole*," McIntyre suddenly shouted, all composure gone. "Did you notice anything about the bullet hole?"

"Yeah! It was in the middle of his fucking chest and covered with blood!"

"There was something else about it, something that meant it was intentional."

"What, for Christ's sake?"

"Burn marks."

Cameron thought back to his target practice days, times he enjoyed with his father and, sometimes, with his friends. He closed his eyes and pictured himself shooting.

Guns make a flash when they're fired and guns leave powder burns. But only when you're very close, not when you're more than a few feet away. Dwyer would never have allowed a stranger get that close to him in a place like that. It had to have been someone he knew very well, and really trusted.

As they approached the hotel, McIntyre spoke, snapping Cameron out of his thoughts.

"This is what we're going to do."

At last! A fucking plan…

McIntyre continued, as though conducting another lesson for him. "I'm turning here. We'll keep along this street and make a left up there. That will bring us in behind the hotel. We'll park out back, where we found the bug. We'll calmly go inside and go straight upstairs. I want everyone together, best be in D'Lorenzo's room. I know Doug is able to get around now. D'Lorenzo wasn't that great when I saw him last. I'll need to brief all of you, then I have to make some calls."

When she parked the car, Cameron got out and waited for her. Walking up to him, she slipped her arm in his.

"We go inside, very casually," she explained in a low voice. "We do not attract attention." As they moved toward the door, she removed her hand and kept a steady pace next to him, as though to keep him from running ahead.

I wonder how many other fucking times she's done this?

Once inside, Cameron noticed that the lobby was occupied more than usual. He thought that strange, especially for a weekday. Then he remembered the restrictions that the government had recently enforced. Unnecessary travel was discouraged, which made travel during the regular workweek significantly less expensive.

Cameron casually scoped the crowd, wondering how anyone could go on about their business like nothing had happened, while someone he knew was dead on the filthy floor of an abandoned warehouse. Angry at the injustice of Dwyer's death, of someone he knew being killed and abandoned where they lay, like road kill, made Cameron want to yell, to hit someone.

McIntyre guided Cameron toward the elevator. Thankfully, it was at lobby level, and the two stepped in. A visiting businessman from Albany joined them and began telling them about his plans to visit Montreal, but unfortunately he had to wait for his company to receive permission for him to cross the boarder and they wouldn't know about that until Friday, and if he traveled on the weekend they wouldn't pick up the additional expense, and that would mean he'd spend his commission before he even made it, and wasn't that a dirty shame and shouldn't somebody do something about it, and what did they think? All of this was unsolicited. The man simply began speaking upon entering the elevator.

Cameron was about to respond when McIntyre bumped him as she leaned over to press the button for the elevator. To the casual observer, it would seem that she merely brushed past Cameron, but he was aware of the sense of purpose to her action. Cameron muttered a casual, "Sucks, man," to their unwitting companion, while noticing that McIntyre had pressed the button for two floors above theirs.

The man continued grumbling and complaining for the entire ride, directing his rant to the universe in general, and speaking as though Cameron and McIntyre no longer existed. The elevator door opened to the floor that McIntyre had selected. Cameron and McIntyre stepped out of the elevator and headed down the hallway. When she heard the doors close, she motioned for Cameron to stand still, then guided him back to the elevator. He was about to push the button when McIntyre held his hand. She was watching the light above the elevator portal to see where it stopped. The elevator landed three floors above where they were.

"I thought you wanted to talk to the others," Cameron whispered.

"I do," she said. "But I want to make sure we're not being followed."

McIntyre had them wait for a few moments. No one called for the elevator. McIntyre was about to push the button when they heard it start to descend, the bell ringing as it landed at each floor. The light indicated that the elevator was headed for the lobby.

"We'll take the stairs," McIntyre said, leading Cameron down the hallway.

"OK. Aren't we taking this a little too far?"

"I doubt it."

"Why worry about if someone knows we're going to our floor. It can't be that much of a secret, for Christ's sake. We've been here how fucking long?"

"That guy just seemed a little too chatty for me," she said, pushing open the door to the stairwell. "I think we need to be as careful as conceivably possible."

"Yeah, but are you going to jump at every person who talks to you?"

"One of the first ways to make contact with someone is to begin a casual conversation. That builds an element of trust. When you trust someone, you let your guard down. When you let your guard down, bad things happen."

"So now you're just going to get jumpy and suspicious of everyone?"

McIntyre stopped abruptly on the landing. She faced Cameron, looking him straight in the eye.

"Dwyer knew whoever did it," she said. "Other than the band, I only know two people. Dwyer and D'Lorenzo. D'Lorenzo is flat on his back right now, and so is Dwyer, for that matter. That means that there's someone running around who knew Dwyer, and who knows us. But *we* don't know *them*. And in case you've already forgotten, some woman just dropped by out of the blue and tried to plant a bug in your room. Yeah, I'd rather take some extra precautions right now. Any arguments?" Cameron shook his head meekly. "No. I didn't think so," McIntyre muttered.

She turned her back to him and stomped away. He watched her hurry down the stairs, and he started after her. Cameron knew that she was right. When the two reached their floor, McIntyre told him to gather everyone for a meeting in Doug's room. They were all to wait there until she arrived.

"Don't open the door unless you know it's me."

Cameron found Rich and Evan relaxing in Evan's room. Clyde was asleep in the adjoining room.

"Get him up," Cameron said. "Meet me in Doug's room. There's some shit going down."

"What's going on?" asked Evan, but Cameron didn't answer.

"I don't want to repeat it," he muttered. "I'll tell you all when we're there."

Arriving at the roadies' room, he knocked on the door. Doug answered, and Cameron was relieved to see that Doug was on his feet, and that some color had returned to his cheeks.

"Hey, man," Doug smiled, weakly. "What's up?"

"I need to come in," Cameron said, moving past his friend. Cameron noticed that D'Lorenzo was dressed and sitting on the edge of the bed with his head in his hands. He didn't look much better than the last time Cameron had seen him.

"You look like shit, man," Cameron told him.

"That's better than I feel," D'Lorenzo said, his head still hanging.

"McIntyre wants to meet us all here," Cameron explained. Before he could continue, Clyde, Evan and Rich arrived.

"What the hell is going on?" Evan asked again. It was more concern than irritation written on his face.

Cameron shook his head. "When we all get here," he murmured. Cameron lit another cigarette, unable to escape from the stares of his fellow band members. He was trying to postpone the inevitable. He had no desire to focus on what he had to tell them. Even as the thought fleeted through his mind, the moments were rapidly ticking away, and he would not be able to delay telling them any longer. Cameron's heart sunk as he heard a knock at the door and, sure that they were safe, allowed McIntyre into the room. There was no putting it off anymore.

"What the hell is going on, Barbara?" D'Lorenzo grunted. "What's with the long faces? Where's Dwyer?"

"Dwyer's dead." McIntyre's voice was flat and even, displaying no emotion. Her body language, however, betrayed her comportment. She stood shoulders up, back straight, and with her chin slightly raised. She avoided direct eye contact with anyone in the room. But she pressed her right arm to her side so tightly that the tension in her fingers blew her cover. Cameron, in particular, noticed right away.

Her statement landed on them like a ton of bricks. The men stood there, speechless with mouths agape. An interminable silence descended upon the room.

"What the fuck are you saying?" shouted D'Lorenzo suddenly. He attempted to stand, only to collapse back onto the bed. Cameron felt a sudden surge of anger. Smacking a plastic cup to the floor, he shouted at D'Lorenzo.

"She means exactly what she said! Dwyer's dead! You stupid fuck! You stupid, stupid fuck!"

"How? When did..." Evan asked, but his voice caught in his throat before he could complete his question.

"We got a call to meet him this afternoon," McIntyre explained.

"Who's *we?*" demanded D'Lorenzo, sitting up carefully. "Why wasn't I told about this?"

"Because you were in here puking you guts out, probably," said Evan. "You couldn't even sit up until we got some tea into you. You still can barely stand."

"Don't you talk to me," D'Lorenzo snapped.

"This isn't getting us anywhere," McIntyre insisted, crossing to Cameron. She turned to D'Lorenzo. "Evan's right. Dwyer did ask for you, but I told him that you were in no condition to do anything. I even stopped in to double-check, but you were sound asleep again."

"So you went alone," D'Lorenzo said, unconvinced. "You know that violates every protocol we've got."

"I'm well aware of that," McIntyre said, testily. "So was Dwyer. He asked me to bring Cameron. He thought it would be of interest to him, too."

D'Lorenzo put his head in his hands; whether from nausea or emotion, no one could tell.

"Did he say what he wanted?" D'Lorenzo moaned. "Do you have any idea what Dwyer wanted to show you?"

"No," she replied. "By the time we got there..."

"He'd been shot," finished Cameron. He rubbed his eyes, trying not to let his sense of loss, or his fears, get the better of him.

"Shot..." gasped D'Lorenzo, looking McIntyre in the eyes.

"Close range," she said, sitting down. "Burn marks around the entry point."

"What about around the body?" D'Lorenzo pressed. The rest of the guys followed with rapt attention the exchange between McIntyre and D'Lorenzo. The band members weren't at all familiar with forensic terms, but they concocted images, all of which were horrifying, from what little they could understand.

"There was none," she said.

"None? None at all?!" asked D'Lorenzo, dumfounded. "There had to have been something! A bullet goes in, a bullet comes out."

"Not all the time," McIntyre replied.

"The body was moved, though," Cameron pointed out, glancing at McIntyre.

Before Cameron could continue, D'Lorenzo interrupted him. "What the fuck do *you* know about this?" he bellowed. "You just play your fucking guitar like a rock star, and shut the fuck up! You don't even know what the fuck we're talking about. You've never even been to a crime scene in your life, unless you were the one getting arrested."

Cameron felt his face flush. Watching D'Lorenzo sitting on the edge of the bed amidst a room full of people that had been taking care of him, his feet and chest bare, his hair disheveled, and hurling expletives at *Cameron* made the rock star angry to the point of pain. Dwyer was dead, shot, and left to rot in a filthy warehouse, and D'Lorenzo was sitting here, as arrogant and obnoxious as ever.

"I know a fuck of a lot more about it than you do," Cameron spat back. "I was *there*! You were here having everyone tuck your fucking ass in bed and hold your hair back while you puked your fucking guts out..."

McIntyre had had enough. She marched to the middle of the room, shouting at no one in particular. "This isn't getting us anywhere, either!" She put her hands to her head and drew in a long, deep breath.

"Maybe he's never worked a crime scene, Don. But you and I both know damn well that I've done plenty. Cameron's right. The body was moved."

"Then there should have been a blood trail showing the path," he insisted. "Or blood drops, even. Did you notice any of those? Did you look for everything that you could possibly find?"

"I did," she said, facing him. The weariness in her sunken eyes astonished the guys. "I looked it over, *all* over, as rapidly as I could. I couldn't see an exit wound. The body was still relatively warm. In fact, and the blood was just beginning to coagulate. It appeared to be sticky and matted on his shirt."

"But how do you know that Dwyer was moved?"

"The pants legs and the sleeves were all bunched up, and so was his coat. They wouldn't have been that way if he'd fallen where he'd been shot."

"That could have happened if he'd struggled at the scene," D'Lorenzo countered.

McIntyre shook her head.

"No. There was no evidence of a struggle. He was killed and his body was moved to the spot where we found him."

"Was it covered or anything?" D'Lorenzo asked, his voice quiet. "Was there any effort to hide it?"

"No," McIntyre replied, shaking her head. "He was left there for us to find."

"No exit wound," D'Lorenzo muttered, shaking his head in disbelief.

"What the fuck does that have to do with anything?" demanded Cameron.

"It has a hell of a lot to do with it," snapped D'Lorenzo.

"How?" Cameron demanded. "How could it possibly have anything to do with it?"

"Because it gives us an idea of the caliber gun that was used," McIntyre explained. "The standard American gun is .45 caliber, like the ones we have."

"So?"

"A .45 caliber like mine or D'Lorenzo's or Dwyer's would leave an exit hole that you could almost stick your fist in," she continued. "This didn't leave one like that. A 9 millimeter bullet would be more likely to go in and bounce around inside. It would make a mess out of his insides but not necessarily come out the other side."

"That worries you, doesn't it?" asked Clyde. He started to fidget in his chair. Clyde wasn't sure that he understood everything that was going on, but he knew that if McIntyre and D'Lorenzo were worried, he should probably be worried as well.

"Yes, it does," agreed McIntyre. "It worries me a hell of a lot."

"Why is that bad?" asked Evan.

"Because a lot of European guns are 9 millimeter," she explained. "The British use them, and so do the French and the Germans."

"And the Russians," said D'Lorenzo, finishing her thought.

D'Lorenzo's words struck them all with surprise. They knew, intellectually, that the U.S. was engaged in a war with the Russians, but the guys never honestly expected to face that reality up close. The war was something they saw on television, or read about in the newspapers, or heard about on the radio. It was something that happened to other people, not to them. Even their recruitment didn't quite seem real, until now. In one instant, their illusions of security vanished entirely, and they were at a loss as to how to cope.

"Wait a minute," said Cameron. "I might not be as knowledgeable about guns as you two, but I do know something about them. 9 millimeters aren't uncommon here. This doesn't mean it was the Russians."

McIntyre nodded in agreement. Even D'Lorenzo didn't argue. Cameron ran his fingers through his long hair, and paced about the room. Lighting another cigarette, he turned to McIntyre.

"Did you call the police?"

"Yes," she said. Her voice was quiet, as though she was trying to keep something from gaining attention, which, of course, attracted everyone's attention.

"And?" Cameron asked. "Do they want us to make a statement, did they ask how we knew about it?"

"No," she said. Her voice carried a sense of finality, as though she was ending talk of the subject, but Cameron didn't let her get away with it.

"What do you mean, "No?" Don't the police want to talk to *us*?"

"No," she said again. "They don't. They don't want to hear from us again. Ever."

"Why the hell not?" demanded Evan. "That doesn't make any sense. There's been a homicide, for God's sake!"

"I know that, Evan," McIntyre said, less than reassuringly. "But our office has taken over. My statement was taken and personnel will arrive to talk privately with Cameron. The local police are not involved in this at all anymore, other than collecting the body and securing the scene. Our people are doing all of the forensic work."

"Who are they sending to replace Dwyer?" asked D'Lorenzo.

"You're not going to believe it," McIntyre sighed.

McIntyre and D'Lorenzo looked at each other, communicating silently. All that the guys could discern was that McIntyre raised one eyebrow and tilted her head to the left. Gradually, though, D'Lorenzo's face changed to astonishment, as he realized what McIntyre was transmitting to him.

"Oh, my God," he whispered. "You don't mean who I think you do…"

"Oh, yes I do," she said. "We get Chuck, the one and only."

"Why the fuck are they doing that?" D'Lorenzo demanded.

"He's the only logical choice," she said. "He helped assemble this mission and he's been the one who gets our reports. He knows as much about this assignment as we do. You and I both know that, for all of his quirks, he's damned good at what he does."

Cameron interrupted. "Who's Chuck?" He wasn't sure exactly why, but something about their dialogue made him very uneasy.

"Chuck Lamont," McIntyre explained. "He's our immediate superior. He's my and D'Lorenzo's contact, just like we are for you guys. He's been with our organization since his discharge from the army about ten years ago. He's worked in Southeast Asia, Europe, and here in the United States. This whole project was his brainchild. He realized how the black market was using the subculture of the rock world to move illicit drugs and alcohol, and thought that if we could recruit bands to help us keep an eye on the black market, then we could close some of it down, especially the outfits that are making their way onto military installations. You guys are involved in one of the prototype missions, but obviously things have gotten out of hand."

"Yeah. I guess Dwyer's getting knocked off kind of threw things for a loop, didn't it?"

"That's not what I'm talking about," McIntyre said. "Dwyer has been reporting on everything that's gone on—your recruitment, tracking down Barre, these two getting drugged, all of it. He worked with our central managers in evaluating all of the intelligence we've sent so far. One of those managers is Chuck Lamont, who's been raising hell over our findings for days now, and my phone call simply tipped the balance. Lamont's on his way up here now, separate from the forensic team. He'll be working with us, taking Dwyer's place as manager, and heading up this team directly."

"What has he been raising hell about?" Evan asked.

"He thought that we've overlooked a possibility," McIntyre sighed. "At first, everyone wrote him off as paranoid, but my gut says he may have been right all along."

"Does he think we've been barking up the wrong tree?" asked Evan.

"No. He thinks that we've only been barking up one tree."

"What the hell is that supposed to mean?" mumbled Cameron. "Will you stop being so cryptic, for Christ's sake?"

"Lamont thinks that we've got two separate and distinct situations on our hands. One of them is the local black market, which is our original target."

"And the other one?"

"He's convinced that we've somehow attracted the attention of the Soviets."

"How could Lamont think that?" demanded D'Lorenzo. "The man's nuts! Why are they even listening to him, for God's sake?"

"The Mustang," McIntyre said. "When word got around that both you and Doug were on this assignment, he knew it was too broad a coincidence to go unnoticed. Dwyer's death seems to prove Lamont's point. Even if he's wrong, he's pressed the issue enough so that the higher-ups have decided to let him run with it to see if his theory holds any credence."

"What do I have to do with any of this?" demanded Doug. He was on his feet and facing McIntyre. Though unsteady, Doug was alert and had been able to follow the entire conversation.

"You had contact with some of the people on the Mustang," she said, calmly and evenly. "So did D'Lorenzo. We think that the Mustang was destroyed by sabotage, and that someone inside our organization helped. Dwyer was convinced that one or the other of you, or even both, might know something about that."

"You're out of your fucking mind," cried Doug. He trembled as he spoke, but whether from anger, panic, or his lingering weakness, no one could be sure. He clenched his fists and spun around to face D'Lorenzo. Cameron and Rich grabbed Doug, mainly to keep him safe from himself; Doug was still quite weak.

"We're not accusing you of anything," McIntyre insisted. "But we think that there's much to discover, and we wonder if you might know more than you're even aware of."

"Bullshit," Doug spat. "After Gus died, you guys came around and bugged me for weeks! You harassed my aunt, went through all of my stuff, followed me around and treated me like I'd blown that fucking thing up myself! You even followed me to his funeral service! I'll tell you what I told them. I don't fucking know anything!"

As Doug shouted, he ceased to struggle against the arms that bound him, and he began to sob. Cameron and Rich released him, but didn't step away. They stayed by Doug's side, unsure of what to do next, and to support and protect their friend.

"Doug, we investigated everyone that had any contact with people on the Mustang," she said, sympathetically. "I worked on that, too. It wasn't just you, and we don't think that you have information that you've deliberately held back. But you and D'Lorenzo being here at the same time aroused curiosity, and we think it might have gotten someone else nervous. Trust me, OK?"

Doug gave no indication that he had heard a word; he was still sobbing. He sat with his head in his hands, shoulders heaving.

"What the fuck did I do?" he whispered. "What the fuck did I do to deserve this? I lose my best friend, I get forced to spend all my time working and looking at the person who got him into that shit, and I have no hope of getting away from it. I go to bed at night and wake up every morning, and spend all my waking moments looking at the living, breathing reminder of it."

He raised his head and glared at D'Lorenzo. Doug's expression sent chills down the guys' spines. Never had they seen such a look of absolute hatred on his face.

"Man, you've got to stop this," Cameron urged him. "If you had died and your buddy lived, would you want him to remember you like that?"

Doug began to tremble once again, his face ashen. He didn't answer, but shook his head, then rose unsteadily and made his way to the bathroom. He didn't bother to close the door. The guys heard the sound of running water, and in the mirror, they could see Doug splashing his face.

"I think we should all take it easy for now," McIntyre said. "Everyone should try to get some rest. We need to get over the trauma of these past couple of days. I hate to bring this up at a time like this, but you guys need to start rehearsing tomorrow. You have a show Friday, remember?"

"We're still going on?" asked Cameron. "I thought this whole thing would come to an end now that Dwyer's, well, you know…"

McIntyre shook her head.

"That was one of the things that I asked about," she said. "Our superiors are committed to this more than ever now. That's one of the other reasons they're sending Chuck in to take over. He's been in music for years, and, as I said, he was the one that designed this entire program."

"Then why didn't he run it?" asked Cameron.

"He was going to come in later," she said. "But they wanted him to be in a neutral position to evaluate the intelligence we gathered, to see if it justified carrying out the whole mission. Trust me. Lamont knows what he's doing. He was the one that picked out your equipment, once we told him what you had."

"If he wasn't nuts, he'd be a great agent," snarled D'Lorenzo.

"He's not nuts," McIntyre sighed. She was obviously quite tired at this point. "He's a little eccentric at times, but I think he's earned that right."

Cameron gave her a questioning glance. He wasn't in the mood for any more eccentricity in his life, and had long grown weary of McIntyre's esotericism.

"Why has he earned that right?" he ventured.

McIntyre smiled.

"He was in Vietnam and worked special ops over there. He saw a lot of stuff that we can't even imagine. Much of it's classified, so he can't talk about it. Even the stuff that he could talk about, he prefers not to."

"Oh, that's putting it mildly," grumbled D'Lorenzo, and for once Cameron was interested in hearing what the man had to say.

"And just what is that supposed to mean?" Cameron inquired.

"He wasn't just special ops," D'Lorenzo explained. "He was Green Berets and the GAMMA project."

"There's no proof of that," interrupted McIntyre. "That is all speculation."

"The GAMMA incident, you mean?" asked Evan. "Didn't that have something to do with torturing civilians?"

"Yes," cried D'Lorenzo enthusiastically.

"No, it didn't," snapped McIntyre. "It involved collecting intelligence and dealing with counter intelligence. A mole was discovered who revealed information about our undercover agents, and dealt with them without clear authority. Everyone involved were soldiers, either ours, or the South Vietnamese's. *No* civilians were involved."

"But this guy Lamont was, though," asked Cameron.

"We aren't sure," she said. "He was in the army and in the region then, and that was his area of expertise. But all of his service records prior to his discharge have been sealed, and they're not open for review."

"That's why nothing got done about that," Evan said. "The government wouldn't release any information, so the people with the charges against them couldn't get a fair trial." Evan turned to McIntyre. "Didn't they drop the charges?"

"Yes," said McIntyre. "They dropped every one of them."

Cameron pondered this for a moment. He wasn't certain how this new development would play out. On one hand, it should be good. They all thought that there was a mole working undermining the operation, and apparently this Lamont fellow had experience in hunting moles. Also, Lamont seemed to possess a sound understanding of music and bands, because the equipment he picked out was the best Cameron had ever seen, much less owned. On the other hand, though, was the issue of Lamont's mysterious background.

How much more of this shit can I take?

Cameron looked at McIntyre inquiringly. "You seem to know a lot about him. How did he get discharged from the army?"

"What do you mean?"

"I mean, did this guy Lamont get wounded and have to come home, or did he get an honorable discharge, or did he get a dishonorable discharge because of all that other shit?"

"No. He didn't get a dishonorable discharge," she explained. "Though there were some higher-ups who tried to do just that. There were no grounds for it, so they dropped the case."

"So, was his tour up, or what?"

"No. He still had some time left, but they thought it was a good idea to get him out. Lamont got a medical discharge."

"Medical discharge, my ass!" cried D'Lorenzo.

"What does he mean?" asked Cameron.

"Well..." McIntyre hedged, then answered, choosing her words carefully. "Some say it wasn't simply a *medical* discharge."

Cameron was losing patience. "Then what the hell was it?"

"A Section Eight."

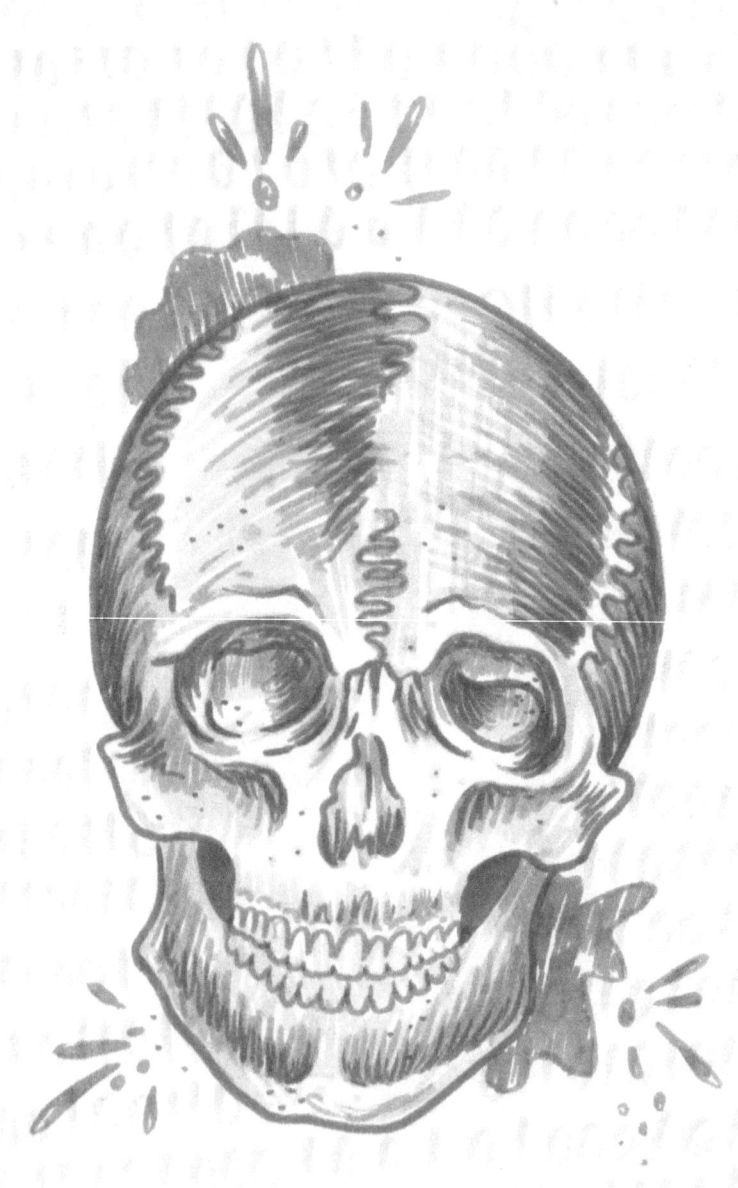

CHAPTER EIGHTEEN
"Coming of Age"

The rest of that day, and that evening, were a total blur for the Roadhouse Sons. A team of specialists arrived to take over from the local authorities and command the investigation of Dwyer's death. As expected, the team interviewed Cameron and McIntyre. Once again, Cameron found himself sequestered in a police station and left all alone in a cold, stark room. He couldn't shake off thinking back to a similar night, the night when he first met Dwyer. How long ago was it? It had only been last September. But now, it seemed like Dwyer and he had known each other forever.

Suddenly, the door swung open. For a brief moment, Cameron expected Dwyer to come walking through, only to find himself looking into the face of an older man in a crisp dark suit. Before Cameron could ask any questions, the other man launched into his interrogation.

Cameron had no idea how long his inquisition lasted. After a while, the relentless rephrasing and repetition of the same questions gave Cameron the uneasy feeling of timelessness. His answers, though varied in phraseology, were always similar and absolute, but minute discrepancies in his responses were seized upon for clarification, and the details hammered until the man was satisfied that Cameron wasn't withholding any particular information. At one point, Cameron tried asking a question regarding the progress of the investigation of Dwyer's death, only to be rebuffed.

"We ask the questions here," responded Cameron's interrogator, without looking at him.

Cameron wondered if this man was the notorious Chuck Lamont, the man with whom he'd be forced to work from now on. That thought did little to console Cameron, only compounding his grief. The older man hadn't even given his name, and wouldn't acknowledge or respond to any of Cameron's questions, regardless of their nature. Cameron was therefore with a sense of abject abandonment, and the feeling of complete isolation grew as the interview droned on. He found himself recalling the incident at the former Safe House, and the alleged calendar in the photo. Cameron surmised what the man was trying to do him, to make him feel isolated and more susceptible by constantly questioning and challenging his responses. Was this another test by Dwyer? The feeling of déjà vu was irrefutable. Cameron felt a surge of optimism and became more animated in his responses. This did not go unnoticed by his interrogator.

However, rather than comment on his observation, Cameron's interrogator took the interview in new directions, now asking questions about the Roadhouse Sons' training and life at the safe house. Then, in a seeming non sequitur, the man asked questions about Louis Barre and the band's surveillance of him. The older man also questioned Cameron about his initial arrest following the show at the Batten Kill Road House, then suddenly, and inordinately, geared the questions to their most recent show. Cameron pictured this to be a tennis match. The room was the tennis court, the table was the net, and the interrogator was on the other side, lobbing balls at Cameron. In Cameron's imagination, the other man was still dressed in his suit, while he, Cameron, wore a tennis outfit. No matter how hard the other man tried to hit the balls, Cameron was always prepared to lob them back.

Me, 20. That guy, love.

A supreme sense of satisfaction grew as Cameron discovered that he was less and less fazed by the questions, and was able to answer all of them clearly and, in his view anyway, succinctly.

"What were you doing at Hart's Tavern?" the older man suddenly asked, jolting Cameron from his thoughts. Cameron, while lost in thought, had missed a ball. He stared dumbly at the other man, who quietly repeated his question.

"What does that have to do with...?" Cameron began.

"We ask the questions, " the interrogator repeated.

What the fuck does Hart's have to do with anything?

"It was just an innocent trip I like to take to relax.," Cameron replied.

How the hell does he know about it?

"I just went over for drinks there once in awhile, I guess," Cameron continued, muttering quietly. Images of the small tavern, now quite familiar, filled his memory and he wished, more than anything right now, that he was on that barstool, a drink in his hand. More importantly, he longed to see Bambi in front of him. The thought of her driving home all alone without him just emphasized his feeling of complete isolation. Cameron's gut began to wrench, the sudden feeling of panic setting in.

"You've been going there on a regular basis," the interrogator said, leafing through the pages in his folder. "Daily. For more than two weeks, in fact."

"I like going over there to unwind after rehearsal. No big fucking deal."

"Did Dwyer know of your frequenting that establishment?"

"Yeah, I guess so," Cameron mumbled.

"You guess so?"

"Yeah, he did," Cameron said, trying to clarify the point. "He knew because I asked for some comps for the show."

"Did he, at any point, express concern over your actions?"

Why should Dwyer show concern over that?

Cameron wracked his brain to recall any incident where he and Dwyer had discussed the Tavern, but he couldn't recall any such time at all.

"Concern? No, I don't think so," Cameron said. But then, he remembered his discussion—almost altercation—with Dwyer about getting the free tickets and backstage passes for Bambi.

"That's not a very definite answer," the older man said, making a notation in his file. The Man didn't bother to look up at Cameron; he simply wrote in his file while pulling at his right eyebrow. This action irritated Cameron. The interrogator's refusal to acknowledge Cameron's presence while clearly and subconsciously employing a personal tic, gave Cameron the feeling that the man definitely knew something that Cameron didn't.

"No. Dwyer didn't have any concerns about it," replied Cameron, his irritation increasingly evident in his response.

The interrogator made no mention of Cameron's potential insubordination, which left Cameron wondering if his imagination was playing tricks on him.

The interrogator pressed on. "Yet in his report, Dwyer expressed concern that you were being careless with the passes, giving them out with no discretion and he felt that this was connected to your frequenting the Tavern."

"That's bullshit!" snapped Cameron. "Dwyer never said one goddamn thing about me going there!"

"Did he ever mention anything about your handing out free passes?"

Cameron hesitated, realizing that this would invariably lead to a discussion about Bambi, a direction in which he did not want this investigation to go. Cameron couldn't discern why, but he felt compelled to protect Bambi from this man.

And all of this crap I'm in.

"Well, yeah. Dwyer thought that I might be handing out too many, I guess."

"You guess? Did he or didn't he. It's not a difficult question to answer."

"OK. Yeah. He *did* wonder if I was sending out too many."

"Were you?"

"No!" Cameron insisted. "I only gave out maybe three or four there."

"There? Then you mean that you gave out more than that?"

Cameron's mind raced. He tried recalling all of the faces of people with whom he'd talked, and of the places he'd been.

"Yeah. I probably gave out a dozen or so leading up to the show."

The older man paused, flexed his fingers, then jotted a quick note in his file.

"You gave out a dozen or more passes. All right. Who received them?"

Again, the man made no eye contact with Cameron, and relapsed into behaving as though Cameron was not even in the room. The man could have been listening to a radio program, for all the difference it made. Cameron's uneasiness grew, and he admonished himself for it.

Steadying his psyche, Cameron snapped, "I gave the passes out in interviews on radio shows, to newspaper reporters, that sort of shit. That's what I'm supposed to do! We give passes to them, they use it to promote the show, and we get people interested and they come to the show. It's done all the time! Goddamn, I had this same conversation with Dwyer!"

This revelation caught the older man's attention. He stopped writing and glanced up at Cameron.

"With *whom*...?" he asked, his tone casual.

"Who do you think, you asshole?!" shouted Cameron. "With Dwyer! He was our manager, for God's sake. Who else would have given a damn if I was papering the whole fucking town with free passes?"

"Why do you think he was concerned about the amount of free passes distributed?"

Cameron's muscles tightened, and his head began to ache. He leaned across the table, barely able to swallow his contempt.

"There are only so many seats in an auditorium," Cameron explained, slowly and evenly. "If you give a seat away, you can't sell a ticket for it. Dwyer's concern was simple economics. He knew the band had to support itself. He might have been an agent, but he was also a fucking bean counter, too!"

"Not anymore," the man said quietly, making another notation in his file. Cameron gasped, agog at the man's gall and disrespect. Cameron fought the urge to belt the man across the face. His exasperation caved to remorse and guilt. The fact that Dwyer was no longer among the living crushed Cameron in the solar plexus. His urge to wound the older man across the table didn't subside. Knowing that the man's irreverence was nothing that Cameron could control or punish, Cameron buried his face in his hands. The interrogator, though, asked another question, as though he didn't sense his own disgusting disregard for Dwyer, or Cameron's resulting angst.

"What was the aggregate monetary promotional value of the passes you gave away at Hart's Tavern?"

"What?" Cameron was nonplussed. He almost looked behind his chair to see if there was a hidden camera in the room. How could this man be so glib about Dwyer's death, and be so mercenary about a world that he could never understand?

Cold-ass motherfucker.

"Was Hart's Tavern an event sponsor for you?"

"No," Cameron said, not understanding the relevance of the question. "We had some local sponsors, but not the tavern. It was too small."

"Then why the passes?"

Cameron hesitated before answering, leaning back in his chair and staring at the ceiling, trying to buy time. His stalling was futile, as the interrogator calmly repeated the question.

"I gave them to a friend, so they could come to the show," Cameron said, bracing for the onslaught of questions that would follow.

"They?" the man asked, inordinately interested, as far as Cameron was concerned. "You mean, you were offering to bring in more than one person?"

Cameron didn't answer, pausing for what he felt was an eternity. He shook his head.

"No," he said. "There was just one. I gave that person the other passes in case they wanted to bring a friend."

"And who was this person, the one to whom you issued the passes?"

Here we go...

It was a fair question, the answer to which would leave Cameron bare and exposed, and the one question that he absolutely did *not* want to acknowledge.

"It was someone that I met that worked there at the Tavern," Cameron said, choosing his words as carefully as possible. "I'd struck up a friendship with them and wanted them to come see the show."

"Was this someone male or female?" the interrogator asked, sanctimoniously folding his hands. Cameron wished that the geezer in the suit would go back to writing in his file, and, for the first time in this inquisition, Cameron welcomed the idea of the man's disregard for him. However, that was not to be the case. The man stared Cameron in the eye.

"She's a bartender there," Cameron answered, reluctantly. Hearing the man refer to Bambi as a non-entity male or female seemed to strip her of her identity and personhood, just as his manner had done so to Cameron. Something within Cameron rebelled complying with the investigation. Bambi was a human being, a treasure to Cameron, and he was going to protect that.

"Do you know her name?" the investigator asked.

Cameron shook his head.

"They call her Bambi," he said. "I never found out her last name, and I never asked." The man in the suit said nothing. He simply nodded and stared at Cameron with that same inscrutable expression that he'd had worn throughout the entire interrogation. Cameron awaited the next question, but it never came. The anxious sense of foreboding gnawed at Cameron, and yet, the next question did not come. Cameron, uncomfortable, was about to shift in his chair, but decided against it. The man was staring at him, patiently waiting for Cameron to show signs of acquiescence, as though Cameron would suddenly break down and scream, "All right! I'll tell you,..."

This is turning into a battle of wills.

Cameron refused to give in. He decided not to move first. What was that Yes song?

It's your move.

Cameron smiled to himself, but no sooner had he made this decision, he began to feel an itch under his nose. He had to fight, with all of his might, the urge to scratch.

Don't make the first move!

He tried to concentrate on anything else possible. His thoughts landed, predictably, on Bambi. His mind's eye saw her smiling face, and smelled the faint trace of perfume in her hair. He recalled conversations that they'd had, relishing the memory of her voice and remembering the feel of her soft, compassionate touch.

The older man in the suit spoke, interrupting Cameron's reverie.

"You knew her enough to give her a free pass to the show, as well as a pass backstage, and yet you never asked her for her last name?"

The question dampened Cameron's spirits like a blast of ice water.

"What are you talking about?" Cameron snarled, resentful of the constant invasion of his sentiments by this man.

"According to these notes, you were given three complimentary tickets and three backstage passes, which remain unaccounted for."

"What do you mean they're not accounted for. How the hell would you know?"

"The passes were to be collected when they were used to enter the backstage area," the man said, referring to his file. "Dwyer said that they were never turned in. Why is that? Why didn't your female friend show up?"

So, Bambi, his "female friend," wasn't there after all, Cameron realized. But he did not have time to linger on his relief. The man in the suit began repeated the question.

"Look, I don't know why she didn't come backstage," Cameron said. "Yeah, I gave her some passes so she'd come see me play. Yeah, I was interested in her and wanted to impress her."

"So interested that you never even bothered to ask her full name?"

The man's condescending smirk enraged Cameron, as did the insinuation about his feelings and intentions toward Bambi. Cameron jumped out of his chair.

"Going somewhere?" Cameron's interrogator said, snapping his head up and looking Cameron in the eye. This action, so quick and deliberate, halted Cameron in his tracks. Cameron's longing to punch the interrogator in the jaw—so hard that he could actually feel the man's flesh and bone against his knuckles—had not subsided. Cameron sat down, hating himself for it, his resentment against this man pervading his every pore.

That will only make everything worse.

"Why didn't she, this Bambi, come back stage after the show?" the man asked, still eyeing Cameron, and smiling at him, as though patronizing the guitarist.

"She said that she brought friends from Winooski and they had to be back for curfew, so she couldn't stay."

"And you believed her?"

"Why wouldn't I?"

The man's smile disappeared, though his stare remained steady.

"I ask the questions," the man said.

Cameron paused, considering the virtue of a smart-ass answer and, not thinking of one readily available, decided to respond simply and in a straightforward manner.

"Yes. I did believe her."

The man nodded, and wrote in his file.

"Do you have any knowledge concerning the drugs given to our agent, Donald D'Lorenzo, or to your associate?"

"Doug. Doug *Courtland*, you mean?" Cameron glowered.

The man glared back at Cameron, affronted by his disrespectful tone.

"You refer to your agent by his full name," Cameron continued. "But you refer to Doug as my "associate." That's wrong."

The man arched his brow, partly in anger and partly in amusement. The look on his face was nothing less than sanctimony. What was it Cameron's mother used to say?

"Sanctimony is a mighty tall tree from which to fall. I hope you have good insurance."

Cameron remained calm and collected. "You drag us into this bullshit spook world of yours and can't give Doug the courtesy you extend to someone so fucking stupid like D'Lorenzo, who can't even keep his own cover story straight? Fuck you!"

"You were duly recruited…"

"Fuck you!" Cameron shouted, cutting the man off in mid-sentence. "You fuckers blackmailed us into this on frame-up charges, and you've acted like you have us by the balls ever since!"

"You'll never get anyone to believe that," the man smirked.

This fucker has me on my last raw nerve.

"I don't need to," Cameron said quietly, lighting a cigarette. "You and I both know it."

"I'm afraid I have no knowledge of that, in fact."

"Fuck you!"

"You may wish to reconsider your attitude. Things don't look that great for you at the moment."

"Fuck...*you...*" Cameron repeated sardonically.

"I will ask you again about the incident involving the drugs administered to these two individuals," the man in the suit said, resuming his interrogation.

"*What* individuals?"

Now it was the other man's turn to be surprised, his mouth agape.

"Mr. D'Lorenzo and your *friend*, of course."

"What's his name?" demanded Cameron.

The man in the suit was incensed.

"What's... his... name?" repeated Cameron. "You know so Goddamn much, tell me my friend's name." Cameron let his cigarette dangle from his mouth.

"You would do well to control your temper..."

"FUCK YOU!" shouted Cameron, slamming his hand down on the open file, his cigarette falling, ashes and all. "You've got everything written down in here! All our comings and goings, and how many times we wipe our fucking asses with our left hand, and how many times we do it with our right. Then *tell me his fucking name!*"

"You will not talk to me in that..."

Cameron lunged forward, sweeping the man's files off of the table with one violent swoop, leaning into the man's face.

"I'll talk to you any fucking way I please!" Cameron shouted, spittle flying from his mouth. "You've tried to dehumanize us since you recruited us against our God-given will! You've treated us like fodder and sent us out to all the places you couldn't be bothered with. By God, I'm fucking *sick and tired of it!* And it will stop *now!* You call the most useless asshole on earth by his name because he's another suit like you, and treat Doug like shit because he isn't? Well fuck that! What is my friend's name?"

The man jumped to his feet, knocking his chair over in the process. He leaned into Cameron, the tips of their noses mere inches apart.

"You really think you want to mess with me?" he whispered. "You might just regret that decision."

"I might," agreed Cameron. "But I guarantee, you'll be breathing hard and having an even harder time walking upright before I'm done with you."

They stared at each other, the seconds ticking by like minutes, like hours. Cameron was certain he was sweating buckets, but didn't care.

"You're actually serious?" the man asked with a smile. He made no other movement.

"Dead serious," Cameron said. He, likewise, made no effort to move or to sit down. The staring match continued, nose-to-nose. The pressure grew.

"Good," the man said at last, and stepped back from the table and shattering the tension. Cameron straightened up, eyeing his interrogator carefully, suspecting at any second to be tricked. However, the man paid him no attention and, instead, bent over to collect his papers. Cameron watched him, squatting as though he was playing marbles, calmly sorting the individual pages, and replacing them in order. Cameron felt remorseful watching the man, ashamed of submitting to raw emotion and reacting in such a purely careless manner. For a moment, Cameron considered offering his help, and even stepped toward the man, but stopped himself. At that moment, the other man stood up and turned to face him.

"Courtland," he said, betraying no emotion.

"What?"

"Doug Courtland," the man repeated. "That's the name of your friend, the other one that got dosed."

Cameron nodded, realizing that he had won a battle, yet he was well aware that he was in no position to press his advantage. The man returned to the table and sat down. Cameron did so, too.

"You were going to help me just then, weren't you?" the man asked, folding his hands on his lap. "Why didn't you?"

Cameron shrugged. "I don't know."

"Oh, come on," the man smiled. "You obviously know what you're doing and you're an expert at all of this. Why didn't you come over and help me?"

"All right," Cameron said, leaning back in his chair and crossing his arms. "I thought it was a trick. I thought you wanted me to come over there, and once I was down on my knees, you were going to pull something. Satisfied now?"

The man nodded, his smile growing.

"Yes," he laughed. "Very satisfied, because you were right. I guess you have learned something after all."

With that, he got up from the table and stood at the doorway. Cameron walked toward the door, too. The man in the suite held his hand up.

"Don't go away," the man said with a wry smile. Cameron watched him leave and felt the same sinking feeling in his stomach when the door closed this time as he did the night he met Dwyer. But now, it was different. Now, Cameron knew that there was a world of shit about to come down on him, but somehow he didn't care. He intended to face it, to fight it, but never again to give in to it. He returned to his chair and sat down, his arms folded across his chest, his mind and thoughts as defiant as his attitude. He began to rock back in his chair in time with the tune he was playing over and over in his head. He studied the walls of the room, all of which were bare. He examined the floor carefully, noticing the specks in the linoleum. At first, it seemed that the specks were random, without any apparent pattern, but as Cameron studied them more carefully, he began to notice a configuration.

Horizontal, horizontal, horizontal, vertical. Vertical, vertical, vertical horizontal. What kind of an idiot laid these?

The flickering fluorescent light made the specks appear to move, and Cameron remembered a game he used to play when he was a child. He would stare at one spot in the grass until all the grass around it seemed to disappear. Cameron did this now, staring at the floor, first at one spot, then at another. He waited, albeit impatiently, for the man in the suit to return, not so that Cameron could learn his fate necessarily, but because he wasn't done with the man. Cameron studied his reflection in the mirror, which he knew to be a two-way glass that had afforded a clear view of the man's exchange with Cameron to anyone on the other side. Surprisingly, Cameron was unperturbed about that.

Just wait until round two.

After what felt like an eternity, the door finally opened, and the man returned with a different file and an ashtray, both of which he set on the table between them. Cameron did not speak or move, nor did he acknowledge the man's presence in any way.

"Here you go," the man said, sliding the ashtray toward Cameron. "I thought you might want another smoke. We've been at this a while."

Cameron said nothing. He removed a cigarette from his pack, lit it, and took a long drag. He exhaled, staring hard through his smoke at the other man, reminding himself of a dragon.

And you sure as fuck aren't Saint George.

"You were with Agent McIntyre when she discovered the body, correct?"

"That's right," Cameron said. "Dwyer insisted on following his own rules of training, so she was not supposed to go alone."

"What rules were those?" the man asked. Cameron thought it odd that the man appeared to be genuinely confused. Cameron was about to provide a full explanation, but wondered if the man wasn't up to another trick. Cameron decided to supply only a partial explanation instead.

"Dwyer taught us that, if we thought that things might be dangerous, we were to go out in pairs. You never go alone to meet anyone, *ever.*"

"But Dwyer did, obviously."

"Yeah, and look where it got him."

Now it was the other man's turn to become angry. Cameron watched the man's skin flush, crimson rising from his neck to his face, but the man did not move.

"Dwyer was an agent with almost twenty years experience," the man snarled. "He's been in some of the worst conditions I've ever seen, and he *always* knew what he was doing."

Cameron, feeling surprisingly empathetic, leaned forward and studied the other man's face. Cameron knew what it was like to lose a friend and a colleague, to see all of a person's talents suddenly come to an abrupt end. Any criticism of a deceased friend diminished their legacy and their memory, but that was not how Cameron meant his comment to be taken for, over time, he had grown to respect Dwyer, and had a lot of reason to believe that the feeling had been mutual.

"There was something that Dwyer told us the night we met him," Cameron continued. "Something that I've never forgotten."

"And what was that?" the other man snapped. Despite efforts to keep his temper in check, Cameron could see the man was struggling.

"Dwyer said that everyone makes mistakes, and that was a given. However, when it happened in his world, sometimes people died. I don't think he was careless. I don't think he was stupid. I think he made a mistake, and his luck ran out."

The man was clearly rankled, and formed a fist with his right hand.

"You were asking about the body, right?" Cameron asked. "That means you've got it and you've seen it, right? Did you notice anything peculiar about it? About the bullet hole?"

"Explain yourself," the other man seethed.

"There were burn marks around the hole. I'm not a gun expert, but I have done some target practicing and know a little bit about guns. For example, I know that if you're more than three feet away, there aren't any burn marks at all, and that the closer you are, the worse the marks are, and the ones on Dwyer looked pretty bad. I thought the blood was already dry, but McIntyre didn't seem to think so. I know that Dwyer would never let anyone get that close to him if he thought there was something wrong, so I *know* he didn't simply fuck up. He would never have been that careless."

The man in the suit was silent, pondering Cameron's explanation. The man's color gradually returned to normal, the bright crimson flush of anger now subsided. Cameron noticed that the man's breathing had become less labored as well, and the man no longer held his hands in the form of fists. The man, still silently contemplating what Cameron had said, opened the new file he'd brought, and began studying several black and white photos. Cameron knew that the photos were of Dwyer's crime scene. He watched the man study each photo. The man breathed deeply, then removed one particular photo for closer examination. It was the photo of Dwyer's chest, showing the wound as a dark blossom on Dwyer's white shirt. The man stared at the photo long and hard. Cameron had the feeling that he was intruding on a private moment, and looked away, trying to give the man a modicum of privacy.

The man returned the photo to the file folder and sat quietly for several moments. At last, he looked at Cameron. "That was a good observation."

"Thanks, but the credit belongs to McIntyre. I never would have noticed that on my own."

"I was talking about your observation of what Dwyer would have done. You're right. He never would have knowingly allowed himself into that situation."

Cameron had no desire to acknowledge the compliment, not because he didn't believe the man, but because he didn't feel that it was right to. This was something about which Cameron would rather have been wrong, and there was no way to admit success without appearing to gloat over Dwyer's death. That was the last thing that Cameron wanted to do.

"I wish I was wrong," he muttered.

The other man nodded and, for a moment, Cameron wondered if the animosity between them was beginning to fade.

"I know you don't have any forensic science experience," the man said. "But I want you to tell me what you found, and be as clear and detailed as possible." The man flipped through the file once again. Cameron noticed that he did not seem to be searching for anything in particular. The man appeared to be struggling with his own emotions. Cameron, feeling a bit uncharitable, still thought that this was strange.

Hell, even D'Lorenzo seemed good at keeping his emotions and feelings in check.

Cameron decided to err on the side of caution.

"Well, first we went to the Civic Center to see if Dwyer had left a signal for us, to let us know if it was safe to meet."

"Did you find it?"

"Yeah. McIntyre found it by the stage door."

"Can you draw it for me?"

Cameron hesitated. In his mind, he knew that these people were Dwyer's colleagues, but he still did not feel secure revealing anything that Dwyer had taught him, or any secret communication left by Dwyer.

"I'd rather not," Cameron said. "No offence, man, but those were Dwyer's secrets."

The man nodded, but said nothing.

"But you say McIntyre did find it on the door?"

"Not *on* the door. She found it beside the door."

"And she recognized it as the "all clear" signal?"

"That's what she said. Safe entry."

Cameron further explained that he and McIntyre proceeded to the designated meeting place, where they found Dwyer's body. When the man asked for specific measurements, placements, such as

Dwyer's body in relation to all four corners of the space, Cameron could only guess.

"We didn't have a tape measure or anything like that," he explained. "And we didn't have much time."

"Why didn't you?"

"Because the body was still slightly warm, and McIntyre thought that meant that whoever had killed Dwyer couldn't have gotten far, and she wanted to get going to look for them."

"But she didn't," the man pointed out. "You both went right back to the hotel and she called it in."

Cameron nodded wearily. "After she looked at the body, she realized that it had been moved there, and the warehouse probably wasn't the actual scene of the crime. She wanted a team who was trained and equipped to study the crime scene to be doing it, so that we'd be able to get everything and not lose any clues or anything."

"Was there a lot of blood?"

"Around his shirt, yeah. But that was the weird part. There wasn't any blood anyplace else. There were no drops of blood, no smears, no anything, at least what we could see."

The man nodded almost imperceptibly as he listened to Cameron speak. He studied a set of pictures, only to stop abruptly, and examine to a set of notes. He asked Cameron general questions at first, then asked more specific ones. Cameron repeated that he was unsure of distances, and asked for a piece of paper and a pen. Cameron drew a rough sketch of the building and of the parking lot.

"We came in here," Cameron said, pointing to the place he'd marked as the front of the building. "Dwyer left another signal there, telling us that things were all right and that the meeting was still on."

"Then what did you do?"

Cameron sighed. At this point, he was exhausted.

"We went inside. The place looked like it hadn't been used for years, all boarded up and shit. The inside wasn't much better. It smelled musty, you know, like an old house that's sat empty for a long time."

"Didn't you think it was strange to have to go in there?"

"Oh, hell yeah, at first anyway. After Doug and D'Lorenzo got dosed, Dwyer and I figured that it might have been someone making the shit. An abandoned place like that would be perfect for making drugs, so I thought that Dwyer had found something. It made sense that way."

Cameron debated whether to mention NAOMI or any of D'Lorenzo's drug-induced ramblings. He also seriously considered whether to mention anything that Dwyer had told the guys prior to his death. Cameron felt that he should mention all of it, but second-guessed himself. After all, the man himself didn't seem to want to talk about any of it.

As if reading Cameron's mind, the man asked, "Were you looking for pot plants or something?"

Well, there's no way around it now, is there?

"No. We were looking for something else, something bigger than that."

Cameron described Doug's and D'Lorenzo's poisonings, and how Dwyer had mentioned that he'd worked on similar cases. Cameron very carefully avoided any mention whatsoever of NAOMI, and of Dwyer's and D'Lorenzo's involvement in that project. Such an operation—one needed to manufacture such poisonous substances—Cameron explained, would require a bigger, less conspicuous place than one needed just to grow pot plants.

"How so?"

"With pot plants, you have to have a light for them if you're not growing them out in the sun. Someone would have seen something like that. If you're just doing a lab, you could do it less noticeably."

"You seem pretty knowledgeable about that sort of thing," the man observed.

Cameron smiled and shrugged.

"I won't deny it. You've probably learned about it anyway. Yeah, I've grown a few plants in my day, but that was it. I never made anything like the shit those two got hit with."

The man in the suit was silent yet again. By now Cameron was used to it, and in fact, had come to expect it. The man was either considering a new line of questioning, or was mulling over the answers he'd already received.

Or is he trying to piss me off with all the delays?

By all means, Cameron had decided to leave the man alone to do what he needed to do. Cameron began reviewing in his own mind everything that he'd just told the man.

Did I leave anything out?

Obviously Cameron had deliberately omitted some particularly crucial information, but was it a good idea to add anything further?

He had already told the man the bare facts of the case, and answered the man's unrelenting questions to the best of his ability.

If I volunteer shit, that might just confuse him.

"I'm going to get coffee," the man said, startling Cameron. "Do you want any?"

"Sure," Cameron said. "Milk. No sugar." He lit another cigarette. The man left. Cameron leaned back in his chair. The man probably did want something to drink, but Cameron also suspected that he was double-checking the information that Cameron had given him. Cameron figured that the man would likely return with a new battery of questions.

Cameron picked up his diagram and studied it once more, his mind wandering back to the reality uncaptured by his meager sketch.

Dwyer's pants had been bunched up around his ankles. His shirt was up by his arms, the back of it untucked. McIntyre deduced that Dwyer had been dragged to the spot where he was found. But Cameron remembered something else, something indefinable. He started to reach for the photos in the folder, and then hesitated. How far did he want to push his luck? After all, these were notes about an investigation that were not meant for public viewing. Technically, though, Cameron rationalized, he was part of Dwyer's team. He agonized over the nagging recollection, unable to pinpoint exactly what it was. Did he remember anything at all, really, or was his mind creating it now? For the first time, he was anxious for the man to return. His previous tricks to distract himself didn't work. His attention returned to the file. Cameron was about to throw caution to the wind and open the folder anyway, when the man returned with two cups of coffee on a tray.

"I need to see those photos again," Cameron blurted out. "There's something I think I remember, but I want to be sure."

The man looked at Cameron for a moment, brow furrowed, then opened the file. He gave the photographs to Cameron. Cameron took them from the man, and nodded in appreciation. He flipped through the first two, which were of the building's exterior and of the parking lot. Cameron then saw the first photograph of Dwyer's body. There Dwyer lay, his light clothes a grotesque silhouette against the dark warehouse floor. Cameron held the photograph for a moment, almost reverently regarding the last memory he would have of the man he had known, had grown to respect, and who had expressed a respect for him. Cameron understood now how Doug felt about Gus Kalbe. Cameron wanted to know who did this to Dwyer. He knew the only way to find out and avenge Dwyer's death was to help Dwyer's fellow agents as best he could. Cameron looked at the next photograph, which was the same scene shot from a different angle. He examined the remainder of the photographs, most of which contained different pieces of evidence found by the crime scene technicians. Cameron finally found the photograph that triggered his undefined memory from that day.

In this photo, Dwyer's body was rolled onto its side, so that his back was clearly visible.

No exit wound.

Cameron noticed, too, to his dismay, that Dwyer's pants were soiled. He felt sadness for this final lack of dignity.

Couldn't they have covered that up?

Then Cameron noticed something that struck him as a bit odd at the time, but upon which he put no importance until now. Dwyer's back was clean.

"There's nothing on his back," Cameron said, pointing to the picture.

"You mean no exit wound?"

"No, man," Cameron said, shaking his head impatiently. "There's no dirt, no crap, nothing. If he had been dragged, his back would be filthy. Do you see anything on it?"

He handed the photo to the man, who studied it carefully, then smiled as he replaced it in the folder.

"That's good," the man said, reminiscent of Dwyer's comments when the band had successfully completed an assignment. Once again, Cameron allowed himself to think that this was just an elaborate test, that Dwyer would walk through the door any minute and tell Cameron how well he'd done. As soon as Cameron allowed himself that remote hope, he let it go, and tried not to dwell on the pain of having done so.

"I want to review the timeline you gave me," the man said.

Cameron took a sip of his coffee, hoping the warm liquid would calm him. He wasn't ready to speak just yet. The man asked Cameron the approximate time of his and McIntyre's departure from the hotel.

"I think it was about one thirty. We went to the Civic Center, but you already know that."

"How long did it take you to get there?"

"About a half an hour."

"So that would have placed you at the Civic Center at approximately two o'clock, or thereabouts. Correct?"

Cameron nodded.

"Dwyer couldn't have been shot much before one o'clock, then," Cameron offered. The man shot Cameron a sharp look. Cameron, ignoring the man's vexation, explained further.

"McIntyre said the body was still warm, and Dwyer wasn't stiff when she shook him. Doesn't it take like four hours or something for a body to get cold and stiff? She mentioned that she had been looking for me, and she found me at a restaurant, so figure that took her about ten or fifteen minutes. That means it was a little before one when she got the phone call from Dwyer."

The man's features didn't soften, but he nodded his head in agreement.

"That sounds correct," the man muttered. "Very good."

Cameron nearly blushed as he realized how grateful he was for the recognition, but froze. He remembered the scene in the safe house when Dwyer was conducting mental exercises, and had warned the band of the psychological need to seek acceptance. "It will hold you hostage to your interrogator," Dwyer had warned.

I'm on my own, even if he's on my side.

"That would also mean that he was shot almost as soon as he hung up with McIntyre," Cameron added. Did that mean that the person was in the room with Dwyer, or right outside? Did Dwyer have any idea what was coming? The man in the suit just sat there, silent, as though waiting for Cameron to complete a complex mathematical equation in his head, without the luxury of paper and pen. Cameron knew that it was highly improbable that Dwyer's superiors had overlooked the possibility that Dwyer wasn't alone when he died.

"So maybe Dwyer wasn't alone when he died."

Cameron's interrogator registered no surprise. He didn't register any reaction at all, in fact.

"I'm going to deliver my notes to my superior, and I'll be right back," the man said, standing and extending his hand to Cameron. Cameron, stunned that the man would simply walk away after what Cameron had just suggested, stood up in response and shook the man's hand, firmly, but without squeezing. Cameron noticed that the man shook his hand with the same grip. The two men looked each other in the eye. The man in the suit gathered his notes and the folder and left the room. Once again, the sound of the closing door imparted a palpable sense of finality. However, this time Cameron was not surprised or saddened by it, but instead, gave it melancholy acceptance.

Yes. I'm on my own now.

CHAPTER NINETEEN
"Point of No Return"

The interrogator—the older man in the suit—never returned to the room. Instead, McIntyre arrived to retrieve Cameron. They left together, returning to the hotel.

"Time to get to work," she said as they stepped out into the parking lot. The cold November wind, as if in agreement, slapped at Cameron's face. To Cameron, McIntyre seemed unusually subdued. Her face was drawn and her eyes appeared sunken and tired, which was not surprising; everyone had been put through the wringer these past few days. Cameron had myriad questions for McIntyre. So many ends that had been left loose, and so many subjects still wide open, but he knew that now was not the time. Regardless of how Dwyer had felt about him, Cameron was not really one of *them*, and trying to be accepted as such would only lead to trouble.

Once out of the building and at the car, Cameron put his hand on McIntyre's elbow and guided her to the passenger's side.

"I can drive," she insisted, trying to free her arm from him.

"So can I," he replied. "You've been through a lot today. Let me do this."

"I'm a big girl and a professional," McIntyre insisted. "This isn't the first time I've had to face a colleague's death, and I'm sure it won't be the last!"

Cameron released his grip, but still held the door open for her.

"Look, there isn't a hell of a lot I've been able to do today to be helpful or useful. Let me at least do this, please."

McIntyre began to speak, but Cameron cut her off.

"Before you give me any of your "I'm just as capable as you are" crap, that's not what I'm saying. Dwyer was my friend, too, and a mentor. Maybe I'm working out shit you guys all worked out a long time ago, but I'm still not sure how to feel about losing him. Do I just chalk it up and carry on, or do I give a damn? Right now, I'm trying to do both, and don't know how fucking well I'm doing at either, so just let me drive. Besides, it will keep me from thinking."

McIntyre hesitated for a moment, climbed into the car, and closed the door by herself. Cameron climbed in behind the wheel, started the ignition, and drove back toward the hotel. The first part of their journey was in silence. McIntyre was the first to break it.

"You've done a lot," she said. Her voice was confident and sincere, and Cameron could tell that she was not trying to patronize him. "My superiors were pretty impressed with how you handled things in there."

"Really?"

"Not the yelling so much," she was quick to add. "But the recall and the detailed answers to the questions. They did notice all of the issues you pointed out, and had just as many questions as you did. They also had the same concerns as yours about the timeline and its implications."

"Really?" Cameron was slightly surprised, yet pleased, and felt a growing sense of satisfaction in what he'd done, not only on the day of Dwyer's death, but during the interrogation.

"Calm down, big boy," McIntyre said, a bit too sardonically for Cameron's taste. "They were impressed because they didn't think you'd amount to shit, and you did a lot better than they thought you would."

Cameron balked and smiled at McIntyre's world-weariness and sudden use of expletives. "Did I handle it like you did?" McIntyre hadn't noticed his expression. She just shook her head.

"No, but you did it better than most lay people do. You actually demonstrated a concerted effort to observe and recall." She began to say something else, but hesitated.

"But, what?" Cameron prodded.

"That was a good tribute to Dwyer that you gave," she said, quietly.

"What tribute?" Cameron tried to recall anything he might have said that could be dubbed a tribute, but he had no idea to what McIntyre was referring.

"When you said that you knew that Dwyer wouldn't have been sloppy or careless, that he simply made a mistake, that it was his luck that ran out. That was a kind thing for you to say, you who has no real reason to be loyal to him. Also, you provided as much salient information as you possibly could, and you brought things to their attention, things that you thought were important. They got to see how much Dwyer had taught you. They were impressed."

"Really?"

"Don't let it go to your head," she repeated. "You did good, not great."

"Yeah, but you said it yourself. I did good!"

McIntyre rolled her eyes. Cameron could tell that she was exhausted. The giveaway was not only her appearance, but her inability to speak briefly and succinctly as usual. She was more emotional, and spoke in run-on sentences.

Cameron parked the car. Rather than say anything, he just smiled at McIntyre and opened the door for her. She got out of the car and walked on ahead of him. Cameron let her go and caught up to her in the lobby. McIntyre was reading a message handed to her by the desk clerk. She had a look of profound concern on her face.

"More bad news?" Cameron asked. He didn't know about her, but he was ready to say he'd had enough bad news to last him a lifetime. Cameron wondered how she could do it, and realized that he didn't know just how long she had been doing it.

"No. Not bad news," she said. "Just news arriving a lot earlier than I'd expected. We need to go to the Civic Center."

"What for?"

"It seems that Chuck Lamont has arrived here much earlier than expected, and wants to meet the notorious Roadhouse Sons. He wants you to bring your instruments. You better go round up the guys. I'll look in on D'Lorenzo and find out when he'll be ready, if at all…"

Cameron and McIntyre rode the elevator in silence. He desperately wanted to ask more questions about issues that he thought of during the interrogation, but didn't feel comfortable discussing with the man in the suit. Cameron hesitated. McIntyre seemed to have the weight of the world on her shoulders, and with the added element of meeting a new team leader, the opportunity to talk to her seemed even more remote. He didn't want to encumber her further.

As the elevator doors opened, she stepped out and headed down the hallway, not looking back. Cameron paused in the hallway, watching her as she entered her room. He wondered what was going through her mind.

Cameron walked down the hall and knocked on the door of Rich's room. No one answered. He went to Evan's room, and finally, to Doug's, where he found everyone gathered together. They were all clearly agitated.

"What the hell's going on?" Cameron asked.

"What do you mean?" said Evan. "Dwyer's dead, you guys got carted off, no one's said anything. What did you expect to find, a friggin' party?"

Cameron sighed. "We just had to go answer some questions about what we'd seen, that's all. It's not a big deal."

"Maybe not to you!" shouted Rich. "We've been sitting here waiting for the door to get kicked in ever since you left!"

Cameron explained to the guys what had happened at the police station. He also told them about the message that McIntyre had received from the mysterious Chuck Lamont.

"Are you up for it?" he asked Doug.

The roadie nodded. Cameron turned to leave.

"Wait a minute," Evan asked. "What the hell is the future going to be now?"

Cameron didn't ask Evan to elaborate. Cameron knew that Evan was as concerned about the band's secret status as he was of the band itself. Cameron's immediate problem was that he had no answers.

"Man, I really don't know," he admitted. "If I had any idea, I sure as hell would tell you, but I don't. I got the impression that they want to keep everything going, but I could be way off. I'm hoping this Lamont guy will have some answers for us."

"What about Dwyer?" asked Doug.

"He's dead, man," said Cameron.

"I fucking know that!" Doug snapped. "But what are they going to do? Are they having a funeral? Does he have a family? Do we send flowers or something? I mean, they don't just pack him up in a box and stuff him on some shelf, do they?"

"OK, listen," said Cameron, closing the door to give them privacy. "I'll just do this once, all right? I'm not going to spend the rest of the day, or any more time, playing twenty fucking questions, do you guys understand me?" Everyone nodded in acknowledgement.

"All right then," Cameron continued wearily. "I don't know about any arrangements. I don't know what they're going to do with us, and I don't know any more about anything than any of you do. Am I making any sense here?"

"Man, you don't need to be so fucking cranky with us!" Clyde exclaimed. "We're just edgy, that's all. Don't we have a right to be concerned? I mean, Dwyer knew his shit and look what happened to *him*! What the fuck is going to happen to *us*?"

Cameron sat down and looked Clyde in the eye.

"Yeah… you do have a right to be concerned, and I have a right to be fucking cranky! I'm expected to lead this team and be the one that Dwyer trusted to keep shit together and keep shit going. Now he's gone and I don't have any fucking clue what I'm doing. I only know one thing's for certain, and that's that I am damn sure not going to let any one of you get laid out next to him."

"How are you going to do that?" Evan demanded.

"I don't fucking know," muttered Cameron. "Yet, anyways. But for now, just get your shit and let's go. We've got a new boss to meet."

Before they could ask Cameron any more questions, he left the room and walked into the hallway. He called for the elevator, stepped in and went to the lobby.

God, I need a fucking cigarette. And a drink.

Cameron stepped outside and lit a cigarette, inhaling deeply. He waited.

I give 'em five minutes.

After eleven minutes, the Roadhouse Sons had gathered their gear and met Cameron outside. They loaded into their respective vehicles, forming a small caravan toward the Civic Center. Cameron had already noticed that McIntyre's car was not in the parking lot, and figured that she was already at the Center. As soon as they pulled into the parking lot, though, he didn't see her car there, either. He did, however, notice the man leaning against the wall by the stage door. Cameron couldn't decide if his gut was reacting with alarm, or with curiosity.

The man was dressed in a well-worn denim jacket, the cuffs folded over and raddled about the seam. He sported a black shirt, faded almost to grey. The man's blue jeans were also faded from long use, and were held up with a wide leather belt bearing a large silver buckle, which was embellished with a rodeo scene stamped in gold. He wore suede cowboy boots, but no cowboy hat. His curly black hair fell loosely past his shoulders, and his skin was tanned, dark as leather. The guys exchanged glances. One could assume that this character's eyes were dark, however, the sunglasses he wore concealed them, making it difficult to guess the man's age. The stranger sipped his coffee as he watched the band members get out of their cars. He said nothing.

Cameron, thinking ahead, had parked away from the stage door. This would buy him time to get a feel for the new boss. Cameron figured that, as he took his time crossing the parking lot, he could study the man. The band members had intuitively followed Cameron's lead. They talked quietly amongst themselves, spouting casual observations about the stranger as they unloaded their gear. Evan and Doug, having no instruments to carry, kept apace behind the others.

The stranger watched them as they approached, still saying nothing. Nor did the band. Cameron made sure that he walked a firm and steady gait.

Not too fast. Not too slow.

He was reminded of an old Western, and began to hum the theme from *The Good, the Bad and the Ugly*, for which Evan gave him a sharp rebuke.

"That's not funny, damn it!" he hissed. Cameron smiled, and stopped in front of his new boss, but said nothing.

"Hello, gentlemen!" the stranger said. "My name is Chuck Lamont. I'll be your new manager."

Lamont's voice was a deep and velvety baritone, and he flashed a pleasant smile. He stepped forward and offered his hand, giving each band member a firm handshake, and a "How do you do?"

"Why don't we go inside where it's a little warmer?" he suggested. "I'd like to hear you folks, if you don't mind."

Before they could agree or dissent, Lamont opened the stage door and stepped through it, holding it open briefly for them, and continuing on into the building. Cameron was the closest to the door, and grabbed it before it could close. Inside, they heard Lamont's boots echo through the empty building, and noticed something unusual. Other than the sound of Lamont's boots, the entire building was eerily quiet. No one else was there.

The Roadhouse Sons followed Lamont onto the stage. He'd set up a stool in the front. A Marshall amp and a guitar case sat next to the stool.

"First off, gentlemen, I would like to let you know that I don't do things the way Dwyer did. I knew him well, and had a lot of respect for him, but I approach things from a very different perspective. For starters, I've had more experience with music than he ever did, and I can whack the axe rather well, if I do say so myself. Therefore, I think my management style will be a little less constricting for you all. Secondly, I don't use last names or formalities unless I have to, and just between us, I try to avoid those situations as much as I can. I'll refer to you by your first names, and would prefer it if you would do the same for me. There is no need for introductions. I've already told you my name and I'm quite familiar with all of you already, as I'm sure you're aware. Now, I know this is a little unusual, but I thought one of the best ways that we could get to know one another is with a little jam session. I realize that we've all had a rough couple of days, but would like to point out that you have a show coming up in a few days, and you've got to be able to top the debut show you did last week, which I understand, by the way, was par excellence."

The Roadhouse Sons stood in front of Lamont, slack-jawed and nonplussed. Cameron, though, was the only member of the band who didn't buy into Lamont's rhetoric right off the bat.

Despite Chuck Lamont's casual and relaxed manner of speaking, he gave the impression of being deliberate and preconceived, and every syllable was delivered with purpose and intent. He couldn't have held their attention any more than if he had slapped his hand against a table with each word spoken.

While still unsure of this new fellow in front of them, admittedly, the more he spoke, the more Chuck Lamont's manner made the band members feel, albeit, slightly relaxed. When he finished, Lamont removed his jacket and, carefully folding it, placed it on the floor next to him.

"Excuse me," said Evan. "But where is everyone? This place usually has at least the janitors and office staff working here. It's deserted!"

"Except for us, it is," Chuck replied with a smile. "We managed to keep this declared a crime scene for the time being, only permitting investigators, et cetera, inside."

"Well, then, what the hell are *we* doing here?"

"I'm an investigator." Chuck smiled, winking at the rest of them. "You guys are the "et cetera." Now, let's get down to business."

He finished his coffee, and giving it one last look to make certain it was gone, set the mug down on his amp. He turned his attention to Cameron.

"Dwyer sent me a tape of you guys back when we were trying to put this whole shebang together," Chuck said, adjusting his position on the stool. "You did a couple of guitar solos that sounded fantastic. I've got to say that I was pretty impressed, and that helped our arguments to give this mission a try, and to select *you* guys as the ones to do it with."

"Gee, thanks. I think." Cameron said, gingerly, eyeing Chuck.

"That was a compliment – really!" Chuck laughed.

Cameron bristled. "Well, I can't help but think that if you'd wanted to recruit us, as you guys like to put it, you could have done it some other way than getting us arrested first."

"Awww, we didn't do that," Chuck said, faux ruefully. "We took advantage of it, I'll admit. Who wouldn't? But, that wasn't our plan at all."

"If you didn't do it, then who did?" demanded Cameron. He felt like someone had shoved his face into a basin of ice-cold water. The suggestion that there was another way to recruit the band into service, one that didn't involve arresting them, *forcing* them, insinuated the possibility that the band could have turned down the job. What was Chuck really saying?

"The police records indicate that there was an anonymous phone call reporting an assault against the club owner and his son, and a theft of unspecified government commodities. Probably made by one of the club owner's flunkies. Like I said, we didn't intend to use that to get you, but when presented with it, we decided that it was not a bad idea, so we let it fly," Chuck said, as casually as if he'd asked for a cup of coffee.

Cameron couldn't believe his ears. "What were you planning on doing then, if you don't mind my asking?"

"We were going to use a more subtle approach." Chuck smiled, devilishly. "You know, dinner, dancing, a couple of drinks. The usual."

"Then why the fuck do what you did?" Cameron demanded.

"Expediency."

Cameron was very surprised to learn that there was a second option for the band's recruitment, but was not at all surprised at the one employed by Chuck and his team. This realization brought Cameron less resentment than it did confirmation; he was too tired of resisting now to honestly give a damn about it anymore.

"Like I was saying," continued Chuck. "I was really impressed with those guitar solos. Would you mind if I took a look at your guitar? If no, I understand, but it sounded sweet and I was dying to see it."

Cameron didn't move, and for a moment the guys wondered if he would refuse. To ask a person one doesn't know to handle something by which the other makes a living is a bold request. However, the band members were struck by the fact that Chuck had provided Cameron with an out. That didn't mean that such an action might not carry repercussions, but already, Chuck's approach was much different than Dwyer's.

Cameron nodded, saying nothing, and reached down to open his guitar case.

His guitar was a 1970s large head-style Fender Stratocaster. Of all the guitars Cameron had ever played, this one was his favorite. The ash wood body was Tobacco Sunburst, fading from dark brown at the edges to a beautiful tanned blonde wood color in the center. The pick guard, originally white, was now yellowed, and heavily scratched, worn from years of usage. The neck was made of rosewood, which Cameron preferred, as it was less likely to warp. A hand tooled leather strap, with colors to match the guitar, completed the ensemble. Cameron carefully handed the guitar to Chuck, who grasped it carefully with both hands.

Chuck ignored everyone else in the room. He held the guitar one way, then another, his attention to it almost reverent. He slid his hand gently up the neck, feeling for the ends of the frets.

"I keep them sanded down," Cameron said. "I like it to be smooth."

"Like cream," agreed Chuck in a soft voice. "Do you mind if I plug it in?"

"Sure. Go ahead."

Chuck's face lit up with a big grin and, taking the end of the cable, plugged it into the amp. Cameron came alive when he heard the familiar click and hum of the instrument as it connected to the monitor, converting it from an inert collection of wood and lacquer to a living source of sound. Chuck reached into his pocket and pulled out a guitar pick. He played each string in turn, tuning them as needed. He began to pick away, playing portions of various songs.

He seems to know what he's doing,

Chuck wasn't playing anything but to justify his earlier proud claim that he was a good musician, but that wasn't surprising. If Cameron had a dime for every person he'd ever met who claimed they were the greatest guitar player since Eric Clapton, he'd have more money than Rockefeller. Cameron tried to stifle a yawn, but wasn't successful. He hoped that Chuck hadn't seen him, but if he had, that he wouldn't take it personally. He was wrong.

"Oh, Chuck's not good enough for you?" Chuck smiled as he continued to play random tunes. "All right then. Maybe this will be a little more to your liking."

Before Cameron could apologize or explain himself, Chuck began to play Jimmy Page's guitar solo from the song *Whole Lot of Love*, his fingers moving up and down the strings, and his eyes fixed on Cameron.

Cameron was about to compliment Chuck when suddenly the music changed. Without looking at the guitar or saying a word, Chuck began to play Ritchie Blackmore's solo from *Highway Star*. Cameron could tell by the distant look in Chuck's eyes that the band's new manager was not just trying to impress them, that playing music was what he loved to do. Chuck's next selection confirmed Cameron's hunch. Chuck worked his fingers through all of the notes, and from the echoes of the *Highway Star*, he fashioned a riff that Cameron recognized, but couldn't place – at first.

It's fucking Jimi Hendrix! The Wind Cries Mary!

Chuck's eyes were closed and, at this point, he was oblivious to his surroundings. Cameron knew exactly what Chuck was feeling; he wasn't simply playing some inconsequential piece of music. Each note and chord was an audible work of art, fashioned and shaped into a thing of pure beauty, not merely plucked from the strings. The man and the instrument were one.

Cameron was about to applaud when Chuck's playing veered in yet another direction, landing on an homage to B. B. King's rendition of the classic *Travelling Riverside Blues*.

Cameron, totally captivated by the music, had to remind himself to breathe. This was not a showboat jam session done to impress a group of known musicians; Chuck's playing was deeply personal and heartfelt. Cameron felt almost guilty witnessing something so intimate. When Chuck strummed the last chord, no one said a word. The last note dissipated into this air. Still, everyone was silent. To speak or to move would be a gesture of obscenity. For several moments, the band sat, dumbfounded, staring at Chuck, whose eyes were still closed in reverie of the music. The silence seemed divine, transporting them from an empty Civic Center to a sacred and holy garden.

It was Chuck who broke the silence.

"How was that?" he asked in a soft, delicate whisper. No one moved; no one spoke. What could they do? Simple phrases and mere clapping seemed inadequate and was in no way sufficient to express what the Roadhouse Sons were feeling. Chuck looked from one face to another. The band understood that Chuck Lamont was expecting a response.

"That was fucking awesome," breathed Cameron.

"Think you could give it a shot?" Chuck asked with a smile, resting his arm on Cameron's guitar, while tossing his pick into the air. As the pick came down, Chuck caught it, and repeated his question. Cameron realized it wasn't a request. It was a challenge. But was it a challenge that Cameron could accept? He hesitated for a moment, realizing that if he backed down, he would lose face with his band and, more importantly, with himself. If he went forward and failed, he could at least say that he had given it a try. Taking a deep breath, Cameron nodded and held out his hand, beckoning for his guitar. Chuck smiled, and shook his head.

"Hey now," he said. "Fair is fair! Why not try it on mine?"

Chuck leaned down from his stool, grabbed his guitar case and handed it to Cameron. Cameron grasped the case with both hands, concerned about its contents. Sure, Chuck could play guitar, but for all Cameron knew, the band's new manager could hammer at home on a pawnshop reject. Granted, Chuck had just played monster riffs, but he did it on Cameron's professional axe, not his own.

Fuck it. No going back now.

Cameron opened the case. His gasp was audible. Inside was something he had heard but never had the chance to play; a 1959 Gibson Les Paul Standard solid body guitar. The body was Heritage Cherry Sunburst with a rosewood neck. Cameron soaked in the view before he handled it. The pickups, the fret board, *everything*, was in beautiful condition, even though it was clearly well used. This was the guitar of a man who appreciated his music and his instruments. Cameron felt confident that it would play well and sound great. He only worried about his performance.

For his entire life, Cameron had favored the deep, soulful sounds of the blues. He was therefore drawn to Strats for their deep, melancholy sound. A Les Paul guitar was totally different, producing a harder, more biting and traditional rock sound.

Removing the guitar from the case, Cameron noticed the Indian blanket design of the guitar strap, adorned along the edge with a small collection of pins. He didn't examine them. McIntyre had said that Chuck had been in the army in Vietnam and had seen the horrors of humanity there; these pins could possibly relate to those events, and Cameron felt he should honor Chuck's privacy by disregarding the them. Guitars, and all the related gear are, to every musician Cameron knew, very personal items.

Best not to look.

Cameron plugged the guitar into the amp, feeling the same thrill as when Chuck plugged in Cameron's guitar. This time, though, the sensation compounded; it was Cameron's soul coming alive. In less than a minute, it would be *his* heart pouring out its music. Cameron wracked his brain trying to summon a playlist and, in an effort to buy time, decided to check the tuning of the Les Paul. To his amazement, and admitted disappointment, the guitar was already perfectly in tune.

This guy knows his shit. He was probably waiting for this moment, I bet.

Cameron gently strummed, his fingers running over the strings, all the while listening to the sounds coming out of his Marshall amp. Every time he stopped, though, each empty space left by the silence reminded him that he needed songs, not noise. His mind was alarmingly blank; he couldn't think of any specific selections. He had to show Chuck that he was up to the task set before him. He *had* to duplicate the performance he had just witnessed, but how? Then Cameron smiled. He knew.

Removing a pick from his case, Cameron began to play, note for note and chord for chord, the entire medley played by Chuck just minutes before. Cameron tried to avoid looking at Chuck, but gave in, eyeing his new manager as his fingers blazed up and down the neck of the Les Paul. Chuck was smiling and nodding his head in time with the music, lightly tapping the toe of his boot.

He's obviously into it.

Cameron didn't allow himself vanity or conceit. To do so would ensure a mistake. Instead, he concentrated on the music, remembering the first time that he'd heard these songs, and feeling, once again, the same thrill and exhilaration that he had the first time he played them in front of a crowd. Strangers had come to hear him play, not just family and friends. Cameron was filled with excitement as he worked the same bluesy sound out of the Les Paul.

The sound that I'm used to...

Cameron played expertly, and without losing the essence of the songs to the harder sounds produced by the Les Paul. He began to sweat as he willed the instrument to obey him.

Cameron had almost reached the end of the medley when he realized that he couldn't just repeat what he had heard. The man wanted to know how good Cameron was, and Cameron sensed that this scrutiny didn't pertain only to his ability to play music. He began the rendition of *Travelling Riverside Blues* and, as his fingers drifted along the strings and frets, he suddenly knew what to do. Having just finessed the Les Paul into yielding to his will, Cameron knew that the only appropriate action before finishing his set would be to run it free. Cameron was in complete control.

This axe is all mine!

Cameron carefully strummed, prolonging the last chord. As it hung in the air, Cameron looked up at Chuck, who was smiling benevolently, as though he was a teacher pleased with his student's recital. Then Cameron launched his surprise.

His gaze still parked on Chuck, Cameron fingered a Paganini-inspired scale. His fingers blithely fluttered up and down the neck as he performed what classical music aficionados and experts refer to as "the Devil's Laughter" from *Caprices Op. 1 No. 13 in B flat major*. At first, Cameron caressed each note, and then cracked them like a whip, the allegretto portion of Paganini's piece now taking on the force of a hurricane. Cameron closed his eyes. Almost mockingly, he played ritardando, as in the beginning, picking slowly, yet ever proficiently. When he felt that he'd done enough, Cameron stopped as abruptly as he'd begun.

Cameron opened his eyes and smiled at the vision before him. There sat Chuck with his mouth open, no longer tapping, no longer smiling. For a millisecond, Cameron thought that Chuck was about to yell at him. Chuck uttered not one sound; he couldn't.

Take that, motherfucker!

A millennium passed. "Holy shit," Chuck suddenly gasped, and he began to applaud. "That was fucking *awesome!*"

Chuck returned Cameron's guitar to him, then plugged his own guitar into its amp. All this time, the other band members had been standing there, waiting, and proud of Cameron, but not knowing what to do.

Thankfully, Chuck called out to them. "Take up your instruments!" For the next hour and a half, the guys jammed, laughed, and became comfortable with their new manager. They shared myriad road stories, and were pleased to discover that Chuck had spent time working as a soundman for various bands in California and in the Northwest. He provided welcome suggestions about amps and PA systems, and was curious to know how they, as a small band, had dealt with various technical situations at their respective venues. The Roadhouse Sons were grateful to have someone willing to listen to what they knew, and who was clearly confident in their abilities. When the men were through with their jam session, Chuck told them to pack their gear and follow him back to their office area.

"We've got some business to discuss," he said, gathering up his coat and cup and heading offstage. The others, albeit a bit apprehensive, followed in due course. They found Chuck seated behind the desk, the desk that Dwyer once used. Surprisingly, no one thought it odd that Dwyer wasn't there, as Chuck fit in with the guys so nicely. In fact, with no disregard toward Dwyer's memory, the band actually felt more at ease with Chuck. As they filed in, he motioned for them to shut the door. He pulled a small envelope from his jacket pocket and dumped its contents onto the desk. A small silver disk resembling a thin coin toppled out.

"That, gentlemen, is a listening device, known in common parlance as a '"bug." It was one of over a dozen discovered here in this office and throughout the building, including the stage, the dressing rooms, and even the bathroom."

"How did you find these?" asked Evan, obviously aghast.

"When we were examining Dwyer's crime scene, we reached the same conclusion as Cameron and Miss McIntyre. There was absolutely no way in hell that the warehouse could have been the scene of Dwyer's actual death. Since the body was still warm, we knew that the site had to be close by. Phone records indicate that the call Dwyer placed to Miss McIntyre came from this phone right here." For emphasis, Chuck jabbed his right forefinger on the handset of the desk phone. "So, we logically began our search here. That was when we found the bugs. We disconnected one, and we've scrambled the others so they won't work."

"Why didn't you disconnect all of them?" asked Clyde. He studied the small object carefully, fascinated by its technology. How could something so tiny cause so much damage?

"We didn't want to reveal that we were on to whoever it was that planted them," Chuck explained. "It's not uncommon for one or more of these to malfunction, or to incur accidental damage. Whoever planted them will find out soon enough that these things aren't working, and they'll try and fix them. That's when we'll be able to figure out who we're dealing with, and decide what to do next."

"Aren't we dealing with the Russians?" asked Evan. "I thought that was what we were here to do."

Chuck shook his head.

"The purpose of this front was to gather information on the black markets channeling illicit drugs and alcohol. The counterintelligence against the Soviets is for the big boys, not you."

Cameron felt some of his earlier regard for the man beginning to fade. Granted, the band didn't possess the vast experience that Dwyer, McIntyre or Chuck did, but Cameron was confident that he and the band could be valuable. Listening to this man talk was belittling, and made Cameron feel like his efforts were insignificant in the larger scheme of things.

Again, I ask… why the fuck are we even here?

"However," Chuck continued. "The best laid plans of mice and men, and me, too, for that matter, often go astray. We've attracted some rather serious attention from some rather unpleasant individuals. That has brought me, and you, to a rather serious crossroads that will require some rather serious decisions.

This friggin' guy and his "rathers." Rather… the grand equivocator!

Chuck continued. "I'm afraid that there is no way that I can honestly ask you to make any decisions without laying all of the information out here for you. In order to do that, I have to inform you that what you're about to hear is considered official intelligence, and you all are still acting as our informants in an official capacity. Should you decide to reveal any of what we're about to discuss, the repercussions to you could be very unpleasant. Do I make myself clear?"

"Man, this is just like fucking Dwyer!" snapped Clyde. "He was always using that blackmail shit on us, threatening us with doing time for shit we never did!"

"Correction, my friend," assured Chuck. "I have no intention of doing that. There is no need for threats. Should you reveal the details of an ongoing counterintelligence investigation during a time of war, there are legitimate consequences that you'd deal with, much harsher than anything we could trump up. Besides, that option disappeared for us when you all agreed to this. The charges against you were dropped, as promised, and that wasn't too difficult to accomplish, considering they were bullshit to begin with."

"Then why did you try doing that shit to us?" Clyde pressed.

"We didn't," Chuck said. "I already told you gentlemen. Someone else did, and we were quick to take advantage of it because we need you guys to carry some credibility in the places we were hoping to use you. The rumors about you will still exist. You won't be any freer from that than Robert Plant is from the rumors that he sold his soul to the Devil for Led Zeppelin's success. However, that's a good thing, really. It gives you a mystique that other criminal elements can feel comfortable around. Should any legitimate source ever do a background check on you, say, for future employment, they won't find anything in your records."

Chuck looked at Evan as he said this. Evan's shoulders visibly sagged with relief, the heavy burden of worry now lifted. Cameron wondered how long Evan had carried that torment with him, and knew that it was because Evan's angst over his absence from his family would not subside until he returned home.

"We want to keep you in that operation," Chuck continued. "We have reports of a channel of black market racketeers running an operation between Montreal and Boston. Burlington is one of their distribution hubs. Other areas are Montpelier, Barre, Brattleboro, White River, Manchester and the North Shore. They bring things up from down south, and down from up north. The Queen City sits in a nice little epicenter for all of it."

"But what the hell are we supposed to be doing?" demanded Evan. "You keep saying you want us to work, that you need us to do things, but we haven't done anything yet, and all of you go on about how valuable we are. Are you saving us for some rainy day or something?"

Chuck shrugged. "I'm sorry," he said, with no real remorse. Cameron was reminded of another lesson from his mother.

"Don't say you're sorry unless you mean it."

Chuck hesitated, as though realizing how callous he sounded. "I thought things had been explained to you better, but I guess they weren't. But then again, in light of all of the shit that's gone on, it probably wasn't a big priority. First off, you guys have already been very useful. Since we recruited you, we've gotten very strong leads on major players in that game. Granted, you were more live bait than active intelligence gatherers, but that's how it works best sometimes.

I'm not going to reveal the suspects right now, because we don't have conclusive evidence, and if we say too much, we might spook them and put the mission at risk. I am going to ask, though, that you guys do more direct socializing with people after the shows. Let *them* hang out with *you*. Don't bring them back here. We'll make one of the nicer conference rooms out front available to you. If you're approached by anyone offering you *anything*, then make your way back here to the dressing rooms. Tell them if they want to make offers, you'd be interested in continuing the discussion in private. We'll have plenty of accoutrements to make it believable for you."

"Like what, for example?" asked Cameron, chuckling to himself at Lamont's pronunciation of "accoutrements."

Uh-koo-ter-mohn!

"Rotgut alcohol, cheap beer and wine that couldn't even pass for vinegar. Don't ask about the champagne, by the way."

"We have to drink that stuff?" moaned Rich. "We got enough of that on the road! You'd think that we'd get something better now. Even if it is a front."

"Yes, one would think," smiled Chuck. "But let's just say that we haven't been able to find a distributor. That word gets around that the Roadhouse Sons seek righteous libations, and lo and behold! A distributor arrives, a friend of someone, let's say, who's willing to do you a favor, for a price, of course. We negotiate a price, and when we take delivery of the illegal booze, either the good stuff or the crap, we also take delivery of the dealer and his minions. Either way, we win. If we get him, then we put the squeeze on him 'til he turns state's evidence against the rest of his network. If we get some flunky, then we recruit them to collect intel on the rest of the operation."

"You like doing that, don't you?" remarked Clyde.

"It's more cost effective that way," agreed Chuck. I'll be honest. The bargaining chip we initially used has been played, and is no longer available to us. I don't need to tell you that things have taken a dangerous and deadly turn. Our little troupe has managed to attract some very big attention from some rather mysterious adversaries concerning the USS Mustang. I want to make one thing very clear. I do *not* think that anyone is withholding any information from anyone or, in *any* way, knows more than what they've already told."

With that, Chuck fixed his eyes directly on Doug.

"I'm serious," he continued. "However, I do think that someone else does not share that opinion, and that someone is trying to cover their tracks. We have evidence that leads us to believe we're being monitored, and have been for a while. Past operations that have failed, ended abruptly, or were otherwise compromised made us suspicious. When we established the dynamic duo of our Mr. Courtland here with Agent D'Lorenzo, that proved to be too much for this someone to handle. Dwyer worked on recruiting and vetting people for the Mustang, and so did D'Lorenzo. Three people, one of them a friend of Doug's, became suspicious that security on the Mustang had been compromised. That friend, Gus Kalbe, tried to contact us. The information never made it to us. That revealed to us that there was one hell of a security breach."

"Dwyer called it a mole," said Cameron. Chuck nodded.

"Yes, that's exactly what it was. We couldn't track down anything that gave us a clue as to their identity, until now. There was speculation that the three people who contacted us tried to pass information, possibly in writing, or communicating via family and friends, but no luck. Do you remember that?"

"Yeah," Doug sighed. "Three of them showed up in town not long after the Mustang sank. They talked to Gus's folks and his sister. His brother was in the army and on his way to Alaska. I don't know if they got in touch with him."

"They did," revealed Chuck. "Go on."

"Well, they spent hours going through his parents' house, asking them to try and recall every fucking conversation they had with Gus. They also took every fucking letter he wrote to them, *and* half the stuff out of his room. All this while Gus's parents were trying to plan a fucking memorial service, because they can't have a funeral because there was no fucking body to bury…"

Doug's voice grew thick, his speech now rapid-fire. The band recognized this behavior as Doug's symptoms of anxiety. They'd seen this a few times before. Cameron was about to calm Doug when Chuck resumed.

"Take it easy, brother," he said. Unlike Dwyer's authoritative tone, Chuck's voice was soothing. "It totally sucks; I won't even pretend that it's any other way. I know exactly how you feel because I've been there myself, too many times, in fact. It hurts, it sucks, but it wasn't personal, believe me. Take a deep breath and let me ask you a couple of questions, OK?"

Doug nodded, breathed deeply, and began to relax. Cameron eyed Chuck Lamont.

He certainly has a way about him. I'll give him that.

"All right then," Chuck pressed on. "You've told us, over and over, that Gus never wrote you or contacted you after he deployed, correct?"

"Yeah, that's right. That's what I've told everybody that 's ever asked."

"I know you did, and your story never changed, so that's why I believe you."

"Well fucking thanks for that, at least!"

Chuck held up his hands.

"I can't help how other people do things," he said. "I only have control over myself and my teams, so don't get upset with me. Deal?"

"Deal…" Doug looked beaten. Cameron could tell that Doug would keep his word, that he wasn't acting sullen for the effect of it.

"Did you and Gus talk at all before he left? I mean, you were good friends and he was taking off for a while, and not just on a short business trip. I mean, he had reenlisted in the Navy, for crying out loud. You must have gone out on the town before he shipped out, right?" Chuck realized that his tone sounded aggressive beyond his intent. He looked at Doug, and made a simpatico gesture, putting his right hand to his heart.

Doug took another deep breath and shook his head. "No," he said. "Gus wanted to stay with his folks, you see. They were older, and pretty upset about having both of their kids in the military at the same time. They kept thinking they were going to be like the Sullivans."

"Who were the Sullivans?" asked Rich. "This is getting pretty hard to follow with all these characters."

"The Sullivans were five brothers in the Navy back during World War Two," Chuck explained. "When their ship was sunk by the Japanese, all five boys were killed. After that, the government made changes so that at least one child in a family could be exempt from military service if another child in the family had been killed in combat. The Kalbes had lost an older son in the Marines in Vietnam. Since Gus was the youngest, he was released from active duty and sent home."

"Then how could he reenlist?" asked Evan.

"Because he was one of the developers of a special type of much-needed radar technology. The Pentagon pulled some strings and got his reenlistment approved, but only on the condition that he go in voluntarily."

"And he did?" asked Rich.

"With some encouragement, yes."

"But wouldn't that take the other son out of service, then?"

"One would think," Chuck sighed. "But to make certain that there was no appearance of a shell game going on, and to avoid unwanted attention, Gus's brother served his term in the Army; well, until he died during the Alaskan invasion…"

Doug looked away, failing to control the tears streaming down his cheeks.

Chuck paused, playing with the bug again, giving Doug time to regroup.

"Is there anything else at all that you can think of, anything we should know?" Chuck asked. Despite the insistence in Chuck's voice, he wasn't forceful. Cameron felt that if Doug withheld anything at all, Chuck's firm but kind method would draw it out.

"No," Doug said, now completely fatigued. "The only time I spoke to Gus was when he left. He said that if anything happened to him and his brother, he wanted me to have his stupid lucky hat."

"Is that the one that you have on?"

"Yeah…" laughed Doug, blushing slightly. "He said that he always got lucky whenever he wore it. He had it on when we won the big softball game, and, um, well… when he got lucky when we'd go out. You know…"

Chuck laughed, waving off the need for any further explanation.

"OK! OK! I get the picture! So that was the only thing he gave you?"

Doug shook his head.

"He gave me his favorite Louis L'Amour book, *Sackett*. He *loved* that thing, and read it maybe a hundred times. It was his favorite possession."

"Why didn't he take those things with him, then?" asked Rich. "I'd have thought he'd want something sentimental to have with him." Doug shook his head again.

"He didn't want to take anything personal with him. They were told to leave everything home except the clothes they wore to the orientation. Everything was going to be provided to them."

"That's weird," said Cameron.

"Not really," said Chuck. "This was highly secret. Even revealing anything about a crewmember's like and dislikes could be deadly. They could be lured into blackmail, coercion or duress. Except for some very high-level individuals, no one even had a full list of all the people on board."

"What was so special about that radar that it needed so much security?" asked Evan. "Seems like overkill, if you ask me."

Chuck sighed once again and leaned back with his arms folded behind his head. He closed his eyes, obviously deep in thought. Several minutes elapsed before he spoke again.

"OK. I'm going to let you all in on a little something. You probably should have been told this already, but obviously you weren't. I warn you, this shit stays in this room. If you breathe, hint, or so much as lisp a word of this to anyone, ever at any time, then you will be in breach of classified information and you will be shot. Most likely by me."

"Well, so much for the carrot approach," muttered Evan.

"This shit is serious," Chuck said in a slow voice. "The Mustang was a radar station with a very specific assignment. And it was not to keep an eye on the Soviets."

"What was it doing there, then?" asked Cameron.

"It was a radar and communications jamming station, and one with a very wide range. This had been in the planning and development stages for some time. Ford initially approved it, but Carter got behind it big time because of his tour of duty on subs. It was supposed to go up near the North Pole, since that would be the shortest route for missiles. From that position, radar could be pointed at Mother Russia and scramble their systems like eggs."

"But the Mustang sank before it could do that," offered Clyde.

"They didn't sink it. They blew it up," corrected Chuck. "And they did do some scrambling before the shit hit the fan, it just wasn't aimed at the Soviets."

"So, then who got scrambled?"

"Do you really think that the United States could be caught so off guard as to let the Soviets walk into more than half of Alaska and a good chunk of Canada too? No. The Soviets had some help. The Mustang ended up targeting our systems, and Canada's, as well. Not only did it knock out our radar, but it also shut down our radio and electrical systems. NORAD and SAC were able to see shit going down, but Alaska and Canada couldn't until the Soviets were banging on the doors. By the time we were able to get forces moving, they already had beachheads established and we got pushed back. You know the rest. The Commies poured into Alaska, our oil poured out, and we have a Resistance movement the French would have been envious of. End of story."

"But how…?" Evan began to ask. He was cut off.

"Traitor," said Cameron. "Judas. Benedict Arnold. Fifth Column. Whatever you want to call it. Someone turned the Mustang against us, and blew it up before it could be turned off, or before they could be captured."

"And their control personnel were left behind to keep that channel open, and to keep mining our intel. They sent all sorts of top secret information back to the Kremlin," grumbled Chuck. "That's why we're convinced they've been targeting you guys. To find out if anyone knows anything, *and* to keep us quiet if we do."

Chuck stood and stretched, letting out a loud, indulgent bear's growl.

"So, gentlemen… If you want to walk, there is no way that we can force you to stay. It's all up to you." Cameron looked at the guys, who were all looking at one another. That Yes song popped into Cameron's head once again.

It's Your Move…

The guys said nothing at first. How could they? Since this entire situation began, all that they wanted was a chance to get out.

And now, here it is…

One of the band's own had been drugged, one of the Feds—who supposedly knew what he was doing—had been drugged, and yet another Fed had been killed. The Roadhouse Sons had every reason in the world to yell "Screw it!" and bail. So why weren't they? No one spoke a single word, but their eyes spoke volumes. Cameron looked at each individual—Doug, Clyde, Evan, and Rich—and they all looked Cameron right in the eyes. They each nodded their head.

"We're staying," said Cameron.

Chuck nodded his acceptance, saying nothing. He sat, deep in thought, repeatedly fingering the now defunct listening device as though it was an amulet. Finally, he spoke. Instead of Americans trying to make a dishonest living selling illegal booze, you now have the possibility of facing a very dangerous and, I should point out, unknown enemy. We know that they've already killed one of ours, someone with nearly twenty years' experience and who has been trained in counterintelligence. I'll say it one more time. If you want to bail out, now is the time. I wouldn't blame you, and I wouldn't stop you. It is your choice."

Cameron said nothing. This was a subject that he and Dwyer had discussed at length and, today, the Roadhouse Sons had come to their conclusions and had already voiced them. There was only one difference. Now, they were presented with an opportunity to choose to participate, instead of resigning themselves to the fact that they must participate. Cameron decided that it made no difference; he was staying.

"I'm in," said Doug.

"Really?" asked Chuck. "I don't want any bullshit reasons, no sentimental attachments to your friend, no desire for revenge. I've seen all those motives before, and watched them disappear at the first sign of trouble. Do it because you want to, or don't do it at all. Is that clear?"

"Yes, sir," Doug said. "It's clear, and it's what I want to do."

"OK, then. No more mention of your friend. You're off the hook as far as your roommate goes. He's heading back for debriefing and getting checked out. You won't be seeing him for a while, anyway."

Doug nodded. He understood the terms and accepted them.

"I'm in, too," said Clyde. Chuck didn't repeat his general admonition; he knew that once was enough.

"We're certainly not the ones they look at first with the draft," said Rich. "They've been pulling other kids into the ranks. I want to do something, too. Count me in."

"Me, too," said Evan. Chuck reminded Evan of his family, but Evan waved it off.

"I'm in," he repeated. "I know the risks. I know the price. I said I'm in."

All eyes turned to Cameron, who simply smiled.

"Do you think I'd stay behind? Hell, yeah! I'm in!"

Chuck looked around the room, smiling broadly and proudly.

"Well, now," he smiled. "This is what I like—going into the fray with a collection of mavericks and truants. That's the only way to fly!"

He stood up and shook each man's hand, congratulating each of the Roadhouse Sons on his decision.

"Now go get some Goddamned rest! But don't stay up too late, or get too wild. I want you hear bright and early tomorrow morning, by nine at the latest. You've got a show in a couple of days, and you've dealt with a shitload of distractions. I want you guys ready to kick this city's ass, even better than you did last time. Today, I heard with my own ears what you can do. I know you're up to that task as much as the others."

Before the band left, Chuck ordered them to examine their hotel rooms for bugs. He reminded them of the procedure, and then left.

"I've got some other stuff to take care of," he told them on his way out. "I'll probably be busy until tomorrow morning. But you're big boys and don't need me to babysit you. See you tomorrow."

Chuck asked Cameron to take his guitar back to Cameron's hotel room, to be picked up the next day. The guys decided to eat dinner, but Cameron declined their invitation. All he wanted to do was return to the hotel for some rest.

"The day's catching up to me," he confessed. The interrogation seemed like it was years ago, but was only that very morning. Since then, he felt like he'd circled the globe and ended up right back where he'd started.

I just need some rest.

As he approached his car, he saw that the driver's side window was partly open. He didn't give it much thought; he opened the window all the time to smoke. As he quickly checked the car's interior to make sure nothing was missing, he noticed an object on his front seat.

An orange.

END THIS NOW!

CHAPTER TWENTY

"Bambi"

His arm kept the dim light out of his eyes, and he gradually began to relax. Upon returning to the hotel, Cameron had checked to see if he had any messages. There were two, both from reporters, and nothing he could have taken care of at that time. He'd followed Chuck's suggestion of examining the room for bugs. Thankfully, there were none. Cameron opened the curtains to let in the last bit of daylight and was beginning to drift off to sleep when he heard a knock at the door.

If I lay here quietly, maybe they'll go away.

The knocking resumed, louder this time.

Fucking housekeeping! I told them to leave me alone unless I call!

He jumped off the bed and stormed across the room, ready to confront this assault upon his rest. He swung open the door, only to find himself staring into the startled face of Bambi.

"Oh, I'm sorry!" she gasped. "We had agreed to meet here. I didn't realize you were asleep!"

Her cheeks turned pink, and she withdrew from him as though expecting a blow. Cameron felt instant shame at his behavior, and even more so when he realized he'd dozed off—when she was supposed to come over!

Shit! I forgot! Can't let her know that.

"Oh, its nothing," he stammered. "We had a long rehearsal and I must have dozed off when I got back here. Please don't think anything of it! Come on in."

Cameron held the door open and stepped aside, waving gallantly to welcome her. As he followed her gaze around the room, he wished he'd let housekeeping in after all. Bambi turned to look at him, smiling as though waiting for him to say or do something next. He quickly closed the door and offered to take her jacket.

"You seem a little flustered," she laughed. "I didn't realize that you were going to be this nervous. I would have dressed better!"

"Oh, no. I'm not nervous," he said, hanging her jacket. "Not at all."

He winced.

We're off to a good start, aren't we?

"I didn't mean it the way it sounded." There was no hiding the surprise on Bambi's face. Cameron stammered on. "It's been a rough couple of days and it kind of has me a little shaky. I actually was looking forward to this, really. It's helped keep me going."

"Good heavens, is something wrong? You act like you had a death in the family!"

Cameron shuddered at her choice of words.

"Well," he muttered, "We sort of did."

Cameron told Bambi of Dwyer's of death, albeit omitting the exact circumstances.

"Oh my God!" she gasped, covering her mouth. "I am so sorry. I didn't mean to be so insensitive."

Her brown eyes brimmed with tears. Cameron's heart broke. He didn't mean to make her feel guilty, and he hated himself for being so careless with his choice of words.

"You're not being insensitive," he assured her, taking her hand. "You had no way of knowing. It was so sudden, and it hasn't been in any of the papers yet, or on the news. It's OK. I didn't mean to upset you. But as you can guess, I'm a little off my game with all this shit that's gone down."

Bambi reached up and gently touched Cameron's cheek. Her hand felt cool on his skin and he closed his eyes, trying to lose himself in the tenderness of her touch.

"I should leave you alone," she said softly. "I didn't mean to intrude."

"No!" he said, quickly grasping her by her arms. "You can't"

Bambi's arms tensed and she stepped back. Once again regretted his actions. Would he be able to do anything right with her?

"I'm sorry," he whispered. "I really am. I didn't mean to be so abrupt. I'm just not thinking clearly right now, but I do know that I don't want to be alone. I thought I did when I was with the guys earlier, but now that you're here, I know that some company would do me good. I didn't mean to be so weird. Please, *please* don't go."

Cameron didn't even try to hide the urgency in his voice, but did his best to tame his delivery. Bambi, though, still regarded him with caution, unsure of how he would react to whatever she chose to do.

"OK..." she said, hesitantly. Cameron wondered if she really wanted to stay now.

Or is she trying to humor me?

"I've been thinking about you since the other day!" he offered.

Oh, that was weak...

Cameron cringed to himself, but plodded on nevertheless. "You've sort of been my life saver these past few days. I know that must sound silly."

"Not at all!" Bambi insisted. Her tone was more relaxed and comforting now. Cameron couldn't tell if she really felt that way or if, because he'd behaved so unpredictably, she was just placating him. "We all have our ways to get through things like this. That is just how you reacted, that's all. I just don't want to intrude if you need to be alone."

Bambi smiled again, this time more sincerely, and Cameron fought tears of relief. She placed her hand against his cheek again and he was instantly reassured.

She wants to be here. If she didn't, she'd leave.

Cameron pulled Bambi close, her head against his chest. He breathed deeply, feeling the gentle pressure of her body against his. He felt the soft silkiness of her hair and the gentle warmth of her breath against his breast. He wanted to lose himself in that moment, to let this be his only reality, one free from Soviets and war and dead bodies, a world filled with only gentleness and peace.

Bambi was the one the break his reverie, though not his embrace.

"Are you sure you're all right?" she whispered. Cameron nodded. He didn't want to talk. The thought of his own speech, so eloquent when in front of a microphone, yet so awkward and clumsy with her today, was unappealing. He didn't want to ruin anything; he'd persuaded her to stay with him.

She caressed Cameron's face with both hands and drew him to her. She closed her eyes and kissed him. Her kiss was light as a feather, her soft lips barely brushing his. He wrapped her in a tighter embrace, offering no resistance. She pressed her lips against his, but with barely more pressure. When she released him, she gazed into his eyes.

"I didn't mean to appear forward," she whispered.

"You weren't," he whispered in response. Cameron traced his finger down the line of her chin, leading back to her mouth. She kissed his fingertips. He held her hand, gently but tightly, and kissed the center of her palm. He pulled her to him and held her tightly. This time, it was she that offered no resistance.

Cameron was thankful that he'd remembered to leave the radio on when he'd left that day. He discovered long ago that the radio, if set on certain stations and at a low volume, was an effective way to discourage people from trying to enter his room. He'd also used it while checking for bugs; it covered the sound of his moving around the room. He never bothered to turn it off, and now found himself moving in time with the music, Bambi eagerly in synch with him.

Cameron smiled as they moved to the beat, holding each other close and swaying, then spinning about the room. The light of day was beginning to fade. The dim glow from the lamp near the door was the only illumination in the room. They danced through several songs, stopping when the station went to a commercial break.

"You're a nice dancer," she smiled. "But that shouldn't be surprising."

"Oh? And why not?" Cameron smiled; he loved her company.

"Because you're also a good musician," she replied with a kiss on his lips. "Of course, you'd have a good sense of rhythm."

"So, you think I'm a good musician?" he asked with a mischievous smile. She gave him a playful tap.

"You're terrible!"

Cameron melted at the sight of her face. The light near the door shined on her, accentuating her radiant fair skin. He hoped that the radio would play a song – and soon. He hated the thought of ending their embrace, but knew that they couldn't just stand there like that.

There's nothing I'd rather do. I don't want to kill the moment...

Unfortunately, the need for revenue triumphed over the encouragement of romance, and Cameron realized that the station was playing a set of commercials that lasted as long as a set of songs.

"What would you like to do?" Cameron asked Bambi, still holding her and swaying to imagined music. "There's a movie playing nearby. I think it's called *International Velvet*. I have some sugar coupons, so I can get you something at the snack bar, if you'd like to go."

"That's sweet," she smiled, pulling him tighter. "But I don't think I'm in the mood for a movie."

"Would you like to go out to dinner, then?" he asked, gently rubbing her back. "I have some gas rations that can get us out of town."

"You don't want to eat here?" Bambi suggested. "I thought the hotel served food."

"Only in the bar," Cameron said, shaking his head. "And that isn't very good. I think they hope people will be too drunk to notice."

"But I take it you don't think that will work?"

"Nope. Their booze is worse than their food. But that's no big deal. I know a cool place in South Burlington. Would you like to go there?"

"I don't think we could get back before curfew…" Bambi looked worried.

True. There is no way in hell I'm rushing an evening with you.

"Why don't we just stay here for a while and get to know each other better?" she suggested. "We can get something at a diner later, if we want."

You don't need to ask me twice.

They stayed in Cameron's room, curled up on the sofa, sharing their pasts with each other. Cameron regaled her with stories of how he and Rich had dreamed of starting a band ever since they were six years old, and of how they'd gone with their parents to hear his cousins play in a local talent show.

"I listened to them do *Teen Angel* and that was it," he laughed. "The next day, we raided my dad's tool shed for scrap wood and nails, got some rubber bands, and made ourselves our first guitars!"

Cameron shared several such stories with her and, feeling that he wouldn't be intruding, he shifted his position on the couch to sit closer to her.

"But I don't want to talk about me all night!" Cameron laughed. "Tell me about you."

"There's really not much to tell." Bambi smiled, shifting her own position so that she sat beside him, facing not Cameron, but the center of the room. "My life isn't nearly as interesting as yours."

"We never think our lives are interesting," he assured her, wondering if her posture was a signal that Bambi was being evasive. "But other people do think so. You thought mine was interesting. I'd like to hear about yours."

Look at me. Talk to me.

Bambi offered coy defenses, avoiding any revelations about her past, but Cameron succeeded in countering each one, his interest in her growing with each attempt. Finally she admitted defeat.

"Ok, you win!" she laughed. "I'll tell you, but don't you blame me if you fall asleep. Deal?"

"Deal," he said, settling in closer and facing her.

Bambi told Cameron about growing up in northern Vermont, about her mother's family hailing from Vermont, and about her father's origins and life in Quebec, where Bambi was born. She confided to Cameron that, for years, she didn't even know if she was an American or a Canadian until she started school in Vermont.

"We spent as much of our time in Quebec as we did here, because my dad traveled to find work," she laughed. "I was shocked to find out it wasn't all one place!"

"So your dad's side are all Québécois?" Cameron asked.

She studied him quietly for a moment, clearly impressed that Cameron, this rock singer, would know the term, let alone pronounce it correctly. She continued with her life story, telling him of how hard it was for her family to make a living. Bambi's father was not well educated, and work was difficult to find. Her mother had to take care of the house and take in laundry and mending to help augment her father's meager income. When the time came for high school, Bambi was subjected to a great deal of pressure to drop out of school and go to work.

"My father even had a job lined up for me already," she said, her voice growing quieter, and her smile fading.

"What was it?" Cameron asked, cautiously. He realized by her change of demeanor that this was indeed a difficult subject for her. He hoped that Bambi understood that he was asking so that she could have someone with whom to share her story, and that he was not just asking out of idle curiosity.

"It was working in a store," Bambi said, looking down at her hands. "I compromised with my dad, and agreed to work weekends and after school. But I *really* wanted to *stay* in school. I knew that would be my best chance to get out of there. My dad was furious at first, but my mother thought I was right. It would be best if I got an education."

Bambi paused at this point. Her eyes held a distant look, as though the memories that she'd just described were unfolding before her once more.

I can never go where she is right now. Don't push. Give her some time.

Cameron allowed Bambi the moments she needed to collect her thoughts. When she was ready, she resumed her tale.

"When graduation time came, things got even more difficult. My dad expected me to start work full-time then, but I'm afraid I had an unpleasant surprise for him. I'd gotten accepted at a college and was going to go. He refused to pay, and went into a towering rage when he found out it was a full scholarship, and there was no way that he could stop me."

"Good for you," Cameron said, and instantly regretted it. He didn't know her well enough to assume a side in a family argument. For all he knew, Bambi and her family had reconciled and all was fine. If Bambi was offended by Cameron's comment, she didn't indicate it. She turned to him with a warm, grateful smile. Cameron felt a wave of relief.

"Where was the college, if you don't mind me asking?" he said.

"Believe it or not, it was in Spain!" Bambi said, proudly.

"What in the world were you going to study there?"

"Art, believe it or not!"

"Oh, I do believe it," Cameron assured her. "See? Now, *that's* interesting! Were you studying painting, or something?"

"Well, yes," she said. "Finally. But in the beginning, I tried studying dance."

"Why'd you change?"

"I broke my leg," Bambi sighed. "It was pretty bad, and looked like I might be sent home. Fortunately, I had a sketchbook that I always carried around with me, and they accepted that as a portfolio. I was there almost two years."

"Did you graduate?"

She shook her head, but said nothing.

"Why not?" Cameron asked, softly.

Bambi hesitated before answering, clearly struggling with her emotions.

Shit. I'm pushing too hard.

Cameron instinctively stroked her hair, then stopped, feeling that he may seem like an emotional opportunist.

"My mom passed away," Bambi said, her voice shaking. "I came home to attend the funeral."

"I'm sorry to hear that," Cameron said, regretting that he'd prompted such a painful subject. He thought of how his family, though initially unsure of his decision to become a musician, was nonetheless supportive and had never tried to force him into some other course of study or work; they'd encouraged him to follow the dream that was meaningful to *him*. Cameron felt a tinge of remorse at how different his life had been compared to Bambi's. Sensing Cameron's rueful discomfort, Bambi revealed the end of her story.

"After I came home, there was no way for me to go back to Spain. I had to work for my father, after all. By now, he'd become a partner in the tavern here in Burlington, and I started working in the kitchen cleaning glasses, and I eventually made it up to being the head bartender. Not what I'd call glamorous, but I suppose that is what I can use my experiences in Spain for."

She looked away, absently picking at lint balls on her sweater. The two sat in awkward silence for what felt like an eternity. The radio played *When Will I Be Loved?*

Oh, God…

Cameron held Bambi's hand. She looked at him, too soon to dab at her eyes, and Cameron could see that she was making a valiant effort to hold back tears. Without saying a word, he stroked Bambi's hair and silently kissed the top of her head. He held her as Linda Ronstadt's lyrics filled the darkness. Cameron wanted to convey to her his feelings – how she made him feel, her uniqueness, and what an incomparable lady she was to him. He wanted her to know that he would really be there for her, now and always. As the last notes of the faded away, Bambi shifted slightly, and scratched her nose in an attempt to fend off sniffles.

"Thank you," she whispered. Cameron replied with another kiss on the top of her head. She pulled him closer to her. He cuddled into Bambi and she into him. Their breathing became one, and he fought the urge to kiss her. He *really* wanted to kiss her. Another song played on the radio, but Cameron paid no attention to it, or to the next one. As the third song began, though, it held a faster tempo than the others. This forced a change in atmosphere, and Cameron fiercely resented it. Fighting the urge to toss the radio across the room, he settled on another course of action.

"Come on!" he said, getting up off the couch.

"Where are you going?"

"*We* are going *out!*" he smiled, holding out his hand. "I'm not going to keep you cooped up in here. Come on."

"But where?" Bambi asked, laughing nervously. "Or are you trying to be mysterious?"

"Let's say… mys*teri*ousssss," he chuckled, beckoning her with her coat.

"You mean you don't have any idea what you're going to do… Do you?"

"Well... yeah!" he laughed. She shook her head and smiled. Cameron realized that she was just as comfortable with spontaneity as he was. It was nice being understood.

"Aren't you going to shut the radio off?" Bambi asked as he closed the door behind them. He shook his head.

"Nah, I like it on," Cameron replied. "It makes me feel like I've got someone to come back to."

"I thought that you would have all kinds of groupies hanging around," she teased as they waited for the elevator. He laughed.

"I won't lie," he said. "We have a lot of them hanging around, though lately they don't, because it's not as easy."

"Why's that?"

"Well, a lot of them used to like to travel around with the band," Cameron explained. "They'd almost make a career out of it. They'd room together and pool their money to buy gas to make it to our gigs, or buy food to make sure we ate, or buy clothes and jewelry to make themselves attractive to us. But once the war hit and travel became so hard, it cut down on how often they could travel. When curfews started, it made it really hard for the girls who lived in one town to go out of their way to attend a show in another, *and* to justify the expense and all the trouble. When you have to keep an eye on the clock to make sure you're home before the streets close, it might not be worth it to go out in the first place."

"So that's why I didn't have to step over any groupies in the hallway?"

"Yeah, I guess!" Cameron laughed.

The elevator doors closed and the pair descended. As Cameron and Bambi stepped into the lobby, they noticed that it was inordinately quiet. A few patrons were watching a rerun of *Adam-12* on television, and another was reading a newspaper. There was no sign of Chuck Lamont or any of the Roadhouse Sons. Cameron made small talk with the clerk as he dropped off his keys. He gently guided Bambi to the door, and held it open for Bambi as they stepped out into the cold.

The dark skies and the few flakes of snow drifting to the pavement cast a sudden and ominous pall upon Cameron's mood. The streets appeared even more deserted than usual. Like most communities, Burlington was doing its part to conserve energy by reducing the use of streetlights. Citizens also contributed by reducing their own domestic use, and by limiting all-night light use in the town's businesses. Cameron saw some random security lights in use, but very few storefronts were lit at night anymore. The Grand Isle Hotel was an island adrift in a sea of darkness.

Shake it off. Just have a good time.

Cameron looked at Bambi and smiled. She smiled back at him. They made jokes about the cold and the energy crunch as they hurried to the parking area. As they rounded the building, Cameron saw a man and a woman coming toward them. The couple didn't seem to notice Cameron and Bambi, but he couldn't shake the feeling that the two walked with a sense of immoderate determination.

Probably just trying to get to where they're going and get out of the cold.

As they drew closer, he noticed that there was something familiar about the man, whose face was huddled into the collar of his coat. The woman had a scarf around her neck, pulled up over the lower portion of her face. She was dressed in a long, heavy coat, with a cap that reminded Cameron of Mary Tyler Moore's tam. The woman also wore expensive dark boots. Cameron said nothing, but nodded politely. He guided Bambi by the arm, heading purposefully toward his car, when the woman suddenly called out.

"Oh, hi, Bambi!" the woman said, pulling her scarf away from her mouth. "Fancy meeting you here!"

"Vicki! What in the world are you doing out on a night like this?" Bambi replied with a laugh. The two women engaged in the age-old ritual that always mystified Cameron—of greeting one another as though they hadn't seen each other in years.

They probably had lunch together this afternoon.

Bambi introduced Vicki and the man to Cameron. For reasons he couldn't quite discern thus far, Cameron felt that it was important to know this other man's name.

There's something about… I can't put my finger on it. This guy's a creep, I just know it.

"Hi, I'm Tyrell Audway," the man said, shaking Cameron's hand with a firm grasp. In order to get a better look at his face, Cameron pretended that he hadn't heard the man. Cameron leaned his head toward the man, hands still gripped, in an unspoken invitation for the man to repeat himself. Audway did, speaking slower and louder, just as Cameron had hoped that he would. Before releasing Audway's grip, Cameron studied the man. Audway wore a black knit cap, from under which sandy brown hair poked out. He wore a heavy Carhartt jacket, severely worn about the cuffs. This suggested to Cameron that the man worked with his hands, the fact of which was confirmed by the calluses that Cameron felt. He glanced at Audway's hands; the cracks in the skin were stained dark.

Motor grease?

Audway wore dark pants and dirty, worn sneakers. Several days' worth of whiskers darkened his face, against which his sharp hazel eyes stood out dramatically.

"Pleased to meet you, Tyrell," Cameron smiled, still shaking his hand. "I'm Cameron Walsh."

At that moment, Cameron remembered where he'd first seen Audway.

"I recognize you, now!" Cameron smiled. Audway tensed.

"You do?" he asked, cautiously. His voice was low but not menacing. Rather, it was the voice of a man uncomfortable with speaking, and who therefore wished to do so as seldom as possible.

"Yeah! You were with Bambi at the concert the other night. Was this the girl you were there with?"

Cameron realized after he'd asked that it was likely not the most diplomatic question, which probably accounted for Audway's reaction. What if it wasn't the woman accompanying Audway?

Then you'll have a lot of explaining to do, and you'll try to get away from us.

"Yes, that's us," Vicki said with a smile. She, too, had a sense of familiarity about her, and as Cameron was trying to place her, Vicki spoke again. Her voice cut through Cameron, causing him to shudder. That was when he remembered where he'd seen her.

She was that hovering waitress at the Catamount!

Cameron made polite small talk as Vicki and Bambi exchanged snippets of gossip. He prayed all the while that Vicki and Audway wouldn't join them. To his dismay, that's exactly what Bambi invited them to do, turning to Cameron only after she had posed the question.

"Oh, no!" Vicki insisted. "Tyrell and I have to be going. We've got an appointment to keep. You guys run along and have a nice evening!"

Bambi asked once again, just to make sure. Cameron wondered for a moment if Bambi was afraid to be alone with him, yet still felt relief when Vicki and Audway declined Bambi's invitation. The two girls exchanged parting remarks and agreed to meet up the next day, since they both had the day off.

As they readied to depart, Bambi slipped her arm in Cameron's and gently began nudging him forward. Cameron needed no encouragement, and gladly walked on. He breathed an inaudible sigh of relief as the other couple headed in the opposite direction. As Vicki and Audway rounded the corner of the building, Cameron looked back over his shoulder and noticed that they were entering the hotel. Cameron frowned, but kept walking.

Bambi had released her hold on his arm and was now a few steps ahead of him. As they approached the car, she reached out her hand to open the door and Cameron hurried to her side.

"Wait a second!" he laughed. "I've got it."

"I can open a door by myself," Bambi said, smiling. "I'm not some helpless woman, you know!"

Oh shit… a feminist.

"I didn't think that you were." Cameron returned her smile. "It's just that I like to be a gentleman. Besides, the door's locked."

With that, he produced his keys with a flourish and unlocked the door. Holding it open, Cameron bowed gallantly with a sweep of his arm, inviting her to be seated. With a shake of her head, Bambi got into the car, pulling the door closed before he had a chance to do it for her.

Ok. Landmine number one to avoid: Don't make her think you're a male chauvinist.

Cameron unlocked his door, crawled in and started the Mustang. He turned up the heater and directed the vents toward Bambi. He blew his breath on his cold hands. rubbing them together for warmth

"So where are we going?" Bambi asked, wrapping her arms around her torso, waiting for the car to warm up.

"I know a nice place not far from here. Do you like Italian food?"

Bambi nodded.

"Great!" he said, blowing on his hands again. "You might not get a lot of meat in the meat sauce, but it's still good."

"It's been so long since I've had meat, I don't think I'd know what it was like anyway."

"Really?" he asked. "Don't you get a ration book?"

Bambi hurriedly turned away from him, and Cameron realized that he'd struck a nerve.

"Yes, but it doesn't go as far as yours do," she said, not looking at him.

"What are you talking about?"

"I'm not an American citizen," Bambi said. "So the government feels its Canada's responsibility to feed me. The problem is, I get a ration book from Canada, but not enough gas rations to go up there to use them, or get new ones. Since you don't report in every month, you have to reapply and wait for them to make certain you're not working a black market deal somehow. We get by, but it's hard sometimes."

Cameron was stunned. He knew that the rations were inconvenient for most people but, thanks to help from Dwyer, the Roadhouse Sons were able to get extra coupons for gas. The band also received coupons for cigarettes and other things deemed nonessential by the government, and even then life wasn't easy. However, he'd never heard of anything like what Bambi described. He couldn't imagine what it was like to be faced with the inability to get what one needed to survive, let alone not being able to do anything about it.

"Does your dad get Canadian rations too?"

"No," she sighed. "He became an American years ago, so he's ineligible for them."

"Doesn't he share his rations with you?"

"He would if he got them," she said sarcastically. "However, he's had his privileges suspended. Now he's on partial rations."

"What the hell are you talking about?" Cameron asked. "What did he do?"

"He tried to make a living!" she snapped. "His regular dealer raised the prices on him more than he could afford to pay. When he tried to buy from a cheaper dealer, the government accused him of getting it on the black market and arrested him. Instead of prison, they gave him a fine that wiped out the little bit he had in his savings and put a lien on the bar for the rest. To top it off, they put both him *and* the business on reduced rations. That's the reason for the limited selection we have."

Cameron didn't know what to say. The car was warm now, but he felt that putting it in gear and driving off would be insensitive. He didn't want that. He wanted to know what she needed, and moreso, he wanted to help.

"Look," he said, choosing his words carefully. "I know it's none of my business, but if there's anything I can do to help…"

"I appreciate that," Bambi said. "But we're watched pretty carefully these days. If we try using your rations, we'll just get into worse trouble. Thanks, anyhow."

"No! I didn't mean it like that. I know that's what would happen. I meant that if you want, I can take you up to Canada to get stuff and get you to the ration office. You know, stuff like that."

Bambi didn't say a word. Cameron pointed to the large green sticker on the lower left of his windscreen – the sticker with the white letter *A* printed on it.

"It's an *A* car," he explained. "It's allowed to be used for nonessential travel. And I've also got a supplemental rations book." He smiled triumphantly. "We're considered good for the public morale, so that's why they allow us the extra travel."

"Must be nice," Bambi said softly. Cameron felt his face flush, and he was glad that she couldn't see him in the dark. He hadn't meant to brag or insult her, but apparently that was exactly what he'd done.

"Look, I'm sorry," he said. "I don't know how you took what I just said, but I was only trying to let you know that I want to help. I didn't mean to insult you or upset you. I was just trying to be nice."

Bambi didn't reply right away. For a moment, Cameron feared that she might get out of the car, but she didn't.

"You're very sincere," she said, patting his cheek. "And I believe you were only trying to help. I appreciate that, I really do. But I don't think there's anything you can do. Besides, that far in from the border, or outside of Montreal, your American rations wouldn't be accepted. But thank you just the same."

Cameron reached out and gently grasped Bambi's hand. She didn't try to push him away. He wanted to maintain contact with her, to never let her go. Intuitively, Bambi leaned over and kissed him on the cheek.

"Don't worry," she whispered. "I'll be fine. This isn't the first time things have been tough for me. I did fine then, and I'll do just fine again. OK?"

Cameron smiled and, turning his head, he kissed her lightly on the lips.

Bambi blushed, and pulling away said, "Now, take me to that restaurant you were telling me about!" She laughed a bit nervously. Cameron didn't argue. Despite their brief and intimate exchange, he still felt unsettled. He wasn't sure why, but finally chalked it up to the fact that this one had differed so drastically from the more pleasant exchanges earlier. He turned on the radio for her, finding the station from Montreal that she said she loved.

"Oh, CHOM has got to be my favorite," she smiled. "My father hates having it on in the bar or at home, so I don't get to listen to it very much."

"He doesn't like rock?" Cameron asked, concerned. Granted, he had no plans to be meeting her father in the foreseeable future, but he didn't need any more strikes against him than he'd already wracked up tonight.

"He doesn't care about that," she laughed. "He's still angry that they stopped being bilingual. He's a pretty die-hard secessionist; supports Quebec independence, favors French as the official language, all that."

"What about you?" Cameron asked. He wondered if he was broaching touchy subjects. After all, everyone knew that politics and religion were the two hottest issues that could stir conflict and controversy. He didn't have any clearly defined opinions himself, but sometimes one only had to make a casual remark to set off someone else.

"I like keeping my views to myself," she said with a sad smile. "Sometimes people don't like hearing them."

OK. That's a relief. Then I won't talk about mine, either.

"No problem here, then!" Cameron smiled at her, hoping to ease the growing tension.

The radio station played on, offering music with only brief commercial breaks, and news bulletins on what the government called the Northwestern Front. There were no reports on any significant victories, but news of military and civilian casualties were covered in depth. When Bambi heard these bulletins, she looked out of her window and became very quiet. Cameron thought it best to leave her alone with her thoughts until she was ready to talk. They drove in silence for a little while longer.

At last, they arrived at the restaurant, a fairly au courant establishment with the usual faux European décor of dark wood wall paneling, amber-glassed windows, and crackle-glass candleholders on the tables. Each table and its matching chairs were constructed of the same heavy dark wood veneer that permeated the walls. The bright orange and gold carpet was an unsuccessful attempt to offset the dimness of the room.

The hostess, a brunette sporting heavy false eyelashes, white frost lipstick and a tight lavender Qiana dress, led them to a table near the fireplace. Cameron made a mental note to tip her well for the cozy seating. The restaurant was sparsely populated, with many empty tables. He and Bambi could hear loud laughter coming from the bar area. He was glad that she didn't ask him to go in there, but then realized that she'd likely had her fill of spending time in bars.

Their time over dinner was spent enjoying a low-grade Chianti, and fare that complied with the new government regulations without being a complete mockery of Italian cuisine. Cameron used some of his extra coffee and sugar rations to buy Bambi some hot chocolate for dessert.

"You didn't need to do that!" She smiled at him over the rim of her cup. Cameron knew that she appreciated his generosity.

"That's why it's special," he grinned. "I didn't *have* to do it."

They talked about the Roadhouse Sons and many of the places they'd toured. Bambi was captivated by Cameron's stories of the road, and of the bands with whom they'd worked.

"I've heard a lot of these guys on the radio!" Bambi giggled. "I can't believe I'm actually talking to someone who knows them!"

"Knows them, got drunk with them, opened for them. You name it, we probably did it at one time or another!"

"Have you guys always been together as a band?"

"I've been the longest with these guys," Cameron said, sipping the last of his Chianti. "Rich and I started putting together something when we were kids. Evan came along after we graduated from high school, and we all decided that we wanted to do this full-time. Clyde came along after we hit the road, and we liked his sound so much we hired him. Doug's the newest one. He's only been with us about three years."

"Who's Doug?" Bambi asked. "I thought you only had four members of your band?"

"He's the road manager," Cameron explained. "He makes sure the equipment is working properly, makes sure everything is set up the way we want it, and that sort of thing."

Bambi appeared to be deep in thought, and Cameron wondered if she was tracking their the topic of discussion.

"Oh, now I know!" Bambi exclaimed. "He's the big one with the black hat, isn't he? He's a little intimidating."

"Yeah, that's him," Cameron said, relieved. He poured the last of the Chianti into his glass, sipping slowly and considering what Bambi had just said. When he talked to her after the last show, she'd told him that she'd never gone backstage.

Doug never comes onstage unless it's a dire emergency, and he never interacts with the crowd unless they're back stage.

When did Bambi ever see Doug? That was a question demanding an answer, and Cameron knew he had to tread lightly to get one.

"Don't let Dougie bother you. He's all right if you know how to handle him."

"And how is that, exactly?" Bambi eyed him playfully.

Cameron leaned in and motioned for Bambi to do likewise.

"Don't make eye contact," he whispered. "And avoid sudden movements."

She stared at him for a moment, and then began to laugh uncontrollably.

"You had me going there for a minute," she giggled. "I thought you had some real advice for me."

Cameron shook his head, chuckling at his own mischief. He sensed an opening for his question, but couldn't quite formulate his wording yet. He forced down another sip of the Chianti, and opted for nonchalance.

"Doug didn't give you a hard time, did he?"

"What do you mean?" Bambi tilted her head quizzically.

"Well, another one of Doug's jobs is to monitor the people that try to come backstage. You said he was intimidating, I just thought you bumped into him after the show. I wanted to make certain he didn't give you a hard time."

"Oh no, nothing like that," she assured him. "I've never had any direct contact with him. I've just seen him come on a little strong at times."

When, where and how?

Cameron saw no point in pursuing his line of questioning, especially right now. So much had gone on in the past few days that he knew was liable to misread every signal that passed his way.

Don't ask her now... too sensitive. Do it with a fresh mind.

The remainder of their conversation encompassed various subjects and incidents in their histories. Cameron wouldn't have realized how late it was were it not for the sudden eerie silence in the bar.

"Shit!" he cried, looking at his watch. "I didn't know how late it was! I better get you home before the curfew goes into effect."

Bambi hurried from her chair and grabbed her coat. Cameron wanted to be chivalrous and help her with it, but every second counted. It was nearly 11:30PM and the streets were mandated to be vacant by midnight. If Cameron and Bambi were caught out on the roads, they could each face a $500 fine, and possibly a night in jail. He knew he couldn't afford either, and was certain that Bambi couldn't, especially with what she'd revealed to him tonight. The last thing Cameron wanted to do was to make more trouble for her.

He led her to the car and didn't wait for the engine to warm up. Instead, he put the car in gear as soon as he started it, and sped toward the hotel. On a few occasions, he barely navigated the intersections before the amber lights turned red. His luck held out as far as cop chases were concerned, but he could've sworn that he'd seen an unmarked surveillance vehicle at least once.

You're just paranoid. Dwyer bought it and you're convinced the boogey man is coming to get you, too. Keep up this shit and you'll drive yourself fucking nuts.

He pulled into the parking lot of the hotel with barely five minutes to spare.

"OK! Which one is your car?" Cameron asked, turning to face Bambi.

"You're kidding me, right?" She was astonished. When Cameron gave her a puzzled look, she laughed sardonically.

"You don't honestly think I have a car, do you? If I had a car, I'd be able to get to Canada and straighten out all of my problems with my rations. Honey, I walked over here."

"Oh, man," he moaned, putting his head on the steering wheel. "I should have known. I should have asked. I am so, so sorry."

Cameron looked at Bambi, pleading. She responded with a smile and a soft stroke to his cheek.

"That's all right," she smiled. "I should have said something. It's not your fault."

"How far away do you live?" he asked. "The patrols probably won't be getting here for a bit. I can get you home and get back before anyone notices. Where do you live?"

She shook her head.

"No, that won't work," she said. "My landlady is the vigilante type and would report me anyway, even if the patrols don't pick us up."

"You're shitting me," he muttered. Then he turned to her.

"If you don't think I'm out of line, you can stay with me if you'd like."

Bambi's eyes widened as she realized what he had said.

"Oh, God! I don't know about that," she gasped, struggling for words.

"No, it's really OK," he insisted. "I'm not talking about, you know, *that.*"

Though I wouldn't turn it down if you offered.

"I don't want you to get the wrong idea about me," she insisted, and he noticed a pleading in her voice. He held his hands up in a gesture of innocence.

"Hands to myself, sweetheart," he assured her. "I'll be a perfect gentleman. I'll even check and see if they have another room, if you'd like!"

"I don't think you'll be doing that," Bambi sighed, pointing out the window. Cameron's gaze followed her finger to the large sign in front of the Grand Isle Hotel. The streetlight illuminated it beautifully. *No Vacancy*. Rather than disappointment, Cameron felt a slight thrill of excitement.

Thank you, whoever you are!

"OK, then. As I said, I'll be a perfect gentleman and keep all of my clothes on. What do you think of that?"

"I'm not going to argue," she laughed. "It's been a long day and I'm beat. I can imagine you must be, too."

Cameron nodded and, as if on cue, yawned. Getting out of the car, he hurried around it to open Bambi's door. Helping her from the car, he placed her coat over her shoulders and put his arm around her to keep her warm. They made their way inside. The lobby was deserted, except for the night clerk, who poked his head out and handed Cameron the room keys. Noticing Cameron's arm around Bambi, the clerk winked and gave Cameron the "thumbs up." Cameron guided Bambi to the elevator, responding to the desk clerk with the middle finger. He was not about to let anyone think that Bambi was some cheap groupie.

As they rode the elevator, Cameron pondered Bambi's contradictions about having met Doug. Cameron finally realized why she was vacillating, but he decided to remain silent for the time being.

The elevator reached Cameron's floor, and he and Bambi entered his room. As he closed the door, Cameron realized that there was something different about the room. It was quiet.

What happened to my fucking radio?

Bambi hung her coat in the closet and went into the bathroom. Cameron used the opportunity to check the radio. The volume was turned to *Off.* Cameron turned the radio on. Music resumed from the same station they'd heard prior to leaving for dinner.

That's fucking weird.

Cameron pondered calling the front desk to see if anyone had asked for him, but he didn't want to talk to that lascivious clerk. He sat on the edge of the bed and took off his boots, trying to understand what had happened to the radio. Then it dawned on him.

Chuck was probably looking for me. He must have Dwyer's pass keys to all our rooms and let himself in. He wouldn't know I like leaving the radio on while I'm gone. I'll tell him tomorrow.

Bambi emerged from the bathroom, her hair cascading over her shoulders in tawny locks that matched Cameron's. She looked even more beautiful with her hair down.

"Well, there goes your offer!" She smiled at him, then giggled.

"What are you talking about?" Cameron asked.

"You said you'd be a perfect gentleman and even keep your boots on," she laughed, pointing at his feet. He smiled and shrugged. The smile faded from her face as she watched him get up off the bed.

"I don't want you thinking bad of me," she said, once again with a pleading in her voice. "I don't usually do things like this."

He wrapped his arms around her waist and pressed against her, leaning his face toward her until their foreheads touched.

"You are such a fucking liar," Cameron whispered.

CHAPTER TWENTY-ONE
"Making Their Move"

Doug realized, as soon as he opened his eyes, that it wasn't something in his dreams that woke him up; it was something in his room. He remained still for a moment, trying to remember what exactly it was that had alerted him. He heard nothing, and continued to lie there, motionless, as if he was still asleep. The room was quiet, yet he couldn't shake the feeling that he wasn't alone. The stillness was unnatural. Doug felt the essence of something tense and coiled, like a snake waiting to strike.

He didn't move, but lay still, waiting to see what would happen next. In his groggy state, at first, he congratulated himself for feigning sleep. Now fully awake, he realized that pretending to sleep would be futile. Anybody monitoring him would know that he snored while asleep, and now he was quiet. Whoever was in the room had already figured out that Doug was wide awake. He debated snoring aloud and simulating sleep, but decided against it. He was on his side, facing the room. To simulate sleep, he had two options, neither of which were very desirable. He would either have to turn on his other side with his back to the room, or he would have to lie on his back, indeed a difficult and vulnerable position from which to deal with any threat.

Doug decided that there was no use waiting, and rose from the bed. He rubbed his eyes and tried to focus. The bathroom light was on, which he remembered turning off. He suddenly spotted the silhouette of a man stepping out of the shadows and into the middle of the room.

"D'Lorenzo, is that you?" Doug asked. He received no response, but saw the stranger raise an arm to strike. Doug thought he espied something in the stranger's hand, but there was no way he was going to wait and find out for certain. Lunging from the bed,

Doug aimed for the figure's mid section and made contact just as the intruder's arm came down, striking Doug in the lower back. The impact was blunt, and thankfully didn't pierce his skin.

Blackjack, Doug thought, but had no time to think of anything more. Upon the impact of his own lunge, he heard the stranger grunt as the wind was knocked out of him. Doug wrapped his arms around the man's waist in a bear hug, and pushed with his shoulder, using his momentum to slam the stranger backward. He tried to locate the doorframe to the bathroom, intending to back the stranger into it and, realizing that he'd somehow managed to get through the open door, Doug tightened his grip in an effort to keep the man from catching his breath. The man stumbled as his legs made contact with the toilet.

The two opponents tumbled awkwardly, and Doug's grip loosened, yet he still held himself in a position of advantage. Reaching up, he tried grabbing the man's hair, but got a handful of wool cap. The man tried twisting out of Doug's vice-like grip. Grabbing the man's head, Doug drove it into the edge of the sink once, twice and then a third time, the thud of bone contacting porcelain like the ring of a bell in a pinball machine.

Doug got a better grip on the man's hat and yanked the man's head back. The stranger's face was now fully lit. It was not D'Lorenzo, though Doug could have sworn he recognized the man. The stranger moaned and closed his eyes. Doug grabbed him by the front of his coat and lifted him to his feet.

"Who the fuck are you?" Doug demanded, shaking the man. The stranger made no response and, in frustration, Doug turned and threw the man out of the bathroom, hearing him hit the floor with a dull thud as he landed. Doug expected the man to be still, but realized as he was starting to turn that the man had caught his wind sufficiently enough to possibly retaliate. Doug rushed out toward the man, intending to pin him down to the carpet. Instead, the man saw Doug coming and stuck his left leg up in an effort to ward Doug off. Without hesitating, Doug grabbed the man's leg and rolled forward over the top of him, pulling the leg with him, hyper extending it. He heard the man yelp and grab his leg as Doug released his grip.

Doug twisted himself around into a crouching position and waited to see what the other man would do. The stranger grabbed his left thigh in both hands and buried his face into the carpet to stifle his scream. Seizing the opportunity, Doug sprang to his feet and rushed over, firmly setting his foot on the back of the man's neck, holding him down. The stranger began to struggle and squirm under the pressure, which only made Doug apply more.

Doug leaned more and more of his weight onto his foot, and with the increased pressure came increased struggle. Doug tried leaning on the bed, but the softness of the mattress didn't provide him with sufficient leverage. He held the man down, but knew he couldn't do it forever. The phone was beside the bed, but Doug had no way to reach it without releasing his advantage. He thought of shouting to attract attention, but knew the hotel was an older building with thick walls and he doubted that anyone would hear him. Doug hesitated a few more moments, and then proceeded to kick the man near his kidneys in an attempt to knock more wind out of him. After several kicks, the man lay still and Doug decided to risk the chance of grabbing the phone. He barely had the phone in reach before he realized it was a mistake.

The stranger began to rise, pulling himself up onto his knees. Doug used the dark room to his advantage. Grabbing the phone, he attempted to bring it down on the man's head. The phone cord stretched from the wall to its furthest extent, and Doug lost his grip and dropped it on the bed. Picking up the phone again with both hands this time, he pulled as hard as he could, and felt the phone rip out of the wall. The man was getting up when Doug crashed the phone down on the stranger's head. Doug watched, wary with panic, as the man sank onto the floor.

The stranger made no sound for the longest time, and Doug was afraid he had killed him. Doug hurried to the wall by the door and turned on the light. He examined the man carefully for vital signs, and felt relief when he noticed the rise and fall of the stranger's chest. The intruder was still alive, but unconscious.

Doug studied the man's features carefully. He noted that the stranger was shorter than he, though it was difficult to be certain, due to the man's odd position. He had a dark jacket, worn about the cuffs, and was also wearing dark jeans and worn, stained sneakers. The knit cap, askew over the stranger's left eye as if in an attempt to hide his identity, revealed greasy, sandy brown hair. The man's heavy growth of whiskers bore further testimony to his lack of personal hygiene. Doug wondered what color the man's eyes were and was about to check, when he realized that he might've hit the man so hard that he gave him a concussion.

Doug grabbed his lighter from the table beside his bed. He lit it and pried open one of the stranger's eyelids. He held the lighter up to the man's eye, and was relieved to see the pupil constrict.

"Watching *Emergency* paid off," Doug said to the prone figure, then sat back on his bed.

He debated with himself what to do next. He realized that he had to notify someone, but how? The phone was now lying on the floor beside the man, its cord trailing uselessly beside it. Doug realized the wonderful opportunity he now had. He could tie the man up, and then get help.

Disconnecting the cord from the phone, Doug rolled the man over and pulled his arms behind him. He decided to check the stranger's pockets for clues to his identity, and found an old bandana in the man's left rear-end pocket. It was slightly stiff, which made Doug nauseous.

"I can just imagine what's all over this thing," he muttered, dropping the bandana on the floor. In the man's right rear pocket, Doug discovered a worn brown wallet. He opened it and found a Vermont driver's license. The name on the license was *Tyrell Audway* and the town of residence was *North Clarendon*. Doug struggled to remember where North Clarendon was, and realized that it was just south of Rutland. At that moment, he recalled where he'd last seen this Tyrell Audway. It was in the same bar in which he'd located Louis Barre.

Without hesitating, Doug grabbed the phone cord, pulled Audway's arms back, and tied them together at the wrists. Rolling him over, Doug searched Audway's remaining pockets for weapons. Doug put on the bed everything he found in each pocket. In Audway's left front pants pocket, Doug discovered a set of keys on a green rabbit's foot keychain.

"Wasn't any luckier for you than it was for the rabbit, was it, asshole?" Doug said.

In Audway's right front pants pocket, Doug found 37 cents in loose change. Doug moved on to the Audway's jacket pockets, still suspecting that Audway was armed. Doug couldn't imagine anyone breaking into a hotel room without some form of protection. He was correct. In Tyrell's right pocket, he felt a firearm. He didn't want to get his fingerprints on it, and was about to reach for the bandana lying on the floor, and thought better of it.

"Not touching that fucking thing," Doug sneered. Heading into the bathroom, he grabbed a face cloth and returned to Audway, still an unconscious lump on the floor. Reaching into Audway's pocket with the cloth, Doug carefully removed the gun and held it up to examine it. It was a small weapon like he'd seen in detective movies. Doug recognized it as a .38 Colt revolver and, opening the chamber, he saw that it was fully loaded. Carefully removing all of the bullets, Doug set the gun down on the bed beside him. In the left jacket pocket, Doug discovered a key to his room. At first, he didn't understand what it was. He couldn't conceive that it could be a key to his room, as he still had *his*, but from the room number on the tag, he realized that it couldn't be a passkey. Befuddled, Doug continued to study the key. At last, it dawned on him that *this* was D'Lorenzo's missing key. Doug knew he needed to get help immediately.

Still in his underwear, Doug looked around the room for his clothes, and saw them crumpled by the foot of his bed. As he pulled on his shirt, Audway began to moan and stir. Doug realized that Audway might try to unbind his restraints. The telephone cord was a good length, but not long enough for Doug to tie Audway's legs together as well. Doug remembered his hunting knife on his belt, and grabbing it, he took the pillowcase off of the other bed and began cutting off big strips of cloth. He tied Audway's ankles together. As a precaution, he rolled the intruder onto his stomach and, pulling Audway's ankles up, Doug was able to tie all of the bindings together with another strip of cloth.

Doug wondered what he should do next. His first thought was to get Dwyer, then the memory of Cameron's voice telling the Roadhouse Sons that Dwyer was dead ran through his mind. He remembered, too, the scene from Rutland, where he and Cameron watched the bodies of the Laverdiers being wheeled out on gurneys. All of this carnage involved finding Louis Barre, whom Doug had last seen talking to Audway, who was now regaining consciousness on Doug's floor.

"No fucking way it's all a coincidence," Doug snarled. He hesitated a moment, his foot poised to strike, but he decided against it.

"Business before pleasure," he muttered. Doug knew that he would have to go get Chuck, as he was the man in charge now. Audway's moans grew louder as he started to come to. Doug didn't want Audway to draw any attention to the room, and looked about for a gag. Spotting the used bandana, he smiled as he picked it up and stuffed it into Audway's mouth, securing it with another strip of cloth from the pillowcase. Pulling on his pants, Doug headed out the door and down the hall toward Dwyer's old room. Once there, he instinctively rapped on the door, employing the designated signal. Doug waited. There was no response.

He wondered if the signal was just something that Dwyer had used, and began to knock more steadily. Still, he received no response. For a moment, Doug feared that Chuck wasn't in his room, and tried to think of what to do next. Just then, the door opened, revealing a bleary-eyed—and very annoyed—Chuck Lamont.

"Dougie, it *has* to be past your bedtime," Chuck grumbled. "Because it sure as fuck is past mine."

"Man, you've got to come quick!" Doug hissed in a low voice. "There's shit going down in my room!"

"Thanks for the offer, man," Chuck yawned. "But I'm not into the group scene, and besides, I'm tired and want to get some sleep. Good night."

Chuck started to shut the door, but Doug stopped it with his foot.

"No, man. It's nothing like that," he said urgently. "I've got a guy tied up in there right now!"

Chuck took a step back, his eyes wide.

"Ok, man…" he said slowly. "I didn't know you were into that shit, but it's not really my thing, you know? So, why don't you just go back to what you were doing and we'll forget this whole conversation ever took place, all right?"

Doug shook his head in frustration, and forced his way into Chuck's room.

"No!" Doug sputtered. "Somebody tried breaking into my room. I kicked the shit out of him and tied him up so he wouldn't get away!"

"Then call the cops," said Chuck.

"I can't!" Doug replied, exasperated. "I tied him up with the phone cord."

Chuck stared at Doug, unblinking. His steady gaze made Doug increasingly uncomfortable. Chuck had recently admonished the band about their bad behavior and lack of hotel etiquette, and Doug knew that this declaration of male bondage was not well-received.

"I also tore up a pillowcase to tie his feet with," Doug confessed. "But I gagged him with his own snotrag, if that makes any difference!"

"Probably not to him," mumbled Chuck.

"Besides, I think he's got something to do with what you've had us working on. This guy was a buddy of Louis Barre."

If Chuck recognized the name, it didn't register. Nonetheless, he asked Doug to tell him everything that had happened. Doug did so, as quickly and as completely as he could, and once again urged Chuck to come back to his room. This time, Chuck didn't argue.

They returned and found Tyrell Audway still prone on his stomach. He was awake now and pathetically struggling to escape from his bindings. Audway looked up at Doug and Chuck as they entered the room, his eyes wide, but from anger or fear, Doug couldn't be certain.

Chuck secured the door and noticed something strange. He could see several holes where screws had been, and realized that the door chain had been removed.

"Hey, Doug, why did you take the chain off?"

"I didn't take it off," Doug replied. "There was never one on it."

"The other rooms have one," Chuck informed him. "I wonder why yours doesn't. Never mind that now. Let's see what our friend has to say."

Chuck instructed Doug to release the binding that connected Audway's ankles and wrists. He rolled Audway over and helped him to a sitting position. Chuck sat back on his heels and carefully studied Audway's face.

"Ok, man. This is what we're going to do," Chuck explained. "I'm going to take that nasty gag out of your mouth. That will help you breath better and let you answer the questions I am going to ask you. But if you try to shout, holler, yell, cry out, or make any attempt to attract attention to yourself, I will make you wish you were never born. Nod if you understand the words I'm saying."

Audway tried speaking through his gag, all of which was incomprehensible mumbling, but Doug and Chuck knew that he was probably swearing, judging from the look on his face.

"That wasn't a nod, Tyrell," Chuck said, shaking his head sadly. "I'm afraid I'm going to have to keep you tied up until they come to get you. You can talk to me, here and now, or you can wait 'til my associates come to get you and you can go someplace and talk to them. Though, I should warn you, they are not as understanding as me. Now, I will ask you once more. Do you understand me?"

Audway stopped moving. He made no sound. His eyes glowered at them. Finally, he nodded.

"That's better," Chuck said with a smile, and removed the gag.

"You fuckers signed your death warrant!" Audway spat, struggling to back away from Chuck.

"Man, I signed that thing so long ago the ink faded," said Chuck, patting him on the cheek. "Now, why don't you just tell us what you're doing here disturbing my friend's sleep, all right?"

"I ain't telling you anything, you motherfucker!"

"You don't really have to," assured Chuck. "I think this has already told me a great deal." With that, Chuck rose from the floor and took Audway's wallet from the pile of items on the bed.

"Did you go through this, by any chance?" he asked Doug.

"No man," Doug insisted. "I just looked for his name to find out who he was. I didn't go through it and I didn't touch anything in it."

"Oh, I didn't think you had stolen anything," Chuck assured him. "I just have a feeling that we might find out a little bit more about him. Oh, what's this? Vermont driver's license made out to one Tyrell Audway. I assume that's you?"

He glanced over his shoulder at Audway, waving the driver's license.

"You leave my shit alone!" Audway shouted.

"Uh-uh, Tyrell," warned Chuck. "You keep your voice down or I'll stick your willey wiper back in your mouth."

Tyrell struggled harder against his restraints and began kicking at Chuck's legs, despite the fact that he was obviously too far away to make any contact. Chuck ignored Audway's feeble attempts at defiance and continued to examine the contents of the wallet.

"I often think parents have reasons for the names they give their kids," Chuck said, facing Doug. "I mean, my name was in honor of my grandfather because they hoped I'd grow up to be like him. My dad was named after a Civil War general because my grandfather was a history buff. I think our friend here was named Tyrell because his mom wanted to get even for a difficult birth. Isn't that right, Mr. Audway?"

Chuck didn't look to see if Audway would respond, and Audway didn't. He just continued to struggle in vain against his restraints.

"You tied those damn things good," Chuck muttered, giving Doug a smile and then turning his attention back to the wallet. As he removed each item, he tossed it onto the bed. He pulled out business cards, a dollar bill and several scraps of paper.

"Oh, what's this? A Vermont fishing license, but it can't be yours. Well, looky here! This fishing license is made out to a Warren Owens of Bennington. I know, I know. You're holding it for a friend, aren't you? But the description matches you, so you could use it if you wanted to, couldn't you?"

At last, Chuck turned his attention to the plastic photo sleeves. He carefully removed each picture and examined it. He held up a photo of a small girl, probably not more than two years old.

"To Daddy, love Audrey. Merry Christmas 1977." As he read the inscription Chuck turned to his captive. "You named your daughter Audrey Audway? You should be kicked in the nuts on principle."

Audway stopped struggling and stared at Chuck, who smiled mischievously.

"I'm just kidding, man," Chuck assured him. "I'm not going to drive you in the balls."

Audway visibly relaxed. Then Chuck continued.

"I'll let Dougie do it. After all, you broke into his room."

"I was looking for something!" Audway shouted, his voice cracking.

"Now, what on earth could you be looking for in here at one o'clock in the morning, I wonder?"

Audway's face became ashen. He tried to lean back against the wall, but misjudged the distance and fell flat on his back.

"Now, be careful, Tyrell," Chuck said in a soothing tone. "Don't hurt yourself, because then Doug and I will have gotten all tired and cranky for nothing."

Chuck removed another photograph from the wallet, but Doug couldn't see what it was of. Chuck placed the photo on the bed and smiled again.

"Well now, what is this?!" he said, removing a folded piece of paper. "Why, it's another driver's license! Is that in case you lose the other one? Oh, wait a minute! We've got one more name to add to the list. Will Eduard Lavelle please pick up a white courtesy phone? Mr. Eduard Lavelle of Sutton, Quebec, please pick up any white courtesy phone. Oh, wait, you can't! We tied you up with the phone cord."

Tossing the wallet and the licenses onto the bed, Chuck sat down on the edge of the mattress and faced their prisoner.

"Dude, you are seriously fucked up," Chuck muttered, rubbing his chin.

"What are you going to do to me?" Audway pleaded, trying to upright himself.

"Me? Nothing!" Chuck said. "It's just that with a choice of names like you were carrying around, you decide to use Tyrell Audway? Man, you are seriously fucked up."

"That was the guy's name," Audway insisted. "The guy I lifted the wallet from!"

"So, what about the other ones. Are they yours or somebody else's?"

Audway didn't answer. Chuck squatted down in front of him in a face-off.

"Oh, come on..." he pleaded in a whining voice. "Tell me your real name, man. Please? I need to know what name to put on the invitation to my birthday party."

Chuck grabbed the toe of Audway's boot and gave it a shake.

"You want to come to my party, don't you?" Chuck insisted. "It'll be fun, man! There'll be cake and ice cream and music. You like music, don't you? Of course you do. Everyone does! Why, I bet you're musical yourself, aren't you? Yeah, sure you are. Why, I bet if given the chance, you'll really sing for us, won't you?"

"I ain't telling you nothing," Audway whined. He tried to inch away from Chuck, who sat there, still smiling like a Cheshire cat.

"Did I mention games?" Chuck continued, his voice taking on a dreamy quality, as though recalling memories of birthday parties from his childhood. Doug, sat quietly, witnessing all of this interaction, and remembered what he'd been told about Chuck. Doug was becoming nervous.

"We're going to have lots of games." Chuck's voice dropped to a conspiratorial whisper. "You want to know what my favorite one is? It's *Pin the Tail on the Donkey*. Have you ever played it? It's really fun. You take somebody and blindfold them so they... can't see... what's going on!"

With that, Chuck grabbed Audway's filthy bandana from the floor and shook it out to its full size. He draped it over Audway's head.

"Then, you move them around so they don't know where they are!" Chuck taunted. "Don't worry. We'll do that later, so we'll just skip that part for now. Then, when they are really out of it, you stick the donkey right in the ass!"

Chuck lunged forward and slammed his fist down on the floor next to Audway's rear end, causing the prisoner to flinch and whimper.

"That was always my favorite game," he whispered menacingly in Audway's ear. "Once, I even got my cousin Seymour to play it with a real donkey. The donkey kicked him halfway across the barnyard. Seymour couldn't do math correctly after that, but I laughed like a bastard!"

Doug became increasingly nervous as he watched Chuck lean closer to Audway, and shifted his position farther away from the two men, uncertain of what Chuck would do next. He did not want to be caught in the fray, and regretted not calling one of his band mates in lieu of Lamont.

"But enough about me," said Chuck, suddenly jumping to his feet. He whirled around and plopped himself on the edge of the bed, laughing.

"Let's talk about you. Let's talk about what you were doing here. You had a crush on my friend here, didn't you? That was why you broke into his room while he was sleeping, wasn't it? You maybe had a rendezvous or something planned?"

Both Doug and Audway stared at him, mouths agape.

"I mean, you know, I guess I can kind of understand the attraction," Chuck continued. "Let's face it. Doug here isn't a bad looking guy, if you're into that brawny type. But Dougie, between you and me, I've got to say that I think you could probably do better than this guy."

"You're out of your fucking *mind*!" Audway screamed. He wriggled, causing the dirty bandana to fall to his lap. His eyes were wide with terror and his face was ashen.

"What the fuck are you talking about?!" shouted Doug, his own face a mask of indignation. He jumped to his feet and stomped over to Chuck. "I've never even *seen* this guy before!"

"Now, Dougie," said Chuck, the mischievous grin returning. "Are you certain of that? Are you certain you never saw him anywhere before, ever? In your whole life?"

"I've never seen that guy!" shouted Audway, nudging his chin toward Doug.

"Well, yeah," sputtered Doug. "I told you I did see him that time in Rutland, but I don't *know* him like you're insinuating!"

Chuck held up his hands in a gesture of acceptance.

"You know, I'm not one to judge," he said with a shrug. "We're all adults here and whatever Tyrell here might want to do is not my business, you dig what I'm saying? I'm not trying to pry into anything, man. Really! I'm not!"

Just as suddenly as he had leapt to his feet, Chuck sprang from the bed and landed on the floor, straddling Audway, the tips of their noses touching.

"Unless, of course whatever you might want to do involves killing one of my friends and trying to kill another. Then it is very *much* my fucking business and you'll tell me everything I want to know or I'll hang you up by your fucking dick and leave you there to contemplate your sins. Do you fucking understand me?"

Audway looked as though he was about to faint. The color drained from his face, and beads of sweat were forming on his forehead. He began to tremble. Doug was afraid that Audway was having a heart attack, and didn't know how he would explain how a dead man in bondage ended up in his room. He reiterated to himself how he wished that he'd first run to one of the Roadhouse Sons. He stood at the foot of his bed, ready to pull Chuck off of Audway, if necessary.

"OK! OK..." whispered Audway finally. "I'll talk! I'll *talk*! I'll fucking talk. Just get the fuck away from me!"

"Oh, you want me away from you," Chuck sneered, leaning in closer until their foreheads touched. "You want to sneak into Doug's room in the dead of night, but old Chuck's not good enough for you? Fine! Talk and I'll stay right here for as long as you do, and as long as you tell me the fucking truth. But you screw up so much as once and I'll be so close to you I'll shove my arm up your ass and do one hell of a Mortimer Snerd imitation, do you dig?"

"Yeah," whimpered Audway. "I dig, man, I fucking dig!"

With that, Chuck sat back on the edge of the bed, his hands folded in his lap and a big smile on his face.

"OK, then!" he giggled. "I'm ready. Tell me a story. Make it a good one!"

"I wasn't after that guy," Audway began, nodding toward Doug. "I didn't have nothing to do with him. I didn't even know he was here. I swear to fucking God! I didn't know he was in here!"

"There's no need for blasphemy, Tyrell. Tsk, tsk, tsk." Chuck admonished, clicking his tongue. "You're in enough trouble without pissing off the Almighty, too. Now, if you weren't here to see Doug, then who were you here to meet?"

"I was supposed to meet Don," Audway muttered. "We had to arrange the delivery of the shipment."

"And just who is Don?" asked Chuck. Doug was about to interject, but stopped himself. Chuck sat bolt upright, his hands still carefully folded on his lap, but his eyes had darted at Doug, who got the cue that he was supposed to keep his mouth shut.

"Don's the guy that's supposed to arrange the delivery for us. I've never met him, I was just told to come to this room and get my contact information. That's why I had the key."

Doug remembered that when D'Lorenzo had returned to the room, he was naked. Even though they later found his clothes in a trashcan, they never did find his key.

"How did you get that key?" Chuck prodded. His body language hadn't changed, but the tone of his voice did.

"He gave it to us at the party, after the show!"

"Go on," said Chuck, his tone menacing.

"We hung around with him after the show. He had some good shit for us to try and said he could get more of that for us and to meet him here the night before the next show to get the details."

"Were you supposed to meet *him*, or someone else?"

"I don't know, man!" Audway l moaned. "I've never done this kind of shit before. I was just told that I was supposed to get here and find out what the drop was."

Chuck looked straight into Audway's eyes, and drew a deep breath. He adjusted his hands as if in prayer, resting his elbows on his legs. Chuck then exhaled and rested his chin on his thumbs. He closed his eyes and sat quietly.

"You've got to believe me, man!" whimpered Audway. Doug saw that he was at the point of tears. Chuck sat motionless, saying nothing. Finally, he sighed and stretched.

"I wish I could, man," Chuck said, yawning. "I really wish I could. But the problem is, you broke our agreement. You lied to me. Here we are, opening our room to you and you fucking lie to me. You take my good nature and you piss on it, and after you piss on it, you grind it in with your feet, and after you grind it in with your feet, you spit out your used bubble gum on it. I'm beginning to think you don't like me, Tyrell."

Audway's lip began to quiver, and his eyes fill with tears. Doug cast an anxious, furtive glance at Chuck, who winked at him.

"Don't hurt me, man!" Audway whispered. "Please! Don't fucking hurt me!"

An expression of shock came over Chuck's face.

"What?" he gasped. "Hurt you? Me? You've got to be kidding, right? Why would I hurt you? Didn't I make an agreement with you? Didn't I say that as long as you told me the God's honest truth, no harm would come to you? Now, why would I hurt you, unless you lied to me? You didn't *lie* to me, did you, Tyrell? You didn't try to ignore the fact that one of these names is the same name as the fellow in charge of the black market trafficking from Montreal, did you? You didn't think that I was too stupid not to see that, did you? Oh, Tyrell... alas... and I thought we had something special."

Audway slumped over, trembling. Tears rolled down his face. He didn't speak.

"You've got balls, Tyrell! I'll give you that!" said Chuck, standing up. "Which is a good thing, because when they get their hands on you they will probably cut them off and stick them on you like earrings. I think this little party has gone on long enough without ice cream. So, since you've told me everything I wanted to know, I think you should keep someone else company from now on. I'm going back to my room to make a phone call."

Chuck yawned and stretched.

"I'll be right back," he said, pointing at Audway. "Now, don't go away!"

Without a word to Doug, Chuck left the room, carefully closing the door behind him.

"That guy's out of his fucking mind!" cried Audway, collapsing into a fit of tears.

"You're fucking telling me!" said Doug, staring at the door.

CHAPTER TWENTY-TWO
"Fading Like a Mist"

"How can you say that?!" cried Bambi, pulling away from Cameron. He looked at her and smiled reassuringly, taking her by the hand and drawing her back to him.

"It's OK," he said. "I understand why you're doing this. You can't fool me."

"I don't know what you're talking about!" she insisted. Cameron felt her arms stiffen as she tried again to retreat from him.

"Oh, come on!" he said. "You tell me about seeing me at a ski lodge and then deny you ever said it, then you talk about seeing my roadie and deny being in the only place where you could possibly meet him, which is back stage! There's only one reason you'd do that."

Bambi looked at him expectantly, her back still tense as she leaned away.

"You don't want me to think you're a groupie," Cameron smiled. "You don't need to worry about that," he said softly. "I don't."

Bambi collapsed against him with a sigh of relief, wrapping her arms around his waist, and resting her head on his shoulder.

"Is that really what you were thinking?" she asked, almost a whisper.

"Fuck, yeah!" he laughed. "What else would I be thinking, you silly girl?"

"It doesn't matter," she whispered.

Cameron put his arms around her and rocked her gently.

"Don't worry about anything, baby," he said softly. "I know you're a good girl. You're not after anything. That was one of the things that attracted me to you. You aren't like the others."

"You make it sound like you've had a lot of experience." Her voice was soft and velvety, yet Cameron couldn't help but notice her accusatory undertone.

"I won't lie to you," he said. "I'm no angel. I've enjoyed the company of many ladies over the years. Some of them I didn't even ask their names, and some didn't even ask mine. You do that long enough, you learn that you want something more than that, somebody who's nice, somebody that you want to spend an evening with, not just spend the night with. Somebody you want to wake up next to, not just fall asleep beside. Does that make any sense to you?"

Bambi didn't answer right away, and Cameron wondered if she understood what he was saying. How could he explain it any further? To say more would be to force the point that he was trying to make, and obscure the feeling he was trying to convey. She was different.

He felt her breath on his neck and savored once more the sweet smell of her hair. He hoped that he hadn't done anything to jeopardize this opportunity.

"Yes, it makes a lot of sense," she whispered. "I feel the same way, and for the same reasons."

"What do you mean?"

"You don't think rock stars are the only ones that get chased after, do you?" she teased. "Barmaids do, as well. If I had a dime for every man that's hit on me, I'd be as rich as Croesus."

"Barmaid," Cameron laughed. "I thought that word went out with the pirates!"

She slapped at his chest and pulled away.

"Are you making fun of me?" she pouted, mockingly. "I was trying to be serious!"

"Oh, I know you were!" he laughed, drawing her head to his chest. "I totally believe you, my little barmaid."

"Ok, now you are making fun of me!" she said, but from her smile, Cameron knew that she wasn't upset. He smiled at her, taking in every feature of her face—her slightly almond-shaped deep brown eyes, her high cheekbones, her tiny nose and delicate mouth, the dimple in her chin, and the creamy whiteness of her neck. Forgetting himself, he leaned down and gave her a soft kiss on the cheek. Then he moved to her lips.

He intended for it to be a simple kiss, quick and innocent. Once he started kissing her, though, he discovered that it was impossible to stop. What was supposed to be innocent soon became passionate. Bambi did not resist, but yielded to him, melting in his arms.

Cameron held her against him, rocking her gently, silently.

"Do you still think I'm not that kind of a girl?" she whispered.

"Yes," he said, and fell silent, letting his embrace do all of his talking. They held each other for a few more moments, until he noticed she tried to stifle a yawn.

"You've got to get some sleep," he said, taking her face in his hands. He held her at arm's length, not to push her away from him, but for one last look. She smiled, and nodded, yawning once more. She looked about nervously. There was only one bed.

"I'll sleep on the floor," she said, trying not to look at him.

"Like hell you will," Cameron said, pointing at the bed. "You sleep there. There's plenty of room for both of us."

Bambi gasped, and began to blush.

"Its OK," Cameron assured her. "You sleep under the covers, and I'll sleep on top of them. I'm not trying to trick you into anything, I swear."

Bambi contemplated Cameron's offer, obviously unsure.

"OK. I can sleep on the floor, then!" he laughed.

"No. That wouldn't be right," she muttered. "OK. I guess your plan will work, but I need to ask you something."

"Sure. What is it?"

Bambi hesitated, searching for the right words.

"I don't have a night gown or anything," she said, the color once again rising in her cheeks. "Can I borrow a shirt from you to use?"

"Well, sure!" Cameron smiled and stroked her flushed cheek. "Absolutely."

Cameron went to his dresser and rummaged around in the drawers. He found a T-shirt that he thought she would like. He'd picked it up a county fair. It was yellow with an iron on transfer of a flying bird silhouetted above a forest of pine trees against a setting sun. Its caption read "Free and Easy." He held it up for her, triumphantly. Bambi's jaw dropped. She stared at Cameron as though he was a madman. He realized instantly the implication of the shirt's message.

"Oh, fuck me! I'm so sorry," he shouted. It was Cameron's turn to blush. "Let me find another one. You don't mind if it's got a few holes, do you?"

"I don't mind *that* shirt," she laughed, taking it from him. "I just realized you hadn't read it before you showed it to me."

Taking the shirt, she gave him a quick kiss on the lips and headed to the bathroom to change. Cameron removed the newspapers and magazines strewn all over the bed and smoothed the bedspread. He fluffed the pillows and adjusted the covers, turning down one side for Bambi, then turned on the bedside lamps. He ran to the light by the door and turned it off. Running back to the bed, he removed his boots and set them in the closet. He took off his jeans, folded them neatly and placed them on the arm of the easy chair. Cameron jumped into bed, and just as he was pulling the bedspread over his chest, Bambi emerged from the bathroom.

Bambi had always concealed her figure under the sweaters that she wore, and now Cameron could espy her slender build as she stood framed in the doorway. Her hair was full, draping down around her shoulders. It reminded him of Farrah Fawcett. He could also see that she wore lace underwear. Bambi demurely carried her neatly folded clothes in her arms. She placed them in the chair next to his clothes, and approached the bed, hesitating. She switched off the bedside lamps and quickly crawled in next to Cameron.

"What time do you need to get up?" he asked.

"I need to be at the Tavern to open it," she said. "I have to be there by at least nine. It's a bit of a walk from here."

"Piece o' cake," he said, smiling, and adjusted the alarm settings. "I can take you over, no big deal."

"You don't need to do that," she said, smiling back at him. "You don't always have to be the white knight, you know."

"I know." Cameron kissed her cheek. She returned his kiss and, slowly stretched out. Cameron watched, noticing that her eyes started to close as soon as her head hit the pillow.

He gently kissed her and then slid, carefully, into a comfortable position and lay there quietly, feeling the pressure of her body against his. This was not the first time he had been in bed with a woman, but this felt different somehow. It felt special. He felt the slight movement of Bambi's body as her breathing became regular and he knew she was asleep. That was the last thing that he recalled as his eyes closed and he drifted off to sleep.

Cameron awoke with a start. He turned over, only to find that Bambi was gone. The room was dark, and her side of the bed was empty. He looked at the clock and noticed that it was a little bit after five in the morning. He lay still, but could hear no sounds. A sense of despair washed over him. He feared that she'd awoken during the night and decided to leave. Cameron replayed in his mind the evening's events to see if he'd misread any of her signals. Each memory resulted in self-recrimination and he knew he wasn't thinking clearly. Rolling over to her side of the bed, he only felt worse as he smelled the faint traces of her perfume on the pillow. Cameron knew that if he didn't get out of bed, he'd torture himself with his thoughts. He decided to get up. Over the years, when he found himself in a state of despair, the only way that he could find any peace was through music.

It was far too early for Cameron to begin playing his Strat. Even the long-suffering hotel management wouldn't tolerate that, but he knew that he could play his acoustic guitar with no problem because its sound was soft enough not to bother any of the other guests.

Cameron picked up the guitar case and opened it. He didn't need to turn on a light. He'd developed a photographic memory over the years and could find his way around a dark room after seeing it lit only once. This gift had enabled him to escape many "coyote mornings" in his lifetime, those mornings when the light of day was less kind to the woman he'd taken home than was the light of the dance hall and, like a trapped coyote, one was willing to gnaw off one's own arm to escape. This talent had allowed Cameron to flee many a room without detection.

But now, it seemed, he was on the other side of the experience. He had remained, and *she* had fled, without leaving him so much as a note or a goodbye kiss.

Or even an explanation...

Cameron picked at each chord, carefully adjusting the guitar string, for a note higher or lower, as required. When he was happy with the sound, he picked at the strings again, allowing himself to fall gently into song. He didn't think about what to play; he just let his heart tell him what it wanted to hear.

Cameron closed his eyes and remembered a piece that he'd written a long time ago and hadn't played in years. His fingers had their own memories, dancing from one string to another, moving one fret to the next, as though they'd been aching to replay the melody.

With each note, he thought of Bambi, and wished that he'd played this song for her. He wondered if he made her feel the way she'd made him feel. He also wondered if he'd ever have another chance to show her. The song's sweet sadness reminisced of something lost, though that was not why Cameron had written it. On a summer night many moons before, one filled with joy and laughter, he'd watched the sun set over a lake, and heard the sounds of his friends around the campfire.

His thoughts flowed effortlessly to that night. Suddenly, he heard the bathroom door open. In the darkness, he knew that he couldn't be seen, nor would the light reflect off his eyes if he opened them slowly. He saw Bambi, still wearing his T-shirt. She settled down on the floor near his feet and looked up at him.

He continued to play, gradually opening his eyes completely. He smiled at her, watching her expression as he played each chord, each note, just for her. Cameron played the last note. It faded away, like the light of the setting sun did upon the waters of the lake years ago.

Bambi watched him, silently.

"That reminded me of Spain," she said softly, reaching out to stroke his leg.

"That reminded me of you," he said, gently taking her hand.

"I didn't know that you played classical guitar, too." She smiled.

"I wouldn't call it that," Cameron said with a grin. "It's just acoustic, really. But I did study with someone who was a big fan of Segovia."

She laughed softly. Cameron looked down at his fingers, thankful that there was no way she could actually see the relief in his eyes at the sound of her laughter. He knew that if he continued to look at her, there would be no way to hide the tears of joy that he was trying to fend off.

"I kept the lights off so I wouldn't disturb you," she whispered. "I hope you didn't think that I had left you."

"It's OK," Cameron whispered back, as much for self-comfort as to reassure her. He continued playing selections from his sunset melody. He watched her, wondering if the smile on her face was for him or for recollections of the verdant hills of Spain. He thought of the narrow streets, Pamplona's running of the bulls, and Rioja in dark bottles on the tables of alfresco cafes. He'd dreamed of going to Spain for years, and poured all of these images into his musical effort for her.

He trembled, slightly, as she gently ran her fingers up and down his bare leg, tracing the curve of his calf muscle beneath her fingernail.

"You've got to get some sleep," Cameron whispered. He ceased his strumming and set the guitar aside. He reached for Bambi's hand. She did not argue, nor did she resist. Cameron led her back to the bed and tucked her in, then crawled under the covers, *all* the way under this time. Once more, she did not argue or resist him. He wrapped his arm around her, nestling her head into his chest.

They awoke much later, in the same position as when they'd slumbered. Reluctantly, he reached over and shut off the alarm. Bambi stirred, but didn't open her eyes. Cameron refused to remind her that she needed to get up. She rose eventually, but not before giving him a good morning kiss.

The two made small talk as they readied for the day. Cameron, in an effort to hang onto the magic of the previous evening, offered to take her to breakfast downstairs.

"It isn't much," he admitted. "But it's a warm breakfast, and not a bad thing to have in your belly to start the day."

"Thanks, but I'm not much of a breakfast person," she smiled. "I'll grab some tea and be fine."

"It's the most important meal of the day," he said, slipping his arms around her waist and drawing him to her. "Or at least that's what my mom always said."

"Mine, too," she laughed. "But I just got out of the habit. I'll make myself some tea when I get to work, like I always do."

He gave her a kiss and smiled again.

"Well, then…" Cameron sighed. "If you're not going to let me buy you breakfast, then you can at least let me drive you home before you go to work."

Bambi pulled him closer and leaned against his chest. She was so content that Cameron was convinced she'd start to purr.

"They are one and the same," she said. "I live upstairs over the bar. I can grab a change of clothes when I get there, and freshen up a bit."

Neither of them made any move to break their embrace, let alone hurry out the door. Bambi's lengthy sigh of resignation was Cameron's cue that she had to leave. However, she didn't move from where she stood and, for a moment, he thought he might be able to convince her to stay a little longer.

I can be a little late for rehearsals. What are they going to do, fire me?

Cameron moved to kiss her. She smiled at him adoringly, but put a finger to his lips.

"No," Bambi muttered reluctantly. "I can't. I have to be going."

She pulled back slowly, enjoying the last lingering effects of their embrace. She sighed again as she stroked his tawny hair.

"Can't you call in sick?" he asked, wrapping his arms around her. She shook her head with a sad smile.

"No, I'm afraid not. I live with my dad and he would know I was lying. He'll have enough of a fit that I was caught out after curfew. If I try that, he will totally loose his mind."

"What, he afraid the Russians will get you or something?"

Bambi shook her head and laughed nervously, releasing her hold on him.

"I've really got to be going," she said, picking up her coat.

"Let me at least drive you," Cameron insisted. "It's going to be cold out and it's a bit of a walk. I can at least do that, can't I? Especially since it was me that had you out so late anyhow."

"I'm not going to argue!" She smiled and kissed him. Cameron noticed that she didn't let this kiss linger as long as she had the others, but it was indeed sincere.

You're reading too much into it. Stop it, or you'll fuck everything up.

Cameron paused just long enough to switch on the radio and ensure that it was still tuned in, once again wondering what had happened to it last night. He double-checked that the door was locked when he shut it, and casually looked at the lock to see if it had been picked. A sound behind him distracted him.

"Well, good morning!" He heard Chuck Lamont's voice. At first Cameron was surprised to see him here, but then he remembered that Chuck had moved into Dwyer's room at the far end of the hall.

"How's it going?" Cameron said. He began the introductions.

"Chuck, I'd like you to meet my friend, Bambi," he said with a smile. Gesturing toward Chuck, he continued. "Bambi, I'd like you to meet Chuck Lamont, our manager."

"You're their manager?" Bambi asked, extending her hand. "I thought there was another guy that was." She looked at Cameron quizzically.

Chuck's smile faded, and he cleared his throat.

"Well, you see, I'm taking over for him," he said. "He left unexpectedly and now it's up to me to sort of keep things moving along."

"Oh, I see," she said, still confused. "Well, it's nice meeting you."

"Oh, man!" said Cameron, snapping his fingers. "I need a couple of passes for the show!"

"Just show passes or backstage ones, too?"

"Oh, both if we can work it out."

Chuck pondered for a minute.

"Yeah," he said. "I think that'll be OK. How many do you need?"

Cameron turned and looked at Bambi, waiting for her to cite a number, but she simply shrugged.

"Let's say three," Cameron answered. Bambi nodded with a smile.

"Three it is, then," Chuck said. "But I need a name to hold them."

"You can just use mine," Cameron said, taking Bambi's hand. Chuck shook his head.

"No can do, man," he said. "You have to be backstage. No running around out front. You don't want to give the crowd a free show."

"Can I just show up early and have you guys let me in the back?" asked Bambi. Again, Chuck shook his head.

"It would be really cool if we could do that," he agreed. "It would make everyone's life easier. But, unfortunately, we need to keep that area cleared until after the show. Just let me know whose name to put on the envelope and they'll be waiting for you."

"My name's Bambi," she giggled, and Cameron was relieved when Chuck smiled.

"I can see why," he said. "But, is that your real name or a nickname? You have to show some form of ID for them, and I don't want you to have any troubles getting these."

"Oh, come on, man!" snapped Cameron. "What's with the interrogation? Just put Bambi on the fucking envelope and leave it at that. Why be such a fucking drag?"

Chuck shook his head. He was firm, but neither Cameron nor Bambi felt that he was being threatening toward them.

"If I do that, how can we be sure someone doesn't come up and claim them? Then how will we get her in? No. Just let me know what your name is and I'll make certain the tickets'll be waiting for you. I give you my word. Honest!"

Chuck gave them a smile and a wink, and Bambi giggled again. Cameron was still upset, but knew that pressing the issue would be futile. He wasn't familiar with every facet of Chuck's personality, but what he had seen thus far indicated that Chuck did not entertain arguments, especially ones involving unsolicited opinions. Bambi looked from Cameron to Chuck, and finally sighed.

"Yvette," she said, leaning against Cameron's shoulder. "Yvette Lavelle."

"Lavelle," asked Chuck, checking his jacket pocket for a pencil. "How do you spell that?"

Bambi carefully spelled her surname for him as he wrote it on the back of a scrap of paper. Chuck gazed at it for a minute, as though admiring a masterpiece. He looked up at Cameron and Bambi and flashed a wide grin.

"There!" he said, triumphantly. "I know I'm being a huge pain in the ass, but I wanted to make sure we had everything we needed. I'll get these over to the box office right away. Just go to the window and they'll have them ready for you. No hassles, I assure you!"

Cameron was about to speak, but Bambi gave his hand a squeeze and smiled at him. She said nothing, and her brown eyes were inscrutable, but somehow Cameron knew that she wanted him to drop the subject once and for all. He did.

"Hey! By the way," he said to Chuck. "You look like crap. Are you all right?"

"Oh, yeah," Chuck said, with a dismissive wave of his hand. "I just had a hard time sleeping last night, that's all. I'll be fine. Don't worry about me."

They said their goodbyes and headed down to the lobby. In the elevator, Cameron slipped his arm around Bambi and drew her close, kissing the top of her head. When she turned her face to his, he kissed her lips. Cameron thought of other girls, the groupies, he'd met throughout the years, and wasn't surprised that he couldn't really remember their faces.

I didn't always ask the names.

Cameron asked Bambi if she wanted some coffee. Once again she declined. She held him firmly by the hand and tugged him toward the door.

"I've got to get going! Come on!" she exclaimed. Cameron didn't resist, at least not much. He wanted to stay with her for as long as he could, even if it meant sharing longing looks over a lukewarm paper cup of coffee substitute.

Life in wartime.

Unlocking the door to the Mustang, he held it open for her. As he walked around the car, Bambi leaned over and opened Cameron's door for him. He lit a cigarette and turned on the radio as he waited for the car to warm up. Out of the corner of his eye, Cameron caught her staring at him.

"What are you looking at?" He smiled and touched her cheek.

"You," she said, smiling back at him. He noted that Bambi's entire being seemed more relaxed now than at any other time since he'd known her. He was relieved and happy to think that he was probably the reason for it. He leaned over and tried to give her a kiss on the cheek, but she suddenly turned her face to his and caught him with a kiss on the lips. He lingered, stealing a second kiss. Bambi didn't resist. Cameron gently pulled away, and touched his nose to hers.

Easing out of the hotel lot, he drove into the street and headed toward Hart's Tavern. They drove in silence, listening to Kansas on the radio. *Dust in the Wind* drifted through the speakers. Cameron glanced at Bambi. She leaned her head against the window, her expression reflective.

"Do you agree with that?" she asked him.

"Agree with what?"

"That we're all just dust in the wind?"

Cameron, caught off guard and admittedly fighting arousal, was in a romantic state of mind. Being pulled into a philosophical one was not an easy transition. However, he didn't want Bambi to replace her opinion of his capacity for sensitivity with one that offered him up as shallow, so he scrambled to recall if he'd ever had a discussion about the song. He was certain that he had but realized, to his own horror, that it was likely conducted under stimulating circumstances and, as a result, he couldn't recall a single profound thought in the sober light of day. Any contribution to the discussion would have to be his own opinion, and he was drawing a complete blank.

"No," he said, finally. "No way."

"Well, why do you think that?"

"Then what's the point of anything, if nothing matters?"

"Well," she hesitated. "If you only have to deal with the right now, wouldn't it be easier to make choices? You don't have to deal with any consequences, right?"

Cameron took a deep breath.

This is seriously fucking up my mellow mood.

"You always have to deal with consequences," he said. "No matter what you believe, shit always happens and you have to deal with it."

Bambi considered Cameron's words, but said nothing. As the silence grew, so did Cameron's discomfort. The song continued with "All we do crumbles to the ground, though we refuse to see..." Cameron regretted ever considering this a beautiful song. The melody, which he had once considered poignant, mindful and meditative, now became pointless, hopeless and depressing.

"I think everything does just crumble..." Bambi said softly. Cameron couldn't help but notice the mournful tone in her voice. "And I think that we do just refuse to see it."

"Well, that's a pleasant note to end our date on," he muttered.

"I'm sorry, but that's the way I feel."

Cameron, suddenly feeling inexplicably defensive, stopped himself short of a snappy response. Last night, Bambi had revealed a great deal of her past to him, a past filled with disappointment and pain, with the forced surrendering of dreams and happiness.

"Life sucks sometimes," Cameron said. "You find the joy among the disappointments and go on from there. They might be a lot, they might be a few, but you find them, you hang on to them and you go on to the next one."

"That sounds pretty shallow," she countered.

"What would you prefer? If you've got something else to put in its place, let me in on it."

"Don't you think there is something bigger to believe in?" she sighed, and pressed on. "Don't you think there has to be *some* purpose to our lives? Shouldn't we be working to change things and make the world a place without all of the oppression and struggle and suffering?"

"Yeah," Cameron said. "Of *course* I do."

"Then why are you doing what you're doing? Why spend all of your time in a band and stuff like that? You should be working to make that a reality."

Now, Cameron was rankled. "And I'm not?!" he challenged. "Just because what I am and what I do don't fit into your definition of what you would like to exist in your perfect world doesn't mean that it doesn't have merit, and that I can't picture it in *my* perfect world."

"Well, what is it that you do that you think makes it so important?"

"I like to try and make people happy," he said. "I like to play music that they can escape into for a minute and forget some of the struggle and crap. I try to give them a way to express their frustration and express their hope for something different. I try to give them some inspiration to move on from where they are to where they need to go."

"Where is that exactly?"

"I don't know," he shrugged. "You have to pick that for yourself. I don't tell people what they should or shouldn't believe, or what they should do with their lives. I hope they do something good, but it's not my call or my problem."

"Then you're just like everyone else," she said, turning back toward the window. "You're just in it for yourself."

"Fuck no, I'm not!" Cameron snapped. "I do what I can, but I have to be responsible for my own choices. I can't be responsible for everyone else's. What am I, God?"

"You should look at the entire scene," Bambi argued. "You focus on the individual because you want to focus on yourself. You think about what you want, not thinking if someone else needs it, too."

"Oh, and there's someone out there having that same concern about me?"

"Well, I don't know," she said. "It has to start somewhere, doesn't it?"

"The whole '"do unto others" thing has been around a long time," Cameron grumbled. "I don't see where it's made that much difference. I'm all for following the Golden Rule and everything, but I'm not under any illusion that everyone's looking out for my best interest all the time. I know my friends do, and I look out for theirs, but I'm not going to put much hope in the guy running the corner grocery worrying about if I have enough to eat or not. He only worries if I have enough ration books to pay for my food."

"That's just typical," she groaned. "That's what the problem of the world is. No one is looking out for anyone else."

"Am I making you walk home?" Cameron said, flatly.

"What?!" Bambi cried, turning to him. "Are you throwing me out?"

"No, I'm not," said Cameron. "That's just what I mean. Am I throwing you out and making you walk home in the cold, or am I using my gas rations and rubber rations to make sure you get home in time so you're not late for work? Doesn't that count as looking out for you?"

"That doesn't count," she said, shaking her head.

"Why the hell not?" Cameron was nonplused. "Just because that doesn't match up to your argument? I'm obviously doing something to help you out."

"You're just doing that because you want to make a good impression on me so we can go out again."

"So?"

"So, that doesn't count," she insisted. "You're not doing it for the greater good. You're just hoping I'll think highly of you and go out with you again."

"And that's wrong?" Cameron felt completely blindsided.

"Well…" Bambi started to speak, then turned away again and finally muttered, "I don't want to discuss it anymore."

No fucking problem!

Cameron was fuming. The warm glow of the morning was replaced by anger, frustration and disappointment. They continued on in silence until Cameron turned down the street to the Tavern. A peculiar sight greeted them.

Outside the front door of the bar, an angry crowd was gathered. In the middle of them all was a white-haired man, yelling and wildly waving his hands.

"Pull over here!" Bambi sighed. It was the heaviest sigh Cameron had ever heard, one full of weariness and resignation.

"What's going on?" Cameron asked.

"Just let me out here!" she insisted. "That's my father. He's probably losing his shit because I didn't come home last night. I don't want you to have to deal with him."

"Don't you think I should at least make sure you don't have to put up with a bunch of shit?" he asked as he pulled to the curb.

"Wow, you really do give a damn…" she said. Cameron wondered if Bambi was being sarcastic until she said, "Maybe I was wrong about you."

Before Cameron could respond, she leaned over and gave him a quick peck on the lips.

"Really, I'll be fine," she insisted. "Sorry about the ride over. That song sometimes gets to me. I'll see you at the show, I promise!"

Before Cameron could say another word, Bambi got out of the car, shut the door and headed along the sidewalk toward the tavern. She glanced over her shoulder and waved, then furtively motioned for him to leave. As she did so, the white-haired man teetered up the sidewalk toward her, shouting incomprehensibly.

What...?! That's right. Her father only speaks French...

Cameron waited at the curb, presuming that Bambi's father wouldn't humiliate her in front of witnesses that weren't in his circle of cronies. Her father turned toward Cameron, glaring at him and speaking rapidly to Bambi. Cameron watched guardedly as Bambi's father approached her, arms flailing, and grabbed her elbow, pulling her along beside him.

Cameron considered getting out of the car and confronting the man, but Bambi didn't seem to resist or show *any* signs of distress, for that matter. If anything, she emitted an exaggerated sigh of frustration, as she rolled her head back and her eyes heavenward. Cameron realized that she'd probably endured this reception many times before. Satisfied that everything was going to be all right, he drove away from the curb.

Glancing in the rearview mirror, Cameron saw Bambi and her father standing in the middle of the sidewalk, face to face, he still gripping her elbow. Bambi's free hand was over her mouth, her eyes an expression of utter distress.

Cameron came to a stop at the intersection and checked for oncoming traffic. When he looked back in his rearview mirror, the sidewalk was empty.

CHAPTER TWENTY-THREE
"Engaged"

"Turn that shit off!" Cameron bellowed, throwing his can of beer at the work crew. It was bad enough that they were listening to the radio while the Roadhouse Sons rehearsed, but the added effrontery of subjecting the band to the Bee Gees singing *Staying Alive* was downright intolerable. If there was any one genre of music that Cameron and the others despised, it was disco.

Many were the posters of *Saturday Night Fever* that had succumbed to the wrath of the band, reduced to a miserable existence as a dartboard, rather than gracing the bedroom wall of some young teenage girl. The unfortunate poster would end its days attached to the wall with glue, spit and venom, subjected to its unfortunate role as the focal point of ridicule toward what the guys considered to be a desecration of genuine music and ability. Ultimately, after barely surviving the frustrations and angers of unappreciative eyes, the last identifiable shred of the poster would be completely destroyed by the various darts, knives, bottles and debris happily hurled at it by the band. Here and now, there was no way in hell that Cameron would tolerate disco playing over, or in tandem with, his music.

"Get that fucking thing out of here!" he bellowed again, lunging toward the startled workmen lingering over their lunches. Rich hurried over to Cameron, grabbing his arm to hold him back.

"Man, come on!" Rich said. "Don't let them fuck you up. Ignore them."

"How can I ignore that shit?" Cameron snarled. "Disco is the fucking GM Pacer of music! I'm trying to put together real music here and everyone's playing that shit around me. Fuck this!"

"Man, just calm down," Rich insisted.

Cameron didn't respond, but glared after the retreating workmen. The afternoon had not been going well. Ever since he had returned that morning, Cameron had been moody and brooding, impatient with everyone and snapping at everything anybody said. He'd left around lunchtime, returned and behaved personably at first, as if he needed the company of his friends. However, that mood began to wear off. He became sulky and melancholy, developing a petulant attitude as the band began rehearsals. He accused the others of playing or singing in different keys, and grew even more frustrated when he himself missed a chord or forgot song lyrics.

A major argument ensued when Cameron suggested exchanging the set list's cover tunes with original songs that the Roadhouse Sons had penned.

"We're starting to get noticed," he justified. "Why not show what we can do? Why should we have people think that we're just a cover band?"

The others agreed with Cameron's idea, but were unable to agree on what covers to eliminate. That led to another episode complete with shouting and hurled expletives of every kind imaginable. Chuck, who stood quietly in the wings observing this discourse, didn't try to intervene. He realized that the band had a necessary dynamic that included moments like these. Eventually, though, he felt that they were wasting precious rehearsal time, and made suggestions that helped the band members reach a fair and reasonable compromise. It was obvious to the boys that Chuck had other things on his mind that would soon demand his attention, and they sensed that their compromise should be an expeditious one.

Until then, though, even Doug was affected by the change in Cameron's mood, and began arguing with the soundmen and the electricians. Once again, lights had been discovered with damaged cords, and there had been problems with the electrical outlets and the circuit breaker. Despite their protests and declarations of innocence, Doug went so far as to accuse the tech crew of deliberately causing problems to garner more pay by creating extra work.

"Don't fucking lie to me!" he snarled, holding up the damaged cord for everyone to see. "I'm not fucking stupid! This thing isn't frayed. It's fucking cut!"

Chuck finally approached them to act as referee and to prevent them all from coming to blows. He looked at the cord carefully and saw that the rubber casing was smoothly peeled back, but agreed with the electricians that it could easily have been scraped by exposed metal and not deliberately cut with a knife. No one disputed that the cord was a safety hazard, but that fact did not suggest malicious deliberation. Ultimately, the damaged cord was mended and everyone's attention turned to the circuit breaker. This nearly caused another outburst from the roadie when the electricians suggested that the repeatedly tripped circuits were the fault of the band's equipment.

"Couldn't it also have been caused by a short circuit from the broken cords?" asked Chuck, deftly positioning himself to prevent an attack launched by Doug. The electricians reluctantly agreed that it could. Chuck realized that Doug's innate defense of the band, while commendable, also rendered Doug more defensive overall, and resultantly quite argumentative. Chuck diffused the situation by sending Doug out for supplies. The cords were replaced and the circuit breaker didn't trip again.

"This would have been a hell of a lot easier if we weren't shorthanded," grumbled the maintenance man. "One of my guys didn't show up this morning. Didn't call in sick or anything. Just didn't show up."

"Is that unusual?" asked Chuck. The other man shook his head.

"Not all that unusual, though he doesn't do it that often. Usually he's been out on a bender, or shacked up with a girl somewhere."

"But not this time?"

"Gave a call to all the girls I had numbers for," said the maintenance man. "They didn't know where he was. If you ask me, he's getting started on deer hunting. That opens in a few days."

Chuck nodded thoughtfully, but said nothing. His attention was diverted once again to the sullen Cameron, who had wondered off to a lone corner and was tuning his guitar. Chuck walked over to him and handed him a guitar pick.

"Man, are you all right?" Chuck asked, approaching him.

"Of course I am!" Cameron hissed. "What makes you think I'm not?"

"Well, for starters you have two cigarettes going in that ashtray, and you've adjusted the strings on that thing so many times, it has to be confused by now. What's wrong?"

"Nothing is fucking wrong!" insisted Cameron, picking idly at the strings.

"No, obviously not," Chuck replied. "This is your usual, charming self."

Cameron shook a cigarette out of his pack and noticed the admonishing look on Chuck's face. Looking down at the ashtray, Cameron shook his head and returned the fresh cigarette to its pack. He slumped into a chair.

"Sorry, man," Cameron mumbled. "Got a lot on my mind."

"We all do," Chuck said. He didn't seem to be accusing or recriminating Cameron. Rather, Cameron got the feeling that Chuck understood what Cameron was going through.

"She runs hot and cold," Cameron muttered.

"Who does?" Chuck asked, confused.

"Bambi…" sighed Cameron. "One minute, I think that she's all into me and cool, and the next minute she gets pissed at anything I say or do. I can't fucking figure it out."

"Don't look at me!" Chuck laughed, holding up his hands. "I am no expert on women, except how to sneak off while they're picking out wedding dresses!"

Cameron felt embarrassment, having revealed his thoughts, and quickly and diligently returned to his guitar tuning.

"Those strings are going to break from sheer fatigue if you're not careful," Chuck teased. "Man, don't worry about her too much. Everyone goes through this shit until they realize where things are going in a relationship. Once you guys get that settled, you'll be fine."

"Like I need one more fucking thing to worry about," Cameron snapped. "I've got the show to think about, I've got the band to worry about, I've got your shit to deal with, and I overheard you guys talking about what happened to Doug last night."

"Man, you are taking way too much on your shoulders," Chuck sighed. "You just worry about Cameron. The band is professional enough to do their rehearsing and totally kick fucking ass at the show. I'll worry about my shit, and call you in when I need to. As for Doug, I wouldn't worry about him. He's apparently recovering very well and settled down over there in all of his magnificent glory."

Chuck nodded his head toward the corner of stage. Doug had nestled himself into a chair and fallen asleep, a small trail of spittle escaping from the corner of his mouth. Cameron shook his head.

Oh, fuck me.

"I'm not shitting you," Chuck said in a low voice. For emphasis, he leaned in to Cameron and whispered. "Dwyer kept you guys in the dark because he was trying to protect you. I don't think I need to do that. I know that you know that I know that you guys have as much on the line as the rest of us do. If there's shit you need to know about, I'll make sure you know. If there's a decision to be made, you'll be in on it with me. I swear to God! *That's* how it will be. I won't spring anything on you that's not sprung on me, too."

Cameron stared at Chuck, perplexed. On an emotional level, he wanted to believe Chuck, but he was so fundamentally exhausted, so soul-weary, that he felt as though he was astrally projected, listening in on someone else's conversation. He simply said nothing. Chuck didn't move, but watched as Cameron played the scales.

"Why did you really ask her name?" Cameron said at last.

"What are you talking about?" asked Chuck, momentarily confused.

"Bambi," Cameron explained. "You asked for her real name for the tickets and passes."

"Yeah," Chuck said. "I told you why I did that."

"Yeah, and it was bullshit. What was the real reason?"

"So she could show her identification…"

"Fuck that," insisted Cameron, calmly. "I could count on all ten fingers and all ten toes as well as my dick and both nuts and still not come up with half the times that I've used a girl's nickname at the *Will Call* window, and I know *you've* done the same thing. You're checking her out, aren't you?"

Chuck pulled up a stool and sat next to Cameron.

"You're a lot more clever than Dwyer let on," Chuck said. "But you need to play things closer to your vest and stop letting people know what you know. Yeah, I'm checking her out, just like I'd check anyone out that starts hanging out with this band. Too much weird shit has happened and I don't want it happening again."

"So you're going to take your precautions and be fucking suspicious of everyone, is that it?"

"Yeah, pretty much," agreed Chuck. "I learn from my mistakes, even if no one else does."

"What's that supposed to mean?"

"It means that the reason the Six-Day War happened in '67 was no one wanted to believe that it would happen. The reason that the fucking Communists are now running around our Alaskan wilderness is because no one wanted to admit the Russians would dare start shit. It was too fucking bizarre to consider. No one wanted to admit that weird shit might go on, because they were all afraid of being wrong.

They didn't listen to their guts and bad shit happened. Dwyer was in that school of thought. I'm not. I'll be suspicious of everyone… until I don't have to be."

"So you're suspicious of *her*!?" Cameron demanded, getting out of his chair and into Chuck's face.

"I'm suspicious of everyone until I don't have to be," said Chuck. His voice was calm, but barely audible, and he enunciated every syllable as though he was teaching the alphabet to a child.

"I don't think that our friends are the ones we need to worry about," insisted Cameron, maintaining his stance. "For Christ's sake! Can't we trust anyone?"

"No, not really."

"You're letting your spook shit get in the way of reality," Cameron said. "You've been suspicious of so much so long, you forget that sometimes you meet someone you can be certain of."

"I'm certain that the key they used to get into Doug's room last night was given to them, and not stolen."

That news hit Cameron like a blast of cold water.

A key?

"I thought someone broke into his room," Cameron whispered. Chuck shook his head.

"No," he replied. "They let themselves in with a key. The door chain seems to have been removed some time ago, I found it in the back of the closet shelf. Whoever had the key did not expect to find anyone in there, or else they didn't expect to find Doug. D'Lorenzo could never account for his missing key, which he said he lost at a party where he got dosed by people he thought were friends."

Cameron sat down. Resting his elbows on his knees, he put his face in his hands. Once again, his world was being shaken up and he didn't know which way to turn.

This is getting to be too much.

"So, what the fuck do we do now?"

Chuck shrugged his shoulders. "Nothing really," he said. "You go on with what you're doing, what you planned on doing. We play our gigs and we keep on doing what we've been doing."

That's an awful lot of doing…

"What about Bambi, though?"

"What about her?"

"Aren't you going to tell me I can't see her anymore? Aren't you going to tell me she's a risk?"

Chuck shook his head. "No, why the fuck would I do that?" he asked. "I'm not your fucking dad. I'm your manager. If you want to see her, see her. I don't care."

"Didn't you just say you were suspicious of her?"

"I'd be suspicious of my own sainted grandmother if she suddenly showed up in my life again without a good explanation. I'll be honest. Yes, I'm doing a check on her. If I find anything, you'll be the first to know. If I don't, then no problem, and hopefully we can prevent this shit from happening again. You cool now?"

Cameron nodded, but didn't look up. Chuck didn't press for further conversation. He understood on all levels the sudden complexities of Cameron's life. The Roadhouse Sons' front man was addled with nervousness before a show and about a new romantic relationship, combined with completely unfamiliar situations involving the entire band, and myriad consequences never before considered.

Chuck left Cameron to his thoughts and went back to the office. He had enough troubling mental activity of his own right now.

Chuck dropped into his chair and stared at the ceiling, trying to make sense of everything that Dwyer had reported before his death. Those reports were oddly incomplete, which immediately led to Chuck's instinctive conclusion that something was seriously wrong. Dwyer was a detail-oriented man. His missions were planned, rehearsed and reviewed to the point of distraction at times, and executed with few complications or surprises. Dwyer had a knack of preparing his associates to expect the unexpected, without distracting them with details and data. As a result, when the unexpected did occur, Dwyer's cohorts were able to adjust and respond to situations accordingly. Dwyer took a lot of chances, some for which his supervisors threatened to cite him, but they almost always paid off. He had enough of a success rate that his few failures warranted only verbal reprimands.

So, what had happened here? This mission had a relatively straightforward objective—collect all relevant information on black market substances utilized in this demographic. Chuck had helped Dwyer compose the proposal, and he'd carefully monitored the recruitment and intelligence development of this band—the Roadhouse Sons. Dwyer hadn't consulted Chuck on any training format or follow-up approach; rather, he implicitly understood Dwyer's decisions. Every one of Dwyer's associates and superiors knew that sending inexperienced people into clear and present danger was to court disaster. The dosing of Doug and D'Lorenzo testified to that premise.

The band actually did well, considering that they'd endured the correspondence school course version of this type of work. Dwyer felt justified in selecting Cameron as the leader of the team, a decision with which Chuck was inclined to support.

On paper, everything should have been working just fine. So what went wrong? How could Dwyer allow himself to get that close to someone that he didn't know, let alone end up shot to death? There was only one answer to the question. He would never have allowed it. Whoever shot him had to be someone he knew.

After reading over the statements taken by the investigating agents, Chuck could rule out everyone on the team. McIntyre was at the hotel, as were the band. Both Doug and D'Lorenzo were flat on their backs recovering from their respective poisonings. Yet, McIntyre's statement cited that Dwyer had told her that he had something to show her, and that she was to meet him at another location. Dwyer had, at the time, obviously felt that he was being monitored. Otherwise, he wouldn't have gone to all of the trouble of leaving the signals, or insisting on a neutral meeting place. He would have told McIntyre to go to the original location, or he would have gone to hers. No. There was a reason Dwyer wanted to rendezvous at a different location.

This cycle of thought brought Chuck back to the listening devices surreptitiously planted at the Civic Center. A search of Dwyer's and McIntyre's rooms turned up clean, but there was a bug planted in D'Lorenzo's room, as well as Clyde's and Rich's. Someone had tried to plant one in Cameron's room and almost succeeded. This was troubling, to say the least. Rumrunners and dealers, even in the black market, weren't that technically inclined, especially the ones that were targeting the concert crowds. That suggested to Chuck that someone else was involved. Was that individual running the dealers, or were they an unrelated threat? There were salient arguments for both sides of the coin.

The amateur clumsiness of how the person gained entry, planted the devices, and quickly aborted their mission would normally have spoken volumes. However, the fact that they were deploying listening devices at all suggested that they were receiving, at the very least, a modicum of assistance—if not instruction—from someone more experienced. Chuck's supervisors had laughed at that idea, dismissing the whole scenario as an attempt by small-time individuals to feign big-time.

"This is Prohibition all over again," they'd said. "Everyone wants to be Al Capone. It doesn't mean it's the Russians."

Chuck wasn't entirely convinced of that. The fact that these people were inexperienced and clumsy meant nothing. The band wasn't experienced either. They were clumsy, and the Americans were running *them*.

Hubris, pure hubris. Chuck sighed. This wasn't the first time he'd dealt with that mindset. The subject matter caused him to think of the unspeakable past, to travel tumultuous, emotional roads and revisit enduring agitations, the journeys of which served no good purpose. He could not allow his mind to embark upon that trek.

Chuck arose and paced the room. There were several loose ends so close to being tied up that he could practically taste them, but each solution remained just out of reach. He stopped in front of Dwyer's old-fashioned coffee percolator. He stood there at the kitchenette for several seconds. Finally, he filled the percolator with water and set it on the hotplate. A nice, hot cup of tea would help him think this through.

There was no reason to conclude that Dwyer's death was an isolated incident. Chuck closed his eyes and let his mind wander for several minutes. His thoughts landed on D'Lorenzo.

For a week before the concert, D'Lorenzo had returned to the room suffering from some type of illness. At first, everyone chalked it up to a case of the flu or a touch of food poisoning. Doug suspected that D'Lorenzo's ills were a result of consuming bad liquor and too many late nights. He'd associated with some of the locals during the after-party and, at some point, had departed with them. This was typical procedure in undercover work, to which Dwyer's notes alluded regarding D'Lorenzo. Unfortunately, D'Lorenzo's reports, as always, were scant of relevant information. This was no surprise to those with whom D'Lorenzo worked, and the actual statement of his undercover assignment status was nowhere to be found in any file.

Chuck was well aware that D'Lorenzo had been under a cloud for some time, due to mishandling several cases. Perhaps he saw his recent undercover work with the band as a chance for redemption and was, therefore, playing everything close to the vest. If he shared the information, then he'd have to share the glory. D'Lorenzo obviously intended to keep the credit for himself. But why would Dwyer allow that?

Chuck watched the steam escape from the spout of the percolator, eyeing it as though it was clear divination. Steam being steam, though, it provided no clarity, just more fog upon the whole situation. He proceeded to abandon any hope of ethereal enlightenment and readied his tea.

Pouring the hot water through the strainer had a relaxing effect on Chuck. It reminded him of his stay in Asia. For a moment, he could feel the warm humidity that caused his shirt to cling to his back. He could hear the hustle and noise of the crowds. The pungent aroma of the tea was replaced momentarily by the smell of the exhaust from the cars and trucks, and the charcoal cookers that the street vendors used. He breathed deep, as much from his memories as from the tea in his cup.

The distraction had the desired affect. In this calmed state, Chuck focused his attention again on Dwyer and D'Lorenzo. Chuck himself had trained them together. Dwyer had been the studious, pedantic one. D'Lorenzo was brash, and willing to take risks. Despite these differences, they knew each other well and were paired up in most of their assignments. They soon had several major successes to their credit. All of this would lead Dwyer to grant D'Lorenzo ample breathing room with little supervision. But things started to go wrong.

At first, there were just minor incidents that were easily overlooked. Then D'Lorenzo began making egregious mistakes and attracting attention. When his job was on the line, it was Dwyer who argued with his superiors on D'Lorenzo's behalf. Dwyer continued to act in full trust, giving D'Lorenzo all the space he needed for a shot at redemption. This dynamic culminated in calamity: the Mustang incident.

Chuck flushed at the thought that he had personally chosen the two for the assignment. His trainees. His project. Following the explosion, Chuck was one of the few people willing to consider a closer look. Some wondered if he was seeking his own redemption.

"I've been dissected like a fucking lab rat already!" D'Lorenzo had argued at a Mustang review hearing held to determine his future. Most of his associates wanted him to retire, while others pushed to have him assigned to a desk job. Chuck, however, on the urging of Dwyer, pushed to take another look at the entire situation. "People make mistakes," he'd argued; "Sometimes, one just has a bad run." Chuck was a proponent of "examining all of the evidence again before making any final decisions." Again at Dwyer's urging, Chuck helped convince their superiors to put D'Lorenzo and Dwyer together as a team, just once more.

"They had a great track record before. Maybe that's a combination we shouldn't have messed with," Chuck had said. Their superiors agreed, albeit reluctantly, to a new assignment under one condition: that Dwyer was placed in charge. Everyone agreed, except D'Lorenzo. He had no desire to go to Vermont, nor did he wish to be anyone's subordinate, but he realized that his options were limited. The alternatives wouldn't be any more pleasant. Dwyer had convinced D'Lorenzo that the Vermont assignment would be the chance he needed to repair his image.

Chuck sipped his tea, wondering if the irony of it all was lost on anyone other than himself. A high profile attempt to crack open the Black Market Triangle that operated from Boston to New York to Montreal placed Chuck in direct contact with a living, breathing reminder of his greatest failure: Doug Courtland. D'Lorenzo had been charged with recruiting and vetting the inner circle of the USS Mustang's crew, and had somehow managed to turn the Mustang into a Trojan horse. Now, that crew, including Doug's friend, Gus Kalbe, was at the bottom of the ocean. Also now, Chuck was face-to-face with Doug, who would never let him forget it. That brought Chuck to another problem around which he couldn't wrap his mind.

What in the world had Dwyer been thinking when he roomed D'Lorenzo with Doug? Even Chuck, with his reputation for taking reckless chances, would have sooner paired a snake and a mongoose than those two. D'Lorenzo's reports were filled with examples of open hostility from the roadie, most of which would have been dismissed as merely petulant, if they hadn't been verified by the reports of McIntyre and Dwyer. D'Lorenzo was called back for examination by his superiors, and Chuck knew that D'Lorenzo would undergo a serious debriefing. Dwyer was dead, and D'Lorenzo was now without his friend and major supporter. The trust that Dwyer placed in D'Lorenzo had, ironically, become a source of concern to their superiors. Where Dwyer had viewed granting D'Lorenzo a free hand as a sign of trust, others saw it as something upon which to cast suspicion. Dwyer's death seemed to seal those misgivings in a tidy bundle. Chuck's superiors promised to bring him up to speed as soon as they had any new information.

Chuck paused, his cup of tea at his lips. He sat bolt upright. He suddenly realized that Dwyer had left signs for McIntyre, leading her away from the Civic Center. He and his superiors had assumed that Dwyer had phoned McIntyre from his office there, and arranged for her to meet him elsewhere. That fact had always made Chuck's gut go off; it made no sense to him at all. If Dwyer didn't think the office would be secure, why would he make any attempts at contact from there?

He wouldn't have, Chuck realized. He went back to the desk for his backpack and pulled out his case notes. Flipping through them, he came across his list of phone numbers from which Dwyer had called in his reports those last few weeks. Chuck's list included the dates and times Dwyer had made the calls, as well as their duration. The majority of the calls came from two listings. One was the number of the phone on Dwyer's office desk at the Civic Center. The other number was Dwyer's hotel room. Chuck noticed that two days before Dwyer was killed, he'd ceased calling from both numbers. Two new numbers were on Chuck's list, ones he didn't recognize. Due to their sudden, and random, appearance, Chuck suspected that the numbers were associated with phone booths.

Grabbing his coat, Chuck stuffed his notebook in his pocket and headed out the door. He didn't bother telling the others where he was going; there was no sense in raising any questions. Outside, the wind had picked up and a few snow flurries fluttered on the breeze. Chuck scrutinized the parking lot and the surrounding area, but saw no phone booths. To his right, the lot was wide open and led directly to the street, giving him a perfect line of vision along the block. To Chuck's left, the buildings formed a visual wall. Chuck spotted an alleyway between the buildings.

Feeling that the alleyway was as good a place as any to investigate, Chuck headed in. As he did so, he thought about his conversation with Cameron that afternoon. Chuck hated lying to him, but upsetting Cameron with the truth would serve no purpose. It wasn't just a matter of simple curiosity; it was a deadly mistake to believe in coincidence in this line of work. The fact that one of the names that Doug's intruder cited last night was the same name that Bambi cited this morning was entirely too much of a coincidence. How could he tell that to Cameron?

Chuck had phoned in from the local State Attorney's office and was awaiting word from his superiors. If Bambi, or Yvette's, name appeared in any legal records prior to now, regardless of jurisdiction, Chuck would be informed immediately.

He hurried down the alley, moving to the side to let a service truck pull through, then stepped out onto the street. To the left, the sidewalk was clear down to the intersection. However, to his right, Chuck noticed the familiar glass sides and blue plastic lights of a phone booth. He also noticed a red headed woman in a waitress uniform crossing the street toward the booth. Chuck hurried over, reaching the booth just as the woman was stepping onto the curb.

"Sorry!" Chuck said through the glass after closing the folding door. He smiled as the woman gave him a dirty look. Turning so that he could watch her with his peripheral vision, Chuck compared the number in the dial center to the number in his notes.

Suddenly, the woman began pounding on the door. "I've got an important phone call to make!" she shouted. The glass muted the volume of her voice, but not to much effect. Chuck held up his index finger, indicating that he needed a minute, but she persisted in pounding. The number on the dial matched the last number from which Dwyer had called. Chuck was about to insert a dime into the phone slot when the redhead's pounding became annoyingly persistent.

"You aren't even making a fucking phone call!" she bellowed. "Get out of there and let me in!"

Chuck realized that he'd have no peace until the woman made her phone call. He pocketed his slip of paper and stepped out of the booth.

"Since you're in a hurry!" he said with a smile and a flourish of his arm. The woman glared at him as she stepped inside. Chuck smiled warmly back, knowing that would annoy her even more. He stepped a few paces away from the phone booth. He didn't want to take the chance that someone else would get into the phone booth before he could. From inside the booth, the woman continued to shower him with dirty looks. She held her hand over her mouth and spoke into the phone. Obviously, he couldn't hear a thing that she said, nor could he read her lips. He wasn't interested in anything she could possibly have to say. After a few minutes, she emerged and pushed past him. As she did so, Chuck caught a glimpse of her nametag. Ruby...

Chuck watched her as she walked across the street and into a restaurant, The Catamount. He recalled that Dwyer had mentioned the establishment. "They have real coffee there!" Dwyer had enthused

"I don't think they'd find you worth putting up with," Chuck said aloud as he watched the redhead enter the building. Stepping into the phone booth, he picked up the receiver and listened for a dial tone. As expected, there was nothing. Dropping a dime into the slot, he heard a series of clicks followed by another dial tone. He hesitated a moment, then decided to proceed with his call. The operator came on the line and informed him that he had to provide additional funds. After he inserted more coins, he heard the phone ring on the other end of the line. After three rings someone answered, and Chuck spoke before the other party had a chance.

"Hey! I'm calling for Max," he said quickly. "Yeah, Max had to go out of town. I don't expect him back, but he wanted me to fill in for him. Man, it sucks doing things by the book!"

"I understand," the other voice said. It was a male voice. No introduction was offered. There was no reason for it. Chuck knew that whomever answered the phone had the responsibility of participating in no conversation whatsoever unless the caller elicited all the correct prompts, and all the correct answers when prompted.

"I was just getting a little lonely," Chuck said, feigning a melancholy sigh. "I was wondering when my brother was coming back this way."

"I believe his train has been delayed," said the voice. "However, if you're really bored, I'd check out the library if I were you."

Before Chuck could respond, the man hung up. Chuck heard another series of clicks before the dial tone engaged.

"One question answered," Chuck muttered to himself. He emerged from the phone booth and hurried down the alley from whence he came. Correctly assuming that even *this* phone was compromised, Chuck had successfully indicated his ersatz suspicions to his unknown contact. "Max" had been Dwyer's code name. "By the book" referred to speaking in coded messages whenever one felt that they were monitored.

Chuck was anxious to know when his superiors would check any of the leads he'd provided. Obviously, and as with any government agency, there would be a delay. Apparently, though, there was certain esoteric information only available from the State

Attorney's office, i.e., the library to which Chuck's telephone contact referred. The library, Chuck decided, was definitely worth a visit.

As he hurried up the alley, Chuck was disconcerted. Something was nagging at him, something about the phone booth. Upon retrieving and reexamining the slip of paper, he realized that Dwyer had made a phone call just before he was killed. The call's duration was less than two minutes. Chuck surmised that it must have been the last call placed to McIntyre from Dwyer. Dwyer realized that, after having made that call, he'd have to hurry to where he could leave the clues for McIntyre to discern their meeting place. Fatefully, this place was the location where Dwyer met his killer.

Considering that Dwyer was dead by the time McIntyre arrived, whoever was listening to the call had no time to form a viable plan of action, hence the haphazard manner in which Dwyer's body was manhandled. This meant that from wherever the calls were monitored, it was near enough to dispatch a killer.

During the last few days, Chuck had studied the buildings in close proximity to the Civic Center. The one directly across from the backstage door was vacant. No hidden doors or secret rooms existed to the best of anyone's knowledge, though recent evidence of secret occupation set the building's owner on edge.

Heading up the block from the theater, one saw a furniture store, a dress shop and a stationer. Heading down the block was a gas station. Around the corner was The Catamount. In either direction were office buildings for various businesses, ranging from real estate to dentistry. Any one of these places could easily harbor a listening station and quickly dispatch personnel as necessary. As Chuck emerged from the alley into the parking lot at the rear the Civic Center, he heard someone call his name.

"There you are!" called McIntyre, motioning him toward her car. "I've been looking everywhere for you! I thought you were rehearsing with the guys."

"I told them to take a break," Chuck replied. "I had some things to check out."

Chuck proceeded to explain what he'd uncovered. He told her that he needed to visit the State Attorney's office.

"I think they've got something for us," he explained.

"Well, I think I've got something for us, too," McIntyre whispered. "We can talk in the car."

As they pulled out of the parking lot, McIntyre turned on the radio and adjusted the dial to a station that only broadcast static. Both doubted that the car was bugged, but there was no point in taking chances. The fact that the phone booth from which Dwyer had called was tapped indicated that their movements were monitored, and not by amateurs.

"What have you got?" Chuck asked, keeping his voice as quiet as possible.

"A phone call to pack up all of D'Lorenzo's things," McIntyre explained, her voice equally subdued. "Our friend is not coming back."

"No shit. Did they say why?"

"Too many unanswered questions and strange coincidences was all they told me. Do you think he has anything to do with this?"

"I doubt it," admitted Chuck. "But only just barely. He had a good record, was decorated. Then he got jinxed and never seemed to get out of it. He's been under a cloud for a long time, and that can make people do stupid things."

"Like shooting a colleague?"

"He's got an alibi for that," Chuck corrected. "Puking his guts out in his hotel room removes him from the list of suspects."

"You don't think he had an accomplice, then?" McIntyre lowered her gaze.

"How long was he working here? Did he have time enough to set up a network?" Chuck didn't hide his supreme doubt that Dwyer was a turncoat maverick. To Chuck, the thought was laughable.

McIntyre hesitated before answering.

"I'm not sure," she admitted. "I don't think he was here before we were dispatched. I *do* know that he was here a few years ago with the Mustang project, but nothing since then."

"How long were you and Dwyer here?"

"About a year," she explained. "We'd been working on the black market angle for some time already, but hadn't gotten anywhere. That's why we were so anxious to try your idea. D'Lorenzo came along only a few months ago."

Chuck considered all of the facts, but didn't say anything. This wasn't getting any clearer. In fact, at best, it was clear as mud.

CHAPTER TWENTY-FOUR

"Surprise"

Cameron shook Doug's shoulder, rousing him out of his sleep.

"What the fuck, man?!" snapped Doug. He jerked away from Cameron and rubbed the sleep from his eyes. "I just fucking fell asleep, too! Get lost, will you?"

"What the hell happened last night?" demanded Cameron, ignoring the roadie's reaction. "Why didn't you tell me someone tried breaking into your room?"

"What?!" Doug stared, incredulously at Cameron. "You fucking woke me up to ask me that? I don't fucking believe you!"

"Hey, I'm the leader of this band and the one in charge here. I expect to know about this shit!"

"First off, you weren't around this morning, and when you were around you had a bug up your ass and snapped at everyone, so I wasn't going to tell you shit. Second, it got taken care of. We caught the guy. Chuck interrogated him and we turned him over to the fucking cops. End of story, thank you and good fucking night!"

Cameron felt his face flush as Doug held him accountable for his bad attitude that morning. He knew that he'd let everyone down and failed at his job. He was determined to rectify the situation.

"Man, listen to me," Cameron insisted. "I'm sorry. I was an asshole and there's no other way to put it. I'm *sorry*. But you've got to tell me what the fuck happened. I don't want to have to find out shit like this from the others, and I might've been able to do something or I could've been on the lookout."

Doug eyed Cameron carefully, weighing his friend's words before speaking. With a yawn, he lit a cigarette and watched the exhaled smoke waft its languorous way toward the ceiling.

"I woke up hearing someone opening the door," Doug began. "I didn't know who it was and they didn't know I was in there. We fought. I tied him up and got Chuck. Chuck interrogated him and we turned him over to the cops, who are probably doing even more."

"Who was the guy?"

Doug shook his head. "I don't really know," he explained. "He had a bunch of phony IDs and didn't own up to any of them. The nearest thing we could figure is that he was looking for D'Lorenzo. He talked about being able to get some good stuff from him and was supposed to meet him."

"Do you believe him?"

"I believe he was expecting to get some shit from D'Lorenzo," Doug agreed. "But I don't know if D'Lorenzo was running something on the side or was setting them up to get caught."

"Do you have any ideas?"

"Yeah," Doug snorted. "I've got plenty. I wouldn't put it past that bastard to do something like that, but I honestly think he might have been setting them up."

"You changing your attitude about him now?"

Doug shook his head.

"No fucking way," Doug said with palpable derision. "But I know that's how they work. I can't let my personal feelings get in the way anymore."

"You're starting to sound like Chuck," Cameron snickered. Doug simply shrugged.

"I guess," he said. "But if that's the case, it's because he's right. I figure if I only look at things the way I want to look at them, then I'm not going to see a whole hell of a lot, and I might've been seeing things that weren't there in the first place."

Cameron nodded. He was amazed that Doug was finally settling in to make all this work *and* accepting it as a reality.

Pretty fucking nice...

"Any ideas where we go from here?" Cameron asked. He was drawing a blank. From the sad shaking of Doug's head, he realized that the roadie was drawing a blank as well.

"All right, man," sighed Cameron. "Try and get some rest, then. We're going to be busy later."

Doug nodded, and put out his cigarette. He was about to lean back in his chair once more, when Cameron slapped his boot.

"Not here, man!" he laughed. "Get into the office and lay down there. Doesn't Chuck have a couch or something in there?"

"No," yawned Doug. "But you're right. Even if I slept on the floor, I'd get more rest than here."

Cameron headed back to the band. No one felt like rehearsing at the moment, and he realized that they needed to take a break. No one showed him any acrimony because of his earlier attitude. For that, Cameron was grateful.

No need to push it.

He pondered going to the Tavern for a drink, but nixed the idea. How would Bambi's father react? Would Cameron's visit solve problems or create more? Bambi had insisted that she would be all right and she'd wanted him to leave right away when he'd brought her home. Regardless, Cameron couldn't escape the urge to find out for himself.

Wandering around the Civic Center, he came to the box office. On an impulse, he asked the ticket girls if Chuck had left any back stage passes and complimentary tickets. Cameron was both surprised and pleased to find out that Chuck had, in fact, left an envelope for Yvette Lavelle.

I guess he wasn't blowing smoke up my ass!

After thanking the ticket girls, Cameron proceeded to the dressing room. Everyone used the term loosely. The so-called dressing room was small and cramped. Everyone's coats and guitar cases were lying about, and Cameron had to walk, and sometimes crawl, over the Roadhouse Sons' gear. Thankfully, there was an overstuffed chair in the room, and it was beckoning him. He collapsed into it.

As Cameron sat there staring at the cinderblock walls, his mind drifted to the brick portico of Hart's Tavern. He needed to go back there; he needed to know that Bambi was all right. But how could he pull that off? There was no way that he could show up there in his car. He thought about how he would overcome the obvious. A yellow Mustang was too easy to spot. Then he smiled.

Another car wouldn't be... They wouldn't even recognize it! Hurrying out the door, he found Rich and Evan jamming on the stage.

"Guys, I need help," he said.

"Don't expect us to argue," said Evan, tapping out a rhythm on his snare. "But the kind of help you need, we're not licensed to give."

"I had that coming," Cameron agreed, holding up his hands in mock surrender. "But I really do need your help with something. It's important."

Quickly, Cameron filled them in the earlier events with Bambi and her possible disappearance, and that he was very concerned that she was all right. He had a plan for going to the Tavern and casually checking on her.

"But, I need your help," Cameron reiterated. He revealed his plan: He would use one of their vehicles to drive to the Tavern under the premise that he was test-driving a new car. The car would suddenly give him trouble, and he'd have to use the Tavern phone. He'd have a beer while he was waiting for them to pick him up, and he could check on Bambi.

"You want us to wait here for your call?" asked Evan. Cameron shook his head.

"Just follow me and park around the block and wait about 10 minutes or so. Then show up."

"Why don't you use your car?" asked Rich.

"They'd recognize it in a minute," Cameron explained. "And there's no way I could explain being over there so soon after dropping Bambi off. But, if I were supposedly test driving a new car, then it's just a little more plausible."

"But only just a little bit," Evan agreed. "You can't think they're that stupid. They'll know something's up. I think you should take someone with you. Explain that they were the ones testing a car and you were with them."

"An even better idea," agreed Cameron.

"What's an even better idea?" Clyde asked as he came up behind them. With a little hesitation, Cameron explained his plan and his motives to Clyde, who decided to go along with it.

"Who's car are we going to use,? Clyde asked.

"Uh… Rich's," said Evan. "You and Cameron can drive that one, and Clyde and I will follow behind."

Clyde shook his head.

"If you ask me, that's the one weak point in the whole thing," he explained. "Cameron being with Rich when they have car trouble would just be too obvious. If I do it with Rich, then we phone from the bar and *then* Cameron shows up, would be a little bit more believable. Especially since Cameron says they've been having our promo pictures there and they would probably recognize us. That would explain why Cameron would be showing up in the first place. He'd be helping out a band buddy. Besides, Rich and I've never been there so it's a little more believable for us to do it."

Cameron agreed, but very reluctantly. He wanted to be the one hanging around in the bar waiting for a rescue ride. He felt uncomfortable with the other guys executing his plan. He felt like they were putting themselves in his position.

Oh, fuck! I'm jealous!

Cameron pushed such thoughts out of his mind and proceeded to sketch a map for Evan, Rich and Clyde, complete with their rendezvous site in case Cameron's plans went awry.

"We should take your car," Cameron said to Evan.

"What on earth for?" Evan asked. It was impossible to miss the reluctance in his voice. Being married, his gas and rubber rations were tied to his wife's. To use any rations unnecessarily meant that Evan's wife would be forced to go without, as well. As a result, Evan and the Roadhouse Sons had agreed that his car would only be used for gig-related travel, or in case of emergencies.

"Simple! You have four doors," Cameron explained to Evan. "If they have to abandon their car and come get us, then they can get in quickly. If we take my car, then we have to get out and they have to climb in over the seats. That would waste lot of time."

"I see your point," Evan said, still hesitating. Cameron knew Evan was seriously concerned about abusing his rations.

"Man, don't worry," Cameron assured him. "If there's a problem, I'm sure Chuck can swing us some more, or I can go with you if you need to gas up or change a tire. I've still got plenty of points left. Relax."

With a smile, Evan nodded and grabbed his coat.

"You promise?" Evan pleaded to Cameron.

"You have my word."

The others were already out the door and waiting. Cameron reviewed his plan once more, for comfort's sake, and gave the guys directions to the bar. Reflecting for a moment, he wished them luck. Clyde and Rich drove off, with Clyde behind the wheel. Even though he had a phony license, the band members knew that this strategy was the only way that the whole scenario could be believable. If the guys were stopped or questioned, no one would believe that Rich wanted to test-drive his own car.

Let's just hope it doesn't get checked.

Evan stalled before heading out of the parking lot. He and Cameron kept Rich's car in view and watched as it turn onto the street toward the Tavern. Evan drove for a few more blocks, and made his way toward the rendezvous site. Checking their watches, he and Cameron realized that they were early. They decided to pull over, park and wait. The site Cameron chose was the parking lot of a small hardware store. There was enough traffic entering and leaving that they could remain there unnoticed.

Cameron's thoughts were on Bambi, and on his hopes that the entire operation would go according to plan. He felt nervous and jittery and began to fidget. In an effort to calm Cameron, Evan tried turning on the radio and talking about various band business. All of this was to no avail. Cameron just kept checking his watch.

"We've only been sitting here two fucking minutes!" he cried.

"It seems that way," said Evan, perfectly calm. "Want to play a game to pass the time?"

"Hell, no!" snapped Cameron.

"I was thinking of that game, *I Spy*," Evan laughed. "You know. I spy with my little eye, and you pick something…"

"I know how to play that fucking game," insisted Cameron, making no attempt to hide his annoyance. "I just don't feel like playing it!"

Evan chuckled at him, and began to study something in the rearview mirror.

"Too bad, because I spy with my little eye something curious."

"Just what the fuck do you mean?"

"That blue car behind us," Evan said. "It pulled in right when we did, but no one has gotten out of that car, either."

From where he was sitting, Cameron couldn't see anything in the rearview mirror. He didn't want to turn around. That would be dead giveaway that he and Evan were aware of the car behind them. If they were being monitored, it was best to pretend that they didn't know it. Fortunately, Cameron was able to see the car from the side view mirror on his door.

"What do you think that's all about?" he asked.

"I have no idea," said Evan.

"Did you notice them following us before we got here?"

"I honestly can't say," Evan replied. "I wasn't paying any attention. I still haven't gotten used to all of this."

"You and me both," admitted Cameron. "I don't always think to look, either."

"So, what do you think we should do?"

Cameron was silent for a moment, mentally devising a strategy.

"Wait here a couple minutes more, then we leave, just like we had planned," Cameron said. "If they're following us, then they won't learn anything much."

"Why not?"

"Because we're not on any secret mission or anything. We're just checking on Bambi, that's all."

Cameron kept track of the time on his watch, and signaled to Evan that it was time to go. As they backed out of their parking space, they were able to nonchalantly steal a glance at the other car. It was a 1975 dark blue Chevy Caprice, with a white top and New York license plates. Two men sat in the front seat. Cameron and Evan were unable to discern if there was anyone in the back. Evan pulled out onto the street and headed toward the rendezvous site. After driving only one block, they noticed the other car pull out and drive up behind them.

"Looks like we have company," said Evan.

"Act natural," said Cameron, watching the other car through his side view mirror. "It might just be a fucking bizarre coincidence. Let's do everything like we planned."

A few blocks further down the street, Evan made a right turn that would take him past the Tavern. Up ahead, they could see Rich's car parked on the street with the hazard lights flashing. Both Rich and Clyde were leaning up against the car with their arms folded.

"What the fuck?" Cameron snapped. "Why are they out here?"

Evan was about to pull over, when he noticed the Caprice coming up right behind them.

"I think they're trying to get our attention," Evan pointed out. Cameron shook his head with irritation.

"Keep going past the guys," he said. "We go around the block once more and then see if they're still here. We'll also see if those clowns behind us are really following us or not."

Evan passed his fellow band members, who simply watched. They gave no indication that they even recognized Evan's car. As they droved past the guys, Cameron realized why they were standing around outside. The bar was closed.

At the intersection, Cameron and Evan looked in their respective rearview mirrors to see what was transpiring behind them. For a moment, Cameron was afraid that Clyde would break form and attract their attention and spoil everything. To Cameron's great relief, all Clyde did was turn and speak to Rich, who continued leaning against the car.

The blue Caprice seemed to be slowing down. Cameron wasn't sure if it was due to approaching the intersection, or acknowledging the stranded car. Evan, who knew to turn right, waited at the stop sign for as long as he felt comfortable that he wasn't garnering suspicion.

"We better hurry it along," suggested Cameron. Evan nodded in agreement. They drove around the corner and circled around the entire route again, after which they began the approach to the bar.

"Pull over here!" cried Cameron. "Here! " he emphasized. "We park here and get out and check it out."

"What if that other car is there?" Evan asked.

"What difference would it make?" replied Cameron.

"A big difference if there's trouble," Evan pointed out.

"You think I don't know that?" grumbled Cameron. "Leave the doors unlocked, or you can wait here with the engine running. I'll go to the corner and check. If there's trouble, I'll wave you away to go back to the theater to get Doug and get help. If there isn't, I'll nod and you come over and join me. Deal?"

"Deal," Evan agreed.

Cameron got out of the car and closed the door quietly. He didn't want to draw any attention to himself. He clung to the building exterior and walked quickly to the corner, surveilling the surrounding area. The blue Caprice was parked behind Rich's vehicle. Two male strangers were standing there, talking to Rich and Clyde. Neither of them seemed very concerned, but they weren't entirely relaxed. The two strangers had their backs to Cameron, and he was unable to see their faces or discern if they were armed. Erring on the side of caution, Cameron waved Evan away. Without hesitating, Evan drove away from the curb and continued down the street. The street had no stop signs, so Evan could drive past everyone without revealing the mission. Cameron was relieved that Evan didn't glance back to look at him. He saw Evan's car turn at the next intersection, and he decided to make his entrance.

Cameron casually sauntered around the corner, his hands tucked into his jacket pockets, and made his way down the sidewalk. If either Rich or Clyde noticed him, they gave no indication of it. As he drew closer, one of the men from the blue Caprice noticed Cameron approaching, and turned to face him.

The man was roughly Cameron's height, but much more heavyset than the lean, thin Cameron. The man's hair was short, not quite a military cut, and he wore black loafers and trousers with a heavy blue jacket. Cameron suspected that the stubble on the man's drooping, unshaven jowls was not usual for him. The man spoke with a thick accent, which Cameron surmised might be French.

"What do you want?" the man snarled, turning to face the approaching musician.

"I came to see what was going on," Cameron said. "Nothing wrong with that. It's still a free country."

"Go mind your own fucking business," the man warned. "There's nothing here that concerns you!"

"Ah, but that's where you're wrong, my porky friend," Cameron said with a smile. "You see, these guys are my buddies. They're due at work with me, but since they're sitting here with their hazard lights on, I can only assume they need assistance."

"I said get the fuck out of here," the man repeated.

"I said no," smiled Cameron.

The man walked toward Cameron and shoved his face in Cameron's, pressing his chest against him. Cameron smelled cigarettes and Aqua Velva, which he found amusing, since it was obvious that the man hadn't shaved. Cameron said nothing, but simply continued to smile. His grin had the desired affect of irritating the man, which made Cameron smile even more.

"Are you guys OK?" Cameron asked, his gaze never wavering from his opponent's.

The second man, who'd remained silent until now, finally spoke. "We were just advising them they should be moving along, They don't belong here."

I wondered when you were going to say something.

"They obviously can't move along if their car isn't working," Cameron said.

"Their car is working fine," the first man replied.

Fuck off, Smelly Man!

"Blinking lights would say otherwise."

The second man stepped forward. He was almost the same height as the first man, but with blonde, longer hair and clean-shaven. He wore engineer boots, blue jeans and a suede jacket with fleece lining. Cameron was taken with how new this man's clothes looked compared to his cohort.

Great... we got Smelly Man and now Blonde Guy...

"You being smart?" demanded the Blonde Guy. Cameron noticed that he, too, had an accent. Cameron shook his head and smiled.

"No," he replied. "An observation isn't an attitude."

"I say it is," said Smelly Man. Cameron shrugged, still smiling.

"You guys all right?" Cameron called out to his friends.

"Yeah," said Rich. "Just some vapor lock. Should be fine now."

"Then let's be getting back," Cameron said. Before anyone could make a move, the Blonde Guy pushed Rich into the side of the car, and Smelly Man pushed Cameron backward.

Shit!

"You're not going anywhere," Smelly Man said.

"You wanted us to leave," Cameron said in a low voice. "We're leaving."

"You leave," Smelly Man smiled menacingly. "The car stays."

"Fuck you!" Cameron said, his ire fully risen.

"We'll see if you have vapor lock or not," Smelly Man said. "We'll bring your car home to you. Now get the fuck out of here."

OK, now I'm pissed!

"We will," said Cameron. "And we'll be taking our car with us."

"Like hell you will!" He took a swing at Cameron. Cameron ducked, and as he stood up, he drove his right fist into Smelly Man's stomach, then brought his left fist into the man's jaw. Smelly Man staggered back, more from shock than from pain or impact. Cameron was not about to surrender any momentum. Lunging forward, he delivered another roundhouse punch with his right fist to the other side of Smelly Man's jaw. Cameron knew that he caused damage with this hit; he felt his knuckles hit the man's jawbone, whereas the previous jaw punch was cushioned by fleshy jowl. Smelly Man stumbled back, flailing his arms to keep his balance.

The other men, regardless of their allegiance, were shocked by the violent exchange. For a moment, they all simply stood there, nonplussed. Almost immediately, though, Blonde Guy came to his friend's defense, only to be stopped by Clyde and Rich. Blonde Guy swung his fist at Rich, who leaned out of the way and watched as the fist hit air. Before Blonde Guy could follow up, Rich charged him with a shoulder block, causing Blonde Guy to fall backward, toppling to the sidewalk. Rich quickly jumped onto his chest and began to pummel him.

Smelly Man, however, was not so easily brought down. Gaining his balance, he lunged at Cameron and swung again. Raising his arm,

Cameron blocked the swing and tried to counter with his own punch, only to have that one blocked. Smelly Man reached out and grabbed the front of Cameron's jacket and tried to swing him to the side. Instead of resisting, Cameron went with the motion and, grabbing onto Smelly Man's jacket, used the momentum to keep the swing going. Cameron pulled his adversary along, pushing him into the side of the Tavern. This only served to annoy Smelly Man, who, with hands outstretched like Frankenstein, made a rush for Cameron's throat. Cameron grabbed the man's wrists in an effort to ward off strangulation. Cameron soon discovered that Smelly Man was much stronger than he seemed to be; he very nearly succeeded at firmly clutching Cameron's throat.

The two men struggled, with Cameron stumbling backward in an attempt to get away from his adversary, despite his stubborn, vice-like grip on Smelly Man's jacket cuffs. As Cameron stumbled into the side of Rich's car, Clyde tackled Smelly Man from the side and pushed him away. Smelly Man pounded Clyde in his back and kidney area, but Clyde didn't falter. Cameron grabbed the front of Smelly Man's jacket and punched him in the mouth. The other man's head went back, and Cameron noticed that he'd busted Smelly Man's lower lip. He punched again, opening the cut a little more.

Confused by the dual assault, Smelly Man was unsure of which adversary to attack first. Before he could make up his mind, they heard the screech of tires behind. Cameron punched Smelly Man once more before daring to seek out the source of the noise. To his relief, it was Evan's car, and as it came to a halt, the passenger door opened and out leapt Doug.

Bounding across the sidewalk, Doug used his momentum to assault Smelly Man with a roundhouse right punch which turned Smelly Man's nearly 300 degrees. For a brief moment, Cameron feared that the roadie had broken the other man's neck, but when Smelly Man shook his head, Cameron knew that their adversary wasn't seriously injured.

Pushing Cameron and Rich out of harm's way, Doug grabbed Smelly Man's ears and pulled his opponent toward his face. For a millisecond, Cameron thought his roadie was going to kiss the other man. Instead, Doug tipped his head and drove it into the bridge of the other man's nose. Blood ran out of Smelly Man's nostrils, merging with the stream of blood from his torn lip. Doug took advantage of Smelly Man's slowed reflexes by gripping his jacket and pushing him back toward the building wall. Recoiling to strike again, Doug was about to punch Smelly Man senseless when suddenly another squeal of tires pierced the air. Doug paid no attention. Instead he delivered a merciless series of blows to Smelly Man's head and face. Cameron had paid attention, though, and looked up to see the horrified face of McIntyre, and a very angry Chuck Lamont emerging from the car.

"What the fuck is going on here?" he demanded, grabbing Doug and yanking him away from Smelly Man. Without being told to, Rich retreated from Blonde Guy, who quickly clambered to his feet. Chuck was about to speak when Blonde Guy shouted something in French to Smelly Man. Putting a hand over his bleeding nose, Smelly Man quickly stumbled toward the blue Caprice and jumped in. Clyde and Doug tried to stop them, with Doug grabbing onto the door handle of the passenger side as the car pulled away from the curb. Chuck ordered them to stop, and Doug released his grip.

"What the fuck were you *doing!?*" Chuck demanded again, each syllable succinctly enunciated for effect. Cameron noticed that Chuck trembled slightly as he spoke.

That's not from the cold.

"They were stalled here," Cameron said, indicating Rich and Clyde. "I came along to see if they were all right. Those guys were giving us a ration of shit and that guy in the blue jacket took a swing at me and I fought back totally in self-defense. The other guy decided to start shit with them and that's when all this started. Doug happened to come along with Evan and tried to help me. It was a good thing you came along when you did!"

"What the fuck were you two doing out here in the first place?" Chuck said to Rich and Clyde, ignoring Cameron.

"I was test driving Rich's car," stammered Clyde. "I was thinking about buying it some time."

"You don't have money, you don't have a license and you don't honestly expect me to believe that shit, do you?" snapped Chuck. The muscles in Chuck's jaw pulsed as he talked, and he clenched and released his fists repeatedly. None of this was lost on Cameron.

He's wound really tight...

"I'll ask again for the last time. What the fuck was going on here?" Chuck hissed. Cameron, Evan, Clyde and Rich exchanged furtive glances. Doug seemed to merely observe this discourse. Like Chuck, though, Doug was actually quite confused. Despite the adrenaline coursing through his veins, he just wasn't as angry.

No one dared speak. "You were here checking on that girl, weren't you?" Chuck said, facing Cameron. Cameron remained silent.

"Get back to the Civic Center. *Now!*" Chuck spat. He walked toward McIntyre's car. Suddenly, he stopped dead in his tracks, turned and pointed at Cameron.

"*You* ride with *me!*" he demanded. "We've got some things to discuss."

Cameron looked at the others. They looked back at him expectantly. He turned to leave and they watched him walk away.

As he followed Chuck, Cameron thought he saw movement in one of the Tavern's second story windows.

CHAPTER TWENTY-FIVE
"Hard Choices"

Cameron watched Chuck lean back in his chair. Chuck just stared at the ceiling. He said nothing and wouldn't acknowledge Cameron's presence. The ride back from the Tavern had been palpably tense, and Chuck was just as silent then. Cameron would have rather argued than endure Chuck's deliberate and mute disregard. McIntyre, for that matter, was just as quiet on the ride back. She wouldn't even look at Cameron in the rearview mirror, which left him feeling more vulnerable than when he was fist-fighting minutes before. When Chuck finally spoke, Cameron exhaled, an audible sigh of relief that filled the room.

"How long had you guys been followed?" Chuck asked, still staring heavenward

"I don't know." Cameron was fidgety. The adrenaline was finally slowing in his veins. "We noticed them just before we were supposed to meet the guys in front of the Tavern."

"Which probably means you had been watched all day," said McIntyre.

"And you only noticed it then?" asked Chuck once more.

"Yeah," muttered Cameron. Chuck and McIntyre were deliberately phrasing their questions in a manner that held Cameron responsible for his enormous carelessness. The perpetual lesson he'd learn from his mistake was sinking in as a result.

"What the hell were you doing there, anyway?" demanded McIntyre. Before Cameron could answer, Chuck spoke up.

"He was checking on that girl, no doubt, trying to be nonchalant about it so he didn't appear either desperate or too eager."

Chuck didn't wait for any confirmation from Cameron, whose cheeks were burning with embarrassment.

"There, of all places!" snapped McIntyre. Chuck turned to face her.

"Like he was supposed to know," Chuck said, calmly. "We didn't even find out 'til a little while ago."

"Supposed to know what?" Cameron asked, visibly concerned. He rarely saw McIntyre flustered or upset. She barely flinched when they found Dwyer's body. Now, she was vehemently upset and very angry.

"We've got a bit of information about some of the people that have crossed our paths of late," said Chuck with a yawn.

"You mean, like the guy you caught breaking into Doug's room?" Cameron asked. That now familiar uneasy feeling came over him again.

"Among others," nodded Chuck. "One of the men that you were having your altercation with was another, unless I am seriously mistaken."

"Which one? Porky?"

Chuck shook his head.

"It was the other guy. I got a good look at him as he was running off. McIntyre got a look at his license plate and she's running a check on that. No doubt stolen, which will help confirm my suspicions."

"Then why didn't you grab them when you showed up?" Cameron demanded. "What did you let them go for?"

"Arrest them how?" Chuck shrugged. "Arrest them for what?"

"Aren't you fucking police officers?" Cameron cried. "Arrest them for assault or some shit! They attacked us!"

Chuck leaned forward on the desk and folded his hands. He studied Cameron's expression closely, but showed no signs of anger. Instead, he seemed perfectly relaxed.

"You know what we are, and we know what we are, but they don't know and they can't know," Chuck explained. "The most that we could have done was make a citizen's arrest, but we still would have had to make a lot of explanations with the cops later, explanations that I would rather not have made. Do you understand what I'm saying?"

"So, you're like undercover or something…" Cameron said. Chuck nodded.

"So are you, by the way," Chuck replied. "Not like us, but no one can know what you are or what you're doing."

"Well, yeah, *that* I know," Cameron assured him. "I just didn't think it applied to you guys, that's all."

"It does," Chuck explained.

"More than for you," added McIntyre.

"What did you find out, if you don't mind my asking?" Cameron said, hoping to change the subject. Chuck and McIntyre looked at each other before answering.

"We found out a lot, actually," Chuck said. "We thought these guys were small potatoes in the group we're looking for. But they're not."

"They're not?" asked Cameron, both interested and concerned. It was one thing to discover information and identify people as much on the fringe as they all were, but it was another to dig below the surface at the inner workings of an outfit like that.

"We thought these guys worked for the main group out of Montreal," Chuck explained. "As it turns out, they seem to *be* the main group, relocated here about a year ago when things were getting hot up there. From here, they can monitor things going on in Boston, New York, Montreal and upstate New York. That Tavern is a main hangout for them."

"How the fuck do you know that?" Cameron was anxious. Chuck and McIntyre knew why.

Chuck shook his head.

"Don't worry about that. If there was anything I thought you should know, I'd tell you. We're looking at the guys running it, nothing else right now." Chuck steadied his gaze on Cameron.

"Bambi's dad runs it," Cameron said. "He's a nice guy. He's not mixed up in any of this shit!"

"Have you ever met him?" Chuck asked.

Cameron sat in silence. "No," he said at last. "But I know he's a citizen!"

"Have you seen his citizenship papers?" demanded McIntyre. "Or are you only basing this on your personal feelings."

"Jealous, sweetheart?" Cameron smiled.

What's the bug up your ass so suddenly?

"Don't flatter yourself," McIntyre replied. Cameron had never seen her like this. She was cold as ice.

"As it turns out, he's right," Chuck said quickly, trying to prevent an altercation between them. "The bar is owned by the old man and, yes, he is a citizen. He's been one for about five years."

"Do you have any dirt on her?" Cameron didn't want to prolong his pretense about a lesser concern for Bambi.

"Don't worry about what I've got," said Chuck. "If you need to know, I'll tell you. I already said that. Right now, we've got to be mindful that we're on the right track, and we're apparently involved with bigger fish than we originally thought. That's good, and that's bad; good because we're getting closer to what we want to know, and bad because we didn't think we'd be the big game."

"So, what now?" Cameron sulked, despite his relief that Bambi was out of the fray.

"Now, you just take it easy," Chuck said, leaning back in his chair. "I'd stay away from the Tavern for awhile. Choose other locations when you want to meet her, but it's best you're not seen over there."

"Do you think the cops will be looking for us?" Cameron asked. Chuck shook his head.

"Nah! No fucking way," he said. "I can guarantee that the cops don't even know what happened, broad daylight and out in the open notwithstanding. These guys run that neighborhood and don't want to attract any attention. I'm telling you to stay away because you stood up to them and damaged their image. That I promise you, will not go unpunished. I can pretty much bet on the fact that they will be waiting for you."

Cameron tapped his pack of cigarettes and fumbled for his lighter. He wasn't feeling any better.

"Don't let it bother you," Chuck said. "We'll be playing Barre next week and stay there for awhile, and then up to the Champlain Valley. By the time we get back here, it'll all have blown over."

Cameron wasn't convinced, but said nothing. There was much more than meets the eye here and Cameron knew it. Chuck was withholding information and McIntyre's unusually cold demeanor and irascible dirty looks confirmed it.

"Man, just take my advice and don't go chasing after that girl," Chuck said. "You're not sixteen, you know. If she's interested she'll be back around."

"That's not it," Cameron muttered. Chuck gave him a quizzical look, which prompted Cameron to come clean himself and tell them what happened when he brought Bambi back to the Tavern. As Cameron spoke, Chuck remained expressionless, but McIntyre melted into her characteristic persona and became less irritated and more concerned. When Cameron finished his account, he waited for one of them to say something, *any*thing, but no one spoke. Finally, unable to stand the silence anymore, Cameron spoke up.

"So, tell me. Tell me the truth. Do you have anything on her?" His voice was quiet but firm. He was not angry or demanding, but it was clear to Chuck and McIntyre that Cameron was not going to tolerate vague, ambiguous answers.

Chuck sighed again and rubbed his eyes. "I didn't find anything connecting her with what we're looking for," Chuck told him. "Are you satisfied now?"

Cameron finally lit his cigarette and relished a deep and lengthy drag.

No, I'm not... but you're not going to tell me any more than that.

"I guess so," Cameron replied, with a shrug of his shoulders. He suddenly felt very tired and just wanted everything to be over. He wanted to feel the weight of his guitar in his hand and his fingers gliding over the frets. He didn't want to be here anymore, forced to deal with all of this. Chuck leaned back in his chair again and cracked his knuckles.

"Why don't you go on and do another sound check?" he suggested quietly. Cameron didn't argue or respond. Rising from his chair, he simply left the room without saying a word. McIntyre watched him as he walked away. She closed the door.

Confident that Cameron was out of earshot, she turned to Chuck. "You should have told him everything."

"Do you think so?" Chuck asked. "I think that would tip our hand too much. I want to see how this plays out, and where."

McIntyre studied Chuck. "I know," she said in agreement. "In a perfect world, I'd go keep an eye on them. They need some breathing room, though. I'm going to get some coffee." McIntyre left. Chuck leaned back in his chair and stared at the ceiling.

Cameron had returned to the stage area and checked the dressing room. He wanted to see the faces of his fellow musicians. Everyone was there, and he could feel their relief when he walked through the door.

"You guys OK?" he asked from the doorway. They each gave a nod or a requisite noncommittal grunt. Cameron was about to suggest another rehearsal, but his curiosity got the best of him.

"What happened when you guys got there?" he asked, closing the door behind him.

"Well, we pulled over like we planned," Clyde began. "We were going to get out and pop the hood and make it look like there was something wrong and we were trying to fix it before heading into the Tavern to call you."

"That would have been a nice touch," Cameron said. He wondered if that also would have blown the plan's timeline, but thought better of pointing it out.

"We weren't even out of the car when you passed us, and that other car pulled in behind us," Rich explained. "They didn't bother asking if we needed any help, they just told us to get the fuck out of there, toot sweet."

"What did you do then?" asked Cameron. He mused over Rich's erroneous use of the phrase. Bambi had told him once that it was actually *tout de suite*.

"We told them that we had a problem with the car and it died out on us. We needed to use a phone to call a friend to come get us. They told us there weren't any phones that we could use, that they knew the car was working fine and that if we didn't get out of there right then, there would be trouble."

"That's when you showed up," Clyde said. "You know what happened after that."

"Did any of you notice that car at all before this?" Cameron asked. They all shook their heads. None of them remembered having seen that vehicle. Cameron felt vindicated, albeit briefly, but kept it to himself. How much glory could he gain by admitting that he wasn't the only one who didn't realize they were being followed? It would be a shallow victory, at best. He turned his attention to Evan.

"You guys got there awful fast," Cameron smiled. "How did that happen?"

"Doug was coming out of the backstage door when I came around the corner. I opened the door and shouted *Fight!* and he dove in. I ran a couple of stop signs getting over there, and you know the rest."

"Is anyone seriously hurt?" They were all fine, physically at least.

"Is this going to be normal shit?" asked Rich. There was nothing different from the way he usually spoke, but Cameron felt the question was accusatory.

"I fucking hope not," Cameron muttered. Rich flexed the fingers of his right hand.

"What's going on there?" Cameron asked, pointing to Rich's hand. Rich shook his head.

"Did you hurt your hand?"

Rich shrugged. "Not the first time," he replied, without looking at Cameron.

"Can you play?"

"Are you worried about the gig tonight?" Rich asked.

"Well, yeah! Of course I am! We have..." Before Cameron could continue, Rich interrupted him.

"I'm not surprised," he said, his voice still calm. "You're worried about the gig. You're worried about whatever mission we're sent out on. You're worried about that girl. When are you going to get around to worrying about us?"

"That is completely fucking unfair." Cameron was surprised at how calm his own voice was. "I never intended for you guys to be in any danger. I had no idea that anything like this was ever going to happen, and it wasn't part of any mission we'd be told to do. It was my own idea, and I was asking you to do it for *me*. I never intended to put you in any danger. If I thought there was any chance of that, I wouldn't have suggested it. Besides, if you thought there might be any trouble, why didn't you speak up and let me know? I would have called the whole thing off."

"We went along with it because we thought it might work," said Rich. "We just didn't figure on anything like this happening."

"Neither did I. Maybe we have to finally accept the fact that the world's changed, at least for us." Cameron stood there before them. He had nothing left to say.

Rich shrugged, but said nothing. He looked directly at Cameron, his gaze absolving Cameron of any blame, despite his own unhappiness about what transpired.

"I'm sorry," said Cameron. "It was never my intention to put you guys in danger doing something for me. I'll be more careful next time." Rich nodded in acceptance.

"Do you need ice for that?" Rich shook his head.

"No. I'll be fine," he replied.

"Then let's head back to the hotel and give all this a break," Cameron sighed. "We could use some rest after this."

The Roadhouse Sons drove back to the hotel. Doug remained for one last check of the wiring and lights, and returned to the hotel.

Cameron stayed. He considered going to the Will Call window once again to see if perhaps Bambi had arrived early to pick up her tickets, but decided against it. Attracting undue attention, even from the girls in the box office, would be counterproductive.

Finally, the demand for sleep triumphed, and he headed back to the hotel, to the place where, only a few hours before, he'd enjoyed the company of the lovely Bambi; a place that was now empty, and where Cameron felt completely alone.

CHAPTER TWENTY-SIX
"Show Time"

As the first sounds of the evening erupted from the Marshall stacks to the rear of the Roadhouse Sons, the stage floor shook and Cameron almost stumbled. He laughed as the sheer magnitude of the pulse pushed him forward toward the waiting arms of the screaming, cheering crowd. The voices of the multitude blended with the notes springing from his guitar. He closed his eyes, his fingers dancing over the frets and along the strings. No one spoke. No one sang. His music was the only sound.

The crowd cried and cheered louder, louder, louder, their souls coiled tightly, anticipating the words, the signal that the song would come alive. They wanted that adrenaline rush, that release when they could completely abandon all inhibitions and surrender to the music. The band felt the crowd's anticipation, and stroked it, playing only chords, masterfully prolonging every note, and working the crowd into a frenzy with each pounding throttle of the bass.

The lights danced hypnotically, in synch with the drum and bass, stimulating the crowd even more. Cameron looked at Rich and smiled as his old friend kept the bass beat ever steady, capturing the audience and holding them enraptured. Rich suddenly turned his back to the audience, but continued playing. Cameron walked backward, dead center stage, then veered toward Rich, leaned in and whispered to him. The audience went wild; they wanted in on this private conference, and started clapping in rhythm, in unison, with the band.

Clyde kept pace with Cameron, tossing his head and shaking his tawny locks as he slammed out rhythm guitar, the backbone to Cameron's solos. The effect was like waving a red cape at a bull. The crowd continued to cheer, now head banging in synch with Clyde. Perspiration flew from his hair, reflecting like raindrops in the colored lights, like sparks of fire cascading from his head. Clyde closed his eyes and emerged himself in the power of band and audience uniting as one.

Evan smiled benignly as he pounded out the beat on his drums, his snare, bass and cymbals blending together to provide the heartbeat of the song, his hands and drumsticks always in the proper place at the proper time, as though guided by the Muses themselves. Like the others, Evan's escape was this music. He no longer simply played it. He yielded to it. Despite his nonchalant demeanor and appearance of effortless musicianship, he thrived onstage. Performing was the only activity that allowed him any distraction from worry about his wife and family.

Cameron kept his mental finger on the pulse of the crowd. He knew that the band had them right in the palm of the hand. The audience was ready to explode with anticipation at any moment. If the Roadhouse Sons delayed that release, they would lose the momentum. Casting a glance across the stage, Cameron gave the nod, that imperceptible gesture that only the band could discern. It was time.

Leaning forward into the mic, Cameron began to sing. He made it count. Every word that he uttered meant no effort wasted. He was determined to that this be the best singing of his life. There was no need. His first words were drowned in the cheers of the audience. It didn't matter. Cameron knew he gave them his best.

At the end of the first song, Cameron and Clyde held the final notes and engaged in a miniature duel of guitar solos, flawlessly stroking and coaxing each note, so much that the crowd was stunned. They knew that they'd walked on hallowed ground; there were some people in the audience, first-timers perhaps, who had no idea that the Roadhouse Sons were such consummate musicians. As the last echoes of the first song resonated, Clyde suddenly plucked his guitar strings and the second song shattered from the speakers. Doug was at the top of his game as the lights blazed forth a new pattern for this song. The crowd, worldly enough to have already witnessed great lighting design, still responded as though they'd never seen anything like it.

The boys didn't tease this time (Cameron was a huge proponent of playing three songs back-to-back without forcing the audience to endure boring interstitial chatter). They plunged into the next song and presented the masterpiece as though it was their personal mission to eradicate the effects and despondency of the war effort. The reality and duration of the war now haunted the band. They craved an escape, and the Roadhouse Sons refused to waver from their commitment to provide relief to the masses.

Cameron watched with sympathy the women who maneuvered their way to the front of the stage. Not all of them were cheap, immoral groupies. They, like he, simply craved a release from the dark and dreary day-to-day wartime existence of rations and sacrifice and the worry about the next meal, and this was the only activity that provided it for them. His guitar was alive in his hands, a White Knight riding to his, and their, rescue, saving everyone from oppressive reality. Cameron's guitar wasn't just a safe haven for him.

Safe haven...

Until now, he hadn't dared to search the crowd for her face. He tried in vain to convince himself that she wasn't there, that she'd changed her mind. As childish as it was, it was the mechanism he needed to ward off disappointment.

He glanced at the crowd, his mind's eye creating sections. He first examined the area directly in front of him, scanning the swirling crowd clapping their hands, singing along with the band, cheering and talking to one another. It was impossible to see clearly. Only the front rows were illuminated by the stage lights. Rows to the rear of that area were darker and the features of the audience less distinct. Cameron felt his heart sink with despair, and he almost missed his solo. Then, like a flash of lightning, the spotlights shone over the audience and Cameron was able to get a better look.

Just keep track of when the spotlight hits again. Then look.

Cameron found that it was a challenge to keep time with the music and track the timing of the lights. He'd never before tried it and, on some songs, the lights were expertly programmed to counter-syncopate with the music

Business before pleasure, man!

Cameron observed that, in this number, the lights always shined on the stage before they hit the audience. Once on the audience, though, the lights covered the center section, the right, and finally the left. However, each motion was timed too briefly for him to see the entire section of the audience. His heart sank once again, as absolute frustration welled up inside him. He followed the sequence of lights once more, trying to discern individual faces in the crowd. It was hopeless. The teeming mass of people seemed to deliberately foil his efforts. It was the first time in his life that he'd ever felt resentment toward his audience.

Cameron threw up his hands, literally. Not missing a note, though, he'd gestured an effort of futility, abandoning his efforts to locate Bambi. Facing backstage, he smiled at his band mates and played again in earnest, blocking everything but the song from his mind. He concentrated on the feel of the frets, on the tension of the strings and the pulse of the bass amp. He turned toward the audience, then looked offstage at Doug, ever loyal, standing by the curtains. Of Chuck and McIntyre, there was no sign.

It's OK…

To ponder their absence was to travel unnecessary paths right now. His guitar solo was the most important matter at hand. As it ended, he inhaled, ready for his vocal solo. It was then that he was surprised beyond hope and comprehension. As he positioned himself before the microphone, there she was, right in front of him. Bambi.

She was dressed in her requisite sweater, her long dark hair pulled back in a ponytail. She waved frantically to get his attention. Fighting back the urge to throw off his guitar and run to her, he smiled, bowed with a flourish, and sang to her his chorus, for all it was worth. She smiled at him in acknowledgment, and Cameron was emotionally soaked with a wave of relief. He pushed back the urge to cry as he watched her move through the crowd, returning to her seat. He wished that she would've danced there, but that was something that she'd never do; in public, she was anything but demonstrative.

Give it time.

The Roadhouse Sons played the gig as though it was their last. The gyrating bodies at the front of the stage empowered each of them. They played like they'd never played before. Each song was innate, freeing them to try new riffs, sounds and interpretations. The entire concert was unparalleled. As intermission drew near, Cameron wanted to signal the band to keep playing but, having never done so, was at a loss. The breaks gave the band a chance to rest their voices and refresh but tonight, the crowd had an effect on them that they hadn't experienced in a long time. The longer they played for this crowd, the more energized Cameron felt.

This is what It's all about. If we break this spell now, we'll never get it back again.

Intuitively, Rich sidled over to Cameron.

"Man, we don't want to quit!" he said.

Cameron smiled. "Me neither!" he cried, and banged into the next tune. Rich moved toward Clyde and yelled into his ear. Clyde's laughed, his face beaming and he, too, played ever so enthusiastically. Cameron knew they wouldn't stop.

We play on!

As they began the next song, Clyde motioned to Cameron that he was thirsty. Cameron, in turn, gestured to Doug offstage. Doug nodded and disappeared. A few moments later, a young man came onstage with a tray of plastic cups filled with beer. Cameron had never seen him before, but surmised that he was a road rookie. The young man clearly disregarded the cardinal rule: Never walk in front of the band when walking onstage.

You won't forget that in the future.

The lad started at the far end of the stage, leaving a cup of beer with each of the band members. He approached Cameron last. Cameron, visibly annoyed, nodded at the youngster, directing him to set down the beer and exit the stage. As the stranger walked off, Cameron tried to remember if he'd seen him before, but couldn't place him. That made Cameron incredibly uneasy.

I've got to tell Doug to be more careful about the help he gets.

Cameron sang another chorus, ignoring his thirst. He suddenly noticed the condensation on the cups. Drinks set offstage on quick demand for the band and under hot lights warm to stage temperature. There shouldn't be any liquid on the outside of these cups.

You're paranoid.

Cameron was about to yield to his thirst when he saw Doug enter the stage from behind the stack of Marshalls, carrying a tray of drinks. In one instant, Cameron's fears became a reality. That young stranger was *not* working for them.

"What the fuck?!" Cameron snapped. Doug stood before Cameron, arm outstretched with beer in hand, a puzzled look on his face. He then caught sight of the plastic cup.

"Who was that other guy?" Cameron shouted, leaning into Doug.

"What other guy?" asked Doug. "I was the only one who went to get these."

"Then some shit's going down!" snapped Cameron. "Get those glasses away from the others! *Now!*"

Cameron turned to look at the others. It was too late. Clyde was tossing his empty cup over his shoulder and Rich was mid-drink.

Doug dashed across the stage and grabbed Rich's arm, slapping the cup out of his hand. Doug whispered into Rich's ear. Rich laughed.

What the fuck is so funny about this?

Cameron's stomach tightened. Rich couldn't stop laughing. He stumbled, yet somehow, managed to continue playing, albeit with less intensity. Clyde, on the other hand, was a totally different matter.

He, too, was laughing and stumbling about and knocked over the keyboard. He suddenly started twirling around, wrapping his guitar cord around his leg. Suddenly, Clyde's head rolled back and his eyes fluttered. Cameron knew exactly what had happened.

Dosed!

Clyde staggered, tripping over his cord toward the edge of the stage. For a brief moment, Cameron thought that Clyde would fall over the edge, but he stopped and began slowly walking backward, brow furrowed and looking down at his feet, nonplussed that he was wrapped in his guitar cord. He attempted to untangle himself. Doug quickly made his way over assist Clyde who, at this point, was flailing about in a dream state. He mumbled to Doug, who quickly hastened past him and ran offstage.

Cameron focused on Clyde. This song was what the band called a "Clyde special," a piece chosen especially for Clyde so he could showcase his chops. Clearly, though, tonight would be no such show. Without hesitating, Cameron began the solo.

He kept his eye on Clyde, simultaneously hoping to make it through the song and corral the band backstage for a brief intermission.

Momentum or not. We need to take five.

Clyde stumbled behind the monitor stacks. Cameron feared that Clyde had passed out, but saw him emerge from the other side of the stack. Cameron's relief was short lived. To his horror, he watched Clyde, wobbly legs and all, climb all eighteen feet to the top of the stacks. Clyde swayed to the music. Cameron was unable to look away. Flashing through his mind were visions of his rhythm guitarist pitching headlong from the stack of amps. Somehow, Clyde defied gravity and stood upright, playing, Cameron had no choice but to play as well.

I have to get help.

Evan, who pulled vocals on this "Clyde special," finished singing and began his drum solo. Cameron spoke into the microphone.

"Doug," he said, calmly. "Doug, my man, please come to the stage."

If the audience noticed anything unusual, they did not show it. The fans gathered at the front of the stage just danced and moved to the music. They watched Clyde and pointed and laughed, all the while cheering him on. Although it was great to have an enthusiastic audience, under the circumstances, Cameron wished that they wouldn't encourage Clyde. Cameron was about to issue another call for Doug, when he suddenly appeared at the opposite side of the stage. He emerged from behind a curtain, holding a bucket. Spotting Clyde swaying on the stack of amps, Doug quickly realized that the situation demanded different equipment.

Before anyone could react, Clyde let out a yell and swung his guitar around in front of him like a scythe, ready to begin a monster guitar solo. Unfortunately, as he did so, he unplugged and silenced his guitar. A few seconds passed before Clyde looked around for the cause of the interruption. He saw the guitar cable on the floor and leaned over to reach for it, but his inability to stop swaying and teetering proved that his senses of perspective and proportion were severely altered.

Cameron gasped and ran toward Clyde, but Doug beat him to it. Grabbing the cable, Doug motioned to Clyde to stay still and, placing the cable between his teeth, started to climb the stack. Cameron, intrigued yet horrified, watched the scene unfold before his eyes.

He looks like King Kong.

After what felt like an eternity, Doug made it to the top and tried to hand the cable to Clyde who, instead of reaching for it, kept trying to swing his guitar around so that Doug could plug the cable into it. Doug tried positioning himself to do just that, but Clyde was unable to hold his guitar steady. Doug's foot slipped and he nearly crashed to the floor, but he was able to secure himself just in time by grabbing an amp handle. He regained his handhold and handed the guitar cable to Clyde who, in a flash of lucidity, was able to grab it and plug it in. The audience cheered and applauded wildly as Clyde's guitar came back to life and a fresh blast of sound erupted from the speakers.

Turning to Evan, Cameron signaled to cut the set and take a break. Evan nodded vigorously; he, too, confused by the scene that just unfolded. As the last chord resounded, Cameron stepped up to the mic.

"Thank you ladies and gents! We're Roadhouse Sons and we'll be right back after a short break!"

Cameron unhooked his strap and unplugged his guitar. He set it on its stand and hurried offstage. Rich and Doug were already backstage and Evan was just steps behind. Doug, surprisingly gentle, was trying to talk Clyde into descending from the top of the stack, but the noise and distractions from the auditorium were too much of a deterrent. Clyde tried leaning down to hear Doug better, but lost his balance. In an effort to regain his composure, he stood up too quickly and teetered so precariously that Cameron was convinced his guitar buddy was going to fall and severely hurt himself. Clyde smiled triumphantly and held out his hands, assuring those below that he was all right. Disconnecting his guitar, he carefully handed it down to Cameron who, at this point allowed himself to relax a bit.

Good! He's not going to try anything stupid.

Then, to his horror, Cameron realized that he was wrong.

Standing up after handing over his guitar, Clyde broke into a big smile, laughing heartily.

"Catch!" he cried, and leapt off the top of the stacks.

"Shit!" cried Doug. He jumped to action, moving into position to stop Clyde's fall. He managed to catch Clyde and the two of them fell backwards onto the stage, somehow managing to avoid toppling any of the surrounding equipment. Upon impact, Cameron heard the air suck out of Doug's lungs. Doug winced as he and Clyde rolled toward the curtain on the far side of the stage. Finally, they rolled to a stop. Doug released his grip on Clyde who continued to roll, a silly smile on his face.

"That was fucking cool!" he laughed. Cameron wanted to scream at him, but realized that it would do no good. Clyde was in no position to comprehend a logical conversation, much less take responsibility for what he'd just done. Cameron grabbed Clyde by the shirt collar and pulled him to his feet and handed him over to Evan and Rich,

"Get him to the dressing room!"

Cameron then turned his attention to Doug.

"Are you all right, man?" he asked, kneeling down. Doug nodded.

"Just winded," he said softly. Cameron grabbed his arm and tried helping him up, but Doug waved him away.

"Give me a minute," Doug wheezed, inhaling deeply. Slowly, he rolled over onto his side and pulled himself up on all fours. Gradually, he was able to kneel and slowly rose to his feet. He bent over to take a few more deep breaths, and then stood erect.

"Are you hurt?" Cameron asked. Doug shook his head, and bent over to pick up his hat.

"I'm fine," he assured Cameron. "Just knocked the wind out of me."

They walked backstage. Doug was limping slightly, and rotated his left shoulder.

"I thought you said you were all right," Cameron said, solicitously.

"I am," Doug assured him. "I just banged myself up a bit, that's all. Nothing serious and nothing to be worried about."

Cameron wasn't convinced. He watched Doug plod slowly to the backstage area, but he himself hurried to the dressing room where they'd brought Clyde. When Cameron arrived, he heard shouting and cries coming from the bathroom. Upon inspection, he discovered Evan and Rich holding Clyde's face into a sink filled with cold water.

"You're fucking drowning me!" Clyde shouted. "I'm fine! I'm fucking *fine!*"

"How many fingers am I holding up, then?" asked Evan, extending three fingers on his right hand.

"How the hell should I know?!" snapped Clyde. Rich plunged Clyde's face into the water.

"Three!" Clyde cried out. "Three! OK? You're holding up three fucking fingers!"

"Let him go," Cameron said. "That's as sober as we're going to get him right now. Someone get him some water, or some coffee."

"I need a fucking drink!" moaned Clyde.

"You do like hell!" shouted Evan, moving Clyde toward a chair.

"What the fuck did you guys put in my beer?!" yelled Clyde, closing his eyes. He covered his face with his hands. "I've never been hit like that before."

"How do you feel?" asked Cameron.

"Like shit!" Clyde snarled. "What did you expect?"

"I expected you to be as sick as D'Lorenzo was, or Doug," said Cameron, studying his friend closely. "Do you feel nauseous? Are you hallucinating or anything?"

Clyde leaned into Cameron. "Yeah, man, I am," he whispered.

"Oh, shit!" whispered Cameron. "Really?"

"Yeah!" whined Clyde. "I see a giant asshole asking me all kinds of fucked up questions! Will you leave me alone?"

Cameron stood up and stormed across the room to examine the cooler of beer. Before the shows, it was always stocked, and he knew that it held a full case of beer, with ice placed on the bottom and on top of the cans. The cans were deliberately placed in a uniform fashion, so that a quick visual inspection would delineate how many had been taken out. Prior experience with former roadies stealing the band's booze had prompted this system, and they simply kept with it.

The cooler held twenty-four cans, twelve atop twelve, and Cameron knew that no one had taken any before the show. The band would have imbibed a little during the break, and they would have some after the show, but not before, in order to avoid burping during the first song. No one, not even Doug, was permitted to take any beer before the show. Cameron had seen Doug bring out four cans at intermission, so that should have left twenty. However, there were several more than four cans missing. Taking a quick count, Cameron saw that there were only eight cans on the bottom and five cans on the top. Cameron's suspicions grew further; the band *always* removed cans in even numbers in order to keep track of how many had been used. Whoever had taken beer from the cooler was obviously not familiar with the system.

Cameron checked on Doug and found the roadie standing up tall against a wall, wearily stretching his back.

"Hey, man! How many beers did you take out of the cooler?" asked Cameron. Doug gave him a funny look.

"I only took four," Doug replied. "Why?"

"There are seven missing," explained Cameron. "Were any missing before you took any?"

Doug rubbed his eyes as he tried to remember.

"Yeah, now that you mention it," Doug said. "There were four gone. I thought it was weird because you guys don't take any before the first break."

"Did you stock the cooler?"

"Of course," Doug said. "I always do!"

"Calm down," said Cameron. "I'm not accusing you of anything. I'm trying to find out what's going on. Someone brought out those plastic cups full of beer. They must have taken the first four out of the cooler then."

"That's impossible," said Doug. "Chuck and McIntyre were watching the dressing room while I was watching the stage."

"They couldn't have been," said Cameron. "They're not here."

"What the fuck are you talking about?!" snapped Doug, suddenly alert. "They were standing right there with me when I went back to the dressing room."

"Man, I'm telling you, they're not anywhere around," insisted Cameron. "I did see them with you, then all of you were gone. I thought they came back here."

"Who brought those other drinks out?" Doug asked, eyes squinted at Cameron.

"Some guy I'd seen standing backstage with you," Cameron said. "A little shorter than you. Messy brown hair, mustache."

"What was he wearing?" Doug stared intently at Cameron.

"He had on a light blue shirt, button front, jeans and worn sneakers. He had some kind of tool sticking out of his back pocket."

"A screwdriver," growled Doug. "He said he was one of the electricians, here to keep an eye on the wiring problems we've been having. I think he said his name was Joe, or something like that."

"Did you recognize him?"

Doug shook his head. Cameron felt his stomach tighten.

"Did you ask him where he came from?"

"Yeah," nodded Doug. "He said he got a call from Everett, the head guy, to come in tonight and work some overtime. I thought that was weird, though."

So do I.

"Do you know where he is now?" Cameron was mustering every possible grain of patience to remain calm. Doug shook his head.

"But I sure as fuck am going to find him!" Doug jumped his feet. Without another word, he stormed past Cameron and disappeared into the labyrinthine backstage area. Cameron followed, but went directly to the dressing room instead. When he arrived, Clyde was changing into a dry shirt.

"How do you feel?" asked Cameron. He sized up his friend, trying to gauge Clyde's condition. Clyde was steadier on his feet and his eyes were less dilated, but he looked like he was about to fall asleep on his feet.

"I feel like I've run a marathon," Clyde said. "But I can play the next set. Just don't dump too many solos on me. OK, man?"

Cameron tousled Clyde's hair.

"You got it, brother," he smiled. "We need to get back out there, but first I want you guys to get all your stuff together, because as soon as the show is over, I want to get the fuck out of here. Doug can handle the tear-down. We need to get back to the hotel."

"What on earth for?" asked Evan. "We sent out those passes for a backstage party and all. Aren't we supposed to stick around for that?"

"We can have them come with us to the hotel," Cameron explained. "There's some shit going down here and I don't want whoever is pulling it to have the advantage. They're thinking that we're going to do it here. If we move suddenly, then they won't have time to rethink their plan, and that'll be to our advantage."

"What do you mean shit's going down?" Evan pressed.

"Chuck and McIntyre are gone. No one's seen them or knows where they are. Someone's been messing with our beers and tried dosing us. The person that did it told Doug he was one of the electricians, here to keep an eye on the wiring problems we've been having."

"So what?" Evan insisted. "He could have been, couldn't he?"

"Doug didn't recognize him, and don't you think it would be odd that they'd bring in someone new for tonight when they've been raising hell about having anyone not in their union working here all this time?"

Evan said nothing. He didn't need to; the fright in his eyes spoke volumes.

"That's what I thought," muttered Cameron. "Make sure our shit is ready to grab and run. I'll go out and stall the crowd for a minute. We've got to get back on stage."

Leaving Evan to handle the dressing room, Cameron headed back to the stage and cautiously peeked out from behind the curtain. The audience was milling about, heading to and from the vendors and leaving the auditorium to smoke. They weren't restless, and so Cameron didn't hurry from his observation point. To do so would get them excited and impatient for the show to resume, and Cameron knew the band still needed time to get their belongings together. Besides, he was trying to spot Bambi. It was nearly impossible for him to single out any one person in the crowd. He wondered if Bambi may have gone to the vendors' area or to the ladies' room. Then he saw her.

She was in the aisle between center and stage left, talking to a man whose face Cameron couldn't see. The man appeared to be young and was pulling on a worn denim jacket with a dirty fleece collar. He wore a knit toque and greasy denim jeans. Bambi appeared to be agitated. The woman standing with her, whom Cameron recognized as her friend from the restaurant, was trying to calm her. Cameron watched the scene unfold, and readied himself to assist her, if necessary. After a few moments, Bambi vehemently shook her head and walked out of the auditorium, her friend in tow. The young man waited for a few moments, then exited as well. Cameron tensed. Was she leaving? She hadn't taken her purse or coat; she'd be back.

"We're ready," said Evan in Cameron's ear. The unexpected sound of a male voice, and one that close, startled Cameron.

"Jesus, man!" he snapped. "Give a body some fucking warning next time, OK?!"

"Sorry," muttered Evan. "But we're ready to go on."

"You got everything ready to grab backstage?"

Evan nodded.

"How is Clyde doing?"

"We got him a stool to sit on if he needs it. He's pretty good, but still a little wobbly. I don't know if he could stand through a whole set."

"Well, we'll be cutting this one a bit short," said Cameron. "We'll tell the crowd that we don't want to make anyone miss the curfew, or some shit."

"Do you think they'll be upset with that?" wondered Evan.

"Probably a little," Cameron said. "But we're not shorting the show a whole lot, maybe fifteen minutes or so. If anyone says anything, we'll say we made that excuse to cover for Clyde's condition. We'll say he's got some illness. The South American Creeping Cruds. I'll think of something!"

"You always do," chuckled Evan. He led the Roadhouse Sons onstage, to the sound of cheers and applause. The band performed a brief sound check, really for the purpose of alerting stray audience members and vendors that the show was about to begin. Cameron, meanwhile, was looking for the person in charge of the lights. He grumbled bitterly about the meager staff. Usually, there was someone stationed on the controls, at the ready to lower the houselights and light up the stage when the band came on. Now, there was no one to be seen. Cameron was about to check the office and the janitor's room when he saw one of the stage hands running, stuffing the last bite of a hot dog in his mouth and washing it down with a beer.

A bottle, not a can...

"Hey! Where's your friend?" Cameron asked. "The one that's been hanging around here?"

"What are you talking about?" the stagehand replied. "It's just me and Everett tonight."

A cold chill ran down Cameron's spine.

"You don't have anyone here by the name of Joe?" Cameron asked.

The stagehand shook his head. "No," he replied, then offered Cameron his hand. "It's just me and Everett. My name's Sam, by the way."

Cameron shook Sam's hand. Sam had short black hair, and wore blue jeans and sneakers. The light blue shirt he wore closely matched the shade of grey that the mysterious Joe had worn. From a distance, or in a crowd, it would have been easy to confuse Joe's garb with the light blue shirt that the stagehands wore.

Cameron spoke up quickly, his examination complete. "He said that Everett called him in to keep track of the lights and make certain there were no problems this time."

Sam shook his head emphatically.

"No way," he insisted. "Everett is so worried about that, he wouldn't trust anyone but him and me to be here tonight. Not that I mind. I need the overtime, with a baby coming and all."

"So, it's just been you two all night, then?" Cameron prodded. "There hasn't been anyone else?"

Sam shook his head again.

"No way! Just us."

"Have you been here all night, then?"

The young man shifted uneasily.

"Well, not exactly," Sam mumbled. "I did step away for a bit. Someone said I had a phone call, but they didn't say from who. My girlfriend is due to have our baby pretty soon and I thought it might have been her. We don't have a phone, so I headed over there real quick."

"So the light board was unattended?"

"No! I told Everett, and he was keeping an eye on it, but he was also keeping an eye on the circuit boards to make sure none of them flipped while you were playing."

Cameron looked down the short hallway leading to the circuit board, which was impossible to see from where he and Sam were standing.

"Well, no big deal," Cameron assured him. "I hope everything was OK at home."

"That's the weird thing. She told me she never got a call, and none of the girls in the front remember taking any message."

"Well, who gave it to you then?"

"Some girl came up and told me that I had a phone call in the office, and left. I thought it was one of the girls up front."

"Had you ever seen her before?"

"I thought that she was familiar, but I couldn't be sure."

"Did you get a good look at her?"

"No," he said, shaking his head. "Once she said I had a phone call, all I could think of was my girlfriend home all alone, and I didn't notice anything else."

That's understandable.

"No big deal, man," Cameron shrugged. "By the way, we're about ready to start the second half, so you better get the lights ready."

Sam smiled and nodded. He adjusted the dials on the control panel in front of him as Cameron took his place at his mic stand. The band employed a few quick tunings and adjustments, and Cameron struck a fierce C chord, signaling the beginning of the second set. The Roadhouse Sons began to play, and play they did. Even Clyde, albeit subdued, still managed to hold his own and keep the sound strong. Bambi approached the stage several times to wave and blow kisses. Cameron considered imparting his famous pelvic twist but, recalling what happened at the last show, decided against it. There was no way to change pants quickly this time. Instead, he smiled and leaned forward toward Bambi and blew her a return kiss.

At the end of the set, the guys went into their usual concert finale routine. At the end of the final song, Evan would draw out the drumbeat and follow up with a portion of Led Zeppelin's *Moby Dick* drum solo. The others would vamp the magic of the final chords, while the audience went mad, lingering on every possible iota of pleasure, if only to temporarily forget the drab reality of wartime. Cameron knew that his audience *needed* to hear the band, to have the song last as long as possible. He also knew that the urgency of the events backstage meant that he had to get the guys out of there as soon as possible, forced by a nameless, faceless fear that gnawed at his stomach like a rat. Finally, the last beat of the drum had sounded and it was over. They had to get out of there.

Now!

"Good night, everybody," Cameron shouted. "We're Roadhouse Sons and thank you for coming!" With that, he turned his back to the audience and headed backstage. As he stepped out of the light, he noticed Doug standing by the stage to take everyone's instruments.

"No luck," he grumbled to Cameron.

"What do you mean?" Cameron asked, confused.

"No luck finding that guy that gave Clyde the dosed beer," Doug explained.

"Don't worry about it now," Cameron said. "Help the guys get our shit and get it loaded into Rich's car as quick as you can. We're heading back to the hotel."

Doug didn't ask for, nor did he wait for, an explanation, which Cameron appreciated. He wasn't in the mood to deliver one. There was still no sign of Chuck or McIntyre. Cameron hurried to the dressing room. He was surprised to find Bambi already there.

"Hey, gorgeous!" Cameron said with a smile. Without waiting for Bambi to reply, he gathered her in a warm embrace and held her close. He breathed in the sweet smell of her, reveling in the feel of her in his arms. He felt her tense.

"What's wrong?" he asked quietly, releasing her.

"Nothing," she said with a forced, nonchalant smile. "Tonight was really cool, by the way. I'm glad there was no mix up getting backstage this time."

Maybe that's it. She's probably nervous about being here.

"Glad you made it, too," he smiled. "Get your coat, though. We're heading back to the hotel."

Bambi's expression changed to one of surprise as she stepped back from him.

"But I thought you said there was going to be a party here," she accused, adjusting the collar of her turtleneck sweater.

"We're moving it back to the hotel," Cameron said. "Clyde isn't feeling too well and he wants to be near his room, so we thought we'd just move everything over there. Besides, the hotel bar would love the business!"

"Oh, well... I guess," she laughed halfheartedly. Her unease was palpable, yet Cameron still wondered if he was seeing the world through his own discomfort right now.

"We could move it over to your dad's place if you want," Cameron teased. "Would that be better?"

"Oh, no!" she cried. "No, I didn't mean that. I meant that I told a couple of my friends that we were going to be here, that's all."

"Oh, well," assured Cameron, putting his arms around her waist, "If that's the case, then we can wait a few minutes for them, or you could go out front and tell them to meet us over there. Want me to go with you?"

"No," Bambi said, hesitating. "I... I can tell them."

"Well, do you want me to wait here for you, then?"

Bambi shook her head. She gathered her coat and purse and Cameron couldn't help but feel that her reactions, her word choices, everything about her tonight, was stilted and strange. Before he could inquire any further, he heard a female voice behind him.

"This where the party is?" Cameron turned around. He didn't recognize the woman initially. She had a face that he was certain he'd seen somewhere before, but he just couldn't pinpoint where. Then it dawned on him. It was the woman from the restaurant, the one he'd espied earlier from behind the stage curtain, but her hair was different for some reason.

This must be the friend Bambi was talking about.

"Hey, there!" he smiled. "No. We're heading over to the hotel instead. More room and we don't have to worry about curfew. You can join us, if you'd like."

The smile disappeared from her face and she began to shake her head.

"Oh, no!" she insisted. "Let's stay here! This is a lot better than some cramped hotel bar."

Cameron laughed.

"No, I think the hotel will be better. You'll see. I promise."

The woman shook her head vehemently.

"No. You have to stay here!" she shouted.

"What the hell is wrong with you?" Cameron's good-natured demeanor vanished.

"Bambi, tell him!" the woman ordered, her voice becoming tense. "He has to stay here!"

"What the hell is going on?!" demanded Cameron. He turned to face Bambi. She stood there, holding a gun in her trembling hands.

"I'm sorry it had to be this way," she whispered. "I really am."

"So am I," Cameron said. He raised his arms, slowly.

CHAPTER TWENTY-SEVEN
"Miss Peel, We Are Needed!"

Doug carefully placed the guitar cases into the trunk of Rich's car, and was about to close the door when he realized that one was missing.

"Hey! Didn't Cameron have two guitars tonight?"

"Oh, shit. Yeah," said Rich. "He had his other Strat with him tonight."

Doug looked around on the ground, in case someone placed it out of his view.

"I think he left it in the dressing room," offered Evan. "Want me to go check?"

"Nah," said Doug, closing the trunk. "I'll go check. I need to grab the rest of our shit out of there anyway."

With that, he turned and entered the building. As he approached the backstage area, he noticed several people standing about, but he didn't recognize any of them. None wore recognizable uniforms, nor were they displaying any backstage passes. Doug realized that they had no legitimate business there. Also, since they made no effort to greet him, and didn't seem to be looking for anything, Doug was even more curious. They behaved as though they were acting as lookouts, but didn't even really notice him. "Pretty piss poor ones, if you can't see me," Doug muttered to himself.

He approached them cautiously. There were three men, all in their early twenties or late teens. Two stood watching the stage area. The third stood with his back to Doug, monitoring the hallway in the direction of the dressing room. The one directly opposite Doug had red hair, fair skin, and was wearing a blue ski vest and hooded sweatshirt. Doug examined him closely. The man was slightly shorter than he, and weighed approximately 130 pounds. The fellow to Doug's left was dressed in a blue and white winter coat with a black ski cap pulled down over his ears. He was slightly shorter than his companion. The hallway lookout was also slightly shorter than the first fellow, and was dressed in a denim coat with a dirty fleece collar. He wore a navy blue knitted toque, from under which greasy dishwater blond hair protruded.

"What are you guys doing here?" Doug demanded, as he crept up to the hallway lookout, who, as startled as the others, spun around quickly to see who had come up behind him. Doug recognized him as the electrician.

"You!" Doug snarled, and reached out to grab him. The young man swung his arm to deflect Doug's grasp and dashed down the hallway toward the dressing room. Doug was about to go after him when then the other two men jumped him. Doug fell into the wall, losing his balance as one tried to tackle him from behind. The other one charged him, punching Doug in the ribs. Bracing himself against the wall, Doug quickly spun himself around so that the assailant on his back was now receiving the punches from his companion. The man released Doug and dropped to the floor, allowing Doug to quickly turn back around and grab the surprised assailant by both ears. Pulling him forward, Doug rammed the top of his forehead into the bridge of the young man's nose, stunning his opponent as a flow of blood gushed from his nose. Grabbing him by the hair on the top of his head, Doug pushed him away and delivered a right uppercut to his jaw. The assailant flew backwards. Doug tried to run down the hall, but the man on the floor grabbed Doug's right leg to prevent him from escaping. Doug delivered a swift kick with his left boot directly into the young man's head, causing the youth to cry out and release him. Without checking on either of them, Doug bounded over the young man at his feet and ran in pursuit of the hallway lookout.

Rounding the corner, he hurried down the hallway toward the dressing room. He heard a gunshot. Forgetting his pursuit, Doug remembered that Cameron was still in there. Running in to the dressing room, Doug saw Cameron struggling with two women, one of whom held a revolver. One light in the ceiling was shot out, but no one had toppled to the floor.

The three continued to struggle. Suddenly, Doug saw the hand that held the revolver aimed toward him. Knowing that now was the only time to chance saving Cameron, he rushed forward, grabbing the woman's wrist just above the pulse point. Doug squeezed as hard as he could. The woman to screeched in pain, and the revolver fell from her hand. Doug grabbed the revolver and yelled, "Stand the fuck still or I'll cock it!" Cameron and his two attackers froze. The woman who had dropped the gun burst into tears, and Cameron put his arms around her to shield her.

"What the fuck do you think you're doing!?" Cameron shouted at him.

"Trying to keep someone from getting fucking killed!" Doug shouted in reply. The other woman lunged toward Doug in an attempt to get the gun. Doug raised his foot, and the woman, unable to stop herself, bounded into it. She fell backward with a grunt, the air knocked out of her. She lay on the floor, crumpled like a rag doll.

"*Vicki!*" the sobbing woman yelled, attempting to free herself from Cameron's grasp. Cameron held her tightly; there was no way that he was letting her go. She, too, went limp.

"She's fine!" Cameron shouted. "You're not going anywhere until you tell me what the fuck is going on!"

The woman buried her face into his shoulder and began to sob even harder. Vicki rolled onto her stomach, gasping. Doug tightened his grip on the revolver. "I'm watching you," he said menacingly. "Don't try to get up!"

"Bambi!" Cameron shouted again. "What the hell is going on here?"

Doug was completely nonplussed. This was the woman Cameron liked. He hadn't been able to get a good look at her in all the scuffle.

"Don't...say...anything..." Vicki gasped, rolling onto her side. Bambi raised her head in an effort to speak, only to sob uncontrollably. Cameron grabbed her by the shoulders and pushed her away from him, holding her at arm's length.

"Why did you pull a gun on me?" Cameron demanded, shaking her.

"I'm sorry!" Bambi sobbed. "I didn't want it to happen this way..."

"Bambi, shut *up!*" cried Vicki, regaining her breath.

"Didn't want what to happen *what* way?" Cameron asked, almost in a whisper. Bambi's sobbing and trembling diminished. Vicki had, at this point, risen to her knees and was rocking back and forth, her arms folded across her stomach.

Doug eyed her in disgust and slipped the revolver into his coat pocket. He waited patiently. He knew that Vicki would try something the second she thought she had a chance, but he'd deal with her without a weapon of his own.

"I didn't want it to end like this…" Bambi said, her voice soft with fatigue.

"Didn't want it to end like what?" asked Cameron. "With my brains plastered all over a wall? What were you trying to pull?"

"They wanted you to stay here."

"Who?" Cameron asked. "Who would care if we stayed or not? It's just a fucking party! They could have come with us to the hotel if they wanted."

Bambi shook her head.

"No. They needed you to stay here. It was all part of their plan."

"Whose plan?!" Cameron demanded. "What the sweet fuck do you mean?"

"Bitch!" screamed Vicki as she got to her feet, her face a mask of pure rage. She reached for Bambi with claw-like hands, but Cameron yanked Bambi out of harm's way. Before Cameron could do anything else, Doug grabbed Vicki around the waist and tossed her to the couch. Vicki landed hard and, with a guttural cry of rage, leapt up to scratch at Doug's face. Doug sidestepped her just in time, and Vicki stumbled past him, tripping on the edge of the rug and falling, face first, into the doorjamb. Right then, the rest of the Roadhouse Sons appeared at the doorway, stunned.

"What the fuck is going on in here?!" asked Rich. "I thought we were moving the party back to the hotel."

"We're not having a fucking party!" Cameron snapped. Rich realized his joke was very poorly timed. Evan tried to lift Vicki to her feet, but was swatted away, as Vicki hurled out unimaginable expletives.

"Do you know what's going on?" asked Evan.

"Fuck if we know!" Cameron said. He turned to Bambi, looking her directly in the eye. She cast her eyes downward, unable to look at him. "I'm trying to get answers here, too! Like, why the girl I've been seeing suddenly goes psycho on me and pulls a fucking gun!"

"What gun?" cried Evan. "*I* was talking about why they're locking all the fucking doors!"

Vicki began to laugh. It was a chilling, mirthless chuckle.

"You're not going anywhere, now," she smiled lasciviously. "The curtain is going down! Once and for all!"

"What the fuck are you talking about?!" Cameron shouted in total frustration.

"Go ahead and tell him now, bitch!" Vicki spat at Bambi. "It won't make any difference!"

"Tell me what?" Cameron demanded. He was being to feel abjectly exhausted.

"You're supposed to stay... h-here..." Bambi stammered. "Somebody was going to do something, and needed you here."

"What? A publicity stunt or something?" Cameron asked. Bambi shook her head.

"Then what?" He drew her close and she looked up at him.

Suddenly, Cameron heard the voice of a demon. "Revenge, you fucking asshole!" snarled Vicki, her voice hoarse and croaky. It was at that very moment that Cameron realized why this woman looked so familiar.

"You were the one that got into my room!" he said in astonishment. "You were the one that tried to put a bug in there!"

"I was wondering when you'd figure it out!" she sneered. "I've only seen you a half a dozen times. I figured at least once you would have recognized me!"

"Fuck you!" Cameron lunged toward Vicki, but Doug stopped him with a hand to Cameron's chest. "What do you need revenge for?" Cameron raged. "You pissed that she's going out with me?"

"Oh, don't fucking flatter yourself! We're getting revenge on whoever you're working for, but *I'm* getting revenge for my brother!"

Cameron was dumbfounded. Did Vicki and Bambi know the Roadhouse Sons were providing intel, and for whom? Who was Vicki's brother, and what did that have to do with the band? Cameron knew this wasn't a case of myriad jealous husbands, boyfriends or angry brothers wanting to take a potshot at him.

"What are you talking about?" Cameron hedged. "We're a rock band. I've never even seen you before you tried to bug my room, and I have no fucking idea who your brother is!"

"You're a lying bastard!" Vicki hissed. "You hounded and harassed him until they found him. Then they killed him!"

"Who?!" Cameron shouted. "Who harassed who? Who killed who?"

"The ones you work for," she said, her voice breaking. "You helped them find my brother and catch him. Then they killed him! Well, it won't do you any good! We're not giving up, and *you're* not taking over!"

"You belong in a fucking booby hatch," grumbled Cameron. "You've got a whole fucking fantasy world going on in your head! We're not trying to take over anything. We're... a... *rock... band!*"

"You say whatever you want," Vicki hissed. "We know you found Louis in Rutland, and you made sure your bosses did, too. My husband recognized you, even though your head was so far up your own ass you didn't recognize him!"

Cameron racked his memory, thinking back to the first mission performed by the Roadhouse Sons; they had to locate one Louis Barre. Cameron remembered Dwyer revealing that Barre had died in an escape attempt, but had no idea to whom Vicki referred as recognizing him. The band never socialized with anyone until they arrived for gigs in Burlington.

"You're on acid," Cameron said, his voice calm and even. "I don't know anyone named Louis, and I certainly don't know anyone you would know." He turned to the guys. "Do any of you?"

Despite being caught off guard ("Blindsided!" Clyde would claim later), they all shook their heads. "No!" exclaimed Rich.

"Deny it all you want, you lying sacks of shit," Vicki shouted through tears. "But they saw you in that store those two old squealers ran, and they saw you here! We know you did it and we know why, and it won't do you a damned bit of good! We're not giving up!"

As Vicki spoke, images of covered gurneys and the body of Dwyer flashed through Cameron's mind. He was about to speak when, suddenly, a strange male voice came from the doorway.

"Don't anybody fucking move!"

Cameron saw a large arm wrap around Clyde's throat in an attempt pull Clyde backward through the door. A struggle ensued, and Clyde pushed forward into the room. With Clyde's maneuver, everyone was able to get a look at the assailant. The man's face was covered with blood, yet despite that, Cameron knew that he'd never seen the man before.

Now, though, the man suddenly held a gun to Clyde's head, and nodding to Doug said, "Going to try and Coco butt me *now*, asshole?"

"You know him?" Cameron asked.

"I bumped into him earlier," Doug grumbled.

"Put your hands where I can see them!" the man shouted. "Don't make any sudden moves!"

This is starting to play out like a bad cop film.

Cameron struggled to conjure a way out of the situation. Unfortunately, none of Dwyer's training covered a situation like this, and Cameron was at a complete loss. He realized that the sensible thing to do was merely cooperate. Slowly, he raised his hands.

"Do what he says, guys," Cameron told them, his voice far calmer than he felt.

Vicki pointed to Doug. "That asshole has my gun!" she told the stranger.

"Get it!" the stranger replied. Without hesitating, Vicki ran over to Doug, patted him down and fished around in his coat pocket.

"Excited?" she sneered. "Don't be! I like men, not boys."

Cameron held his breath, afraid that Doug would take the bait and retaliate. Thankfully, Doug just stood there, passive. Cameron dared to hope that they'd all get out of this alive.

"Let's shoot them now!" Vicki put the muzzle of her gun next to Doug's temple. Doug swallowed hard but maintained his composure.

"No! Frank said to take them downstairs first," the stranger insisted.

"Fuck that!" Vicki croaked. "We're going to shoot them anyway! Do it now and get out of here!"

"I'm not pissing him off!" the man snapped. "Get them downstairs."

"What downstairs?" Cameron asked. "We're on the ground floor and this is solid. There is no downstairs."

"Then you're not as fucking smart as you think you are, are you?!" spat Vicki.

"Who's Frank?" Cameron asked, refusing to show any irritation.

"He's my brother," said Bambi, softly. When Cameron turned to look at her, she was weeping.

"Shut up and get moving!" the man shouted. He nodded to Vicki. "You lead them. I'll follow to make sure no one tries anything stupid."

"Speaking of stupid..." Vicki grabbed Bambi's arm. "You'll be my insurance."

Cameron's resolve broke and he lunged toward Vicki, who quickly stepped out of Cameron's reach.

"Try that again and there'll be consequences," Vicki sneered. "And in the mood I'm in right now, I'll make sure you're last, so you can see the rest of them die first!"

Cameron stepped back and raised his hands in submission. He glanced toward Bambi, attempting to hide his fear. Bambi's weeping turned to a sob, and she cried uncontrollably.

Vicki, eliciting not one iota of sympathy, shoved Bambi through the door and marched her down the hall, occasionally pushing her to walk faster. They all fell into suit, passing the office used by Chuck and, at one time, Dwyer. Cameron was dismayed to see no light coming from under the door. Chuck and McIntyre were nowhere to be seen. Cameron recalled the discovery of Dwyer's body and realized that, if someone as experienced as Dwyer was killed doing this line of work, what chance of survival had the Roadhouse Sons?

Cameron's mind regaled all of the things he was going to miss. For some reason, more than anything else, he wanted an ice-cold Coke. He tried not to laugh aloud at his own absurdity. He caught Rich's eye and saw fear riddled all over his old schoolmate's face. Cameron realized that the guys were looking to him for guidance. He looked at Evan, who was bearing up well, though apprehension was etched over his entire being. Cameron recalled Evan's lovely wife, and memories of holding Evan's adorable newborn daughter. Clyde was squinting to discern where they were walking, but his breathing was labored and panicked. Doug remained eerily calm. Cameron feared that his roadie would try to perform heroics that might get them all killed. This scenario was something for which they were never prepared, and Cameron fought reluctant anger toward Dwyer and McIntyre.

They arrived at a door marked *Authorized Personnel Only*. Bambi opened it. Inside were pipes and valves. Behind the pipe work was a flight of stairs leading downward. Other than one basket-covered light, which Bambi had switched on, there was only one light at the top of the stairs. Cameron wondered if he would be able be to cause confusion by flicking the stairway light on and off in an attempt to trip up their captors and make them drop their guns, but the stranger seemed to read his mind.

"You lead them down ahead," the man said to Vicki. He gestured toward Cameron. "I'll wait here with this one until you're all down. If anyone tries anything, he gets it!"

Cameron, defeated at the loss of their chance to escape, carefully made his way down the stairs. They all followed Vicki to a landing, from which a shorter flight of stairs descended. For no apparent reason, Vicki grabbed Bambi. Bambi yelped. Vicki held the gun to Bambi's temple.

"It's OK," Vicki called up the stairs. "We made it, no problems!"

"You got us covered?" the man called back. "Yes, I do!" Vicki bragged in reply.

Cameron watched as Clyde and the man made their way down the stairs. Cameron felt lost and helpless. Frustration mounted as he the others arrived at the bottom step. Once everyone was assembled, Vicki switched on a light. Cameron saw that there was a space behind the stairs, revealing a door. It was painted to resemble the cinderblocks of the walls. Even the doorknob was covered, aiding in the camouflage. There was only one giveaway that a passage existed, and that was a warning sign posted nearby. Beyond that door were high voltage machines. Cameron fought a wave of nausea as Vicki opened the door and shoved Bambi through it.

If I make it through this, I'll kill you myself, and with my bare hands.

As they filed through the door one by one, Cameron was surprised to find that there were, in fact, no machines of any sort in the room. It was simply one long corridor with no other discernable exits. Bare light bulbs, some hanging precariously and others held in place with crude fasteners, lined the walls. At last, they came to a partially opened door. One again, Vicki shoved Bambi. Cameron bristled.

"Did they give you any trouble?" All ears turned toward the raspy voice emitting from inside the room. As Cameron came through the door, he was shocked to see Blonde Guy, his face still abraded and bruised from the encounter with Rich at the Tavern.

"They settled down!" snickered Vicki.

"I take it she started getting soft again," Blonde Guy snapped, directing his attention to Bambi. "I'm getting pretty fucking sick of your shit!"

"Leave me alone!" Bambi shouted. She wasn't as afraid as she'd been upstairs. Blonde Guy raised his arm toward Bambi in a backhand gesture, but shook his head, dismissing the idea.

"Shut that door," he said, waving his hand dismissively at the fellow manhandling Clyde. "And let him go. He's not going to do anything."

Cameron watched as the man released Clyde and shut the door, which didn't latch. The man turned around, failing to notice that the door was slightly ajar. Cameron felt a glimmer of hope. He looked around the room to see if anyone else had noticed. Nobody noticed, or, at least, didn't let on if they did. Cameron then examined the room itself.

It was furnished like a small apartment. There was a bed, four chairs and a table upon which were several beer cans. Bland and boring pictures hung on the walls. The light in the center of the ceiling was similar to the one in Cameron's hotel room.

Doug suddenly spoke. "Hey, I've been here before," he said.

Blonde Guy laughed. "Yeah, we brought you here with your friend. Dosed you pretty good to get you down here, but we'd hoped that it'd be worth it. Should have known better."

"What the fuck are you talking about?" demanded Doug. "What friend?"

"That guy you were working with," Blonde Guy snapped, impatiently. "It's no use denying it. He told us everything! He knew more than you did about this shit. I don't know why we wasted our time with you."

"What exactly did he say?" asked Cameron. He was hoping to stall for time and discern these goons' strategy. Had they discovered the real purpose of the Roadhouse Sons?

"Don't fucking play stupid with me!" Blonde Guy shouted, grabbing a beer from the table. Cameron noticed that the beer was the same kind they'd bought for their dressing room cooler. He already felt as though that world was a million miles away, as if it had already been years since they'd last performed.

"You fucked things up for me since we met you," Blonde Guy continued. "But now, we're done."

"Who's we?!" demanded Cameron, hiding none of the exasperation in his voice. "What the sweet fuck are you people talking about? I've never seen you before until I saw you at the Tavern the other day!"

Blonde Guy looked at Cameron as though he hailed from another planet.

"Have you ever been to Rutland?" he asked.

"Yeah," said Cameron. "I've played there and passed through it lots of times. What the hell does that have to do with anything?"

"I had a nice little operation going in Rutland," Blonde Guy explained. "Until you came along, that is. You made too much trouble for me and I had to shut it down."

"Shut what down?" Cameron was exhausted.

"Quit fucking with me!" Blonde Guy shouted. "Your boss told us everything. We know you're trying to take over, or were. But it doesn't look like you're going to do it now, does it?"

They think we're running drugs and trying to take over their territory!

"Our boss? You mean D'Lorenzo?" asked Cameron, testing the waters.

"The big guy with the black hair and the big fucking mouth," said Blonde Guy, tossing the beer can on the floor.

That would be D'Lorenzo. What did that bastard tell them?

"He said we wanted to take over?"

"He said you were looking to find out who was running shit and was going to be shutting them down. Now, that would be me, but I don't think things are working out the way you planned."

You're right about that.

"You met him in Rutland?" Cameron asked. Blonde Guy shook his head and reached for another can of beer.

"No," he said. "I've seen him elsewhere and it was easy to tell he'd been looking for us. He didn't make much secret of it, even when he wasn't using shit."

Cameron recalled Dwyer's warnings about a mole, and the incident of the crude attempt at picking the lock to the safe house, and wondered if the entire operation hadn't been compromised from the beginning.

"He got *high* with you?" Cameron asked, genuinely shocked. Cameron's bewilderment amused Blonde Guy, who guffawed loudly.

"Him!?" Blonde Guy cried. "Ha! He had too much of a stick up his ass to admit he did that shit, even when he was as strung out as a pearl necklace! He didn't do it. We slipped it to him. Of course, it wasn't all that bad. We found out he was telling the truth on being able to get us some of the good shit. The problem was, he couldn't tell us how to make it, and we couldn't figure it out. We tried a few times and it was either too weak or too strong. He did make a good guinea pig, though."

"And *me!*" growled Doug. Blonde Guy threw his had back, laughing.

"You weren't that good of a guinea pig, ass munch," he explained. "You were a belligerent pain in my fucking ass!"

That's our Doug…

"What did he do?" Cameron asked.

Blonde Guy whistled. "He tried to kill that guy at least twice. We had to slip him a tranquilizer to calm him down, finally. Then we dropped him off where he could find his way home and didn't waste time with him again."

Blonde Guy pointed at a large painting hanging on the far wall.

"See that ugly thing?" he asked, grabbing Doug by the collar. "I had to hang that over the hole you punched in the fucking wall! I couldn't bring any sheetrock down here without attracting attention, so I had to resort to that!"

Cameron held his breath as the man shook the roadie, fearing his friend would decide he had nothing to lose and slip into attack mode. Thankfully, reason prevailed and Doug did nothing more than clench and unclench his fists.

"Where are we?" Evan asked. Cameron noticed the tremor in his voice.

"Where the fuck do you think you are, asshole? You're underneath the Civic Center."

"Why do you want to be there?" asked Evan, trying to remain calm.

"Ease of distribution," Blonde Guy smiled menacingly.

Now I get it.

"You're not content running the booze here. You're doing that other shit, too," Cameron challenged. Blonde Guy smiled and nodded.

"I make it here, I sell it here," he said, with a wave of his hand. "And I'm not handing it over to you either, motherfucker."

"Is that what D'Lorenzo told you?" asked Cameron.

"D'Lorenzo?" Blonde Guy asked. "Oh, you mean the double-crossing piece of shit? Yeah, that's some of the shit that he talked about."

"Double-crossing?" Cameron said. "What the hell are you talking about?"

"He wanted in on the action," Blonde Guy clarified, heaving in exasperation. "He said he could get us better shit than the pot and hash we were moving, so we listened to him. He did bring in some good stuff. I'll give him credit for that. Of course, we tried it out on him first, and that's how we learned he wanted to get rid of us. I never let on that we knew, but we kept our eye on him to see if we couldn't get rid of him and distribute the shit ourselves."

Blonde Guy checked his watch.

"Almost time," he smiled, finishing his beer, tossing the can to the floor.

"Almost time for what?" Cameron's gut was in his throat. Out of the corner of his eye, he noticed the door move slightly, and wondered if it was caused by a current of air, or if someone was on the other side, listening.

"Revenge," said Blonde Guy. "You guys killed one brother and made another go missing. I can't have that. I'm French-Canadian and we prize family above everything."

Bambi, who'd been silent all this time, suddenly laughed derisively.

"You are so full of *shit*!" she scoffed.

"Watch your fucking mouth, little sister!" Blonde Guy warned. "Or I'll send you home to your mom."

Bambi bristled, and turned her back on her brother.

Blonde Guy snickered. "Right now, my two favorite sisters are all I have left of my wonderful family, or should I say a stepsister and a half sister. You killed my brother Louis, and my brother Eduard went to meet your friend and never came back. As if that weren't enough, you tried making moves on my stepsister and attacked me in front of my own place of business. No. There's no two ways about it. You guys have gone too far, and now you're not going anywhere else."

"Why wait?" demanded Cameron. "Why not just shoot us and get it over with?"

The Roadhouse Sons gawked at Cameron, mouths agape. Cameron ignored them. So did Blonde Guy.

Blonde Guy smiled. After several seconds, he said, "Because you can still find bullets after a body has burned. I figured I'd come to your dressing room and congratulate a fine band on a wonderful performance, and offer you a little something to help you unwind. I sent some out earlier, but you didn't fall for it, apparently."

That explains the beer.

"After we got you good and wiped, there was going to be an accident. I have a firebomb hooked up to a timer. You were going to perish in a fire and they were going to find your burned bodies in your dressing room. After all, what is suspicious about a rock band being passed out, or having drugs in their system, eh? But, as usual, you had to go and fucking spoil a nice plan, and so I had to improvise, and fast."

"So, why here?" Cameron asked. "Why get rid of your hideout?"

"Yeah… it's a sacrifice…" Blonde Guy sighed in faux agony. "But when we burn this shit hole, they'll probably poke around for the cause of the fire and find our sacred hideout."

Blonde Guy suddenly faced off with Doug, knocking the roadie's favorite hat from his head. Blonde Guy swung a fist at Doug, but stopped just short of Doug's face. When he spoke, he practically spat in Doug's face.

"You damn near fucked that up on me, too!" Blonde Guy seethed. "A fire triggered by an electrical short would have been perfect, but you kept finding the faulty wiring and raising a ruckus until we fixed it! But tonight… tonight I was able to get someone to pretend to be an electrician to get all set up tonight! Lucky you!"

"Lucky?!" yelled Cameron. "That's not the fucking word I would have chosen."

"Probably not," shrugged Blonde Guy blithely. "I want another beer." He looked around the room, and there were no beers to be found. Blonde Guy was suddenly belligerent.

"Fuck this shit!" he shouted, kicking a can across the room. He stumbled, but caught his balance. Cameron noticed that Blonde Guy was swaying, and wondered if the brute had been sampling his own product. Blonde Guy turned to his young hoodlum friend. "Go to the dressing room and get me some fucking beer!" he bellowed. "They've still got plenty up there, and they won't be needing it soon, but me? I'm fucking thirsty!"

The young man just stood there, perplexed. "But… what about these guys?" he mumbled in fear.

Blonde Guy sputtered, now in a towering rage. "Give me the fucking gun, then!" he bellowed. "Vicki and I can handle these assholes ourselves! Make yourself fucking useful, for a change!"

The youth hesitated, then walked over to Blonde Guy to surrender the gun. As he did so, the door flew open with a huge bang. Everyone in the room shouted or screamed in terror. For a split second, Cameron thought Blonde Guy's explosives had detonated, but it was Chuck at the door, gun drawn and ready to fight. The young man, gun still in hand, turned suddenly to discern the source of the noise. Chuck ordered the youth to drop the gun, but the young man, frozen with fear, did not obey. There was a loud bang as Chuck fired at him. The young man screamed in pain as the bullet hit his arm. A spray of crimson flowed through the air as the bullet entered his bicep. The young man, now ashen, dropped the gun and toppled to the floor in pain. Cameron heard one of the women scream. As if on cue, Chuck stepped aside as McIntyre entered the room.

Blonde Guy attempted to dive for his gun, and fell to the floor. He reached for his gun, but it was just beyond his grasp. McIntyre yelled at him to freeze, but Blonde Guy defied her and reached for his gun again. McIntyre fired one shot, narrowly missing Blonde Guy's ear. She fired a second shot as he reared up and tried again to grab his gun. This shot hit him in the chest. Blonde Guy's expression was one of shock and surprise. He hung there for several seconds, as though suspended by invisible wires. His head fell back, and he thudded to the floor. Vicki and Bambi screamed in unison, horrified and hysterical. With no warning, though, Vicki decided to strike back.

Raising her gun, she randomly fired several shots, none aimed at any particular target. Cameron and his fellow band members dropped to the floor. As they did so, Cameron heard several shouts of pain, and instinctively called out to see who was hurt. No one answered. He was about to call out again when he heard Vicki scream and saw the gun fly from her hand just as Chuck swung a hard kick at her. Vicki was knocked to the floor. Cameron leapt to his feet and dashed over to Bambi, grabbing her.

"Are you OK?" he asked, scooping her up in his arms. Bambi was shaking uncontrollably and began to sob. She was unable to speak. Cameron held her tightly, ruing that there was no way he could assure her that the ordeal was finally over. The others arose from the floor. Doug was the first to get up, followed by Evan. Clyde and Rich eyed each other, seeking confirmation that it was safe to stop hugging the ground. Only the youth, whimpering in pain, and Blonde Guy, dead, remained down.

"Let's get them out of here!" Chuck ordered. He grabbed Vicki, yanked her arms behind her back and handcuffed her. McIntyre retrieved Vicki's gun and motioned for Doug to assist the young hoodlum.

"Come on," Doug grumbled, grabbing the youth by his collar. "They shot you in the arm, not the legs." The young man awkwardly scrambled to his feet, clutching his arm and babbling hysterically.

Bambi was still a wreck. Her whole body trembled as she sobbed inconsolably. Cameron held her tight. He caught Chuck's disapproving eye. Chuck nodded toward the door, saying nothing, but his expression spoke volumes. He was not at all happy with Cameron's attention to Bambi.

Fuck you!

Cameron led Bambi toward the door, shielding her face from her dead brother, but Bambi looked back anyway, and erupted into another mournful wail.

Chuck and McIntyre led everyone down the corridor toward the stairs. Cameron was so relieved to be alive that he felt gratitude for every detail he espied. The cinderblocks in the wall, the light fixtures overhead, even the sounds of their weary footfalls echoing in the corridor were music to his ears. No one spoke. Except for the weeping of the two women and the whimpering of the wounded youth, there were no sounds but their collective footsteps.

They finally reached the top of the stairs.

The hallway's so quiet...

Cameron expected to see people milling about post-concert. The clock on the wall revealed that they hadn't been downstairs for even an hour.

"This place is deserted," murmured Evan.

"They had it evacuated," said Chuck. They told everyone there was a gas leak in the furnace room. We heard that from the custodians outside."

"Guess they didn't want anyone to get hurt when the shit went down," said Clyde.

"Except us," muttered Rich.

Cameron said nothing, his head still reeling from the events downstairs. He braced Bambi in his arms and helped her into a chair.

"No stopping," snapped Chuck. "We need to get out of here! Now!"

Cameron was about to argue on Bambi's behalf when Chuck shook Vicki.

"What time is it set to go off?" he demanded.

"Like I'm going to tell you," she said, spitting in his face. Unflinching, Chuck shoved Vicki forward by the scruff of her neck and turned to McIntyre.

"Better make that phone call," he said. "Looks like things are going to get a little more exciting before we're done. Everybody out!"

They all scurried toward the exit. Doug paused, then ran back to the dressing room. Chuck shouted at Doug to come back, but the roadie didn't obey. Furious, Chuck was about to head down the hall after him, when Doug emerged from the room with a collection of duffel bags.

"They left their shit in there!" he shouted at Chuck.

"You don't disobey me again!" Chuck bellowed, handing off Vicki to McIntyre and stomping toward Doug. He pressed himself against Doug's chest.

"It's my job to look after this band and its property!" Doug shouted back, pushing back against Chuck. "And I'm going to do my fucking job!"

"Give it a rest, you two!" shouted McIntyre. "We don't have time for pissing contests! We've got to get out of here."

Glaring at one another, the two men ceased their chest-butting faceoff and headed toward the door with the others. They stepped out into the cool night air, and into a sea of curious onlookers.

"Fuck!" spat Chuck. "Just what we need. A goddamned circus."

They made their way to McIntyre's car, and placed Vicki and the young man in the back. Chuck closed the door as Vicki began to hurl expletives at him. The youth was still crying. Chuck ordered Rich and Evan to stand guard at the car. He shook his head and clucked his tongue as the young man began screaming in pain.

"It's on the outside of your arm," snarled Chuck. "It's probably only a graze. Be a man, for Christ's sake!"

Cameron led Bambi to Rich's car, and helped her into the back seat. He stood by the open door, shielding her from the onlookers' gazes, but Chuck would not be put off.

"We need to talk to her, too," Chuck said. Cameron detected no anger in Chuck's voice, but nor was there any sympathy or understanding. Chuck spoke plainly, matter-of-factly, and with cold resolve. Cameron couldn't abide by it.

"She needs a minute to pull herself together," Cameron said, positioning himself between Chuck and Bambi. "You know what she just went through. Give her a minute to catch her breath, for God's sake!"

"Get out of my way and let me handle this," Chuck said. "You're in too deep, too close, and you don't know what the fuck you're doing. Now please step aside."

"Leave her alone," warned Cameron. Before Chuck could respond, there was a commotion behind them. The rear door of McIntyre's car opened and the wounded youth emerged, brandishing a gun. He was shouting angrily, and fired two shots in Chuck's direction. One bullet hit the building, and the other shattered the windshield of Rich's car. Bambi screamed, and Cameron pushed her inside and down onto the car floor, slamming the door closed.

"Get down!" he shouted. He pushed Chuck behind the car. Chuck drew his gun and, creeping low to the ground, made his way around to the other side of the car toward the front of the vehicle. Peering out, he could see the young man running across the parking lot toward the building, but Chuck was unable to get a clear shot.

"Fuck these people!" he cried in frustration, and charged after the young man. As Chuck was about to dive for his legs, he heard a queer, loud snapping sound. The windows of the building exploded outward. Cameron looked up. There was a split second of surreal silence. Shards of glass floated through the air, almost in slow motion, catching and reflecting light. People screamed and ran about wildly. The parking lot became a mass of confusion as flames sprung from the windows, illuminating the entire parking lot in an eerie amber glow.

The force of the blast knocked Chuck and the young man to the ground. They struggled to their feet as people scrambled past them. Chuck, despite the chaos around them, caught hold of the young man and threw him back on the ground, knocking the gun out of his hand. They both lunged for the weapon, but the young man was faster.

He grabbed the gun and pointed it at Chuck, when suddenly Clyde appeared out of nowhere. Clyde tried to wrestle the from the youth but, startled, the young man struggled and pulled the trigger. Clyde screamed in pain and released his grip on the man, falling and rolling around on the ground. He'd been shot in his left arm. Chuck recovered and brought his hand down in a fierce chop against the young man's neck. The youth fell, limp as a rag. Chuck heard Cameron shout.

"Get back here, you idiot!"

Chuck saw Doug rush into the building.

"Oh, fuck!" moaned Chuck. "What now?"

Racing toward Rich's car, it was everything Chuck could do to restrain Cameron from following the roadie into the burning building.

"What the fuck is going on?!" Chuck demanded.

"We heard someone call for help," Cameron said, his voice trembling. "The asshole went running in there before I could stop him!"

Cameron struggled to break free from Chuck's grasp.

"You can't go in there!" Chuck shouted. "Wait here!"

Before Chuck had run five feet, Doug emerged from the building, a man dragging in tow. Cameron recognized the man. It was Sam, the electrician's assistant. Doug lay Sam on the ground by Rich's car, and collapsed, coughing.

"Everett," Sam wheezed. "Everett's still in there!"

"Where is he?" asked Chuck.

"He went up to check the lights," Sam wheezed. "They were acting funny as we were shutting things down, and so he went to check on them. Then everything exploded and he fell. He's on the stage. You got to get him out!"

"Calm down," Chuck soothed. "The fire department is on the way. We'll get him out!"

"No!" Sam insisted. "He's hurt! He's hurt bad. You've got to help him!"

"We'll help him, son," assured Chuck. "Don't worry."

Without saying a word, Doug stood up and dashed toward the building, dropping his hat as he ran.

"Get back here! Fuck!" Chuck screamed.

"I'm going in after him!" shouted Cameron.

Chuck was livid. "Like hell you are! You stay right fucking here!"

"He isn't strong enough to carry a grown man out, especially if the guy's unconscious," insisted Cameron. "That's just dead weight!"

"Well, it'll be a hell of a lot more than just one person's dead weight if you go in there," yelled Chuck. Cameron pushed past him, but Chuck grabbed him by the coat and shoved him against the car.

"You're not going anywhere," he warned. Cameron went limp. Chuck's eyes were fierce with resolve, and Cameron knew that protesting was a lost cause. Cameron slowly nodded in agreement.

"You fucking mean that?" Chuck asked, his grip still firm. Cameron nodded again, and said nothing. Chuck scrutinized Cameron's expression and, satisfied that he was honest, released him. Holding his hands up where Cameron could see them, Chuck took two steps back. Cameron smoothed his coat and brushed the dirt from his pant legs. Then he bolted toward the building before Chuck could catch him.

"God damn you!" Chuck's screech blended with the approaching sirens as Cameron ran as fast as his legs would carry him.

He reached the building and saw that flames were fanning across the drop ceiling, but the doorway was mostly clear. Pulling his coat over his head, he tried to get his bearings as he stepped through the door. The familiar sight of the hallway was gone, and the scene that greeted him was straight from his nightmares. He hedged forward a few steps, but was unsure of exactly where to go. Cameron moved cautiously down that corridor, realizing that he was heading toward the dressing room. Then he remembered the dead body of Blonde Guy and turned to move in the other direction. Cameron walked for a few feet along that passage. Just ahead of him, chunks of burning fabric dropped to the ground. He knew that he was heading toward the stage. There was no sign of Doug.

Cameron called out the roadie's name, but heard no answer. He pushed on, despite the heat and smoke. He thought he could see a shape a few feet in front of him, and feared that Doug had stumbled, overcome by the smoke. Hurrying forward as fast as he could, Cameron saw that it was not a person, but a pile of debris that had fallen from the ceiling. He was about to step around it when he saw something that chilled him. Sticking out from the rubble was a hand.

"Doug..." he said. His friend's name croaked out in a choke of a whisper. There was no answer. Before Cameron could move forward to investigate, another portion of the ceiling fell, some of it landing on the pile before him, and some behind. Finally admitting to himself that the situation was simply too dangerous, Cameron covered his face and rushed out of the building.

He stumbled into the parking lot, gasping. The November air was so cool that it stung his lungs. Rich and McIntyre were anxiously awaiting him. He was aware that they were speaking, but he was unable to hear them. The roar of the flames still echoed in his ears. They leaned in to talk to him. The entire scene was spinning before him. Then everything went dark.

CHAPTER TWENTY-EIGHT
"Carry On, My Wayward Son"

The early morning light was as glaring to Cameron as the fluorescent lighting in the hospital had been. Treated for smoke inhalation and released, he then found himself taken in for his statement by Chuck and McIntyre.

"Fucking give me a rest, man!" Cameron complained. The last thing he wanted to do was relive the previous night, especially since he could hardly stand up.

"While it's fresh in your mind," insisted Chuck, opening the back door of McIntyre's car. Through the open door, Cameron could see two people sitting in the car, and was surprised to find Bambi and Evan in the back seat. Bambi's eyes were red and puffy, her face a portrait of despair. She held her hands in her lap, clutching a decimated tissue. Cameron slipped into the back seat, too, and once seated, reached for Bambi's hand. She recoiled and turned her face toward the window.

I don't blame you.

Chuck and McIntyre got into the car. They drove away from the hospital in silence, passing the downtown buildings of Burlington. Cameron watched all the people go about their daily routines as they'd done countless times before, and would inevitably do ad infinitum. They were completely secure in their routines, ensured of normalcy, and Cameron resented them for it.

"Are you all right, man?" Cameron asked his drummer, only to be told by Chuck to remain silent.

"No talking," he said.

"What the fuck?!" demanded Cameron. "We're being arrested now?"

"Just keep quiet," Chuck repeated, and then turned his attention back to a file he was reading. They drove on, the silence almost stultifying. When they arrived at the police station, McIntyre and Evan steered Bambi toward one room while Chuck led Cameron into another. Cameron watched as the others walked down the hall, their backs to him. No one turned around. Chuck coughed discreetly to get Cameron's attention and motioned him inside the interrogation room and into a chair.

"All right," Chuck said. "I kept you guys quiet in the car so you wouldn't influence each other's statement, or hers. Now, let's hear what happened."

Cameron rubbed his eyes and sighed wearily, then drew a deep breath. He told Chuck that dosed beers were brought to the band during the show by someone impersonating one of the employees. He explained that, after realizing the beers were drugged, he'd decided to move the band to a place where he could better monitor them, and that Bambi tried to convince him not to do so. Cameron hesitated to mention Bambi's gun, but he realized that he had to. In doing so, though, he made it a point to mention that Bambi had aimed the gun at Cameron, yet hesitated to shoot, and that Vicki, therefore, tried grabbing the weapon from Bambi. Cameron emphasized that the only reason Vicki didn't harm or kill anyone was due to Doug's timely intervention.

Cameron then told Chuck of how they'd all been forced to go downstairs to the room where Blonde Guy was, and how Blonde Guy and Vicki kept accusing the band of taking over Blonde Guy's territory and killing off this crew. Cameron revealed that Blonde Guy was Bambi's brother and that the band was being blamed for killing her other male sibling.

"Then McIntyre arrived and saved us." Cameron paused, exhausted, then his ire rose. "What the fuck were they talking about?" Cameron asked. Chuck yawned and stretched. He leaned back in his chair and closed his eyes.

"Blonde Guy, as you call him, was actually Francis Lavelle, a small time hood from Montreal that got chased out of there for trying to take over someone's bootlegging operation. He got lucky when he found an outlet for some of the cheaper shit the big guys were stuck with, and made a deal with them to unload it for them to keep them from dumping him in the St. Lawrence Seaway. He caught our eye when he tried to grow his operation, hitting a lot of the clubs between here and Boston, and started carrying drugs instead of sticking with the booze. At first, it was just simple drugs and cheap booze, but then he tried to get creative and started manufacturing shit himself. About a dozen or so people died from his toxic experiments, and things took a more serious turn when he tried infiltrating New York. That would have brought in the Mob and made things even worse, especially if they discovered they were stuck dealing with something that was going to be attracting a lot of attention by killing their customers."

"So, that's when you tried getting into his network?" asked Cameron. Chuck nodded.

"Dwyer and McIntyre busted their ass trying to do that," he explained. "Francis must have been pretty spooked by his run-in with the Montreal boys, because he was fucking suspicious of everyone, including his own family. Every undercover agent we tried putting in there didn't get past hello, and only a few of them were able to score more than a bag of weed. We were able to make some progress as dealers, but any time we tried to position ourselves to get evidence on any of the big shots, it wouldn't work. They ran like rabbits."

"So that's where we came in?" Cameron asked. Chuck nodded again.

"Yeah," he continued. "I got the idea at a party I was jamming at. Everyone wanted to hang around with the band. I pitched that idea to my big guys and they jumped on it. I advised them as they developed it. It obviously worked, too."

Cameron agreed begrudgingly with a grunt.

"So why did Lavelle think we were trying to take over? They said they knew who we were and all that shit. What the hell did they mean?"

"D'Lorenzo," Chuck sighed. "He was the one that we were running as a potential supplier of some better grade junk than the smaller dealers were selling. We were trying to get their attention by waving the drugs under their noses, as opposed to just cut-rate booze. They could make more money drug running, and they were interested, especially when they really saw how lucrative it was. They passed the word on to Lavelle, along with some of the goods, and that seemed to work. We needed you and the band to track how successful we were, because if we started asking questions, then the dealers would start asking questions. and we'd be right back where we started. Maybe even worse."

"Was that SPECTER they were telling us about?" Cameron asked. Chuck nodded angrily.

"We had no idea that idiot D'Lorenzo started using that again. We thought he was going to use the regular stuff we kept for these types of operations. Instead, the Asshole-In-Chief thought that if he could get them to take SPECTER, the truth serum component of the drug would get them to spill the beans on the rest. Obviously, it didn't work that way. Not even fucking close."

"Obviously," mumbled Cameron.

"The irony is, it seems he got caught in the same net he tried to snag them with."

"What do you mean?"

"They slipped the stuff to D'Lorenzo to see if he was selling them the real shit, and in the process, discovered the secret side of what they were dealing."

Now I get it!

"Then he probably told them about the whole plan, right?" Cameron asked, shaking his head. "They were watching us the whole time we were watching them."

Chuck nodded.

"That's exactly it," grumbled Chuck. "Every time he would go to meet with them, they would slip him something and learn a little bit more."

"Is that what made him sick?" Cameron queried.

"I doubt D'Lorenzo was getting sick from the stuff he'd given them. Remember, Lavelle thought he was a manufacturer, too, and obviously decided to create his own, cheaper version. From what Dwyer reported and D'Lorenzo has said, they were probably using him to experiment on dosage."

"Do you think that D'Lorenzo really told them anything?" Cameron asked.

"We're pretty certain that he told them everything that was going on in Rutland, and probably gave away our plans for here, too, because they were waiting for us."

"How do you know that!?" gasped Cameron.

"For your consideration," Chuck said, imitating Rod Serling. "Witness one Vicki Withers, waitress at the Catamount, an eating establishment in close proximity to both the hotel and the Civic Center, and one of the few venues in the Queen City to serve real coffee and not just any regular Maxwell House, but a particular brand of coffee that is, or rather was, the personal favorite of one Mr. Gordon Dwyer... Mr. Dwyer, therefore, preferred, over any other, that location in which to conduct his business. Surprisingly, both Ms. Withers and the coffee were recent additions to the Catamount, both arriving there roughly three days before your arrival in Burlington. Previously, Ms. Withers was employed at another Queen City enterprise known as Hart's Tavern. Coincidence? Maybe… in the fucking Twilight Zone."

Cameron was stunned silent. The mention of Dwyer compounded the actual danger of the previous evening. He shuddered to think.

"Did D'Lorenzo tip them about Dwyer's signal?" Cameron asked.

"What signal?"

"You know. Using the color orange," Cameron said, a bit exasperated. "Remember the note on orange stationary that Dwyer received right before he was shot? And what about the orange on the seat of my car the first day we met you?" Chuck shrugged. Cameron realized that Chuck was already thinking the same thing.

"That's some of the shit we're looking at," Chuck explained. "We're trying to get some answers from everybody involved, but until we learn for sure one way or another, we have to consider it a very real possibility."

Cameron knew that in addition to Vicki and the wounded youth, Chuck's higher-ups were also questioning Bambi. He pictured her alone with a pushy agent in an interrogation room. It was a pretty picture, yet, no matter how hard he tried, he couldn't push the image out of his mind.

"Bambi said Vicki was her sister, or half sister, or something," Cameron said, his voice close to cracking.

"Yeah. It seems Francis had a nice little family operation going on. He ran it, and his closest associates were his sister, Vicki, and his brother Eduard, the one who tried to break into Doug's room. There was another brother, Louis, and your friend Bambi."

"She said her dad was mixed up in some stuff, too. Do you think *he* was really the leader of it all?"

Chuck looked at his file again; he was silent for some time before answering.

"He took the fall for some stuff," Chuck said, looking at his notes. "But there is a big question as to whether he had anything to do with it, or if he was just covering for his son."

"That Louis you mentioned... is that Louis Barre?" Cameron was trying to fish for just how much information Chuck had on Bambi. "They kept talking about how we got rid of him, and how they knew what we did in Rutland."

"That's more of D'Lorenzo's handiwork, it seems."

"How so?"

"He gave us the wrong name," Chuck explained. "It was really Louis Lavelle. The name Louis Barre was some misinformation they fed him to see if he was going to double-cross them, and when Louis got nabbed, they knew who did it."

"He died, didn't he?" Cameron asked, his voice almost a whisper. "Louis, I mean. Dwyer mentioned something about him dying during interrogation."

Chuck didn't answer right away.

Why are you being evasive?

"Why won't you answer?" Cameron snapped impatiently. "I said Dwyer mentioned it! It can't be that much of a secret, then."

"No. You're right," Chuck replied. "And, yes, there was some kind of an incident and Louis Lavelle tried to escape and, in all the confusion, he got shot. I honestly don't know any more than that."

Cameron accepted his explanation with a shrug.

"So, does all this mean that D'Lorenzo was the mole Dwyer was telling us about?"

"Beats me," admitted Chuck. "On the one hand, I'm tempted to say no, and say that the only real betrayal was an undercover operation into a smuggling ring,"

"But..." Cameron prodded.

"But, on the other hand, there was a lot of shit that these guys were doing that drug dealers and smugglers don't typically get mixed up in."

"Like what?"

"Like the listening devices and phone taps that we uncovered," Chuck explained. "They don't usually get involved to that degree. That suggests that someone else was giving them the idea, or doing it themselves."

"You think D'Lorenzo had something to do with that?"

"That's what the chief muckity-mucks are trying to find out right now."

"You mean, D'Lorenzo's been arrested?"

"I mean, he's being held for questioning in all of this shit, and will probably be answering a whole ration of other questions about other dealings, too."

Cameron was at a loss. He looked down at his hands and traced with his eyes the lines on his palms and fingers. He said nothing. His mind was reeling with thoughts of Gus Kalbe, the Mustang mission, Dwyer, and the horrific events of the previous evening.

Cameron finally spoke. "Do you think D'Lorenzo was trying to take over that operation?"

"What do you mean?" Chuck was perplexed.

"Well, you keep saying someone was trying to give the Lavelles an edge, and that they kept thinking we were trying to take over their operation. Add them both together, and it seems to me that D'Lorenzo was trying to set up his own thing."

Chuck shook his head.

"If that was the case, then things would have either been done a lot better, or a lot worse. D'Lorenzo is an asshole, no question about that, but he didn't used to be, and I can't forget that. He would take huge risks, but then, so do I. The difference is, I take them with a specific end in mind, and he simply kept throwing shit against the wall until something stuck. However, he was still a lot more thorough than the leaders of this operation were. Nope. Someone was watching us, but not running them."

"Any idea who?"

Chuck shook his head again.

"Not a clue," he said. Then, as if anticipating Cameron's next question. "And no, I am not ruling out the Russians. I'm just not going to start a Red Scare. I wouldn't put it past the KGB to try running bad shit and encourage members of gangs and families to try going rogue to start trouble. They wouldn't be sad for suddenly causing us to deal with a whole series of turf wars, but I can think of a lot better ways they'd want to use energy and resources, to be honest."

"So you don't think D'Lorenzo is a double agent?"

"Smarter folks than me are going to have to figure that one out," Chuck said with a smile. "I did my time sticking up for him. Someone else can have a shot at him now."

"So he has been arrested." Cameron made a statement; he didn't ask a question.

"I mean he's being interviewed. Closely!"

Cameron wished that he had a cigarette.

Either that, or a nice cold beer.

His mind flashed to last night and the cans of beer in the cooler. He recalled that the phony employee gained access by telling the actual electrician that he had a phone call. Cameron also remembered that Chuck and McIntyre disappeared at that same time.

"Where did you guys go last night?" Cameron asked.

You deserted us…

He tried to suppress his resentment and doubted that he was successful.

I don't care if you know how I feel. I'm sick of pissing ice cubes.

Chuck answered with deliberation. "We got an urgent call from the State's Attorney. The information we'd been looking for came in, finally."

"Everyone had phone calls last night," Cameron said with a tired laugh. "How do you know yours wasn't a trick to get you out? That's how they got rid of the real electricians. Was yours bullshit, too?"

Chuck was overtly defensive. "First off, I don't jump at every possible lead, especially if I suspect for even a minute that it might be a wild goose chase. Secondly, they used the proper identification," Chuck replied. "Furthermore, as I said, they were there waiting for us with the information we wanted. I can't imagine someone like Lavelle being able to pull that off so successfully and so high up when the other activities are so amateur and so hit-or-miss."

Cameron accepted Chuck's admonishment without comment, but couldn't help wondering if the whole evening would have been different if Chuck and McIntyre had been present the entire time. Cameron trembled.

I gotta get this shit out of my mind!

Chuck hadn't asked Cameron any questions about his account of the previous night's events. Cameron, on the other hand, had questions that he wanted to ask.

But I don't dare…

There was no way to delay it any longer. He had to know what happened to his fellow band mate. His voice was barely audible as he broached the subject.

"Is there any word on Clyde?"

"Yeah, there is," said Chuck, closing his file. "And the word is lucky."

"Lucky?!" cried Cameron, swiping Chuck's file onto the floor. He could no longer hide his rage. "You call what happened to Clyde lucky? *Lucky*?! What the fuck is wrong with you?"

Chuck jumped to his feet, his eyes ablaze. "He's lucky that the kid he was wrestling with didn't have any idea how to clean, load or shoot that gun, or how to get the right kind of bullets! That damn thing was so dirty and corroded, I'm surprised it didn't blow up in his hand! There were only four bullets in the gun in the first place, and they were the cheapest ones he could've had. Clyde is lucky it got him in the deltoid and didn't end up in the bone. Then he'd most likely be disabled for good. As it is, he's got a fucking serious wound, but he won't lose the arm and he didn't get killed. Sometimes, that counts as lucky." Chuck plunked down into his seat, scowling.

Through all of Chuck's vehement discourse, all Cameron saw was Chuck's mouth moving. What he heard was incomprehensible. The only word that registered with Cameron was "killed." Once again, the rubble and the acrid smoke of the burning Civic Center taxed Cameron's mind and matter. His heart sank. Cameron tried to speak, but he couldn't find the words to ask the question. To blurt it out seemed so cold, but he had to summon the strength to ask.

"Is... is there any word on, I mean, did you find anything out about...?"

"About what?" Chuck was still smoldering, and belligerently impatient.

Cameron's initial impression was that Chuck knew the information Cameron sought, and was deliberately insensitive. Cameron fell silent, mustering as much courage as possible. He was about to ask a question, the answer to which he may not want to hear. He became light-headed and his breathing accelerated.

"Did they find that old guy?" he blurted.

"You mean the electrician? Everett?" Chuck asked, his voice more sympathetic now. "Yeah. They found his body on the stage. They're still examining him for cause of death. He was pretty badly burned, but they figure he was caught in the explosion when the first device went off. He probably got blown off the catwalk. If it's any comfort, he was most likely dead before he hit the ground. I know from talking to him that he had a bad heart."

"The first device?!" Cameron was nonplussed. "Exactly how many devices were there?"

"There were two that went off while we were there, and one more that went off after we left to get you guys to the hospital. They found a fourth, but that one apparently had a faulty timer and didn't go off when it was supposed to. By the way, that one was in the dressing room."

The depth of Lavelle's plan leveled Cameron. Despair swept over him as pressed himself to ask the one question he wanted to avoid more than anything. But Chuck had stated "you guys'" when referenced the trip to the hospital.

This isn't real. It didn't happen.

"Do you have any word on…?" Cameron couldn't continue. He sat there, staring at Chuck imploringly, yet dreading the impending answer. Chuck didn't speak. He picked up the file and all its contents from the floor and stood upright, then hurriedly grabbed his coat from the back of his chair.

"Let it go…" he said plaintively. Chuck's voice was soft, but he spoke with a palpable tone of finality that rendered Cameron nauseous. Unable to fight the gag reflex, Cameron began to tremble. Clenching his fists, he tried to quell the inevitable, but ran to the wastebasket and vomited.

"No!" Cameron wept openly. "I'm not letting it go, damn it! He was my friend! I was his boss, his leader, and I have a right to know what happened!"

Chuck, almost at the door, halted, his back to Cameron.

"I know that," Chuck said. "And I'm not trying to be cruel. I know what you're going through, because I've been there plenty of times. I just don't want you to make me paint you a picture, that's all. Accept it and let it go."

There's no denying it anymore, then. No more pretending. He's gone.

"He kept his promise," Cameron whispered, wiping his mouth and putting his head in his hands.

"What?" Chuck asked. He turned to face Cameron..

"He promised me he'd help me make sure we got through this in one piece!" Cameron raised his head, his eyes wet with tears. "He promised me that when we watched them take the Laverdiers out of their store in fucking body bags. We promised each other we'd never let that happen to the Roadhouse Sons. He kept his promise, but I guess I broke mine, didn't I?" Cameron hung his head. His shoulders heaved with each sob.

"That was a promise neither of you would have ever been able to keep!" Chuck said, his voice stern instead of comforting. He stomped to the table and leaned into Cameron's face. "I'll tell you right now you'll fuck yourself up if you ever try to hold yourself to that. You did the fucking best you could have done in a situation that you'd never been in before, and that was probably compromised from the very beginning, to boot. You did it alone, for all practical purposes, and not only did you accomplish the objective given to you, you only had one loss to your team, and that was on an unrelated rescue effort, not part of the mission. I know teams that would cut off their low hanging nut for results like that! I'm sorry if that sounds harsh, but you'll tear yourself up and go fucking nuts if you blame yourself for this. Take my advice and learn to take your happily-ever-after wherever, whenever and however you can, and don't say a Goddamned thing about the rest."

Cameron stared blankly, his tears ceasing. Surprisingly, he understood Chuck's decree, but had no idea how to follow it.

"Get some rest," Chuck said with a weak smile, his tone calmer. "You've been through hell and back. All your circuits are fried. I'll have one of the officers take you home. Sleep as much as you can because I'm pretty sure I'm going to need your help later, and I'll want you on top of your game."

Cameron didn't argue. He pushed himself away from the table, barely able to stand. Every muscle in his body ached, screaming for slumber. He stumbled toward the door. Chuck was afraid that Cameron would collapse.

"Wait," said Chuck, reaching into his coat pocket. "I thought you might want this."

Cameron stared at the black trucker cap. It was Doug's hat. Doug never parted with it. Cameron hesitated before taking it, childishly reasoning with himself that if he didn't take it, then Doug wasn't really gone. Cameron hands trembled. He cupped them together and Chuck gave him Doug's hat. They stepped out into the hall.

Evan was by the coffee machine, sipping coffee substitute. He and Chuck exchanged benign greetings, and Chuck left to find the officer in charge. "Sergeant!" he bellowed. "One of my men needs a ride!"

"How are you doing, Ev?" Cameron asked. He longingly eyed Evan's coffee drink.

"I feel like you look," Evan muttered, leaning against the wall.

"Oh, you poor bastard," Cameron said, trying to make a joke. He remembered that the last time he'd said that phrase was to Doug. Cameron no longer saw the humor in it.

"Any word on Clyde?" Cameron asked Evan.

"He's in recovery," Evan said. "The bullet didn't fragment, so that was a good thing, and it went into the deltoid muscle. He's got stitches, and he'll probably have to rehab it, but it doesn't look like it will keep him from playing."

Good news, at long fucking last.

Evan noticed the cap in Cameron's hand. Cameron gave it to him, and Evan pondered it for moments, then handed it back to Cameron.

"I called my wife earlier," Evan said, looking down the hallway, avoiding Cameron's gaze. "McIntyre told me not to say too much, but I was afraid she'd hear about the fire on the news and be worried. I told her it happened after the show and we were all fine. I didn't go into any details."

"I bet she was relieved."

"Yeah... She was..."

Fortunately, Chuck returned with an officer in tow, sparing the two men any further attempts at small talk. Cameron was genuinely happy that Evan's wife was all right and that Clyde wasn't seriously hurt, but his mind was numb and he was beyond exhausted. He just wanted to collapse on his bed.

Chuck introduced them to the officer and the three of them stepped out into the parking lot. No one spoke during the ride back to the hotel. The silence was broken only by the crackle of the patrol car's radio. When they arrived at their destination, Cameron, Chuck and Evan thanked the officer for the ride, and each went to their respective rooms.

As Cameron closed the door, he scanned the room, wondering if it had really been just a short while ago that he had shared it with Bambi. It felt as though a millennium had passed. He placed Doug's hat on the stereo, and adjusted the volume on the radio to his favorite sleep setting. For a moment, he thought of turning it off, but he'd had his fill of uncomfortable silence. Kicking off his shoes, he fell back onto the bed and stared at the ceiling. Within minutes, he dozed off into a fitful slumber.

Cameron awoke to the ringing of the telephone after what seemed like only a few minutes of sleep. He checked the clock on his bed stand. It was after five o'clock in the afternoon. He'd slept for several hours.

"Did I wake you?" said Chuck's voice, with a chuckle.

"I got some sleep," Cameron replied with a yawn. "Not that it seems to have done any fucking good."

"I sympathize, man. Believe me!" Chuck replied. "Listen, I need you to meet us at the, uh, library as soon as you can. We're going to need your help with something."

"What do you need my help for?" Cameron asked, wearily. He had long harbored the hope that they would simply return to rock band status once their recruitment assignment was completed. With this call from Chuck, that hope was fading fast.

"I don't want to spoil the surprise over the phone," Chuck explained. "Just get down here as soon as you can. Another thing; make sure you go down the back way and try to be as inconspicuous as possible. I've been getting phone calls from the hotel that there've been a shitload of reporters hanging around the hotel lobby trying to get a story. I had the hotel staff send the reporters over here this afternoon and we gave them a statement, but I don't know if any are still hanging around. If they are, tell them you've got nothing to add and get the fuck out of there. Got it?"

"Got it," Cameron assured him. Chuck mentioned the library once more and hung up. Cameron sat on the bed and plopped back, lying there for a moment in an attempt to get his bearings. Outside, daylight was gone, hurried along by the overcast sky and the looming storm. The light in the room was dim.

I want it that way.

Cameron fumbled around in his bureau for a clean change of clothes and a jacket. The one he'd been wearing reeked of smoke from the night before.

I'll have to get that cleaned.

On the way out, he paused to turn up the volume on the radio. Doug's hat sat atop the stereo. The track light illuminated it from above. Around the stereo itself were beer cans and a pack of cigarettes. Cameron smiled at this inadvertent yet appropriate memorial to his roadie. He saluted this, Doug's shrine, then quietly slipped out of the room.

He saw no one in the hallway. He hurried down the rear stairwell and, before exiting into the parking lot, he opened the door slightly and peered out. The coast was clear. Wasting no time, he ran stealthily to his car and scrambled in. As the engine warmed, he innocently checked his mirrors, scanning the parking for anyone watching him from one of the other cars. Not only could nosey reporters be lingering, but some of

Lavelle's vengeful crew could be lurking, as well. Cameron recalled Lavelle's crony, Smelly Man, from the fight at the Tavern, and realized that that fellow was nowhere to be found the previous evening. Having a suspect unaccounted for was a valid cause for concern.

Cameron drove from the parking lot, periodically checking his rearview mirror to see if anyone was following him. On the day of that fight at the Tavern, Lavelle had taken Cameron by surprise, and he would never let that happen again. Satisfied that he wasn't being tailed, he drove on to Chuck's rendezvous site. Following the designated street pattern cues, he took a deliberately circuitous route and made several unnecessary turns, doubling back occasionally. This way, he could discern if he was being followed. He eventually arrived at the State Attorney's office, approaching from the opposite direction than if he'd used the shortest route.

Chuck was waiting for him inside. He'd changed his clothes since that morning. The dark circles under his eyes told Cameron that Chuck didn't get any shut-eye. Nevertheless, Chuck greeted Cameron with a smile and walked him to a side office.

"I wanted to update you on things before we went in," Chuck explained, collapsing onto a sofa, his eyes squeezed shut.

He must be exhausted, too.

Chuck made no effort to open his eyes as he spoke, confirming Cameron's assessment.

"I've been spending damn near the whole day on the phone," Chuck said, fatigue evident in his voice. "It seems your little girlfriend has managed to attract some attention here and in Ottawa."

"Ottawa? Cameron asked. "What the hell for?"

"She's a Canadian citizen," Chuck explained. "She's here legally and all, but has gotten into trouble on Federal charges. Obviously, we had to let them know about the events of last night, but there had been some interest before."

"What kind of interest?"

"Remember when I got her to tell me her name?" Chuck reminded him. "You knew I was going to do a background check, right?"

"Yeah. So? You must not have found out anything if this shit was able to go down."

"I'll ignore that, for now," Chuck muttered, his eyes still closed. "The fact is, I did discover something about her, but nothing about her brother until we ran the plates that McIntyre took down when we broke up that fight at the Tavern. We still didn't have anything to connect her to him, just more reasons to keep our eyes open."

"So what did you find out?"

"Were you aware that she had spent some time in Spain?"

"Yeah," said Cameron. He reminisced about his first date with Bambi. "She was there a couple of years, I think. She told me she came back when her mom died."

"Did she tell you anything else about it?"

Cameron struggled to remember details of what he and Bambi had discussed. He remembered that she said she was a dancer, and he remembered their dinner, but he couldn't recall much about their conversations.

"I think so," Cameron said at last. "I think I remember her saying she studied art, or something."

Chuck nodded.

"She was part of a select group referred to as Los Niños, and she studied at a private institute run by a woman whose name was Señora Diana Isabella de Reyes, a truly fascinating woman. De Reyes was believed to be a mistress to both Picasso and Hemingway. She fought in the Civil War, Spanish, not American, by the way. She also spied on the Nazis during the Second World War, and is the only person I know of to publicly tell Franco to fuck off and to not get in trouble for it! She was a painter and a poet, as well as a dancer and close friend of Isadora Duncan."

"The dancer?" asked Cameron.

"The dancer, mother of modern dance and a Soviet Citizen," Chuck corrected.

"She was a Communist?!" Cameron gasped.

Chuck yawned indulgently. "I have no idea if Duncan herself was. I know she was married to a Soviet poet at one point. However, if you are asking about de Reyes, then the answer is yes, she was, or rather, *is* a Communist. A very active one, by the way, and a leading advisor to Santiago Carrillo, the Secretary of the Partido Comunista de España."

"What's that?"

"The Communist Party of Spain," Chuck replied. "They became legal in 1977, and within a few months had over two hundred thousand members, so that should tell you how popular they are. Of course, even before they became legal, they had a lot of members in their party, including your little friend."

Bambi's a Communist?!

Cameron couldn't comprehend, let alone accept, such an idea. He felt as though he'd been sacked with a ton of bricks.

She's not a spy!

Then he remembered the arguments Bambi had incited, only to drop them at a turn on a dime. Did that mean she had betrayed him and the Roadhouse Sons? Was she spying on the band for the Russians?

"Don't get so upset!" Chuck said. "The PCE, as they are called, are known as Eurocommunists, and of whom Señora de Reyes is a leading proponent."

"What's Eurocommunist mean?" asked Cameron. "I thought a Communist was a Communist."

"You and J. Edgar Hoover," sighed Chuck. "You really need to pull your head out of the sand. You're naïve. Maybe I'll take you to Plattsburgh one of these days and buy you an ice cream. Eurocommunism is a wonderful school of thought devoted to promoting liberal democracies. Its premise supports constitutional monarchies, and ever since the Soviet invasion of Czechoslovakia in 1968, Eurocommunists have been dead set against the Soviet version of Communism and are proving to be more of a pain in the ass to Brezhnev than anybody gives them credit for."

"How?"

"By being even more vocal in their opposition and condemnation of the Soviets than Voice of America. They are also very active with Communist parties in other countries, and have managed to gain some influence with China and North Korea, which has helped keep them at least on the sidelines so far. In short, they're the good guys."

"So, what does that have to do with Bambi?" Cameron asked, still not convinced of her Communist status.

"Because, while we do have some members in the PCE, we don't have anyone in a high level position, and certainly no one with access to Carrillo. However, he spends almost as much time at de Reyes's home as he does his own."

Cameron sensed where the conversation was leading, and he would not tolerate it.

"Bambi didn't have anything to do with that shit!"

"Los Niños was a select group that lived and studied in de Reyes's home. One of the only ways to get in there was by being a

Communist, and before heading to Spain, she was a member of le Parti Communiste du Québec while in high school."

"What the hell is that?" demanded Cameron. His patience was rapidly waning.

"Man, you have got to start watching Public Television more," muttered Chuck. "It's the Communist Party of Quebec. Little Bambi joined it when she was sixteen! Apparently radicalism was a trait of that family."

"What the fuck makes you say that?" Cameron sneered. "Some more fancy reports?"

"As a matter of fact, yes and no," said Chuck, shifting his position and finally raising his eyelids. "Some of it came from the Canadians, and all of it was confirmed by Bambi and her sister, what's-her-name."

"Vicki!" snapped Cameron.

"Oh, yeah," Chuck yawned. "Miss Personality. Anyway, their family life was not the inspiration for *The Waltons*, in case you hadn't figured that out yet. Her biological father died when she was still a baby. Her mom married Laurent Lavelle, a widower with two kids, Eduard and Francis. Apparently, Vicki was born shortly thereafter. Bambi, or Yvette, and her brother are what are called Metisse, or mixed race. Her mom was an Indian and her dad was French. They weren't all that accepted socially, and things were hard. It didn't get better when her mom married Lavelle, because he was a radical member of the Quebec Party and a strong advocate for separation from Canada, and that wasn't popular with the English bosses he was trying to work for. If I start to snore, just kick me. OK?"

"Oh, sure," said Cameron.

Right in the fucking balls!

"Where was I?" snorted Chuck. "Oh, right. Their dad. Anyhow, he drifted around trying to find work to support them. The mom tried holding things together while the dad tried to find work. Sometime around then, her mom got pregnant again and lost the baby when she developed some complications and couldn't get medical help because the doctor supposedly didn't like her kind. She lost the baby. After that, the mom suffered a breakdown and began to develop more radical ideas the harder things got for her and her family. Eventually, she joined the Communist Party herself. This didn't go over too well with the old man, because he had been a decorated sailor in the Royal Canadian Navy during the Second

World War. He had other problems to deal with, namely Francis, his son from a previous marriage."

"Is that when Francis started getting into this whole ball o' wax?" Cameron asked. Chuck shrugged and yawned again.

"I don't think so. I think that happened a long time before, but it was right around this time that Francis started showing up on police records. He was his father's oldest son, so all of his dad's attention went toward him, and he spoiled the kid rotten. Kept covering for him, going broke paying for lawyers, the usual routine. It seems Francis got involved with cigarette smugglers and that's when he got into the big time. By then, Bambi had gone to Spain, though, so she was out of it all."

Cameron was extremely relieved to hear that. The rest of Chuck's tale, though, left Cameron numb.

No wonder she was so sensitive about things… nothing but shit her entire life.

"Bambi told me her mom died. That's why she had to come back," Cameron offered. Chuck gave him a "thumbs up" sign, all while draping his arm over his eyes.

"Yes. She died of pneumonia about two years ago," Chuck said. "Her dad was out of work and had just spent the last of his savings, so there was no way of getting proper medical help in time. That's when things really became dark. Vicki had a major breakdown and decided to join the Symbionese Liberation Army. However, it wasn't active anymore, and certainly not in Canada. This is where the brother comes in."

"Let me guess," said Cameron. "He convinced her to work with him and he would help her start her own little revolution. Is that about right?"

"Very good!" smiled Chuck, opening his eyes and staring at Cameron. "Did she tell you that?"

"No," said Cameron, shaking his head. "I remember hearing about the SLA on television, and remembered hearing someone say that they only resorted to serious crimes so they could fund their revolution. It seems to fit in this case."

Chuck gave Cameron another "thumbs up"

"Yes, it does, unfortunately," sighed Chuck. "Francis played his sister like a violin, convincing her that the big score was just around the corner. Then they could finance a social revolution. She tried to be a radical Separatist right around that time, and that was when the old man finally tried to get out of it and move down here. Unfortunately, Francis figured out a way to forge his signature, and used the Tavern as a front for his black market operation. However, it seems Francis had a wire crossed with his Midas touch, and so everything he touched turned to shit. The old man gets nailed for a crime that he never committed, but there's not enough proof to send him to jail, and he gets fined almost to death, severely hampering any chance Francis might have had to use the Tavern as a front."

"Bambi came to help take care of her dad, didn't she?" Cameron asked.

Chuck didn't answer right away. This made Cameron very nervous.

"Didn't she?" Cameron repeated, more force in his voice.

"Not really," Chuck said. "According to what we've learned from her, as well as her sister, she did come back for the funeral and did come to stay with him, but planned on returning to Spain. However Francis learned about her being in the Communist Party and threatened to turn her over to us if she didn't cooperate with him. She'd be deported and would probably never be able to get back into the country. She was afraid she'd never see her father again. Besides, the Communist Party hadn't become legal in Spain yet and she really didn't look forward to going back to Canada alone."

"What's going to happen to her now?"

Chuck took a deep breath and sat up. Leaning forward, he studied Cameron closely. Chuck's intensity wasn't enough to mask his fatigue.

"That is where you come in," he told Cameron.

"Me? What the fuck can I do? I don't even know what the hell is going on! There's still a whole bunch of shit that I can't figure out. How can I possibly be of any help to you?"

"We need you to convince her to work with us," Chuck said. "Washington and Ottawa both think this is a great chance for us to get someone into the PCE. We may never have a chance like this again. Do you know what they call de Reyes in the PCE? *La Popessa*, the Female Pope, because of the influence she has. Bambi was in de Reyes's close circle of students. We'd be sending her back to school, and to de Reyes. She'd be a channel for us to get information on what's going on, and to pass on assistance if they needed it. It wouldn't be like what we brought you in for. We'd be helping that organization as much as spying on them."

Cameron felt nauseous yet again. His gut wrenched in his throat. How could they ask him to do that to Bambi, or to anyone? How could they ask him to put someone through what he had just gone through? Cameron decided to refuse.

"How do we know she isn't a spy already?" Cameron asked. "There are still the unexplained warnings we got. There's still the phone taps, remember? You said you were going to try and find out more about them. Well? Did you? You want me to get involved in this when there's still a hell of a lot of unanswered questions. And before you jump on my ass, no, it isn't just because I've got feelings for her! I've got feelings for my two friends that are dead, too, and I don't want to be adding a third to the death toll!"

Chuck nodded, but said nothing. He rubbed his hands, considering a response, but Cameron didn't let Chuck get a word in edgewise.

"Besides," Cameron said, swallowing hard, "How do we know she wouldn't be fucking with *us*? If she was what you said, if she's got that much of a beef against everything she associates with the shit she's gone through, and I know for a fact she does, how can we be sure she won't head right to the Reds and have a good fucking laugh at us?"

"We don't know," said Chuck, matter-of-factly. "We take our chances like we always do. Then, we monitor the situation and the individuals involved with the information provided to us and, if it checks out, we keep running them. If it doesn't..."

"If it doesn't... Then what?" Cameron demanded.

"Then we stop running them," said Chuck.

"How do you do that?"

"Now *that*... that is none of your business," said Chuck. His jaw muscles tightened. Cameron's gut went into his throat again.

What's he hiding?

Cameron decided that he had nothing left to lose at this point. "How do you...?"

"Don't!" warned Chuck.

Cameron, albeit reluctantly, decided not to pursue his question any further.

"You still didn't answer my other question," Cameron pressed on. "You know. About the bugs."

"I have good news and bad news about that," Chuck said, leaning back on the couch. "Which do you want first?"

Cameron laughed derisively. "Good news and bad news are pretty relative. Give it to me any way you want."

"All right, then." Chuck yawned yet again. At this point, Cameron wondered whether Chuck was exhausted, or pointedly bored. "Here goes. We have admission from Vicki and Eduard that the bugs planted in Doug's and D'Lorenzo's room were planted by them. D'Lorenzo had given them sound surveillance devices—without approval, by the way—to get information on competitors. They decided to turn it around. They thought it would be a good idea to listen in on D'Lorenzo and find out what he was up to. Francis wanted to check you out because he was convinced that you were already seeing his sister, and he wanted to see if there was anything he could use on her."

"But why spy on his own sister? That doesn't make any sense."

"Because they didn't trust her," said Chuck, with a smile. "They were convinced that she would run away the first chance she got. That was why they wanted to bug your room, and why she either had to see you at the bar, which was monitored, or meet at the Catamount where Vicki worked, so that she could monitor Bambi's conversations. Not one of them, including that kid we're talking to, thought she was committed to their mission. They wanted Bambi to get friendly with you, and dig for information. What happened between you two was exactly what they didn't want. As it turned out, she cozied up to you, and there was a huge risk that you could or would help her get out."

Cameron remembered his and Bambi's date at the Catamount and how rude the waitress was. He remembered, too, the first time the band dined there, and how Vicki hovered at their table. Chuck's opinion that D'Lorenzo had possibly compromised things long before they arrived sent a chill down Cameron's spine. And he had no choice but to face what Chuck revealed about Francis ordering Bambi to befriend Cameron.

Was that all a fraud, too?

"Was that the good news or the bad news?" Cameron wished he could dry up and blow away in the wind.

"Take your pick," shrugged Chuck. "As for the taps on the phones, the note, and the orange, none of them have any idea about all that."

Cameron was quiet. He felt blind-sided. He didn't know how he felt about trusting Chuck now. "Do you have any ideas about all that?"

Chuck sat up. His face was emotionless. "We have no choice but to consider that bugs were planted by a hostile organization," Chuck replied, flatly.

"Did the Lavelles know anything about the Mustang mission?"

Chuck shook his head.

"They admitted hearing D'Lorenzo and Doug fighting about it. That was when Doug punched the wall, apparently, but they didn't understand what they overheard. They thought D'Lorenzo had wrecked Doug's car."

"Do you have any more information on the Mustang, by the way?" Cameron asked.

Chuck shook his head. "None," he replied.

"So, what do we do about it, then?"

Chuck smiled. "Not a fucking thing; for now, anyway. I'd let that go, too, if I were you."

That was like asking Cameron to stab his parents, cut up the pieces, and offer them up for sacrifice. Never in his life had Cameron been able to leave unanswered questions dangling, and there was another one that required an answer.

"What about Dwyer? Did they have anything to do with his death?"

Chuck raised an eyebrow and glared at Cameron

Why do I hit a brick wall every time I ask about Dwyer?

"So, why keep me involved? Why keep the Roadhouse Sons involved? I thought all we had to do was get you the information you wanted, and then we were through. *Then* we could go back to our lives"

"I'm sorry if that was how it was presented to you, brother," said Chuck. "I really truly am. But the fact is, there was no way that it could have been a one-shot deal."

I knew it. In for a penny, in for a pound.

"All right then," Cameron sighed. "What do you need me to do?"

Screwed again without the benefit of intercourse.

"Convince Bambi to work for us. If she does, she'll not only have support from us, but the RCMP Security Service has signed off on the deal, as well."

"What the hell is RCMP?"

Chuck grinned. "They are the Royal Canadian Mounted Police Security Service, the Dudley Do-Rights of the Canadian intelligence community. Red jackets, horses, the whole nine yards. You can spot them easily enough. They're the ones with the dark glasses."

"Really?"

Chuck slapped his knee, guffawing. *"I'll save you, Nell.* Fuck, no! Now, when we found out about your girlfriend, I was told to go see if she was willing to consider this offer. Not at first, so she seemed, but with recent developments, I think she might be more amenable to it."

"Why?"

"Because, otherwise, she's facing serious charges with crimes connected to the death of an undercover officer, to drug trafficking, and to bootlegging, all of which carry additional charges by the U.S. Treasury Department. That doesn't even include charges at the City of Burlington and the Vermont state levels. That's shit piled on top of shit! *Including,* but *not limited* to, arson and multiple wrongful death charges, due to the fire last night. Those are just with our branch! I have no idea if the Canadians are going to do anything."

Who's the carrot, who's the stick? It all depends on how you look at it, I guess.

"But, why me really? I don't even know her that well. I like her a lot, sure. And it's true she's not the groupie type; that's why I gave her the time of day."

Chuck smiled awkwardly. "Well… First off, you've been tiptoeing through her tulips for a bit already. I don't mean to be sticking my nose in where it doesn't belong, but secondly, I personally think she really likes you and trusts you. We're betting she'll listen to you more than to us."

Every nerve in Cameron's body screamed for him to evacuate. *Right now!*

There was no way that he could willingly introduce someone to his circumstances. For all intents and purposes, he and the band had been blackmailed into service, and sitting before him was Chuck, asking him to do the very same thing to someone else. That someone was a person for whom Cameron cared deeply.

No… Bash his fucking face in. Then leave!

To do so would resign Bambi to a fate much worse than Chuck's proposal. They really weren't asking her to do what Cameron and the guys were forced to undertake. She'd be returning to a place that she loved, and she'd live amidst a group to which she'd secretly belonged. She'd also be working toward her beliefs. By conveying useful information, she'd be helping her simpaticos abroad just as much as Chuck and his higher-ups.

Pass me a shovel. I'm feeding myself naïve bullshit… The lesser of two evils?

"OK!" Cameron mustered only a whisper. "We'll do it."

Chuck said nothing. Finally he nodded. The two of them rose to leave.

"One thing," Cameron said, pausing at the door.

"What's that?"

"Why are we here instead of the police station?"

Chuck hung his head. After several moments, he looked up at Cameron and removed a folded piece of paper from his shirt pocket.

"I've been carrying this around with me since I took over from Dwyer." He handed the paper to Cameron. It was a list of telephone numbers.

"These are all the numbers that Dwyer called in the two week period before he was murdered. The first one was his hotel room. The second was his office at the Civic Center. The third one was a phone booth near there, just across the street from the Catamount. I met the lovely Vicki at the Catamount the day I located and scoped that site, but she didn't know who I was. I'm not surprised, because D'Lorenzo had no opportunity to contact them before I got here."

Cameron fought confusion. "What does all that have to do with anything?"

"All of those phones were tapped," Chuck explained. "I had no gauge about that last number, because I had no idea where it originated from until today. I happened to call from it this morning when I checked with my higher-ups. As I was dialing, I looked at the number in the middle of the rotary and thought it looked familiar. I checked my list after I hung up and it matched. There was just one problem, though."

"What?"

"When I went back to use it again later that morning, there was a double clicking noise when I picked up the receiver. It hadn't been there before. Sometime during the day that line was tapped."

"Shit," whistled Cameron. "Does it have anything to do with this?"

Chuck shrugged. "How does anybody ever know? I can't be one hundred percent certain yes *or* no," he admitted. "We're still trying to find out. If it was tapped, then we got out of there just in time. My thanks, though? All the information on the offer for Bambi was made out of this office."

"How do you know this phone isn't bugged?"

"I've had them checked," Chuck said, smugly. "Regularly, too, I might add. We want to make certain there is at least one secure line for us in and out of Burlington!"

Why don't you just look in the mirror and rub yourself with butter?

"Who do you think planted the tap this morning?"

"Dwyer and I have one thing in common," Chuck said. "Neither of us wastes time speculating. I won't worry about anything until I've got something to worry about. We're checking that situation out now, and when we find something, we'll act on it. In the meantime, and much to my chagrin, the latest events have been chalked up as anomalies. Fuck that! We have work to do here."

Chuck jumped up from the sofa and opened the door with a flourish. He led Cameron down the hallway. Cameron's stomach churned with every step. With every physical and moral fiber, Cameron wanted to scream, "*Forget it!*" But he didn't. He followed Chuck down the hallway to a conference room. McIntyre and Bambi were waiting. Cameron was simultaneously relieved and nonplused. Both women wore different clothes than they'd worn that morning. Both appeared to be consummately weary. McIntyre was poring through a black leather journal, ignoring everyone around her. Bambi was sipping from a mug of tea. She was agitated. Cameron's heart sank. Her face was not only marked with exhaustion and fatigue, but also despair. Her eyes were, from all her weeping, a fiery, blood-shot red. Her hands shook. Cameron wondered if she'd eaten at all that day, and felt guilty for having returned to the hotel for rest.

What was her night like?

Chuck presented a chair and motioned for Cameron to sit. He explained to Bambi the charges against her. She trembled, slightly at first, and more as he proceeded. Cameron worried that she would crack under the pressure. Suddenly, though, Chuck ceased his inquisition..

"That sounds pretty bleak, I know," Chuck explained to Bambi, his voice soothing and sympathetic. "But, I think we can help you if you're interested."

"Help *me?*" Bambi asked, no expectation in her voice. Cameron fumed.

They ask the question like they're about to play a horrible joke on her. She's already figured out the punch line.

"How can you help me?" Bambi asked, her voice weary.

Chuck didn't answer. He turned to Cameron and nodded his head in Bambi's direction. Chuck cued Cameron about their previous discussion.

Cameron had no idea how to broach the interrogation. "Do you remember when you were telling me about Spain?" Bambi nodded, displaying no emotion.

"You liked it there a lot, didn't you?"

Bambi nodded. "Would you like to maybe go back there? You know... Kind of get away from all of this shit here?"

"Go back?" she asked, more as an accusation than a question. "How can I go back to Spain? I can't even make it up to Canada to get my rations! Are you serious? How can you ask me that?"

"I am serious," said Cameron. He described Chuck's offer. Far from smiling, Bambi's expression was hard.

"You want me to go and spy on my *friends*? You want me to betray everything they say? And do to *you*? And in exchange, you'll give me the wonderful opportunity to be a Judas? Go to Hell ! I'd rather go to jail!"

"No! That's not what we're asking you to do!" Cameron insisted. "It would be a two-way street. You could let us know how we could help and, you know, how to... work with them!"

"Work with them?" she laughed. "I though you were fighting Communists!"

Chuck intervened. "We are. The same ones you guys were fighting. The same ones that Carrillo condemns every day, and the same ones that Señora de Reyes denounced at her performing arts exhibition in Madrid yesterday."

At the mention of her former mentor, Bambi's eyes softened.

"They told me she was the biggest supporter of the Prague Spring," Bambi said. "She wrote a beautiful poem about it. They tell me that she went into a towering rage when the Soviets invaded in 1968."

"I bet she did, if she's anything like I've read of her," laughed Chuck. "Would that poem be *La Esperanza Muere Al último*, by any chance?"

"Yes!" gasped Bambi. "It translates to *hope is the last to die*! How did you know about it?"

Chuck grinned at Bambi. "I like modern poetry," he said, coyly. "I also like her poem, *Mover Cielo y Tierra*."

Bambi was delighted. "To move Heaven and earth!" she laughed. "Some of the girls sang that at one of Señora's dinners. It was so beautiful, even Señora cried."

"Wasn't it about doing everything possible to make the world the best that you can?" Chuck asked, his voice barely audible.

Bambi nodded. Then she began to weep.

"Don't you think that this might be a way for you to do that very thing?" Cameron asked. He, too, spoke softly, in the least intrusive manner that he could fashion. He was careful not to violate the privacy of her memories. Bambi looked at him, wiping her eyes.

"Its not that simple," she said, choking. "It's not just spying on my friends. How can I leave my father? He's alone now. Francis is dead. Louis is dead, and the rest of us will be going to jail, probably for the rest of our lives. Certainly for the rest of his!"

"Would going to prison make him feel better?" Cameron asked. "You don't think he wouldn't be happy knowing you were in Spain? Someplace away from this mess?"

"He does have family in Canada, still," Chuck pointed out.

"That he's not permitted to see!" Bambi snapped. "They made it a part of his probation that he could not leave the country, and the Canadians were all too happy to agree with that!"

Cameron looked at Chuck, who made a clicking sound, and then leaned forward.

"All right," he said. "We have signed statements from your sister, your brother and their accomplice, confirming that your father was innocent of all the charges against him, and that Francis used your father's ration coupons, as well as the coupons for the Tavern, without your father's knowledge or consent. I can get all the charges against him dropped. That'll restore his privileges."

"The Canadians won't go along with that," Bambi sniffed dismissively.

"What I'm permitted to offer are jointly sanctioned by the State's Attorney and the Attorney General for Lower Canada, and with the full approval of their superiors. This opportunity originates in both Washington and Ottawa."

"I don't believe they'd do that," Bambi said, shaking her head. "They'd never offer me that deal…"

"Why not?" Cameron interrupted. "They offered one like it to me."

No sooner had he blurted it, Cameron realized the weakness of his argument. He had no true comprehension of what Bambi had endured.

"You're not like me," she said with a cold smile. Cameron bristled.

"What the hell does that mean?" Cameron was defensive.

"She means you're not Metisse," said Chuck, folding his arms. "You don't know what it's like to be a kid rejected by two cultures."

Bambi's eyes narrowed. "And how would you know?" she challenged.

"Do I look Irish?" Chuck smiled. "My mom was a Cherokee and my dad was French, not unlike you. I got it all thrown at me. I was picked on in school, and everyone calling me Tonto, and yipped the war whoops, I got only the crappy jobs, you name it. But I managed."

McIntyre, who'd, as always, remained silent the whole time, slammed closed the book in her hands. A resounding echo hit the walls of the sparse room. "But you had something going for you that she didn't. You're a man. She's not. You still had a few breaks that she didn't."

Chuck's eyes grew wide with surprise. Cameron muffled a laugh.

It's like he forgot McIntyre was in the room!

Chuck said nothing and just sat there, a bit slack-jawed. Cameron was relieved. He'd feared for a moment that an argument would ensue about women's lib and the ERA, pure anathema to him. But McIntyre just smiled at Bambi and reopened the book, which as it turned out, was Bambi's sketch journal from her years abroad.

McIntyre pointed at a page in the book. "I really like this one." From where he was seated, Cameron couldn't see anything, but Bambi smiled.

"That was the daughter of one of the gardeners," Bambi explained. "Her favorite toy was that ball. One day, she was just sitting there chattering away at it and I sketched it while she was having a long talk with it. She was so engrossed that she never noticed me."

"You captured everything so nicely," McIntyre said. "Was this early afternoon? You even did the shadowing so well I can tell the time of day. You certainly have a talent."

"Thank you!" Bambi blushed. "Yes, it was just before lunch. Right after that, her mother called her home to get cleaned up."

"It seems a shame to let that talent go to waste," Cameron said. Bambi eyed at him. She said nothing. Cameron used her silence as an opportunity to continue the original conversation.

"We're not asking you to change your views or beliefs," Cameron continued. "We're not asking you not to do anything you haven't done before."

"Except spy on my friends," Bambi muttered.

"You don't think the Reds haven't got someone there keeping an eye on things?" Cameron argued. "I can guarantee that if we've thought of it, so have they. Especially since you guys have always been such big critics of the Soviets."

"He does have a point," McIntyre said. She held up the sketchbook. "But just think of the wonderful chance you have to go back to this."

"With strings attached!" Bambi accused.

"And there weren't any strings the last time?" Cameron pointed out. "Didn't you have to belong to a Communist group before you could go to Señora's school? That seems like strings to me."

Bambi studied the mug of tea in her hand, slowly rubbing it between her palms. Moments of awkward silence passed.

"Every offer we have made is sincere." Chuck finally spoke. "And the Canadian government is endorsing this as well. If you say yes, then I go down the hall to the State's Attorney's office and we can start things rolling right now. Tonight. You will be officially released on your own recognizance and allowed to go home to your dad. We'll assign someone to work with you and help facilitate your return to Spain, and establish your communications with us. We'll do everything we can to help you and your family, but this offer isn't good forever. We need to know now."

Bambi began to sob. Cameron reached out and put his hand on hers.

"Every promise they made to me, they kept," he said. "I know it isn't an easy choice. But would going to jail really be any better?"

"No," she whispered. "It wouldn't."

Cameron had just recruited. He wanted to crawl out of his skin and hide.

"I just have one question," Bambi said, her lower lip trembling. "Will I ever be able to come home again?"

"Of course!" said Chuck with a grin. "You're going to art school, not exile! You'll be able to move freely. Just keep us posted on your whereabouts. Your case officer will work all of that out with you."

"She won't be working with us?" asked Cameron. Chuck shook his head.

"No. Europe is not part of our bag," he explained, getting up from the table. "We work our magic stateside. So, will you accept this offer?"

"Yes,…" Bambi nodded. Tears stained her cheeks.

McIntyre carefully closed the sketchbook and handed it to Bambi.

"Those are lovely," McIntyre said with a smile. "I look forward to seeing your work in a gallery one of these days."

Bambi smiled demurely and blushed. Cameron's heart melted.

For the thousandth time…

"I'm going to go with Chuck and start the paperwork," McIntyre said. "Do either of you need anything?"

"No… Thank you," said Cameron. Bambi shook her head. Chuck and McIntyre left the room. Cameron and Bambi were finally alone. Cameron stared at the door for a few moments, waiting to see if Chuck and McIntyre would come right back, and because he needed a few seconds to think. He'd hoped to have some time alone with Bambi. Now that his hopes were realized, he didn't quite know what to do about it. So many thoughts and emotions fought for supremacy. He could not deny the feelings he had developed for her since he met her, but at the same time, two of his friends were dead. One was wounded because of Bambi's brother, and due to her involvement.

How do I deal with that? What do I say now? There couldn't possibly be anything to say…

Cameron turned to Bambi and examined her expression.

What is she thinking?

Bambi was timid now. Gone was the fire and defensiveness of a few moments before. Now, she was just as vulnerable as he was.

"Are you all right?" he asked, stalling for time until he could think of a better question. He did genuinely care.

"I'm as good as can be expected," she whispered, looking away.

"Have you been able to make any phone calls?" he asked. She shook her head.

"I've been being questioned all day," she said. "They did get me a lawyer, but the State's Attorney must have said something to him, because he left after a while."

Cameron nodded. He suspected that some pressure had been brought to bear, but kept this to himself. The best plan of action, right now was to adhere to Chuck's advice about not worrying until something worrisome presents itself.

"Have you talked to any of your family?" She shook her head.

"No one… How is your friend?"

Clyde or Doug?

"Clyde got hurt in the arm."

"Is he OK?"

"I guess he's doing all right."

No more feeble attempts at small talk…

"Was any of it real?" Cameron blurted out his question. He was neither confrontational nor angry. Bambi said nothing.

"Were any of your feelings real?" he repeated.

"Yes," she replied, looking him square in his eyes. "I really liked you once I got to know you, and it was pure hell when they had me spy on you. You know, like you're asking me to do now?"

"That isn't fair! It's nothing like that. Your brother was trying to stop us from stopping him. We're asking you to help us keep people out of the war and stop a threat to anyone opposed to Russia. You don't even support them, for God's sake."

"It seems like the same from where I sit," Bambi said. "I'm being asked to keep tabs on something. I can't just live my life!"

"You're being asked to help watch something that will be harmful to a lot more than a drug pusher's business this time! You're being asked to help us support a group that wants to do something about this war. From where I sit, that is a big, big difference!"

Stay cool!

Bambi held her breath, and gazed into her now empty mug of tea. The silence was palpable, and awkward.

"Can I ask a question?" Bambi's voice was flat.

"Sure, go ahead."

"OK, then," she said, eyeing him again. "Can I ask *you* if any of it was real?"

"Yes, you can ask. And, yes, it was real."

"You weren't just interested in me because you were supposed to be finding out information?"

"No," Cameron insisted. "You weren't even on my radar. We thought we were just supposed to hang around with people at the parties and find out where they were getting their stuff and pass it along. Then we were done. How it turned out was none of our doing, at least not intentionally."

"I didn't mean to spy on you, either." Tears welled in Bambi's eyes. "When Francis found out that you were coming to the Tavern, he asked if anyone was showing an interest in you. He wasn't happy that it was me. He thought I would try and run off with you."

Cameron smiled, but said nothing.

"His original plan was to have Vicki take an interest in one of you, but that didn't seem to be likely, so he began pressuring me to be more interested."

Cameron didn't know how to respond. Bambi quickly sensed that.

"It wasn't all that hard, if you want to know the truth," she said with a shy smile. Cameron smiled back.

That feels better.

"So, let me ask you this. Did you ever really see me in Stowe?"

Bambi blushed and shook her head.

"No," she replied with a smile. "I never did. Eduard did, and told us about it. Francis and Vicki wanted me to use that as a way to get your attention."

"So, why did you go back and forth on that?"

"I guess I was trying to warn you that something was up," she said, meekly. "I didn't dare come right out and say it. Francis would have killed me, and I'm not just using a figure of speech."

Images of Dwyer and of Doug flashed through Cameron's mind. He knew that she was probably right.

"I appreciate that," he said softly.

"Appreciate what?" she asked, a sudden cynical tone to her voice. "Appreciate that I was interested in you?"

"Yes! I appreciate that, and I appreciate the fact that you risked a lot to try and warn me."

They sat in yet more awkward silence for several moments. Finally, Cameron nodded to the sketchbook on the table.

"What's that?" Cameron asked.

"This is my sketchbook." She pulled it toward her and fingered the cover for a few moments, lost in thought. Then, she slid it across the table to Cameron.

"Would you like to take a look at it?"

"Sure," he said with a smile, carefully opening the cover. Inside, the pages were covered with pen, pencil and ink drawings. Spanish country scenes, people, and other slice-of-life images, the majority of which were in black and white, graced each leaf of paper.

Cameron flipped each page, clearly astounded by her talent. He stopped at a page which featured a drawing of a lone woman.

"That's one of me," Bambi giggled as Cameron. Indeed, there on the page was a seascape scene. In the foreground was Bambi, her hair loose and windblown. She was sitting on a rock with one leg drawn up, her hands folded around the front of her leg. The other leg was folded under her body. Behind her were clouds, birds, and the spray of a wave striking rocks.

"That was from a picture a friend took of me when we went to the beach one afternoon. I hadn't gone in the water yet."

"Was this a lake?" Cameron asked, captivated by the picture. He didn't want to turn the page.

"No," she explained. "It was the Mediterranean. Valencia is on the Mediterranean coast. That's where the school is."

Cameron continued perusing Bambi's drawings. The pencil sketches were quite detailed, some so much so that they were easily mistaken for photographs. He could tell that some were works in progress; others were simply rough sketches that she'd never completed. Cameron noticed one distinct element in each and every drawing. They depicted happiness, be it amongst a group of people on a picnic at the beach, or on the face of a small child with a toy, or in Bambi herself. There were absolutely no brooding, Gothic images.

"Do you think he really read her poems?" Bambi's voice startled Cameron out of his reverie.

"Who? Chuck?" he asked. "We've never talked about it. But if he says he did, then I bet he did."

"And he said he liked her stuff, too," Bambi said, her voice melancholy and reflective. "If he told the truth about that, do you think he's telling the truth about everything else?"

Cameron nodded, but didn't say a word. He was about to speak, when Chuck and McIntyre suddenly reentered the room.

"We've got the paperwork started," Chuck said with a wan smile. He nodded toward Bambi. "You have to come with us now to complete your statements."

Bambi looked from Chuck to Cameron. She was shaking.

"It's all right," reassured McIntyre. "Just a little while longer and you'll be free to go home. You can come with me and we'll get all this tidied up."

Cameron eyed Bambi. Not knowing what to say, he simply smiled and took her hand, giving it an encouraging squeeze. Bambi enclosed her hand around his. They stood there for several moments. McIntyre cleared her throat. Cameron realized that Bambi had to leave. He released her hand and rose from his seat.

"Wait!" cried Bambi, her voice quivering. She flipped through the pages of her sketchbook. She stopped leafing through it and tore a page out and handed it to Cameron, her hands trembling. "I want you to have this." The paper fluttered in her hand as she passed it to him. For some inexplicable reason, he was reminded of a turtledove.

It's her self-portrait from the Mediterranean...

He gave her a kiss and a strong, lengthy hug. He was lost in her touch, in her body, in her warmth. He heard someone cough. He wasn't sure if it was Chuck or McIntyre. It didn't matter. The moment was broken. Cameron released Bambi from his embrace. She began to weep. She gathered her sketchbook, and followed McIntyre from the room. Cameron choked back tears.

Chuck closed the door and turned toward Cameron

"Are you all right?" he asked. Cameron nodded, swallowing hard.

"You've had a tough day," Chuck said, patting him on the back. "Go to the hotel and get some rest. We can start putting our plan together tomorrow."

"What are you talking about?" Cameron was nonplused.

Can they honestly expect us to do more? We're broken...

"The Roadhouse Sons still have tour dates, in case you've forgotten," said Chuck. "And we've got a rhythm guitarist who's on the injured list for God only knows how long. We've got to decide if we're going to cancel the dates, deal with insurance adjusters, all that sort of thing. I'm afraid the exciting part is over. We've still got reality to contend with. But all that can wait till tomorrow. Like I said, go to your room and get some rest."

Cameron didn't argue, nor did he look at Chuck. He simply nodded and exited the interrogation room. Once outside, the cold pre-winter air cut into his lungs. Despite the shock of it, he welcomed the discomfort. He turned up the collar of his jacket to block the wind. He had no gauge of the time, yet he didn't look at his watch. He climbed into his Mustang and revved the engine. He knew it was late, but didn't give a damn about the curfew. He pulled out onto the street, half-heartedly checking his rearview mirror to see if he was being tailed.

Follow me all you want. I have no idea where I'm going.

He drove around Burlington for some time; no singing, no radio, no sound. Then, suddenly, he found himself craving a human voice. He turned on the radio. News commentators discussed mass suicides of the Jim Jones disciples in Guyana. Cameron wondered how so many people could become so completely enthralled with someone that they could surrender their own critical thinking. Then he remembered Vicki's homicidal devotion to her brother, Francis. That mindset still made no sense to him.

At the radio station's commercial break, another reporter commented on the continuing eulogies for the late Margaret Mead. While the station replayed the dry, bromide professional recollections of Mead's colleagues, Cameron reminisced about his high school travails. He reflected upon the time when he attempted to prepare a report on Mead's book, *Coming of Age in Samoa*, and the firestorm that erupted when his spinster teacher caught him reading it. He was uncertain of the book's premise and its impact. At that young age, all that he knew was that Samoa was a tropical island and there were grass skirted, dancing women on the cover. This particular memory fostered maudlin thoughts about beaches and warm, sunny days and, suddenly, his thoughts drifted back to Bambi's Mediterranean self-portrait. A flood of emotions encompassed him.

Cameron pushed a different channel selection button. He wanted music. He caught the closing chords of a song and then that station segued to a commercials. Cameron felt assaulted by the local supermarket advertisements touting Thanksgiving holiday specials. These same ads issued vague admonishments for its listeners to remember to retain fat and cooking grease for the war effort. Cameron was utterly disgusted when that ad was followed by another one encouraging people to buy government bonds. He changed the station. He thought about Dwyer, Doug as well as Bambi.

I don't feel like I have a whole hell of a lot to be thankful for.

Turning onto Lake Street, he drove past the parks, now streetlamp-free, darkened for the war effort. He chose another station on the radio, relieved to finally hear music. He thought of the dark waters of Lake Champlain. As he drove along listening to the music on the radio, snowflakes drifted in the beam of his headlights.

It's early for snow...

As he slowed for a stop sign, the song on the radio captured his attention, his emotions, his soul.

The mournful melody of *Dust in the Wind* by Kansas blasted from the Mustang's speakers.

All we are is dust in the wind... Don't hang on... Nothing lasts forever but the earth and sky...

Cameron's eyes welled with tears. He remembered the conversation he had had with Bambi about this very song in this very car, in a very different lifetime not long ago. Snowflakes drifted past his headlights, vanishing into oblivion. He thought of the destruction—the chaos—in which he was now situated. The realization of his own naïveté regarding his romantic notions about the ways of the world, all ersatz images taken from television and the movies, smashed his psyche.

All we are is dust in the wind...

"Fuck you..." he whispered aloud. He jabbed the channel selector buttons once again. The song was more upbeat, seeming out of synch with the previous song and Cameron's mood. It took him an inordinate amount of time for him to realize who was singing. As if in mockery, the sounds of Kansas burst forth from the radio, the lyrics assaulting his ears.

Carry on, my wayward son. There'll be peace when you are done. Lay your weary head to rest. Don't you cry no more..."

"Fuck you!" he screamed. He turned off the radio. Cameron was finished, spent. There was no peace awaiting him.

And I doubt I'm done crying...

Cameron began to shake uncontrollably. The events the last twenty-four hours had finally caught up to him. He was so exhausted that he could barely keep his eyes open. He turned the Mustang around and headed for the hotel.

Once there, he parked his car and stumbled into the lobby. Somewhere in the recesses of his mind, he vaguely heard a desk clerk greet him, but he offered no reply. There were no reporters in the lobby, nor were there any hangers-on or typical lobby denizens at that time of night. He ran down the hall and beckoned the elevator. He pushed his floor button and leaned against the wall, closing his eyes as the car ascended to his floor. He briefly contemplated stopping at Rich's room to see if there was any word on Clyde.

Or...

He changed his mind, figuring that Rich needed rest as well.

Cameron stumbled down the hallway to his room. He swore that the hallway grew longer every time he went out. He unlocked his door and stepped into his room. He didn't bother to turn on any lights. The only illumination was the single track light over the stereo.

I like it.

He walked over to the stereo to place Bambi's Mediterranean sketch there beside Doug's hat

My new shrine.

Cameron froze. Doug's hat was gone, and in its place was an orange.

An Excerpt From Roadhouse Sons – Book Two: Renegade

This wasn't what he thought dying would feel like. Instead of lingering in a bed in a sterile hospital, lonely in some nursing home, or even in a comfortable bed surrounded by greedy heirs and fat grandchildren, he felt the wind caress his cheeks as it blew through his hair. He was strangely calm, even oddly reflective. He looked, for the last time, upon the magnificent colors of the sunset as it cast its glow upon the city of Seattle. He was glad that this would be his last vision. The war effort had dimmed the lights of Seattle, giving all who loved the evening skyline a sense of loss, as though grieving a longtime friend. But the setting sun reflected off of the buildings and gave the appearance that the lights were on. He felt the thrill of relief now. He was grateful that his last memory would not be clouded by grief.

He relaxed; all of his the earlier tensions ebbed away. The arguments, the fighting and the shouting all seemed like they happened to someone else. The accusations no longer rang in his ears and he no longer vainly uttered his denials. He wiped the corner of his mouth where he felt a trickle of blood, then chuckled as he realized what he was doing. Soon it wouldn't matter anymore.

He thought about what they were doing in his apartment now; going through his things, laying bare the mementos of his life for the world to see. Would they appreciate them as he did? Or consider from whence they came and what recollections would be associated with them? He doubted it. They weren't the sentimental types.

He vaguely remembered an engagement he had the next day. He was supposed to meet Chris for drinks. With regret, he realized that he hadn't informed his friend of the sudden change in plans. But that was all right. Chris would find out soon enough. That probably wouldn't make any difference anyway, either. Not to him at least. Not anymore. That very thought made him smile. Nothing would make any difference to him anymore. He was free at last. Free from the threats hanging over him. Free from the retribution that he feared so much. Free from the rough hands that had grasped at him. He relished that freedom. The only surprise was the end. The end had come much quicker than he'd thought... almost as quickly as the pavement that rose up to meet him.

www.ingramcontent.com/pod-product-compliance
Lightning Source LLC
Chambersburg PA
CBHW020918020726
47495CB00002B/246